Dedicated to Al and Marcia, my incredible grandparents and the people I hope to live up to. Thank you for always believing in me. Love you, always.

CONTENTS

PREFACE

THROUGHOUT MY LIFE, it has always seemed necessary to reach various landmarks in order to continue on whichever path I have chosen to take. Sometimes the milestones are places, sometimes they're achieving particular goals, and sometimes it means getting a little beat down before getting back up.

I'm standing here clutching my stomach with one hand, waiting for a wave of sickness to pass, while my other hand is gripped around the source of my apprehension.

The past two years have brought us closer to this moment, and now watching him off in the distance, I can't help but recall a time when we had no idea what our future would hold. Everything was new, surreal, and fit nicely inside of a little dream. If we had known what was to come, would we have continued running toward the unknown? Or would we have high-tailed it in a safer direction? It's hard to tell.

Our lives began to unfold shortly after we both left the institution, when we were hopeful for a new life no matter what that would mean. We were quick to learn that a new life isn't as great as it may seem.

CHAPTER ONE

A NEW LIFE

CLASSICAL MUSIC SETS THE MOOD in this dimly lit, tiny restaurant we often find ourselves in. Since we don't have a kitchen to use, we've gotten to know the local eateries pretty well.

Regardless of our living situation, I still feel like a princess who has been rescued from a prison tower. I never imagined having the opportunity to escape my imprisoned life. Sometimes I have to remind myself how lucky I am to be away from it. When things change fast, it's easy to forget about what was left behind.

I twirl the last piece of spaghetti around my fork and look up to see the love emanating from Alex's crystal blue eyes. The look never changes. It's as if he can't get enough of me. On the other hand, it could be that he's trying to take every part of me in now while he can. I'm not sure which, but it makes me feel loved.

I smile at him as I place the last bite in my mouth. Without a second passing after I've swallowed my food, Alex shoots his hand up in the air, waving over the waiter.

He finished his meal ten minutes ago, and he's been impatiently waiting for me to finish. His fingers are drumming against the table and his foot is tapping nervously against the floor.

"Are you okay?" I ask, reaching my hand out to him.

He slides his fingers in between mine and grips my hand. "Just ready to get out of here." He waves his hand at the waiter again.

The waiter notices Alex and runs over to the counter, fumbling around and ripping the top piece of paper off his order pad.

Alex places a handful of Euros over the bill and pushes his chair out with an assertive thrust. "Ready to go?" he asks.

He laughs and relief fills his face. "I'm serious," he says. "You're not mad I picked it out without you?" He places his hands over my shoulders and runs them up and down my arms. His eyes soften, but they're still filled with worry.

"Mad?" I slap his arm. "It's perfect." I wrap my arms around him and fling my legs around his waist. "It's a dream come true. Our own little place in the city," I giggle. "Why would I ever be mad about this?" I trail my lips around his face, careful not to miss a spot.

He locks his arms around my back and rests his head on my shoulder. "Big relief," he sighs.

I pull my head back. "You're crazy if you thought I wouldn't."

An apartment in Paris with the love of my life? Or a guarded room at a mental institution? Tough choice.

"I've been anxious all day." He places a soft kiss on the nape of my neck. "It will be a good holding place for us." His words send me through a loop and drag my mind back to the precise place I was trying to keep it away from.

I release my legs from around his body and place my feet back on the ground. I take a couple of steps backward and shake my head in confusion. "What do you mean?" I press my hand into the side of my cheek. "I thought—or I was hoping…"

He grabs my hand and pulls me back in. "You were hoping this could be a permanent residence." He places his finger under my chin, lifting my face. "You're the one who wanted to go back and deal with things. Remember?"

I shrug my shoulders and let my focus fall toward the ground. The truth is, I don't know what I want. I want everything back at home to be okay, but I want this life too.

"I've been having so much fun here that I started to forget about what we did leave behind," I say. "I hope we can fix everything when we go back home in a couple of weeks." I fidget with the hem of my shirt, avoiding his normal response to this issue.

He drags his fingers through his hair and shakes his head with frustration. "We don't know how bad this situation is yet." There it is, the same response I always get. It's everything I already know. It doesn't matter. "I don't want to make any permanent decisions right now. That's all," he sighs. "I'm sorry, Chlo. I didn't mean to bring your mood down." His hands slide down my back and rest over the waistband of my pants. "Can we forget the last five minutes?" he pouts. "Come back up here and kiss me." His lips mold into that crooked grin. He knows the affect it has over me. Damn him.

I wrap my arms back around his neck, bringing my lips close to his ear. "I'll see what I can do." I press my lips gingerly against his neck and release my arms. "So, where's my bedroom?" I giggle. He groans.

"Down there." He points down the short hall. "I'll show you."

He pushes the door open and I expect to see four white walls with no furniture. However, this room is fully furnished: a king sized bed, mahogany furniture, a white plush area rug, and Parisian paintings cover the walls from top to bottom. My jaw drops open, surprised and in awe. The furniture isn't what makes this room so unique though. The view is like nothing I've ever seen. The Eiffel Tower, sparkling and beaming with all its glory appears less than a mile from our apartment.

I spin back around to face him and place my hands against his chest. "When did you have time to do all of this?" I run to the window and fling open the French doors, welcoming the scent of fresh rain. "How did you manage to afford this place?" I lean over the side, looking at the street lined with bakeries and stores. "Do I even want to know?" I laugh.

He tries to inconspicuously pull a price tag from the hanging curtain. "I've had jobs here in the drift over the years and never really much of a reason to spend the money...until now."

It's a dream inside of a dream.

He pulls me around to face him. "Glad you like it," he smiles.

I reach up and brush my lips against his cheek. "This is amazing. You're amazing." I pinch my lip between my teeth, noticing how he looks even more beautiful under the glow of the Eiffel Tower.

His eyes drift to my bitten lip. He clears his throat and takes a step back. "I think I'm ready to call it a night. Are you tired?" he asks.

Not really. I could stare at both of these views for the rest of the night. "I guess."

He walks over to the bureau and pulls out a couple of the drawers. "I filled these up with the new clothes we just bought. I hope you don't mind."

He's taken me to nearly every clothing store in the city. It's almost as if he's been trying to give me and show me everything I haven't had in my life. I never had the opportunity to pick out my own clothes or wear anything that resembled a fashion trend from this century. Now I have enough clothes to fill my dreams for a lifetime.

I reach inside the top drawer and run my fingers over the folded clothes. "I was wondering where all of our clothes were being sent," I grin. I continue to fumble through the drawers, searching for something to wear to bed.

My cheeks fill with warmth when I pull out a silky black nightshirt. I can see Alex trying to hide his excitement. I'm not doing as good of a job hiding *my* nerves. "I'll be right back."

I slip into the bathroom. Oh boy. Okay. This is it. Get a hold of yourself, Chloe. What am I saying? He's probably not even thinking about *that* next step right now. It's too soon. Maybe not. It's been a year. Breathe. If it happens, it happens. If not, oh well. I change my clothes and pull in a deep breath before opening the bathroom door back up. It's fine. I'm fine. He's fine.

I walk out and immediately look for a distraction to give me some more time. The living room light is still on. I take another deep breath and flip the living room light switch off.

I turn back toward the bedroom and notice he's already shut the light off in our room. Maybe he's just really tired.

I reenter the room and see that it isn't as dark as I had thought. The sparkling lights from the Eiffel tower reflect off the walls. My nerves ease as the glow pulls me back over to the window. I press my face up against the glass, hypnotized by the view. My mind never lets me down.

Two warm hands slide across my shoulders and down both arms. A rush of goosebumps cover my skin. "I thought you were going to sleep," I say in a soft voice, holding my focus on the blinding lights.

"How can I sleep when you're standing here looking as beautiful as you are?" He places his lips on my shoulder. "Sleep can wait." The stubble on his chin electrifies the skin on my collarbone.

"It's late." He tugs on my arm. "Let's go to bed."

I turn around, frozen, staring into his glowing eyes, knowing that everything is right in the world. He moves in closer then lifts me into the cradle of his arms and walks me over to the bed. I'm lying here speechless and motionless in place as he climbs over me to his side of the bed.

He traces his fingertips down my arm. "Are you okay?" he whispers.

"Yeah. Why? I thought we were going to bed?" I'm not sure he's buying that.

He leans over and slides his heavy arm around my waist. His lips trail kisses from my ear down my neck and over my shoulder. "Good night, beautiful." His words tickle my skin.

"Good night!" I chirp.

Real smooth, Chloe. I'm such an idiot.

I lie in bed wide-awake for a while, pondering my thoughts, nerves, desires…and his. My mind is restless, but my body is pretty comfortable lying so close to his.

"Are you asleep?" I ask, my voice hushed.

"No." His voice is deep and smoky. "Are you okay?"

"I'm just having trouble falling asleep."

"Me too," he says. "Hey Chlo?"

"Yeah?" I turn onto my side to face him.

He places his fingers on the side of my face, brushing his thumb over my cheek. The intense look in his eyes does something to me. A rush of warmth fills my face. His eyes—those eyes—they're methodical as they drift down to my lips. He moves in closer, placing one hand behind my neck and the other on my hip. I can sense the desire growing within his grip as he leans in, letting his lips float over mine. Our noses brush against each other's, sliding into place as if they are the last two pieces of a puzzle. The mint on his breath cools my lips and sends chills up my spine. My pulse quickens with anticipation. Unable to restrain my urge, I close the gap between us, sucking every last bit of air out of the little amount of space left between us.

Our lips move together in perfect sync. His hand skates from my neck up to the back of my head. The air in my lungs goes flat, and my head starts to spin. His fingers twist into my hair, forcing our lips to press harder and our breaths to become shorter. My gut is doing summersaults, and my heartbeat is dancing to its own rhythm. The uncontrollable motion between us causes a moan to escape from his throat, and the sound is like a melody designed for only my ears. I didn't know I wanted this as much as I do at this very second, and I feel like I don't need anything more in my life than I do him right now.

His fingertips trace down my leg before lifting it over his, snaking our bodies into a tight knot. The friction between us increases the heat with each movement, and I lose all sense of control. I press my fingers into his shoulders, holding him in place, forcing an entrapment of oxygen into a chokehold between us.

I hesitate only for a second before pulling myself on top of his warm body, locking my eyes into his as if I was confessing my undying love to him with just a look, with just my breath, with just my lips. His hands sweep under the hem of my shirt and up my back. He holds his grip tight, claiming me as his. I surrender to his touch, and lower myself onto him. His head cranes around mine, and his lips blow warm air into my ear. The feeling warms my insides, electrifies my nerves, and holds my pulse hostage. I feel like he wants to say something, but words aren't necessary. His breathing speeds and slows against my skin. Why are they slowing? I need to hear the want through his incessant breath. Keep breathing for me, I plead in silence.

"Chloe…" he whispers, breathless. He glides his hands down my hips. "We shouldn't." His face presses against my neck. "Not yet," he exhales, releasing a sigh. "I shouldn't have let things get this far. It's not the right time…I'm sorry."

Right time?

Embarrassed and overwhelmed, I flip over onto my side, wrapping myself in the sheets. I want to cry from the combination of emotions gnawing at my stomach. *I* shouldn't have let things go that far. I should have kept things simple. We don't even know what our future holds. We could be dead soon.

CHAPTER TWO

HAPPINESS LOVES MISERY'S COMPANY

THE SUN PEAKS THROUGH OUR WINDOW, waking us from a night I partially want to remember and mostly want to forget. Regardless of my recent embarrassment, I still want to lie here staring at him, waiting for his eyelids to reveal the two most beautiful blue crystals I've ever seen.

When he finds me looking at him, a smile tugs on the corners of his lips. "Morning, beautiful." His voice is raspy and lustful. He wraps his arm around me and tugs me in against him.

"I'm sorry about last night." His lips drop to my cheek and then trace up to my temple. "Sleeping next to you, wearing that..." He glances down at my silken shirt. "It was a little harder than I thought it was going to be."

"Yeah," I say, my voice hardly audible.

"Are you mad?" Worry clouds over his perfect smile.

"Mad?" I gaze up at him. "A little embarrassed." I lock my eyes on the comforter to avoid his look. "I'll be right back." I get up from the bed and grab his hanging sweatshirt from the closet doorknob.

He lifts himself up on his elbow. "You're embarrassed?"

I cover my face with my hands. "Yes," I stifle an awkward laugh. "I'll be right back."

I walk into the bathroom and stare at my flushed face in the mirror. Get a hold of yourself, Chloe. You're acting like an idiot. So what if it didn't happen last night. Maybe it's best that it didn't. I just wish I knew why he stopped. Maybe I made him stop. Maybe it's the workings of my own mind. Maybe I'm the one who isn't ready.

A splash of cold water trickles down my face, and I pull my hair up and twist it into a high knot. I lean forward against the base of the sink and stare at my own reflection, wondering what's happening inside of my mind—how this can feel so real. There isn't a day that goes by when I don't question the validity of the reality I live in.

Cold and warm. Love and hate. I'm not given an option to choose, but I want this. I want Alex. I want Paris. I want to be loved. I don't want what I left behind. I don't want that to be the base of everything that is real. Because anything that is real is bad. Evil.

I pad along the hardwood floors into the kitchen, searching for words to break the tension I'm feeling. "Do you want to go for a run this morning?" An opportunity to burn off this awkwardness is the best thing I can come up with.

"Love to," he grins.

*   *   *

I feel myself begin to wear down after a half hour of running along the river's edge. I'm out of shape. My muscles ache and my lungs burn. I try to push through the pain, but my head is aching now too. The pain fleetingly increases until I feel a pulsating throb on the side of my face. Maybe I'm dehydrated.

I try to catch up to Alex, but the pain swells with each step, and the ache is debilitating. I grip both sides of my head and a cold sweat covers me, forcing me to my knees. I can't figure out what's going on. This isn't pain from dehydration. This is something more.

I choke out to Alex, "I need to go home." I continue coughing through my gasping breaths. "My head." Little colorful spots sway around me like floating bubbles, and my head feels heavy in my hands.

He sprints over to me and drops to his knees. "You okay?" He cups his hands around my cheeks and tilts my face up to look at him. "What's going on?"

"A pain. In my head." I scrunch my eyes tighter and pull myself up against a nearby rock.

"Did you have any water before we left?"

"No."

He reaches his hand out to help me up. "You're dehydrated."

By the time we reach the last block before our apartment, the headache disappears almost as suddenly as it appeared.

*   *   *

Alex reaches into the refrigerator and pulls out a bottle of water. "Drink all of this." He hands it to me.

"Is this yours?" I hold the bottle up. "We didn't go food shopping."

He chuckles quietly. "I had the kitchen stocked with the necessities." Of course he did. He opens a couple of the cabinets above the counter to show me what we have. "You hungry?"

"Starving." I open the refrigerator door, curious as to what he had it stocked with. Yup. Necessities. "How about some eggs?" I remove the egg carton from the fridge. "I'll make them."

He places his hand over his stomach and grins. "I would love that," he says, as he pulls out the milk and butter. "You sure you're feeling up to it?" He places the items down on the counter. "Besides, how are your cooking skills?"

"I'm fine," I say as I rummage through the lower cabinets for a bowl. "I'm better than the cooks at the institution." Truth be told, I've never cooked anything before. Crazy girls aren't allowed near dangerous kitchen appliances. I've been a spectator for long enough though. I think I can manage to scramble up some eggs.

He raises an eyebrow and laughs. "Good enough for me. I think." He brushes by me and slaps his hand against my butt. "Get cookin', beautiful."

Frustration washes through me again and warmth tinges my cheeks. Am I the only one feeling unsettled about last night? He seems even more relaxed now than he was yesterday. Now I'm twice as uptight as he was.

He's been eating quickly, and I've been eating slowly, replaying everything in my head until his voice snaps me from my haze. "I'm impressed, Chlo," he says, shoving the last forkful into his mouth.

"Thanks. I guess it's not bad for my first try," I grin. "I'll have to try my cooking skills on something a little more advanced next time."

"You've never cooked before this?" he laughs. "You knew not to cook the eggshells, right?"

"Oh. Was I not supposed to?" I scoff. "Silly me." I slap my palm against my forehead.

* * *

I wish I had a magic button to shut off the horrific movie that replays in my head. The recollection of my final memories in the institution haunts me daily, sometimes hourly. I don't think I can ever forget the look on his face. The pain I felt. Or the fear in Alex's eyes. It was unreal, but at the same time, unbelievably real. I've tried to convince myself that I'm safe here. But I'm only fooling myself. I couldn't be further from safety. Even though these thoughts take up a permanent residency in part of my mind, today I have an extra bad feeling—like something is creeping up on me. Maybe I just feel guilty for being *this* happy. It's almost like we're cheating in a game. Except this is not a game. I'm not sure how long we can keep this up—playing house in this illusory world. I'm confident that everything will catch up to us eventually.

"You're spacing out again. Are you okay?" Alex tugs on my hand.

I shudder at his words. "I'm fine. Don't worry about it," I say, trying to brush him off. "What store should we go into next? We need a throw rug for the living room."

He tugs on my hand again and spins me around to face him. "Worry about what?" he asks. His eyes are full of concern and I know I'm about to ruin his day. He tries to pretend this is all okay—hiding and masking the truth of our existence. I know this is his only reality, besides the whitewashed mind that inhibits the part of his physical being. But this isn't my only reality. My mind is still connected to my body, and I'm far more aware of my actual existence than he is.

I cover my eyes with my hand and pull in a sharp breath. "I meant to say that I'm not worried about anything." I look down at the cobblestone sidewalk, feeling ashamed for lying.

"I know you're worried," he says. "Can't you try not to think about it?" He purses his lips into a pout as if he were a child begging for ice cream. It's not that easy to forget about the threat our lives are under.

I nod my head with agreement, but my mind is screaming no. Nothing could make me forget. "I'll try," I say, knowing I don't sound too convincing.

There's anguish in his eyes and the stress lines that I've caused are becoming more prominent on his forehead. He deserves to be happy too, especially after I uprooted his life.

"All I *want* is for you to be happy." He pulls me into him and rests his chin on the top of my head.

I inhale the soapy coconut scent from his shirt and close my eyes. "I want *this* life to be our real one—our permanent one. That's all," I whisper.

"We'll get there, I know it," he says. I wish his words reassured me.

"How are you so sure about all of this?"

He sweeps the back of his thumb across my cheek and his lips pull into a partial smile. "Trust me." He intertwines his fingers between mine and pulls me to continue walking. "After your birthday, we'll go back and check things out."

We made a deal back when we first ended up here. I wanted to go back right away, but he insisted we stay. Lingering in a constant state of unconsciousness doesn't bother him like it bothers me. He's used to this. I'm not. It's almost like we're in a conjoined coma.

* * *

We spent a few days arguing about what we should do—whether we should stay here, or go back to face our complications. We ended up compromising and decided to stay here for a few months until my twentieth birthday. After that, we'd go back. He's looking at this time here in Paris as a break. But I'm counting the days down until the end—whichever end that may be.

I don't want to wait another week until my birthday. "I want to go back now." My abruptness surprises him.

He releases my hand and places his hands into his back pockets. "You don't want to wait until after your birthday?" I never did. He knows this.

This is the first time he's hinted at agreeing to move up the *end* date. I don't care about my birthday. They've all sucked anyway. What's one more crappy birthday? I'll root for year twenty-one.

"I can't help but wonder what Franco's doing to us. You aren't wondering the same thing?" I'm trying to rationalize my hopefully impractical thoughts, but I'm not sure it's working on him or me.

"If you want to go back…we'll go." I can tell by his disconcerted expression that his words aren't quite matching his true feelings. I know it's the last thing he wants to do, but I think we need to.

"I do." I wrap my hands around his forearm, pulling it from his back pocket. "I want to get it over with." I'm just not sure what *it* is.

"We'll go," he says in a low gruff. He turns around and starts down a different direction from which we were originally headed.

"Where are you going?" I follow in his footsteps, trying to keep up with his fast pace. "How are we going to get back?"

"Tomas." The name floats above my head and then falls on me like a brick.

"Are you insane?"

He throws his hands up in the air. "You have a better idea?"

"No," I say. There must not be another option if he's turning to my uncle. He hates him more than I do. I wonder if Tomas is even still here.

After the trouble he got us into last year, I'm not sure how well any conversation will go over with him. My stomach is churning with apprehension. What do we say to the man who's more than half of the reason we're in this trouble?

We slow down as we approach the old beaten door of Tomas's office. With a soft fist, I apprehensively listen for a hint that he's in there. Although, I'm starting to hope he isn't here. Alex is standing guard behind me with his arms crossed over his chest, already angered.

I pull him to look at me. "Take it down a notch," I say. "You want him to help us, right?" Then again, maybe he doesn't want him to help us.

The office door creaks open, and Tomas sticks his head out of the small opening. He looks staggered and panicked to see us standing before him. "You. I cannot help you. Sorry, dear."

Tomas attempts to close the door in our faces, but Alex steps in front of me and stops the door. "We're coming in, Tomas." He pushes the door back open. "Are you going to move out of the way, or am I going to make you?"

"Alex!" I shout. I try to grab a hold of him, but my attempt to keep him in place is useless.

"Okay. Okay," Tomas says. "No need to get physical." He waves us in, bowing before us. "Come in." His movements are skittish and he works diligently to keep a safe distance between him and us.

"We need to talk," I say.

He steps back into his office and slams the door behind him. "What is it, dear?" he asks, pulling his chair away from his desk. He sits and sweeps an array of pill bottles off of his desk and into his top drawer. I don't even want to know.

I pull up another chair and set it down in front of his desk. "I have something to tell you."

Tomas is staring down at his hands, picking dirt out from his fingernails. "Talk away." He raises his eyebrows and nods his head from side to side. "Is the rabbit hole not treating you well?" He couldn't sound more disinterested in what I have to say, but I have a feeling that might change in a moment.

"I met Franco." The words spew out of my mouth. His eyes dart up to meet mine, and his pupils are fully dilated, appearing as if he's lost in thought.

It seems to take him a minute to digest what I said. "Pardon me?" His voice sounds strangled. "You must not be that ridiculous, dear," he laughs. "That is quite impossible." He pulls a mirror out of his top drawer and checks his reflection, tilting his chin in various directions. I can't imagine what he's looking for. "I'm very much aware of *who* I am at all times," Tomas drones. He drops the mirror back into the drawer and slams it shut. "Franco has not been around for many years, not even during your lifetime."

I'm doing my best to remain calm, knowing that hostility won't get me anywhere, but I obviously need to supply him with more proof of the current situation Alex and I are both in.

I stand up from the chair and place the palms of my hands down on Tomas's desk, bringing my face closer to his. "I beg to differ. And Alex can attest to this." I feel a storm of rage bubbling in my stomach. I know what I saw, and I know what I heard.

Tomas's hands tremble over his lap, and I watch as he tries to swallows a large lump in his throat. "I am Tomas. I am not Franco. I am not Simon. I am not James. I am one person, Tomas. Tomas is who I am." I wonder what is he doing? I look over at Alex, who doesn't look confused, just enraged. Tomas repeats himself three more times before letting his head fall into his hands.

Alex walks over to Tomas's side, places his hands on each armrest of his chair, and hovers over him, using intimidation as his tactic. "Franco has taken Chloe and I against our will. I'd be happy to brief you on what *you*…I mean…he did to us."

Tomas nods. "Please don't spare any detail." He lifts his head and laughs as if this is a joke. "A fairytale at last." He waggles his eyebrows. "Begin at the beginning, please."

Alex rests on the edge of Tomas's desk. "Last April, Franco approached Chloe in the hall at the institution. He wanted to speak with her for a few minutes."

Tomas reaches over to a tin on his desk that holds a few pens, pencils, and a pair of scissors. He pulls out the pair of scissors and dangles it from his pointer finger. "Please continue," he says.

Alex raises an eyebrow and continues. "I had been waiting for Chloe to meet me." He looks at me with a tinge of sadness still fogging up his beautiful eyes. "But when she didn't return, I went looking for her." Alex slides off the desk and paces around behind Tomas. "When I walked up to her room and saw that the door had been closed and locked, I knew something wasn't right."

Tomas lets the scissors fall from his finger. They hit the desk, causing a loud thud against the silence of the room. "And?" Tomas urges.

Alex slides onto the chair next to me and lets his head fall. "I busted the door open. Chloe was in the corner. Her hands were bound. Her mouth was gagged. Bruises everywhere. And blood was dripping from her nose." Alex pulls in a shuddered breath and places his hands on his knees. His fingers are pressing so tightly his knuckles turn white. It's clear that the anger and resentment hasn't lessened since that day. I'm glad I don't remember any of it.

"Ah-huh," Tomas says. He pulls a pen from his tin cup and a pad of paper from his top drawer. He looks inspired rather than sorrowful.

"I tried to help her. I tried to calm her down—to stop her shivering and her tears." His hand moves from his knee to mine. He's holding onto me as if he thinks I might leave. "But it was only seconds before a shadow appeared on the wall. I knew he had come back for her, and most likely me as well."

Tomas doesn't look up from his note taking. His hand is moving at a rapid rate, and his expression doesn't even twitch. Alex stands and swats the pen out of Tomas's hand. He clenches his fist around the collar of his shirt and directs his attention to his face. "Give me the respect of looking at me when I speak to you, before I remind myself that *you*…are Franco."

"Okay." He places his hands up in defense. "Go on."

Alex releases his fist from Tomas's shirt and sits back down. "He kicked my knees in behind me, shoved my head down onto the bed, and tied a gag around me. Both of us were incapacitated within fifteen seconds." Alex leans back in his chair, folding his arms over his chest. "I want to know why he left us alive." More silence floods the room, and Tomas's face shows nothing but confusion. "I'm sure Franco has a reason for it. Don't you agree?" Alex prods.

"Anything is possible," Tomas sings. He dances his pen in the air and shoves it behind his ear.

Such a quack.

Alex hasn't blinked or shifted his eyes from Tomas's. "Are you going to help us, or what?"

I stand from my chair and lean against the front of Tomas's desk. "When we woke up, we were here in Paris, forced into a permanent drift," I say. "It's a reality that we both love, but it's also a reality that can't keep us alive."

"We need to get back somehow," Alex says.

Tomas drums his fingers on his desk. His eyes are stale—lost in thought. He flings open all of his drawers in search for something.

His mind, maybe.

"You still want to do this?" Alex asks me, ignoring Tomas's floundering behavior.

I kind of have a sick feeling now. Maybe we shouldn't. Then again, if we don't, who's to say we're not already in trouble, or worse. How are we being fed and kept alive? I'm scared to know these answers. What if I'm already dead and this is my heaven? I hate being left with no choice.

Tomas jumps to his feet. His chair bounces off from behind his knees and crashes into the wall. The red veins in his eyes brighten and his eyes ping off of each corner of the office. "That explains it!" he shouts, his words sounding like an *ah-huh* moment. "I've been feeling quite enigmatic for a few months now." He rakes his fingers through his messy hair and grips at the roots. His face flushes and the wrinkles around his sagging eyes swell, making his eyes appear smaller. "A problem. We have one." He presses his finger into his temple firmly. "Franco is a murderer. You should stay away." Um. Yeah. That's why we're here, genius. Have we not made that clear? Alternatively, does he just now comprehend everything we had said?

"Stay away?" I yell. "We're being held as his prisoners somewhere. What if he just decides to kill us? Being here won't do us any good."

Tomas stops for a brief moment, looks up in thought and rushes to the other side of his office. "You do have a good point, dear." He pulls some cords out from behind a bookshelf. "You should go." A pile of books fall to the ground as he continues digging something up from a heap in the corner. "But I must warn you." He heaves a pile of junk over his shoulder. "Franco won't be happy to see that you broke through his intentions. However…" He jerks upright and scratches his fingertips through his greasy beard. "If you still insist, I suppose I could gas you both."

"What will that do?" Alex asks.

"It will cut through your state of unconscious. A negative times a negative equals good things." His eyebrows dance around on his forehead again. "The gas will only last you fifteen minutes or less, but that should give you enough time to assess the situation." He finally spots what he's been digging for and wrestles with a pile of equipment just sitting in the corner of his office.

"Don't you think we should discuss this first? Alex shoots me a harsh look, making it clear he's still not convinced.

Tomas drags a piece of machinery toward us and pulls two oxygen tanks out from behind his back. "Get comfortable for your ride to loonieville," he says, smiling.

Alex drops down into the chair next me and slides his body out to the edge of the seat so he can lean back into a comfortable position. Tomas shoves two oxygen masks on our faces and snaps the elastic behind my ears. He then takes the two loose tubes connected to each of our masks and attaches it to a tank that is labeled, 'narcotic gas.'

Tomas leans over in front of me and places his cold gangly fingers over my shoulder. The smell of his breath matches the sulfuric scent of the office, and I feel stomach acid burning up my throat. "Count backwards from twenty. That should do the trick," he instructs. "Good luck, kids."

Alex and I count backward, echoing each other. The sound of Alex's voice faded when he reached fifteen. And by the time I counted to twelve, darkness set in.

Black to white, whiteness to a blur. Drifting to the cold…

The sensation of falling downward through a spiraling tube sparks an instance of nausea, following a high-pitched squeal that bites at all of my senses. My blurry vision turns into a thick fog, and Tomas's office blurs into something far worse than what I had anticipated. I wish I could rip the gasmask off my face, but the plastic is melting into my skin, leaving my vision clear.

And in a horror movie.

CHAPTER THREE

GHOSTS OF THE ASYLUM

WHERE THE HELL AM I? No, no, no, no, no. This can't be happening. *Okay, Chloe. Breath,* I remind myself. It's only fifteen minutes. I can do this.

Feeling a flurry of fear sneaking up within every fiber of my body, I reach my hands out to feel my way through the obscurity.

I take one step forward. I'm walking across a padded floor.

I take four more steps. *I reach a padded wall.*

I trace my fingertips around the square room.

Another padded room.

A darker padded room.

An abandoned padded room.

It's pitch black. Only gloom pours in through the bar covered window.

"Alex?" I whisper, crossing my fingers, hoping that he's near.

No answer.

I flutter my fingertips along the wall, circling the room around me. My sluggish vision adjusts to the opaqueness as I notice another bar covered window staring at me from across the room. Another room, maybe. One I might find Alex in.

I pull myself up on my toes to look through the window. "Alex?" I whisper again. My eyes search for his dark shadow.

Shit.

He's on the ground with his feet straight out in front of him, handcuffed against a wall.

He's unconscious.

His head is cocked over to the side, resting on his shoulder, and he's staring right through my eyes. His chest is moving, so at least I know he's alive…physically. Maybe I should have assumed his mind would not function here.

Lucky him.

I'm not handcuffed to a wall, but he is.

My heart quakes against my sternum. My stomach feels like stone, and my throat is clenching in on itself. I walk to the other bar covered window, completely horrified. I curl my fingers around the damp, ice-cold bars, and I pull myself up, pressing my face against the metal to look out.

The hallway is just as dark and abandoned as this room. The walls are painted a sea green. They're cracked and peeling, and old rusty handcuffs hang from chains that line the wall. I peer down the other end of the hall, somewhat curious and somewhat petrified as to what I might see. The words "help me" are smeared along the wall in what looks to be blood.

Against my desire, I take in every detail of this deserted passageway, hoping to gain insight on where we might be. But I'm lost and dumfounded. An abandoned institution is the best I can come up with.

Sounds of footsteps arise from the depths of the barren walls, and the dissonance increases with each footstep, warning me that someone is coming. The hallway only has two directions and I don't see anyone in either.

I'm going crazy.

I could only hope.

The footsteps stop, as does the beating of my heart. I close my eyes and pull in a deep lungful. But I inhale someone else's warm, stale breath. My eyes snap open, and two large bulging brown eyes stare back at me. My chest caves in. My lungs struggle to move, and I fall backwards.

I wish I was unconscious. Now I wish I were dead. Please leave me alone. My insides are screaming with fear.

I need to cry.

I can't—he'll hear me.

My lungs hurt from holding my breath.

I don't want to breathe.

I don't want him to see me try.

A metal clink warns me that a key is being shoved into a lock. The door to my cell creaks open and I feel pressure on the padded floor .that surrounds my head. I squeeze my eyes shut, scrunching every muscle in my face, wishing and praying he will go away.

Just leave me here to rot. Please.

Vivid images of my worst nightmare play like a movie reel in my head. But I don't need the movie. If I open my eyes, it will be real.

My head lowers further into the surface of the padded floor. He's too close.

I can hear him breathing.

He can hear me breathing—or trying not to, rather. He nudges my head with the toe of his polished dressed shoe, startling me to gasp for air.

"You are fully conscience," he cackles with amusement. "You're not so much fun when you roam around this room like you're brain-dead—like a zombie. You're just like your stupid boyfriend now. You're welcome." He continues laughing. I'm somewhat conscious here even though I'm fully conscious in Paris? Great. I guess I *am* like Alex now. I'm not sure it's so bad, though. A permanent happiness? If only I were safe here. I know *that's* not the case.

He lifts me up by the back of my shirt, and I peek out through my half lidded eyes, forced face to face with Franco again. He shoves his other hand into the inside of his coat pocket and pulls out a syringe. "Dinner and drinks?" he snorts. "Fine. Since you're awake, I'll let you enjoy your food." He snaps his fingers three times. I hear the sound of a squeaky rolling cart bumping down the hallway. The sound grows louder for what seems like a minute before she appears in the gloomy dimly lit opening of the cell. She's petite, frail, and still as damaged as I saw her last. Ashley, the girl I once referred to as the serial killer looking girl, is now working with the serial killer. Except, it doesn't appear to be at will. She looks terrified, beaten, and weak. "This is Ashley. You remember her from the common area I'm sure, right?" He grips Ashley by the arm and drags her into the cell. "Ashley has been keeping you and Alex fed, and she will continue to do so until I tell her otherwise." He releases her and shoves her back toward the rolling cart. "Isn't that right, Ashley?"

"Lost. Scared. Dying," she says in her familiar voice. She returns with a plate of hospital food and a bottle of water. "Dying." She repeats.

"Where are we and why are we here?" I yell, flinching away from his grip. Although, I have an idea.

"We're below the institution. I need to keep you alive, love. So here are your nutrients and a little something for your hydration."

"Why are you keeping me alive?" I seethe through my clenched teeth. "And Alex, why him?"

"Oh, love. I need you two. You are going to save me." He smiles, flashing his overly white bright teeth. His smile is so large I can see a silver cap on one of his side molars.

"If you need me, why are you so horrible to me?" I ask, honestly curious why he's so cruel.

He releases the back of my shirt, letting me fall to the ground. He hovers over me, his eyes blazing into mine, his left eye giving a slight twitch. "You are your mother's daughter." The corner of his twitching lip pulls up into a smirk. "What other reason do I need?"

I cry silently, still wishing I could wake up. But then I realize, I am awake. This is my reality.

My living nightmare.

He glides the palm of his hand over his perfectly slicked down hair. "You are not as sweet as you pretend to be, love." He takes a few steps back and leans his back against the wall. "I can see right through you."

With the space between us, I take the opportunity to scoot back against the opposite wall. It gives me the illusion of space. An illusion is all it really is, though. "I'm nothing like my mother. I can assure you of." I swallow my fear. "As a matter of fact, I hate her. More than anything."

Please believe me.

Please.

I pull myself up to my feet, still keeping a supportive grip on the wall behind me. "However she treated you, she has also treated me."

He moves forward, closing in on me. My knees are weak and they want to give out. But I hold myself still, forcing short spurts of air into my lungs. He stares at me, hovering with his lip curled to one side. "What did she do to you?" he asks, barely moving his mouth to speak.

"I've been locked up my entire life," I say. "With the exception of being dragged down to the institution twice a week." My words sound garbled, as if I was choking on them.

He tugs on the bottom hem of his black suit jacket, straightening it to lie flat. His eye twitches again. "I don't believe you," he says. His voice is complacent and calm. "You are a good liar." His unmoving smirk makes me squirm. "Just like your mother."

My mother? He thinks I lie like her? Am I even capable of such a trait? I'm not lying. I have been a prisoner. Anyone could look at me and recognize that.

Anyone, but him.

I stare up into his dark sinister eyes, terrified of his next move. He pulls open the right lapel of his jacket and retrieves another syringe. With gentle force, he reaches down for my wrist and pulls it up in front of me. I don't fight him. It's not worth it. I'm putty in his hands, and I'd rather face the outcome of whatever is in this syringe. "Do you want to eat first?"

First? Before what? Ashley approaches me with some kind of sandwich. My stomach doesn't feel empty, but it doesn't feel full either. Unsure of how well Ashley has been taking care of us, I take a couple of bites and wash it down with the opened bottle of water she's holding. "Are you going to feed Alex?"

"Dying," she says in response.

"Please feed him," I beg.

"I've already told you, I need you both alive. He will be kept fed," Franco growls.

It's clear my meal is complete as he wraps his hand around my bicep and holds the needle an inch away from my skin. "Chloe," he rumbles my name. "Do not tell your boyfriend about what happened here."

He punctures the needle into my skin. I welcome the pinch, knowing that it has to take me somewhere better than here. "You should know that I do not like to be betrayed." He lets my sleeve drop back into place. "It never ends well." His laugher booms in my ears. "Or, I guess it does *end* well...for me."

He leaves me, liquefying onto the padded floor. Light shines through me, and sulfur burns my nose. I endure the grotesque aroma, knowing where I'm heading.

*   *   *

When light fills my vision, I find myself sitting in the chair that I had fallen asleep on in Tomas's office. I grip the armrests with force and my eyes dart over to Tomas. I pull my gas mask off and drop it on my lap. "How long has it been?" I ask, panic quickening my voice.

He snatches the gas mask from me and checks his watch. "Thirteen minutes." With a confused look, he checks the dial on the gas tank. "How did you get back sooner than Alex?"

"Franco injected something into me, and then I blacked out again. He's holding us hostage in two separate padded rooms. They aren't the padded rooms we've seen before though."

Two minutes pass before I see Alex's eyes twitch below his eyelashes. He's waking up. Relief overwhelms me.

I fall to my knees, clawing at his legs, trying to snap him out of it. "You okay?" I ask, on the verge of tears.

He pulls the gas mask off his face and squints one eye half open. "I don't know what happened." He looks groggy and seems puzzled. "Everything just turned black until now."

I run my fingers up and down the side of his stubbly cheek, rousing him to focus on me. "You didn't see anything?" I ask..

He pushes my arm away and grabs a hold of my shoulders. Angst fills his eyes. "What happened? Are you okay?" The words leave his mouth as a shout. But I know it's not me who he's angry with.

"Nothing happened." I force a fake smile. "Everything is fine."

A lie.

I hate lying to him. I just wish it were the truth. I wish I was in denial and could believe to make him believe.

"You're a horrible liar," he says. "Tell me what's going on." His voice calms an octave, but veins bulge from both sides of his face.

"We're not dead." I shove my hands into my pockets. "That should be all that matters, right?" I sound a little too chipper.

More like a little too fake. I can already see it on his face. He doesn't believe me.

He throws his gas mask onto the ground and steps out from the cords below him. "That's not all that matters!" he shouts. "Dammit, Chloe. Tell me what you saw."

I can't tell him. I don't know what Franco will do if I did, and I can't risk that. I already know we're not getting out of those padded rooms without going through hell, and any attempt to escape him will likely guarantee that we'll become the new ghosts of the asylum. It's not happening.

Alex pushes off the window and trudges toward me. "We aren't leaving this office until you tell me what the hell is going on." His actions are unsteady, and he's completely freaking out. I've never seen him act like this. "Why is this a secret?"

Left with no words, I rush toward the door. I need to get out of here. I don't know how else to avoid this interrogation. He can't know. Franco made that clear. "I've had it." I stare back and forth between Alex and Tomas. "I'm leaving."

If he knew I was protecting him, he wouldn't be acting this way. He should learn to trust me a little.

With anger blistering through me, I whip the office door open and slam it behind me. My brisk walk carries me multiple blocks until I stop to catch my breath. I'm somewhat surprised that Alex hasn't come after me. Now I'm just more infuriated. He has no right to be mad. I'm just trying to protect him from something he has no control over. He should just thank me for dealing with the issue. I'd love to be able to block it all out like he can.

My long heavy steps return me to my apartment, and I'm still trying to convince myself I'm right in this situation.

I pound the back of my head against the wall in our furnitureless living room for over an hour, and my anger still doesn't settle. I wonder where he could be? I doubt he stayed to hang out with Tomas.

I pace the empty room for another hour, racing after my unruly thoughts. I'm tired, and I want this to be over. I plop my butt back down on the floor, pulling my legs in tight against my chest. As I bury my face into my knees, I hear what I hope are footsteps leading up to our front door. A key clinks into the lock, and the doorknob twists. Still unsure of what to say to him, I pull myself up to my feet and fold my arms over my chest.

Alex looks at me for less than a second and nods his head, disappointed by my attitude. He walks by me and continues toward our bedroom.

How dare he?

With rage piercing through every nerve, I stomp down the hall and follow him. I leave a few feet between us. "What's your problem? Haven't you ever heard of discussing a solution, rather than just taking control of everything without even acknowledging my feelings on the matter?" I slap my hands over my hips.

He tilts his head to the side, looking as if he's baffled by what I'm saying. He takes a small step closer to me, tightening his eyes so that his forehead crinkles. "I'm sorry, but I don't really care about your feelings right now." He removes his wallet from his back pocket and tosses it onto the dresser. "Do you want to know why?"

"Why Alex?" I lean back against the closet door. "Why do you not care about your girlfriend's feelings? Not important enough to match yours?"

He sits down on the edge of the bed, clasping his hands between his knees. "That's exactly right," he laughs silently. "More like, it's because you won't share them with me. You just decided to leave me in the dark like my goddamn brain does. So, thanks for that."

That hits straight to my heart. I'm a piece of shit. It was never my intent to hurt him. But what the hell am I supposed to do? I still can't tell him what happened or who knows *what* will happen to us.

"That's not it," I say. "I'm protecting you from something you can't do anything about. You should be thanking me." My words sound harsher than I mean.

He clasps his hands around the back of his neck, looking even angrier. "Thanking you?" he squawks. "I want to protect you too, Chloe. Do you have any clue how hard it is on *me* to know that I'm useless anytime we get into serious trouble? What kind of boyfriend am I?" he questions himself. "A shitty one, that's for sure."

He flings his feet up on the bed and leans his head back against his folded arms. "Plus, that was very childish of you to run out of Tomas's office like you did. What's gotten into you?"

I feel like a kid who just got scolded. I look down at my hand and pluck at the threads on my bracelet. "I can't believe you didn't come after me," I whisper, knowing I shouldn't be saying it.

He waves his hands at me as if he were shooing me away. "Chloe, quit it with the drama."

I hate how angry he is. I hate how this is our first real fight and how much it hurts. "Where did you go?" I ask softly.

"I stayed and had a drink with Tomas," he says matter-of-factly.

A drink? I feel a sense of disbelief that Tomas is his newfound comrade. "Oh nice. Are you two best buddies now? What, were you sharing magic formula recipes with the great wizard of hell?"

"You're the one who left me there with him," he justifies, shrugging his shoulders.

I don't want to sit here and argue with him anymore. I'd rather go back to pacing around the living room.

After shooting him an irritated look and getting no response, I turn toward the door. But before I reach the doorway, he lets out a snicker.

I whip my head around with fury, glowering at him. "You think this is funny?" I shout. "How is anything about our first real fight funny?"

His anger transforms into smugness, but I'm not sure I understand why. "Come over here and calm down, will you?" He continues laughing with just his breath.

"No!" I shout. "Not until you quit laughing. This isn't funny." I stare up at the ceiling trying not to break my scolding grimace. He's just too cute to be this angry at and I feel a gurgle of giggles trickling up my throat. I suddenly want nothing more than to end this stupid argument. But I need to maintain a sense of seriousness with the situation too. I can't just give into him. I need to know that he's going to let this go.

"Come here," he says again. He pats a spot next to him.

"Why?"

"Tomas gave me an idea as to what happened. It sounds like we're in quite a pickle," he teases. "Tomas also said that if Franco wanted us dead, we'd be dead."

I inch forward, but I can see he has more to say. "What else?" I ask.

"Look, I know you want to stay here and forget about what you just saw, so I'm not going to ask you any more questions about what happened to you. I'll let it go. We'll stay here, living this life until we have a reason to go back. We can just hope that there isn't a reason *to* go back. If Franco wants to keep us hostage for the rest of his life, so be it. It will just allow us to remain here, together and happy."

I shouldn't have said anything to Tomas. Crap. What if Franco finds out? What am I saying?

Tomas is Franco. I doubt they converse. I want to laugh at the idiocy of my inner dialogue, but I'm still too upset.

Why would Tomas tell Alex, knowing he's putting us both in danger? Now I get to spend every second looking over my shoulder. At least I'm sure Alex doesn't know the real reason why I didn't tell him what happened. If he knew of the given threat, I don't think he'd so easily let it go.

I continue edging toward him, still questioning if this is really over. "Well, thank you for understanding," I say, placing my hands on my hips. "I'm sorry for storming out of Tomas's office."

He grins, the half-crooked grin that makes me weak. "You don't have to apologize, Chlo. But it's okay, I forgive you." He pats the bed again.

I stop walking toward him. "I am mad that you didn't come after me," I say, teasing with a slight smirk.

"If you didn't run off, I wouldn't have to run after you and you wouldn't have to be mad at me for not running after you. So technically, you're the only one to blame." He winks, exposing his two perfect dimples.

My anger turns into embarrassment as I can see his point. I roll my eyes up toward the ceiling, not wanting to see his grin. "Point taken."

"Now that we have all of this crazy stuff out of the way, do you forgive *me* for being a little too harsh?"

"Maybe."

He purses his lips and narrows his eyes at me. He seems to be getting a thrill from my sarcasm, and he leans forward, reaching for my arm. His fingers wrap around my wrist and he pulls me onto the bed with him.

With my hands pressed against his chest, I push myself up, forcing space between us.

"Chloe…" he says, propping himself up against the bed.

"What?" I ask, biting my lip, trying to coerce him in.

His expression turns serious and somewhat pained. "You're killing me," he groans.

* * *

We're lying in bed and my stomach is complaining for dinner, but I watch as the sun fades away and the lights of the city appear. The shadows on the walls force my mind to wander back to the padded cell—memories of Franco's beady eyes zap a shroud of fear through me. What is he doing to me there? What does he want from me? Can I really just sit here and pretend I didn't see what I saw? I mean, keeping Alex in the dark—can it really be what's best?

Alex nudges my nearly unconscious body. "Do you want to go take a walk and grab a bite to eat? I'm starving," he says, brushing hair off my cheek.

"Now?" I whine. I don't see myself climbing out from the warm comforts of the bed any time soon.

"Not until you tell me you forgive me," he says. "But after that, yes."

"Eh...I still need to think about it," I grin. "Besides, this bed has me trapped in its warmth."

He whips the covers off me and gives me a playful look. "Not so warm now?"

I groan and throw the heap of blankets at his head. "Fine," I laugh.

I comply with the cool breeze floating in from the window and bounce off the bed, making my way into the bathroom to freshen up.

I study myself in the mirror, and I suddenly feel as bad as I look. A wave of dizziness crashes into me and I grip the sink for stability. I got up too fast, but not fast enough to cause a bloody nose. I watch as a trickle of blood drips from my nose. I look at myself, studying the red raindrop dripping over my lip. This can't be good. I grab a wad of toilet paper and press it up against the base of my nose to stop the bleeding. I don't feel any pain, but I'm not sure if pain accompanies a typical bloody nose. I've never had one before. Maybe it's the climate change here. If only I could be naïve enough to think that.

I continue cleaning myself up and pinch my cheeks to avoid Alex asking why I look so pale. There's no need to worry him with a bloody nose. He worries so much about everything else.

I walk back into the bedroom and find Alex clutching the side of his head. I feel frozen at first, trying to piece all of this together. I think I might know what's causing our concurrent bouts of bodily distress.

"You okay?" I run my fingers through the ends of his hair. "What's going on?"

He nods. "I just have a weird headache. It must be from getting up too fast. I think it's going away though. Don't worry. I'll be okay." He continues rubbing the pain from his temple.

Dammit, Franco. We've become his mindless dartboards.

CHAPTER FOUR

THE TWISTED RIVER

I WONDER IF PARIS LOOKS THE SAME outside of my mind. It's a dream. An amazingly beautiful dream.

Alex hands me a crepe wrapped in paper. Our nightly ritual—now a distraction from the reality I want to forget about once again.

"Ready?" he asks.

"For wh—"

The light show erupts into the sky. It startles me and whisks my breath away. The thrill gives me an emotional reaction. It doesn't matter how many nights in a row I've seen the Eiffel Tower beam with sparkling lights, the beauty and grace of the synchronized illuminations bring happy tears to my eyes.

Beautiful.

Everything is so beautiful here.

It was as if it was lit just for our showing. People are scattered across the lawns, picnicking, drinking, laughing, and romancing. I try to take it all in, knowing full well that every day could be my last here. Whether I die or remain a prisoner in a padded cell, I need these memories to live on within me. I continue scanning the swarm of people taking in the breathtaking moment when I notice a woman walking through the crowd with a massive birthday cake—one large enough to feed an entire restaurant. The French words to "Happy Birthday" grow in volume, and as the sound catches on the wind, the entire landscape fills with hundreds of people erupting into song. My heart flutters with shyness for the person on the receiving end of the song. The thought of this many people wishing me a happy birthday at one time would make me run and hide. The woman with the cake shifts her direction and walks toward us.

She's walking toward *us*.

I tug on Alex's arm, pulling him out of the woman's path.

But she follows us.

The singing increases in volume and my cheeks begin to burn. She's within a couple of feet from us, and I realize that they are all singing to me.

This entire lawn full of people is serenading me in French, wishing me a Happy Birthday.

I can't stop the hitches in my breath or the tears trickling from my eyes. The second the song ends, hats are thrown into the air, and clapping hands create a roar of thunder. They all yell, "embrasse-la." I'm not quite sure what that means, but I have an idea.

Alex's lips brush against my ear. "First, blow out the candles." I can feel his smile grow across my cheek.

I focus my attention on the massive cake, and I suck in as much air through my lungs as possible. I blow the hundreds of candles out as fast as I can. As the last candle singes, Alex's hands find my cheeks. His fingers curl around my ears, and he pulls my face close to his. The hollering continues, all still shouting, "embrasse-la."

"What does that mean?" I whisper.

His lips cover mine. His hands slide down my back and he wraps his arms so tightly around me that the embarrassment of everyone watching us fades away. They all blur into the background, leaving us here, alone, in front of the dazzling tower that's lit just for us.

For me.

His lips move around my mouth and his tongue dances around mine. He pulls away slightly to whisper, "Happy Birthday, beautiful."

"My birthday isn't for another couple of days," I remind him.

He shrugs. "It's your birthday week. I would celebrate you every day if I could. At least I have an excuse this week."

"I can't believe you did this for me," I say, my voice trembling. The emotions overcome me, reeling through the memories of each forgotten birthday, each year that I sat at my window making a wish on a star instead of a candle, each year where all I wanted was someone to love me. This may only be in my dreams, but all of my wishes have come true. The stars in the sky have been good to me.

He wipes a tear from my cheek. "The people like to celebrate here. I called a local bakery, asked for a little help, and got this." He spreads his arms out to the sides, indicating all of the wonderful people who joined in for a moment of celebration.

The woman hands the cake to Alex, smiles and disappears into the crowd. It's clear why they call this place The City of Romance.

After sharing our cake with anyone who wants a piece, Alex doesn't spare a second before wrapping his hand back around mine, and pulling me away from the crowd and toward the tower. "Where are we going now?" I laugh.

"You'll see when we get there," he grins.

We come up to the Seine river—the place of our fist kiss. I remember the smooth touch of his skin and the warmth of his lips as they touched mine. My heart didn't know how to react. It pounded against my ribcage with excitement, with eagerness. I wanted to freeze that moment and make it last forever. I wanted us to last forever, and that is still all I want now.

"I love it here," I say, nestling my back against his body.

"I fell in love with you here," he says, turning me around to face him. "I never really told you where we were when I felt those words spouting from my soul. I knew it was too soon to tell you, though. It happened before we even had our first kiss," he sighs. "It was like this epiphany came over me. I mean I had always loved you, even when we were kids. I loved you as my best friend, the little girl who was just like me. Then I loved you when I saw you re-appear at the beach. I immediately felt the same connection to you as I did when we were kids. It was like nothing had ever changed." He drapes his arms around me and presses his forehead against mine. "Then when we finally reconnected, different feelings started to grow within that love. When I caught you gazing at me on the boat that day, my heart felt like it was going to explode. I could see the look in your eyes. I could tell you felt it too. It was that moment that I knew there could not be another description for the way I felt, other than being absolutely and incessantly in love with you." His lips drop to my nose.

I knew that moment when he kissed me was the best moment I'd ever had, but knowing what was behind that kiss, just somehow made it even better.

His lips move over to my cheek and then to the corner of my lips. "I like to reminisce," he whispers against my mouth.

He presses his lips against my bottom lip, sending a rush of eagerness up through my stomach. I squeeze my arms tighter around his back, pulling him into me with a sense of desire that can only be quenched by his mouth right now. I never would have thought that each kiss could be more intense than the last one, but clearly, it can.

As air becomes a necessity, we pull away, still deep within each other's stare. He glides his hands up to my face and runs his thumb across my lips. "I am so in love with you, Chloe. Even more than that day when I thought I couldn't possibly feel any more than I was feeling at that second."

I grip each side of his face, looking deep into the depths of his beautiful eyes. "Thinking back to that day now, I'm pretty sure I was falling in love with you then too. I just had no idea what love was supposed to feel like yet. But, you didn't fail to show me," I say. "Plus, I also needed to make sure you were a good kisser," I laugh softly against his lips.

Breaking our embrace, he pulls me over to steps that lead into the water, which reflects the Eiffel Tower as we sit. It mirrors the picturesque view hovering above us.

I nestle my head into his shoulder and feel infused with peace. Dream or not, this is all real to me. "This is beautiful. I love our little spot here."

He wraps one arm around my neck, pulling me in closer to him. "The perfection of the river barely compares to your beauty, but I do like it here."

"You're kind of cheesy, but I like it. Keep it coming," I say. "I wish I could stay here forever…with you." As the words come out of my mouth, I know I just set myself up for another reminder of how temporary this place is in our lives.

Just temporary.

"I can't promise we can stay *here* forever, but I can promise you that *I'm* here forever. That is, if you want to be with me." He turns his head toward me and his eyes lift expectantly, searching for a reaction.

I can't tell if he's asking me if I want to be with him forever, or if he's inquiring whether I've made up my mind yet. When I think about forever, I can't consider the thought of not having him in my life. I would be miserable. I would be half of what I am. I wouldn't be me. I'm only twenty years old, but love like this doesn't just disappear. It grows and I can't imagine feeling more love for him than I do now.

"I want nothing more than to grow old with you. I love us and I love that we are the only two in the world that understand each other. We're lucky to have found each other." A smile consumes my face. "Have you ever considered the thought that maybe our lives were pre-designed for us and that it was planned for us to be together?"

"That's exactly how I've always felt," he says, taking my hand with his and pulling it up to his mouth.

"What do you think we'll be like when we're eighty? You know, other than old and wrinkly," I ask.

With a serious look on his face, he squints his eyes, looking through me, as if he were looking into the future. "We'll be more in love than we even are now, and lots of people will look up to us and love us. I know we're going to build an incredible life together, and this right here is just the preview of our story," he says, focusing back on my eyes, but still mesmerized by his own thoughts.

I lift my hand up and look at my empty ring finger. "Maybe… we should get married," I say, laughing at my own joke.

He pushes my hand down to my lap. "Maybe you should leave that part to me, Chlo." His response is more serious than I anticipated.

Well, that's embarrassing. I shouldn't have said that. "I'm sorry. I didn't mean to make you uncomfortable. I was kidding." The words come vomiting out of my mouth.

Why would I say that? I'm not even twenty and we've been together for less than a year. *That was just stupid, Chloe.*

His eyebrows scrunch together, looking as if I just punched him in the stomach. If only he knew how stupid I felt right now. "You were kidding?" he asks.

Awkward. So very awkward.

"Not exactly, but I didn't mean to make you feel uncomfortable. I know we've only been together for a year," I say, feeling as though I'm losing my breath with each wrong word that flies out of my mouth.

He arches both eyebrows upward and a shy smile tugs at his lips. "You didn't make me uncomfortable. Besides, we've known each other a lot longer than a year. It's just that…well, talking about getting married isn't something I take lightly." His words come to an abrupt stop and he averts his gaze out at the water.

I fidget with the hem of my dress, feeling tongue-tied. Does that mean—is he planning to ask me to marry him? The thought hasn't really entered my mind. I'm so focused on trying to remain in this state of mind that I never considered having the option of marriage.

This is insane.

I'm insane.

No, wait—he's insane.

I wonder if I'm even ready for marriage. I mean, I suppose it won't change much, except for my last name. My mind begins to swirl with beautiful emotions. Most women spend a lifetime searching for the man of their dreams, but I seem to have found mine within my dreams.

Mrs. Alex Levette, I silently croon at the thought. It does have a nice ring to it.

Ring? I wonder what *that* would look like? It *would* be my dream to get married here in Paris. I wonder what my dress would look like? There are so many details to think about. I feel like screaming from excitement, but then he'd know what I'm thinking. I can't do that.

Alex waves his hand in front of my face, snapping me out of my daze. "Earth to Chloe." He rocks my shoulders back and forth. "What are you thinking about?" he laughs. "Wait." He nods his head with an impish smile. "Let me guess...you're planning our wedding out in your head?" His dimples glow under the reflective lights, making me want to tell him the truth. But then he cocks his head to the side and he gives me that, *you're crazy,* look.

I let out an exaggerated scoff. "Nooo," I huff and roll my eyes, trying a little too hard to hide the fact that, yes, I am most definitely planning our wedding in my head. "Don't be ridiculous. I'm just enjoying the view." I try to look out past him at the water, but I know he knows what's really going on in my head. He's totally calling my bluff. "Right. Let's go, you crazy girl."

He wraps his arm around my shoulders and leads us back up the stairs toward the bridge. "Where to, Mrs. Levette—I mean Miss Valcourt." The smirk on his face lets me know how much fun he's planning on having with this, while I get to sit back and wait. It certainly won't help that I'm the most impatient person in the world.

"Let's go to the café." I sprint forward and take the lead. "I could go for some hot cocoa."

"You and your hot cocoa," he snorts.

*   *   *

It's funny, no matter what decade we're in, the café always remains the same—the décor, the furniture, and the menu never change. I think that's what I love about this place.

Alex pulls out a couple chairs from around one of the tables along the outside of the cafe. When we come at night, we like to sit outside and people watch. It's kind of the thing to do around here, and it's nice. Plus, the spaces are tight and we're forced to sit close together.

"I bet you they're on their first date," I whisper in Alex's ear, subtly pointing at the couple in front of us.

"It couldn't be that great of a first date if they're already saying goodbye." Alex looks down at his watch. "It's only eight o'clock."

"Yeah, but look...he's about to kiss her," I chant.

Alex nods and wrenches his lips in a painful line across his face. "Ah, I don't think she's going to bite the bait." He continues watching, squinting one eye.

The man leans in to kiss the woman, and she pulls away. Instead, she leaves him with a friendly but distant hug and then waves good-bye as she struts off in the opposite direction. She left the poor guy with his head hanging low.

"That's so sad," I squawk.

"Told you," he shrugs, acting as if he's dealt with it before.

"What, are you a love expert now?" I slap his arm.

"Chloe. Do you know how many times I tried to kiss you and how many times you turned me down?" Pink fills his cheeks. "I think I'm a little knowledgeable on the subject."

"I think, twice?" I ask, scrunching my nose.

"Three times. But who's counting?" he smirks.

"I only remember two. The first time was when we saw the shooting star, and the second time was on the Ferris wheel? When was the third time?"

"Wait, you knew I was trying to kiss you both of those times, and you looked away?" He throws his napkin in my face.

"I was nervous," I squeal and throw the napkin back at him. "So? When was the third time?"

"You're a pain in the butt, you know that, Chloe?" he says, wrapping his arm around my waist. "The third time..." He thinks for a minute and leans back in his chair. "It was when you were in a coma. I wanted to find a way to wake you up so badly, I was so desperate that I was willing to pull the whole prince charming shit just to see if a kiss would wake you up." He laughs, covering his eyes with his hand.

"So, did you?" I ask, now wondering if I might have been unconscious during my first kiss.

"Nah," he smirks, slapping the air with his hand. "I figured you could use the sleep," he grins.

"Seriously?" I slap my hand down on his knee. "I could have woken up sooner."

"It's fine," he sighs. "I got to stare at you for an entire day. It wasn't so bad." He clasps his hands around the back of his neck, sinking further into the chair.

I wrench my fists around the collar of his shirt and pull his face close to mine. "Don't ever do that again."

He shrugs his shoulders in a playful cowardly way as if I might hurt him. "You should probably stay away from climbing trees then." He leans his head back, easily pulling his collar from my grasp and lets out a loud throaty laugh.

"Yeah. Well..." I cup my hands around his cheeks and press my lips against his. I tease his bottom lip with the tip of my tongue until he responds with a quiet groan.

I win.

I pull away, and I see excitement flicker within the sparkle of his eyes. "We should probably go home," he whispers raggedly as if his voice has been stolen. By me.

"Not yet." I sit straight up, replacing my napkin smoothly over my lap. "It's not the right time yet, remember?" I still haven't figured out what he's waiting for. I feel like I've caught him trying to hold himself back from me. I'm just not sure why. He hasn't given me any real reason.

He groans again, but this time with an exaggerated whine at the end. "Always a pain in the butt."

"Hey now, I'm not the one being a pain in this situation." I give him a dubious look. "Why don't you tell me what exactly we're waiting for?"

I can tell my question changes the mood instantly, and I know I've stumbled across unchartered territory with him. He had to assume I'd ask at some point.

"You deserve your first time to be real. Not in a dream." His words cause a storm of pain to cloud the inside of my heart. A real life with Alex isn't possible. His mind doesn't function well enough to acknowledge me in that way. It could never happen. Is that what this is, an IOU for never?

"Chlo." He places his finger under my chin and forces me to look at the struggle swirling within his beautiful eyes. "I know what you're thinking. I'm still trying to work this out in my own head. I just…I just need a little time. I want every part of us to be real. I want every feeling to be real. And sometimes I forget that everything can only be real within our dreams."

"I understand." Kind of. I force a smile. I'm sure it looks exactly how I feel.

He closes the space between us and kisses me softly. "I don't think you do understand," he says in a deep husky voice that I don't normally hear. "You don't know how badly I want you. All of you. Every single part of you. And let me make one thing clear." His voice lowers to a whisper and he moves his lips close to my ear, tickling my skin with his cool breath. "It will happen someday, whether it is in or out of my control."

"I'm yours, Alex. Whenever you want me, whether that's today or…someday."

He grins in response, and I'm wondering if I changed his mind.

Before any further questions about our non-existent, but very much desired sex life continues, a flamboyant, blond-haired, too much make-up wearing waitress who always seems to wait on us when we're here, struts over to us with her order pad in one hand and a pen twirling in her other. Every time we come in here, it never fails, she hands me a menu, keeps her eyes locked on Alex and then finds some excuse to put her hand on his shoulder. He always rolls his eyes and clears his throat, but she doesn't seem to get it.

I watch as the girl tries her usual tricks, and it suddenly makes me wonder if Alex has ever had a girlfriend before me. He's never mentioned anyone, but it hasn't exactly ever come up either. I think I would feel too weird bringing it up now.

Alex drones a loud, annoyed, and abrupt "Thanks!" to the waitress as she snatches our two menus out of his hands. The volume of his voice snaps me out of my wandering thoughts. Alex's annoyed attitude seems to entice the waitress. She turns around with a smug smile and saunters back into the cafe.

"Why were you being so rude to her?" I ask.

"She's annoying," he shrugs. "That's all." He unfolds his napkin and fidgets with it. I can't argue with that.

The waitress reappears within seconds it seems, and her eyes immediately lock on Alex. I'm surprised the distraction hasn't caused her to drop the huge tray of glasses she's carrying on her shoulder.

As if my mind could control the glasses on the tray, they all begin to tremble against each other as she leans over to place our food down on the table. My eyes are focused on the wobbling glasses, watching as one tips over and crashes to the floor.

Maybe she could quit looking at my boyfriend and concentrate on her job. I roll my eyes and clear my throat. She's frozen. Not moving. What is this girl's problem? "Hello?" I call out, hoping to break through her unmoving stare. She doesn't respond. But I see now that she isn't looking at Alex anymore. She's looking over his shoulder to the street.

Oh.

That's what she's looking at.

Now I'm looking too.

Staring, actually.

Why does this seem to be happening in slow motion? There's nothing anyone can even do. It's like watching a lion attack a mouse in slow motion.

A small two-person car seems to have broken down right in the middle of the busy intersection. They're trying to re-ignite the car. I can see the desperation and utter fear in their eyes, which are bulging, staring at what's coming toward them. They both shove their hands in front of them as if to stop what's coming. But nothing can stop the large truck speeding toward them.

I feel like it's been an hour since we started waiting and watching, yet it's only been a second or two. But that's all it takes, a second. There was no time to yell, no time for the small car to start, and no time for the driver of the truck to even lift his head and notice what he was about to do. It was all...too late.

The impact is ruthless. No one likes to watch a car accident, but watching it from fifteen feet away is even worse. I wonder if the people in the car are okay. How could they be? The truck must have been going thirty miles an hour, and the car is molded around the nose of the truck.

Before I can gather my thoughts for a suitable reaction, Alex sprints toward the mess. It's clear that he's a doer and I'm a thinker.

I approach the scene with caution, but Alex is already in the process of trying to rip the car door off the driver's side. I watch, feeling helpless as I notice that the driver is a man in his late twenties and the passenger is probably the same age. She doesn't look conscious, but the man is screaming for help. After minutes of prying the door open, it finally breaks free from the hinges and dangles by whatever tiny pieces of metal are still holding it together. Alex lunges into the car and drags the man out to the street.

"Call an ambulance!" Alex screams.

I'm still like a frozen block of ice, unable to react fast enough. I manage to push myself through the terror and run into the café.

Everyone is lined up against the window, staring as spectators. Will they live or die? That's the question in everyone's eyes. I have to find a phone. I have to call the ambulance.

When I return, Alex is pulling the woman out of the passenger seat. He's yelling at her, pleading, "Stay with me! Stay with me, you hear me. I can't lose you again."

I can't lose you again? Does he know her? I didn't think he knew anyone here. Why would he be saying that? He's hovering over her, attempting CPR. As he pumps on her chest in between breaths, I watch as he begins to panic. He's losing his grip.

Adrenaline spikes through my body. I have to help. I don't know how, but I have to try. I approach the man lying by himself in the middle of the road. His head looks as if it's floating in a pool of blood. His eyes are open, but I don't think he's conscious anymore. He stopped screaming, and he isn't moving. He isn't wincing from the incredible pain I assume he's in.

I press my two fingers on the artery of his neck, searching for a pulse. I've only seen this done on TV, so I'm not sure I know if I'm even pressing in the right place. And I hope to God I'm not. Everything beneath my fingers is still. Too still. I slide my fingers up, down, and across his neck, feeling for any type of beating sensation. But there's nothing.

Dread sets in. I've taken this man under my care. I have to save him. I watch Alex continue his attempt at CPR, studying his every move so I can try it myself. I pound the heels of my hands into the man's chest. I lift his chin, hold his nose, and blow into his mouth. And repeat. After each cycle, I search for a pulse.

Not even a flutter.

The blood pooling around his head is worsening. I slide my hand over to the other side of his head, searching for the wound. It isn't hard to find. It's large, gaping, and blood is spilling out like an overfilling bucket of water. I remove my sweater and compress it against the wound—something else I saw on an emergency show. It's my only idea. I'm sure this man would love to know that I'm using techniques I learned from watching a stupid TV show. Although, maybe he would appreciate my efforts since no one else is coming over to help.

Finally, I hear the blaring sirens approaching. They come to a screeching halt in front of us and the paramedics rush to our sides. I inform them of my attempts and they tell me I did everything I could. Even so, I feel like a complete failure.

They take over, forcing me to back away and become a spectator once again. I watch carefully as they place two paddles on the man's chest. His body convulses in response, giving a glimmer of hope that maybe whatever they are doing is working. "Again!" one of the paramedics shouts. I can almost feel the pain and jolts in my own chest. Sparks feel as though they are igniting within me instead of him. I think I'm on the peak of an emotional breakdown. They place the paddles on his chest again, and once more, his body convulses. "Nothing," one of the paramedics announces. "He lost too much blood. No pulse."

"Nothing over here either," says the paramedic who's working on the woman.

The paramedics confirm my fear with a nod. My heart is breaking as I watch them cover black tarps over the bodies. That's all they are now, bodies. I've read about death, who hasn't? I've seen death on TV, but I've never watched someone die.

I walk to Alex, suddenly far more aware of the blood of a dead man clinging to my pale skin. I have this overwhelming feeling that the world is caving in on me. Everything is echoing around us. The gravel and glass beneath my feet crackle and crunch with each step. The sirens echo in the distance, playing a haunting melody. The gas fumes are potent and burn my nose. I wish my senses would shut off and allow me to focus on the one thing I need to focus on.

Alex.

The zombie-like figure of the man I love stands before me, emotionless and dazed. He doesn't move a muscle until the last ambulance is out of sight. I slide my blood covered fingertips down the length of his back. I know he must feel like I do. A failure. He's probably questioning why this is happening, here in our dream. It's hard to believe my mind would be capable of so much destruction.

I guide Alex away from the scene and back toward the café. His steps are robotic and his eyes are stretched open and unblinking. I can understand.

We sit down in front of our two cold, hot cocoas and pastries. I watch as the rest of the spectators make it back to their seats, all looking stiff. Most of them are conversing about their assessments of the situation. They're making up their own stories for the man and woman. Some assume they were newlyweds, and some think they were on their first date. But they all agree in their feelings about the truck driver who just walked away without a scratch. They're speculating he was drunk.

Alex is still staring at the cleared scene. The cars have both been towed away, and the debris is being swept. I place my hand over his and arch my neck around to look him in the eyes. "Did you know her? I heard you say *'I can't lose you'*."

He looks at me with grief pouring through his darkening irises—eyes that don't look like they belong to him. I'm not sure if he can't find the words to respond, or if there are too many words to respond with. He ignores my questions and continues glaring out at nothing. Empty stares. Non-verbal. And then it hits me. No. Please, God. No.

"Alex, please let me know you're coherent right now," I plead, reaching the brink of panic. I don't know what I'll do if he turns into the person neither of us can control again.

He nods. Relief comforts me. "I'm here," he mumbles, his tone distant and furtive. But he's speaking, and that gives me relief.

"Why won't you answer me then?" I plead for insight.

Again, he doesn't respond or even look at me. Instead, he pushes his chair out from the table and stands up. He whips his head toward the café doors, yells something in French to the waitress, and runs out of the restaurant.

"Alex? Come back!" I shout after him.

I follow him down the street, but I'm unable to keep up with his pace. He looks as if he's running away from something, and I hope it isn't me. As soon as I reach the end of the road, I lose sight of him. I circle around, looking in every direction, but I don't see a trace of him anywhere. He's never acted like this before. *I'm the only idiot who likes to run off.* I scold myself for making him feel the way *I* feel right now.

At a quick pace, I retrace my steps toward our apartment hoping to find him along the way. But I don't. I go back to our apartment alone, saddened by his behavior.

Two hours later, I'm at a loss for a possible explanation. With despair tugging at my heart, I climb into our cold empty bed. I slide my feet under the blankets and lean back, forcing myself to stare at the bland white ceiling.

I have to block out the flashbacks of the car accident. My mind is never going to rest tonight. Between that and endlessly wondering where Alex is, I've assumed he must have known the woman who died.

As I'm running through ideas on how to find him, I remember he gave me that dumb cell phone a few weeks ago. I thought it was funny when he gave it to me. I even handed it back to him. I didn't see the purpose of having a phone if I had no one to call. He made me keep it though, and said it was for an emergency. An emergency in my dream. I laughed at that too. Now I realize I shouldn't have.

I pull the phone out of the top drawer and hold the power button on until the screen flashes with thousands of colors. I don't even know how to use this stupid thing.

I'm lame.

It can't be that hard. A picture of a phone—I'll start there. I tap it with the tip of my index finger, waiting for something to happen. A picture of Alex pops up next to his name, one of only two names in my phone, Tomas being the other—like I'd ever want to call him. I want to laugh, but I can't right now. I press the icon on the screen, and my heart races with anticipation in hope that this little device might actually do something of use for me.

Four loud rings chime in my ear, then, "Hello, you've reached the voicemail of Alex Levette. Please leave a message and I'll get back to you as soon as possible." The message I didn't want to hear, followed by a long annoying beep. What's the purpose of this thing if I'm here having an actual emergency and it doesn't work? All it's doing is pissing me off more.

I try my hardest to remain calm, but I'm far too worried, confused, and angry. I can't believe he would do this to me. I'm sure he knows how worried I am.

After dialing his number for a tenth time, the phone rings twice again, but then abruptly stops. I hear static, followed by breathing. "Alex, are you there?" I ask firmly, trying to conceal my building anger, but failing at doing so.

No response. Just a click. I look at my phone, and it says *call ended.*

CHAPTER FIVE

TRUE STORY

THE BED WEIGHS DOWN, forcing me to roll to the side. I peel my eyes open from a hazy sleep and glance over into the darkness. I flick the lamp on and look at the alarm clock. "It's three in the morning?" Is this a joke? I groan. "What the hell, Alex?"

He rolls over onto his back. His eyes are bloodshot and puffy, just as they were hours ago. His face is washed out and his lips are quivering in a straight line. I can only assume he's trying to avoid looking into my heated gaze because his eyes are glued to the ceiling. Wasn't I at the same scene? Did I not witness the same disaster? What gave him the right to run away after?

"Well? I'd love an explanation for your disappearing act," I say, propping myself up on my pillow.

He looks at me. My heart starts drumming up emotions when I see the strange look in his eyes, a look that could only be described as broken. I wish I could take back the harshness of my last statement. It's obvious that he's in some kind of turmoil, and regardless of my annoyance, I need to find out what's going on with him before I lash out any further.

"I'm sorry." I place my hand down over his tensed arm. "I didn't mean to come off sounding angry. I was very worried about you. You've never just left me like that before." I perch myself up on my knees to face him. "Please, I'm begging you, talk to me."

He shoves the heels of his palms into his eyes. "You're about to be a lot angrier with me," he says, his voice crackling with anguish.

At least he's speaking, but a looming concern punches me in the gut. I'm not sure I could be any more pissed off than I am.

I don't move my eyes from his. I'm not sure why it's taking him so long to speak, but the suspense is making my stomach twist in pain. Is this going to ruin our relationship? Is this going to cause me to think differently about him, to feel like I've been with a stranger, or worse?

"I haven't been completely honest with you," he says, keeping his eyes trained on the bed sheets.

There it is. Our relationship hovers on the brink of destruction. He's been lying to me.

"What?" I ask, feeling the air being stolen from my lungs.

"Everything," he responds. His voice remains soft and sullen, and tears trickle down his reddened cheeks.

I feel sick and I want to leave, but I want to stay and hear more. How could everything be a lie? What does everything even consist of? Us? Him? Me?

"What does that mean?" I ask, trying to speak through the lump in my throat.

He places his arm over his eyes and leans back against his pillow. "I wasn't always like this."

"Like what? I don't understand." Like me? Mute? Perfect? What?

"It was a cold snowy night. We had just left some kind of party."

"What are you talking about?" I ask, trying to make sense of his story. What does this have to do with lies?

He doesn't blink. He just stares across the room as if he's watching a movie in his head. "My parents and all of my family and friends were there. I can't really remember what the party was for though." He smiles at his memory.

His parents? Is this about his parents? The ones who left him to rot at the institution? Why would he be speaking of them like this? They're horrible for leaving him.

"I thought…"

He doesn't acknowledge my interruption. "The party ended late and I was starting to fall asleep," he laughs softly. "I had made a bed out of two chairs and wrapped myself up in my jacket using it as a blanket. I remember thinking I would be an inventor someday because I had figured out how to put together a makeshift bed." He nods with a look as if he were appeasing a small child's wild dreams.

"My father woke me up and placed my winter jacket around my shoulders, helping me slide my deadweight sleeping arms into each sleeve. 'It's time to go, Al,' he said, ruffling his fingers through my hair. He always called me Al, and he was the only one who did." The smile on his face almost makes me forget about the part where he's been lying about something.

"Al?" I ask. "Is that what you've been lying about? Your name?" I could live with that. "I like the name, Al." I offer a smile. But he doesn't reciprocate or look at me.

"My mother always called me Alexander. 'It's a mouthful, but a worthy one,' she would always say when I'd asked her why she didn't just call me *Alex*.

"Oh," I say. "Okay, so Al, Alexander, you have multiple nicknames. I don't see the harm in that." I know I'm trying to convince myself that the lie could be so simple.

"Chloe, please," he says, his eyes begging for understanding. "When we walked out of the party that night, I remember my mother telling me to try and fall back asleep in the car. She said the ride was going to be a little long since we had to drop a couple of people off. I remember my aunt being in the car. I loved her—she was one of those cool aunts who was always more like a friend than an aunt. She was my mother's younger sister by about fifteen years, making her closer to my age than my mother's."

"You have an aunt?" I ask. "I thought you didn't have any family?" Is that the lie? Please let *that* be the lie.

He sighs, sounding frustrated, probably because I keep interrupting his story. I don't want the truth…I don't think.

"Yes. I have an aunt." His words sting with coldness. "It was seconds before I drifted off in the car and seconds before I was awoken. The blaring headlights startled me awake. I remember the horrible noise of my parents' screams. The sound shocked all of my nerves into a motionless state. The look on my aunt's face was clear as day. It was the last thing I saw before impact."

"Impact?" My heart sinks into my hollow stomach. "What do you mean by 'impact'?" Even though I think I know what it means, I'm not sure if I want to hear the rest.

"Did you know that the word impact has two meanings? One of them, defining a crash, the other is the effect of something. I experienced both definitions at once." He pauses and his breath runs dry.

My eyes widen and fix on his. "Were you in a car accident?" I reach my hand over to his chest.

He sniffs in to hold another tear back. "An accident. I could call it that, but he was drunk. The other driver—the one who hit us head on with his truck. I doubt he accidentally drank that night. Therefore, the accident could be deemed purposeful, right?"

"Of course," I agree with that. He's like this because of some drunken asshole? That's worse than being born this way.

"I didn't remember any of this...until tonight." I wrap my hands around his. They're trembling and hot. "I never saw my parents again. They died. I tried to convince myself that they had forgotten about me, because it hurt less."

No. Why did that have to be the lie? He lied to me about something he lied to himself about. I would much rather have heard that he was lying to me about something that would just hurt me, not him. "I'm so sorry." That's the best I can come up with, and I know it's not enough. I know he needs to hear more than I'm sorry, but what can I say?

"Tonight, when I saw the man and woman near death, I thought it was my parents for some reason. I thought I was getting a chance to save them. Strangely, the only thing going through my head was that if I was able to somehow save them, maybe that would prove my parents *were* still alive."

"Is that why you were saying '*I can't lose you*'?" I ask, scrunching my face with empathy.

"I thought it was my mom," he cries. He's crying. He can't cry. He's the strong one—my rock. He doesn't cry. But tears barrel down his cheeks. Now mine, as well. "When the man and woman were pronounced dead tonight, so were my parents again." I suck in a stiff breath. "I know this supposedly happened twelve years ago, but I swear...it feels like it was yesterday. That's what caused me to feel that way."

I pull in a shuddering breath of my own and brush away the tears pooling under my eyes. I have to be strong for him. He needs me right now. I wrap my arms around his neck, squeezing so hard that it releases some of my own tormenting emotion.

With a gentle nudge, he pushes me off of him, and places his hand on my knee. "I can't talk anymore tonight. I'm sorry," he says. "I just—I just need to be alone with my thoughts right now."

I kiss him on the forehead and run my fingers through his soft blond waves. "It's okay. You can talk to me whenever you want. I'll always be here."

I shut my bedside lamp back off, and I wrap my arm around his chest.

I hold him against me until the sunlight begins to drape over the windowpane. I feel like I should prepare myself for whatever mood he might be in. I don't know how to act around him now. It's as if our relationship just shifted.

He springs out of bed before my eyes have adjusted to light. "Mornin' Chlo," he says, cheerfulness permeates his voice, almost like nothing happened last night.

"Good…morning?"

He stretches his arms above his head. "Can I make you breakfast?"

I raise an eyebrow at his weirdness, or lack thereof. "I'll have some juice…and some unscrambled eggs-planations."

He throws his pillow at me. "Did you really just say that? 'eggs-planations'?"

"I did," I grin and nod. "But really, how are you *this* okay after what happened to you last night?" I don't understand how anyone can just turn their emotions on and off like a light switch.

"I said I didn't want to talk about it anymore. Can we skip the 'eggs-planations' and have some pain-in-the-ass-cakes?" His perfect lips form a pout, and I can't say anything other than okay to that face.

"You're not as funny as I am. You shouldn't try to compete," I smirk.

He picks up a load of towels from the laundry bin and throws one after another at me until I fall backwards onto the bed in defeat. He clambers over me and holds himself a few inches above my body. "I may have had a shitty night last night, but I still love you." He leans down, his lips brushing softly against mine, and then he opens his mouth slightly and bites down gently on my bottom lip. The feeling sends shocks down to my stomach and I feel the need to pull him onto me and make "someday" today.

*   *   *

My first glimpse into Alex's past shows a world of disaster. I have so many questions that I want to ask him. I want to know what happened to him in the accident and what happened to his aunt, if he even knows?

"Pancakes?" he asks, interrupting my thoughts.

"I still want eggs."

He cocks his head to the side and curls his lips into a coy grin. A look of apology, maybe. With slow strides, he approaches me and wraps his arms around my neck. His eyes become stern as they peer into mine. "I'm sorry for leaving you alone at the café last night. That place is supposed to be one of our favorite spots, and I changed that. I should never have acted the way I did, and I apologize...from the bottom of my heart."

"It can still be one of *our favorite spots*. The café didn't change, the café will never change, but the world will always revolve around it. Just don't ever leave me there again." I stretch my body over toward his and kiss him on the nose.

"Thank you," he whispers in my ear. "In the mood for a run before breakfast?"

*   *   *

I hope the wind will blow my thoughts away.

The first couple of miles prove to be what I needed, and I feel better already. This road is quiet, peaceful. There are no cars or any other runners. It's nice to have the road all to our selves.

Focused on the miles of empty dark pavement, I see a set of headlights peak up over the hill. It's sunny out, and I'm not sure why they need headlights at nine in the morning.

With my eyes set on the approaching car, I see an older lady driving the black sedan. She can hardly see over the steering wheel, and she's going slower than I'm running.

As she approaches our side, I'm taken down to the ground with a powerful force. My head slams into the pavement and a shooting pain sears down my neck. When I fling my eyes open, I see that I'm lying beneath Alex. He's screaming, "I have you, Chloe." He presses his forehead into my shoulder, holding me down with force. "You'll be okay, don't worry."

When I have a second to comprehend what's going on, I watch the black car continue by us. Words aren't even coming to my mind. All I can do is look up at Alex with incomprehension.

"What are you doing?" I manage to ask.

"I thought...I mean...the car was going to..." he mumbles into his hands.

"The car was going to what?" I shout, gripping the back of my head, feeling a throbbing pain. I don't mean to sound angry. But that was totally uncalled for.

"I thought the car was going to hit us. I was trying to protect you," he says, almost questioning his own motive.

I pull myself off the ground and brush the dirt off my backside. "Alex, are you okay? That car was nowhere close to hitting us."

"Wow. Sorry, Chloe. Shit. I was just trying to protect you." He gives me a look as if I just insulted him. "This is how you act?"

"You threw me onto the ground and jumped on top of me to protect me from a car that was at least twenty feet away from us. So yeah, this is how I'm acting."

He turns around and starts jogging in the opposite direction. "Let's just go home. I'm done," he says, leaving me without an opportunity to talk. Done with what?

We go most of the day without exchanging more than a *yes* or a *no*. Things are uncomfortable between us, and I hate this feeling. Just last night we were talking about spending the rest of our lives together, and now I couldn't feel more distant from him.

* * *

It's official. We've gone an entire day without having a conversation. How long will this go on? How long can this go on? How many apologies can I accept for his behavior? I get that he's repressing some horrible nightmare he lived through as a child, but I'm here for him and I'd support him. He just won't let me in, and for what reason? There isn't one.

I lie as close to the edge of the bed as possible, facing the wall, hoping he'll get the point. But he doesn't. We continue to lie in silence, as we should, since we're going to sleep, but it's as if we still both know we're just being silent rather than dozing off.

It must be midnight when I feel his arm reach around me. He pulls me into him. My heart speeds up with anticipation, wondering if he's actually going to say something. But he doesn't. He just holds me with his jittering hands.

I've tried to fall asleep numerous times tonight, but each time I surrender to my fatigue I'm awoken by an unconscious gasp or whimper from Alex.

CHAPTER SIX

TRAUMATIC STRAIN

THE ONE THING THAT CONCERNS ME the most is that he told me he was lying to me about *everything*. Yet, nothing he told me the other day was proving anything from the past to be a lie. Sure, I didn't know about his parents' untimely death, and he said he'd been left at the institution and forgotten about. But he believed the lie himself until the other day. I can't help but to wonder if there is still more.

* * *

I'm lying in bed alone. There isn't a remnant of warmth left on his side of the sheets. Why today, on my birthday would I have to wake up alone?

It's way too early to be trying to crack the code on Alex's past, and I need more sleep. I could sleep all day, and I just might. I plop back down and curl up against Alex's pillow. It smells like him. I know I can trick my brain into believing it's him. I'll sleep better thinking that.

* * *

I'm not sure if I'm sleeping, awake, or in between. I just know it's that place where you're not awake, but not quite asleep either. It sucks, and it's similar to falling asleep with your eyes open. It usually only happens when my mind is on overdrive, and I'm pretty sure my mind is now officially off-roading.

The door opens, feet tiptoe in, and a heavy object is placed down beside me on the bed. I pull myself out of my half sleep place and allow my nose to do the detective work. Familiar with the scents, my eyelids give up the battle and I glance over to see a croissant, a to-go cup, and a red rose lying on a tray next to me.

I sit up, trying to place my thoughts in order when I focus on Alex sitting on the edge of the bed with his adorable crooked grin. "Morning, sleepy head," he says. His voice is timid.

"Where were you?" They're the only words I can muster up that go together in a sentence.

"Don't you worry about that," he says, leaning over to place a gentle kiss on my forehead. "Happy Birthday."

He seems...normal. I hope he's feeling normal. Although, I'm not sure I can hang with the table tennis game going on in his head.

"Thank you," I smile. "You didn't have to go get me breakfast." I blow on the steam spilling off the cup. "I was wondering where you were when I woke up. I thought you...you..."

"Were gone?" he cuts me off, looking disappointed in himself. "Chloe, I promised I wouldn't leave you again. I'm so sorry. I thought I would make it back in time before you woke up this morning. I feel horrible for leaving you the other night, and I feel even worse about yesterday morning." He takes the coffee from my hands and places it back down on the tray. He fills my empty hands with his. "I know my apologies are becoming redundant and useless, but sorry is all I can say, that, and thank you for putting up with me. I know it's been a rough week for you too."

I place my fingertips on his cheek, tracing his sun-brightened freckles. "Don't worry about it. I know you're having a hard time and I'll do whatever it takes to help you through this. That's what love is, isn't it?" Please just snap out of your funk. Please.

He leans over, presses his lips against mine, deliberately making me melt back into the bed. "Well, I guess you really do love me then," he murmurs in between kisses.

I pull my face away from his a bit and grip his face in between my hands. "Yes, I really do love you, every single crazy part of you."

He sits back up and hands me a couple of napkins. "Okay, eat up. We have a busy day ahead of us."

* * *

"What's the surprise?" I laugh.

"We're almost there, don't worry," he says, squeezing my hand a little tighter.

"Aw," I grin. "The café? We're having dinner at the café?" I was hoping this was where we were coming. I couldn't think of a better place to have my birthday dinner.

He laughs with only his breath. "Something like that…"

What is he up to now? He opens the café door, and we walk into a dimly-lit ambiance. It's usually a little brighter and a lot livelier. I don't see any other person in here.

"I think the café might be closed." I tug on his hand, pulling him back toward the door.

When he doesn't respond, I pull him to turn around and look at me. A wide grin stretches across his face. Without another word, I hear, "Surprise!" from an overly cheery, high-pitched, lovable voice—a voice I've missed. She flicks the lights on, and flings herself onto me, squeezing the air out of me. "Happy Birthday, Chloe," Celia sings into my ear.

Shocked, I cup my hands over my mouth. "What are you doing here?" I wrap my arms around her neck.

She pulls away and grabs my hand with both of hers, still bouncing up and down on her toes. "I wasn't going to miss your birthday, silly girl."

I glance back to Alex. "Where are all the customers that would normally be here?"

Alex walks over to one of the tables and straightens the already perfectly placed condiments. "Well, when I told Albert, the restaurant owner, it was your birthday and I had a special surprise for you, he made a deal with me."

"A deal?" I give him a wary look.

He nods. "If I agreed to work here a couple of nights a week, he would let me have the place to myself just this once. I've been thinking about picking up a couple of shifts here anyway. So, it all kind of worked out. There will be a private dinner served, followed by one last surprise." The excited look in his eyes tells me he's been planning this for a while.

"I can't believe you did all of this for me." I know I'm grinning like an idiot, but this is unreal. "Are you sure you want to start working again, you know...with everything that's been going on lately? It's not like we really need money...here in our minds." I spin my finger around my head for effect. Really though, who would want to have a job in a dream? I laugh.

"I like it here, and I like to keep busy. You know that. Don't worry about me. Tonight is your special night," he says, skimming past my question.

Celia drops my hand from hers and looks over to Alex. "Alex?" she says. "What have you been having a hard time with lately? Why am I just hearing about this now?" Her words seem anxious and her face crinkles with worry.

He shoos her off with a snort, minimizing the seriousness of what he's been going through. I wish he *would* talk to her about it. Maybe it would settle whatever it is that's going on in his head.

"It's nothing. You don't need to worry about it, okay?" he says to her with a not-so convincing look.

With the creases tightening around her forehead, she gives him a motherly glower. "Well, we'll talk about this later. I don't want to upset Chloe on her birthday."

Alex brushes her interrogating look off, and shuffles his hands together with excitement. "Want to eat first, or do you want your gift?"

"I can't believe you got me a gift after the day you've given me. You like going overboard, huh?"

"Okay, I'll be right back," he shouts, while jogging into the backroom.

The lights flicker off again. A spotlight appears on the one empty wall across from the front door.

A spotlight? What is this?

"Alex? What's going on?" I yell into the back room.

The back door swings open and he comes running back out. He makes his way over to me, wraps his arms around my neck, and faces me toward the spotlight. "You know how you can't remember anything from when we were kids?" he asks.

Apprehension overwhelms me with where this is going. "What is this?" I'm not sure I want to see whatever this is.

He doesn't respond. Instead, a movie flickers under the spotlight.

Celia walks up to me and puts her arm around my waist. "I found this when I was cleaning some stuff up last week. I had forgotten all about it until then. I had taken a video of you and Alex a couple of days before you stopped coming to visit us. I thought it would be special for you to see what you can't remember." She squeezes me a little tighter.

I'm trying to conceal the mix of emotions bubbling in my stomach. The second the image appears on the screen, warm tears prickle my eyes.

I see a little girl, me, wearing a pink and purple polka dotted bathing suit, flip-flops, and arm floats. I have two springy bronze pigtails, millions of freckles, a missing front tooth, and a smile that could light up a room. "Alex," I squeal. "Come back here." My seven-year-old self shouts and giggles.

Now in view, I see a seven-year-old Alex with bright blond hair flipping out from under his red baseball hat, rosy cheeks, and a water gun in hand. "I'm gonna getchya, Chloe," he shouts in a growly voice, shooting me with his water gun. I shriek and sprint around the pool.

Alex stops chasing me when he sees me running out of breath and takes a quick breather himself. He removes his hat to wipe the sweat off his head, and bewilderment shadows my thoughts.

"Alex…what happened to your head?" I ask, nodding and almost wishing I didn't have to know the answer.

His arms release from my neck, and Celia's arm releases from around my waist. "I don't…I have no idea…Celia? What was wrong with my head?" Panic saturates his voice, despite the video being thirteen years old.

She places the palm of her hand over her forehead. "Oh boy. I didn't even see this part," she explains, clearly struggling to compile her thoughts into an answer. "Alex honey, why don't you shut the video off for now?"

He lowers his head toward the ground and grips the back of his neck as he ambles into the backroom. He switches the spotlight off and turns the lights back on. He returns just as slow and sits down at the nearest table, lowering his head into his hands.

"Celia, what's going on?" I plead for an answer. Any insight.

"What happened to my head, Celia?" Resentment chimes in his voice, but I'm not sure the person he should be resenting is Celia.

"Alex, do you remember the car accident you were in? The one where your mom and dad got hurt?" she asks.

"You mean the accident where they..." He visibly swallows the lump in his throat. "Died?"

Celia nods her head in agreement. "Alex, they did die." She places her dainty hand around the back of his neck, lowering her face to his. "You refused to believe it for so long, I was forced to play along with what you believed. Honey, do you remember who was with you in the car?" she presses.

"My parents and..." He looks down at the table and fidgets with a napkin. "My...aunt?" he questions.

A slight smile grows on her lips. "Do you remember anyone else in the car with you besides your parents and aunt?"

"No. I don't."

It's as if his comprehension is releasing some kind of agony within her. "Do you know *who* your aunt is?" she asks, still looking at him with hope.

He nods. "You're my aunt?" Alex asks, confirming his realization.

"Do you remember what else happened?" She squeezes his shoulder.

Realization is now stinging my heart too. I never would have assumed that to be the case. I'm not sure it clears anything up, though. I'm actually pretty sure that just confused the hell out of me.

"The last thing I remember..." Alex whips his head over to look at me and his eyes widen as if he remembers something. I can't understand why he's looking at me the way he is. He doesn't break his gaze for what seems like minutes, and I start to wonder if he's looking at me, or through me. He clears his throat and snaps out of his hollowness. He turns back to face Celia and says, "The last thing I remember was the look on your face right before impact." Alex looks up at her, waiting for the answer to a question he never wanted to ask.

Celia kneels next to Alex and places her hand over his knee. "Alex, honey, when the accident happened, your head went through the side window. It shattered the glass."

I feel like a shard of glass just punctured my stomach and my heart. I can't just sit here and listen to this horrific story—the demise of his life. It was so painful he blocked it out, and now he's being forced to relive it.

Alex places his hand on the back of his head. His eyes are large and his skin is pale. "Is that how…?"

His incomplete sentence makes perfect sense to Celia. She nods in agreement with sadness veiling her emerald eyes, transforming them into a murky green hue.

"Unfortunately, I wasn't wearing a seatbelt. So stupid. I went flying through the front windshield." She pulls in a deep breath. She must be remembering her own horrible memories.

It allows Alex a minute to comprehend what she's saying, but instead of being upset, he looks eager to hear more. "Then what? What was my prognosis? What happened to you? Tell me. I need to know," Alex demands.

Celia stands up and paces around for a moment. She clasps her hands behind her back, focusing and unfocusing on the wooden floor. I think this is becoming too much for her.

She's a saint. She's spent most of her life concealing this painful truth from the one person she loves, only to now be forced to break his heart all over again.

She stops and looks over at Alex. "Honey," she sighs. "You had significant brain damage. They had to operate on your brain to stop the bleeding. They ended up having to remove a small portion just to keep you alive. The part they removed was the size of a tiny sliver, and that's what caused you to be who you are today." She sits back down in front of Alex and cups her hand around his cheek. "The doctor always explained it to you as having a *fissure* right smack down the middle of your brain. You actually thought it was pretty funny each time the doctor said it, but that was only until the day you became completely non-responsive." Her words stop, and her eyes stop blinking. She nods as if she's forcing the painful memories away.

Alex looks down at his clenched hands. "So that's the reason I'm like this? I have a fissure in my brain?" he confirms.

Her head barely moves. "They couldn't really figure out what pushed you over the edge from coherency to a permanent incoherent state. It happened very suddenly about five weeks after the accident. They tried many different treatments to help you get back to a stable state, but nothing worked. Their final diagnosis was that you had a permanent chemical imbalance that was enhanced by the damage to your brain. Not even the strongest medication helped you," Celia explains, sniffling her tears back. She pulls a tissue from her pocket and presses it up against her nose. "I'm sorry, honey."

Alex's complexion is growing paler. "But, what happened to you? You said you went flying through the windshield," he asks, pushing her to continue the story.

"That's correct," she says. "I have brain damage as well. It was a bit different than yours though. It left me unable to speak, or hold a short-term memory for more than fifteen minutes. It's a miserable way to live, but thankfully, you and I both know how to drift out of our minds and into a better reality. You see, within a weakness can come strength, and when one reality closes, another one opens. That is why we are here like this, happy. Free."

"That's beautiful, Celia," I say, placing my hand on her shoulder. With so much confusion, a valid answer stands within. It all makes sense now. Finally.

"Wait!" I shout. "Where did you live before the accident?"

Alex looks up and nods with question. "I don't know." His gaze flees to Celia.

She nods as well. She walks over to her purse on a nearby table and pulls something out. She keeps it concealed behind her back as she makes her way back over to us. She pulls her hand out and places a Polaroid picture in front us. It's the same picture I found in my closet, and the same one he had in his closet. It's the picture of him and me in front of the elementary school in Southborough, Massachusetts.

"When was this picture taken?" I ask. My heart leaps into my throat.

"You two were best friends in school." She smiles. "You were inseparable from age five until seven. Chloe, your mother, my sister, and I were very close. We had tea every day while we watched you two play outside. You were always chasing each other, always laughing, and always playing little pranks on one another. You were two peas in a pod." Celia lets out a small laugh, while wiping a tear away. "I guess it's pretty clear that nothing would keep you two apart."

We've always known each other. Even before I started drifting. I started drifting so I could find him, because I missed him, because I loved him. "Hey, wait. How do you remember all of this—our childhoods, Alex's diagnosis?" I ask.

Well, I have my long-term memories, but the damage to my memory doesn't seem to affect me in the drift. I believe my subconscious picks up things, and I remember it here."

"Wow." Alex finally snaps out of his state of shock. He laces his fingers through mine. "I don't even know what to say."

"Alex, I know I'm not your mom, but I promised your mother, my sister, that if anything were to ever happen to her, I would do anything in the world to take care of you. I did the best I could, and I hope I didn't let you or her down."

Alex doesn't respond. Instead, he wraps his arms around her neck and squeezes.

"Celia," he says. "You've given me an amazing life. You saved my life, and I will be forever grateful." Alex seems to be doing the convincing now. The parent to child role sounds reversed as he assures her that she has done right by him, allowing him to live with his own beliefs.

He turns to look at me, and says, "I'm so sorry. I had no intentions of the video turning out the way it did. I wanted to give you the gift of remembering, and unfortunately, I remembered too."

*   *   *

The food was a bit cold, but we all sat at the table as Celia and Alex shared stories about our days of tag, playing house, and the funny things we said and did as children. It was amazing to be filled in on the gaps of my life. The memories feel so close now that I have a small view into my past. Alex also told Celia all about the car accident the other night, what happened, and how he reacted. She didn't look surprised, more sympathetic than anything. Everything feels like it's out in the open now, like there aren't any more secrets. I guess that's a good thing, or a step in the right direction at least.

"So, when's your first day of work?" I ask.

"I start tomorrow actually. Are you okay with this? I know I should have talked to you about it first, but it was all tied in to my big secret." He looks uneasy, questioning my response.

"I think this will be great for you," I say. "Congratulations on the new job. I'm happy for you." I hope my smile doesn't look as forced as it feels.

I'm not sure I'm as happy about this as I'm pretending to be, but it looks like I'll have to get over my unwarranted concern about him working with the wandering-eyed waitress.

CHAPTER SEVEN
SOCIAL SURVEILLANCE

"YOU'VE BEEN PRETTY QUIET the whole way home. Are you okay?" Alex asks, wrapping his arm around my hips.

Crap. I didn't want him to ask me that. I need to get rid of this annoying thought in my head. My thoughts are out of control. I'm stronger than this. I have to be. He'd think I'm crazier than he already thinks I am if I told him what was bothering me.

"Of course I'm okay. Are you? It was just a lot to take in tonight, huh?" I babble, trying to brush by the topic.

"It's the strangest thing. I actually feel as if I have some kind of clarity back in my life. I blocked out a lot of what really happened when I was a child, and I feel like it's okay to remember it now," he says, sighing deeply with relief.

I'm not sure I can understand. I guess realizing that you weren't actually dropped off at some hospital and ditched by your parents might be a nice change of perspective. At least he can rest knowing that his parents still loved him when they died. If my parents died tomorrow, I'd still know that they don't give a crap about me.

* * *

Sleep isn't coming so easy tonight, but lying here awake, listening to Alex's heavy rhythmic breaths is calming and keeps my thoughts at ease. My eyes are glued on the intricate golden strands on the back of his head. I run my fingers through it and glide over what feels like two flattened folds of skin that have been rigidly sewn together. My analysis is kind of frightening, and while I'm sure that's not the case, it's unnerving that it feels that way. It must be where his incision was. I'm surprised I haven't noticed it before, but I guess I wasn't really looking. He must not have thought much of it either if he never thought to question why he would have an abnormality on his head.

I feel my throat welling up, saddened by thinking about him as a seven-year-old experiencing the trauma he was forced to live through. I think I'm also just realizing that we aren't the same. Alex wasn't born with this condition like I was. But, why did he say we both came from a long line of drifters or *wanderers*, as he called it? I feel kind of alone again. I know comparing the origins of our condition is superficial, but it *was* comforting to know that someone else was born like this too.

Alex rolls over and places his arm over me. "Chlo? Why are you still awake? You okay?"

I sigh, warning him that I'm not. "Do you remember when you told me that you came from a long line of *wanderers*?" I can't hold in this question all night. I know this probably isn't a good time to start digging for answers that I don't really need, but if I don't ask now I know I'll never fall asleep.

"Yes, I do remember that," he says, seeming to question himself as well.

"How is that possible if your drifting capability came along with your head trauma?"

After sitting and thinking for a few minutes, I see clarity appear on Alex's dark and shadowy face.

"My ability to drift wasn't caused from the accident. It was the accident that gave me the need to drift. Everyone has their own reasons for escape.

"That makes sense." I think. "When did you drift for the first time?"

"Right before we got hit. Celia masked her face of terror and said, "Close your eyes and imagine you're somewhere warm, like the beach."

"Quicker than it took for us to get hit, my eyes opened and I was on the beach. I guess that's why I don't remember what happened to me. Celia really did save me from a life of bad memories."

* * *

I watch as Alex moves around the apartment, ironing his white button down shirt, combing his hair into waves, and shaving his stubble. I'm going to have to find something to do with myself while he's at work. I can't just sit here, bored. Bad things will happen.

"Excited for your first shift at the café, tonight?" I ask. My excitement definitely sounds forced. Hopefully not so much that he notices. This will be fine. I can find a way to occupy myself for a few hours. Some space is good. Unless someone else is within his new space, like a blond waitress who has too much interest in him. This sucks.

"I am excited, actually," he says, his face is stern while he concentrates on ironing out the crease on one sleeve. "I liked working there before. Ya know?"

"I know," I say. Is it because of her though?

"I mean, it'll be a little different, working in a different era and all," he winks. "I liked working in the 1940's. People were friendlier." He looks up and raises an eyebrow. "Although, the tips weren't that great," he laughs.

I mirror his humor, laughing a bit. I wonder if he'd be so excited about working at the café if he knew what was happening to us back home. I can't quite share in his excitement, and I'm starting to feel too alone with my thoughts.

"I'm going to go get us some lunch down the street. I'll be back in a few." He kisses me on the forehead and pulls a sweatshirt over his head.

*   *   *

After lunch, we somehow manage to nap most of the day away. We wake just as the sun is starting to set. As I peel my eyes open, I see Alex frantic and bolting around the apartment. He's getting ready to leave. He's so hot in his uniform, and with his hair slicked back the way it is, it just makes this harder.

"Chloe, are you awake, or sleeping with your eyes open again?" he teases, bopping his head around in front of my glazed over eyes.

"Yup," I croak. "Just waking up."

He walks over to my side of the bed, fussing with his tie. "Okay, well if you are awake, could you help me straighten this thing?"

I pull my limp and tired body up to my knees so I can reach his neck. The closer I get, the stronger the scent of his intoxicating cologne becomes. I don't want to send him off looking and smelling this good.

After I straighten his tie for the third time, he sits down next to me on the bed. He slaps his hand over my knee and looks me in the eyes. "I need a kiss for good luck," he says, pulling me onto his lap.

He wraps his arms around my chest and wiggles me from side to side. "What are you going to do to keep yourself occupied tonight?" He kisses my cheek. "I don't have to worry about you, do I? I know how you like to look for trouble." The vibration of his gentle laugh tickles the back of my ear.

I shrug at his question. "I'm probably just going to run to the bookstore and grab a girly romance book."

As he slides me off his lap and back onto the bed, he takes my chin in the cup of his hand and steadies my face in front of his. "I love you." He pecks my nose with his lips. "Thank you for keeping me fissure free here in this dream of ours." He leans over again and places a lingering kiss, making me crave more. That might have been his intent by the look of the snide grin stretched across his face. "I'll see you in a few hours, beautiful."

* * *

Drumming my fingers on the bed had gotten boring about an hour ago. I can't seem to concentrate on the book I picked up at the store. I'm bored out of my mind—or within my mind. Who gets bored in their own mind?

I take a walk but I go in circles, finding myself in front of the café. Why not? I have nothing else to do. I'll read my book inside. Even if he wasn't working, I'd come here. It's where I like to go when I have nothing to do. Am I being weird? Showing up on his first night of work? I can't imagine he'd really care. Whatever. I'm going in.

As I push open the café door, my heart starts racing with dread as I wonder what Alex's expression will be. Maybe this isn't a good idea. I might embarrass him—his girlfriend showing up at his first shift. It does sound kind of dumb, but it's too late to just walk out now.

Alex turns around after shoving his order pad into his pocket and acknowledges me at the door. "Chloe? What are you doing here?" he asks, *not so* ecstatically.

I fidget with the strap of my purse and look down at the book in my hand. "I got bored sitting at home…so I went for a walk and ended up here. I'll sit over there in the corner. I won't bug you." I smile to conceal my growing nerves. I didn't think he'd be this aggravated to see me. If I were the one working I'd be happy to see him.

He lifts up a large bucket of dirty dishes and brushes by me. "All right, whatever makes you happy," he says. His words sound frigid, or maybe I'm imagining it.

I find a seat at the furthest table in the corner and open my book to give the appearance that I'm not paying attention to anything else going on in the café.

Maybe I'll actually give this book a shot. The first few pages drag me into the story, and I lock my eyes on the words for minutes without any interruption—until I hear the front door open.

Little black skirt, tight white blouse, red lipstick, dark eyeliner, and two sodas in hand. I was kind of hoping she didn't have the same shift as him. No such luck there.

"Hey Al," she chirps. "Here's your soda." Her voice sounds like it belongs to a teenage cheerleader.

My face fills with heat, and my nerves are exploding with anger. *Al*? What gave her the right to give him a goddamn nickname after only knowing him for three hours?

"Leave it on the counter. Thanks," he replies with a less than excited sound in his voice.

I can't tell if he sounds like that because I'm here or because he really doesn't give a crap. All I know is, I can't move my eyes from staring right into the gloss of her hooker red lips, watching as she stares at the back of Alex walking away from his last table.

As Alex disappears into the backroom, my existence catches her eye and immediately makes for an uncomfortable situation. I force myself to look back down to my book, knowing that if I had magic powers, my eyes would be burning holes through all four hundred of these pages.

Suddenly, my book is swiped from my hands and Alex sits in the chair across from me. "Chloe, you look like you're about to kill someone. I know you're not reading."

I fold my hands together over the table. "Sorry, *Al*. Hope I wasn't bothering you."

He cocks his head to the side, realizing what I just said, and bows his head to the table. "Chloe..."

"I didn't know you liked to be called Al? You should have told me," I say in a soft voice, fumbling with a straw wrapper that I've managed to rip into thousands of pieces.

He presses his fingertips onto the table and leans toward me. "I don't like to be called Al," he whispers. "Kiera's dumb."

"Kiera?" I question her name like it's a cuss word.

"Yes, most people have a name," he laughs, a weird laugh. A nervous laugh. Am I missing something?

"Why was she getting you a drink? You just *officially* met her a few hours ago. Right?"

He slides my book back across the table. "Chloe, I really can't do this right now." He pushes the cuffs of his sleeves up to his elbows. "I'll be home in two hours." Is he telling me to leave?

"Yup. See you then. Sorry for bugging you." I take my book and purse and hustle past him and out the door. I can feel his eyes burning into my back, but I don't care. That was a real asshole move. And now I'm crying. In the middle of the street. In Paris.

* * *

I've now managed to lie here in our bed for two hours, staring point blank at page six of my book. And I've suddenly come to realize that this bed is not comfortable without Alex in it. I get up and look out the window to see if there's any sign of him walking down our street. He said he'd be home around now.

I stand on my toes to see further down the street, and I see him turning the corner. His eyes are set on the pavement below his feet, and his hand is pinched around the back of his neck. Something's bothering him. Probably me.

Right as he's under our window, I see him stop and pull his phone out of his pocket. He answers it, says something, and looks up toward our window. He catches me watching him. Without another word to the person he's speaking with, he shoves the phone back into his pocket. I hear loud thumps ascending the stairs. My heart mimics the noise.

The door flies open, and Alex walks in at a brisk pace. "Chloe, have a seat," he demands. He's pale, worried. Mad, maybe. His expression is distant, that's all I know for sure.

We both sit on the new furniture that arrived earlier today, and he turns to face me with his large glossy eyes. "I've known Kiera for a while," he says, clasping his hands together over his knees. He lowers his head. He can't look at me. "I know I should have told you, but I knew you'd freak out if I did. It was wrong not to be honest with you."

I pull the throw pillow over my lap and clutch it to my stomach. I focus my eyes on the varying patterns, wishing I could get lost within them. I can't look at him. "How do you know her?" I ask, forcing my voice to sound fearless.

He leans forward with his forearms resting on his knees. "A few years ago, before you had started re-appearing on the beach in San Diego, I visited Paris a number of times, quite often actually. It was both in current time and in the earlier decade to visit with my great-grandfather. I love it here. And just like you, I was drawn to our café."

I nod. "Okay, and?"

I can see him looking at me now, but I still can't meet his gaze. Not until I know what's going on.

"Kiera has been working there since we were both sixteen. To make a long story short, I asked her out and we kind of tried the girlfriend/boyfriend thing for about a year, but I ended it shortly after that. The girl is nuts. I couldn't deal with her flamboyance and her constant cheeriness. It was annoying and it is still annoying."

I think that's my cue to look up at him. But I'm too upset that he lied to me about her. "Okay," I say. How is she here in my dream? I'm pretty sure I wouldn't have imagined her.

"Chloe." He places his bent finger under my chin and lifts it so I have to look at him. "She never meant much to me, but I think I meant a lot to her. The first day I saw you reappear on the beach, I came straight here and broke things off with her. I told her there was someone else, even though you had no idea who I was. I just knew that if I had a chance of having you back in my life, I wasn't going to have some bimbo on the side."

I don't know what to say, except, "Okay."

"Even if I never got to talk to you, or be with you, I still would have left her. We are not meant to be together. It's clear and simple."

Am I supposed to be okay with the fact that he decided to voluntarily work with her? Should I not think that's weird?

"Hmm," I say.

"Please say something?" he pleads with desperation in his eyes.

I lock my eyes on his and narrow them, allowing him to see my anger and hurt. I feel numb inside. I thought we were open with each other, didn't hide secrets, and we were the only two people each other knew here in this place we created. None of that is true now. "How is she a part of this place we refer to as a dream? Is she part of my mind?"

"No. She's part of mine. Our worlds and our minds have merged. We're a part of each other's dreams, and that means the past comes along with it." He shrugs with his clear explanation.

"Who were you just on the phone with downstairs?" I ask.

He leans back down on his elbows and rakes his fingers through his hair. He exhales a loud sigh and looks back up at me. "She's psycho," he says. "She called me and asked if I could come back and walk her to her car. I told her no, obviously. She's trying hard, but I assure you, she won't win. Not now, not ever."

"How did she get your phone number?" I ask.

"Our numbers are all posted on the back wall so staff can call each other if they need coverage. Like I said, she's psycho." He places his hand down on my knee. "Look, if you want me to quit, I will. I understand if you're uncomfortable with me working there."

"I just don't get why you would even want to work there with her in the first place." My eyes can't stay focused on his. They drift down to the comforts of the patterned pillow.

"I honestly didn't think she was going to continue acting the way she was. She means nothing to me. I should have been honest with you before I accepted the job though. But again, there is nothing between us, nothing at all." His words sound pleading and true. Although, his words don't lessen the pain.

I'm angrier with her than I am at him right now. She's the problem. "I don't trust her, and I never will. I don't like her, and I don't like that she calls you 'Al' or gets you drinks. I don't want you to quit your job because of my jealousy, but I would appreciate it if she wasn't buying you anything and she didn't call you nicknames," I say. "I would also appreciate it if you were honest with me. All of the time." I look back at him, allowing him to see the sadness in my eyes. He should know I'm hurting and that his actions caused me pain.

"First, I didn't ask her to buy me a drink. She did it on her own. I didn't even drink it. It was some weird orange stuff, and I hate orange drinks. Second, I have asked her to stop calling me 'Al' more times than you could even imagine. Like I told you, my dad used to call me that and I don't want anyone else to take that away from him. I explained that to her tonight, but she's so clueless that she didn't even care."

I feel the angry tension my face is holding ease. I'm searching for a way to make this better, to make it acceptable, livable. "I want to meet her," I say. Why did I just say that? I don't want to meet that stupid bitch.

"I don't think that's going to help anything. It will probably just fuel her. But you're always welcome to come in during one of my shifts and sit with your romance novel and sip on hot cocoa." His lips curl into a hesitant smile, testing the waters to see if I'll bite the bait. "Thank you for loving me so much that you actually worry *that* much about losing me. It's flattering."

I raise one eyebrow. "Oh please, you're just my meal ticket." I nudge my knee into his.

Relief floods his face. Am I letting him off the hook too easy? I do believe him. I'm angry, but I trust him.

"Well then, you better be nice to me, Chloe Valcourt," he says, grabbing the front of my shirt and pulling me on top of him. Without a second to interject or get the last word in, he covers his lips over mine.

With each kiss becoming more intense and insistent, his hands slide down to my hips. His tongue slips into my mouth, moving around in graceful swirls that cause a fluttering ache in my stomach. I grip my fingers tightly around the curves of his forcefully flexed

back, squeezing, trying to release some of the building angst. I won't
be able to come back from this again. I need him. I need him to need me.
If he had any hesitation, I think it's becoming unhinged as he grips the
hem of my shirt, pulling it up and over my head. My skin prickles
with a warm sensation as I feel his body compress against mine. I
pull his shirt off, pressing my bare skin up against his. The friction
between us could start a fire.

His lips work against mine as he backs up against the arm of the
sofa, pulling me up with him, allowing me to secure my legs around
his waist until we're twisted together. My pulse hammers through
my body as my insides cry for more. It's as if we're running out of
time, and this can't happen fast enough. The urgency in his moves is
similar to an animal attacking its prey. His efforts are gentle, but
wild and untamed.

He stands effortlessly, still holding my clinging body around his
with one arm. The other hand is tangled up in my hair, keeping our
lips sealed. He stumbles across the living room, knocking us into
walls as he blindly carries me down to the bedroom. Our lips are in a
boxing match, but neither of us is winning. My lips are burning and
swelling from the intensity, but I only want them to burn more.

My heart pounds so hard against my chest that I can barely
breath. He gently lays me down on the bed, never taking his wanting
eyes off of mine. With careful moves, he climbs on top of me, holding
himself only inches above me before he lowers his lips to mine while
fumbling with the top button of my jeans. Just as the button separates
from the loop, a buzzing noise escapes from Alex's pocket.

I sit straight up, pushing him off of me. I rip his phone out of his
pocket. "Her again?" I ask, looking at the number.

"What the hell? Should I answer it?" he asks. His words are
timid and his eyes are filled with worry, for me, not the person on
the other end.

"Nope," I snap back, pressing the talk button.

"Chloe speaking," I say into the phone. "Hello?"

"Hi, is…ah…Al there?" A now less confident trembling and mousy
voice squeaks into the phone.

I hold the phone in front of my face so I can get a direct shot into
the speaker. "First off, his name is Alex, not Al. Second, this is his

girlfriend, but I'd be happy to give him a message," I say sardonically, placing the phone back up to my ear.

"There's ah…no message, sorry for bothering you," she says in a weak voice. The phone clicks.

"What did she say?" Alex asks.

I hand his phone back to him. "She wanted to talk to you, and when I told her I'd give you a message, she said she didn't have one. Then she hung up."

"I think I need to quit the café. I don't think I should work in the same place as her. She's on a whole different page of crazy," he says, raking his fingers through his hair.

"She's not going to attack you." I re-clasp the button on my jeans. "You can keep your job. I'm not so worried about her anymore. She'd scare any guy off in a matter of minutes if that's how she acts."

I'm still not thrilled about this situation, but I can see that Alex isn't either. We're on the same page at least. It gives me relief and a reason not to worry, as much.

With the moment lost, I walk over to the bureau and pull out another shirt to pull over my head. "So, have you had any other girlfriends I should know about?" I ask pointedly as I straighten the tight fitting shirt over my hips.

Alex leans back against the headboard, tilting his head toward the ceiling, letting out an annoyed sigh. "No, she was just about all I could handle. Plus, once I knew you were back, I knew we were meant to be together and I didn't need to look any further," he grins.

The phone rings again.

"Seriously?" I shout.

Alex rips the phone off the bed and clicks the button. "What?" he snaps. I smile at his tone. "What do you mean?" His eyebrows pull in. "Okay, stay right there, I'll be right down." He clicks the end call button and looks up at me with unease, probably because there are daggers shooting from my eyes. I pull in my breath in an attempt to control my growing rage from the thought of him agreeing to do something for her.

"What's her problem now? And where are you going?"

"Her car was broken into and one of her tires was slashed. She said she doesn't know who else to turn to. I guess her dad is out of town. Should I go?" he asks.

It's not like he didn't just already agree to go down and help her. But, whatever. I'll go too. "Yes, but I'm coming with you," I snap back, grabbing my purse.

With his eyes focused on my face, looking as if he's trying to analyze every thought running through my head, he grabs a t-shirt from the closet and slips it over his head. "I'm just going to put her spare tire on. She can go deal with the rest. I'm not playing boyfriend to her, don't worry." He pulls his baseball cap over his head and stretches his neck to each side. I'm pretty sure she's the pain in his neck.

*   *   *

The multi-colored cobblestones are now black as night, and they shimmer from the misting rain. It's cold and musky out, and the scent of old cigars wafts through the stale air. This isn't the Paris I'm used to. This alley is unfriendly and looks as if danger lurks in each nook of the surrounding buildings. It's an odd place to park a car, especially since the café is five blocks closer to a main street.

"Why the hell are you parked down here, anyway?" Alex yells over to Kiera.

"I needed the exercise," she says, biting down on her bottom lip. Trying to look cute, I think.

"Seriously?" I say under my breath. "Hi Kiera, we haven't formerly met. I'm Chloe, Alex's *girlfriend*." I extend my hand out to shake hers.

She seems taken back by my gesture, and with much hesitation, wraps her loose fingers around my hand.

"I've heard an awful lot about you," she says, snarling at me.

This is going to get weird. I can feel it.

"Knock it off, Kiera," Alex snaps. "Do you want help or not?" He turns to look at the damage on her black Mini Cooper.

She walks over to show him the blatant slash on the tire. "It's this tire, right...here," she points, bending over right in front of him.

What the hell? I should go shove my boot right up her ass. Alex ignores her extra attempts to get his attention, walks over, and crouches down behind the car, out of sight.

Kiera must have gotten bored of Alex ignoring her since she's bouncing back over to me. "So Chloe, I take it you weren't too happy tonight." She pulls out a compact mirror from her purse, flips it open, and puckers her lips. "You know, to see that I'm working with Alex, and all?" she teases with an obnoxious smile and an annoying giggle that sounds like it should come from a Smurf.

"I couldn't care less. I'm not insecure in my relationship," I lie, only wishing I was that confident. What did Alex ever see in her? She's kind of pretty. But her attitude, laugh, and arrogance detract from her looks, big time.

"Yes you are, or you wouldn't have come to spy on him earlier. I'm a girl too and I know how your mind works," she says, popping her gum in my face.

I can't conceal the laughter that's about to erupt from the depths of my stomach. She thinks she knows how my mind works. The top neurosurgeons in Massachusetts don't know how my mind works. Putting aside the fact that she's actually right, she's still awfully conceited to think she has me pegged.

"If that's what you want to think," I shrug, trying my hardest not to let her know she's under my skin.

"Look, Chloe. I won't go after your man, okay?" she says with large eyes, ones I'd probably believe on a stranger. Hers though, I don't trust. I don't trust one word that comes out of her mouth. "I appreciate you two coming to help me tonight. I had no one else to call, honestly."

Crap. Now I kind of feel bad for her. That is, if she's telling the truth. I divert my gaze past her, and I notice that her driver's side window was broken into as well. Maybe she isn't lying.

I brush by her and meet Alex behind the car, finding that he already has the flat tire off and he's getting ready to put the spare one on. I shove my hands into my back pockets and watch his strong large hands move so fast that I can hardly see what he's doing in the darkness.

"You're good at that." I place my hand over his tensed shoulder and rub my fingers over the knots. I know what I'm doing. She knows what I'm doing. And I'm winning this round. I lean over and brush my lips up against Alex's ear.

A soft laugh escapes his mouth. He drops his head and the metal tool to the ground. "Chloe," he whispers. "Wait until we get home."

I wrap my arms around his neck and kiss the top of his head. "Sure baby, I'll wait until we're home, in our apartment, together," my words come out much louder than Alex's.

Before looking over to see her expression, I hear sobbing. Come on. She's crying now? Alex rolls his eyes and exhales loudly. He grabs the collar of my coat and pulls me down. "She's unstable. Very unstable. Please don't push her, Chloe. I told you, it doesn't take much to fuel her behavior." He releases my jacket. But I don't move. "Please, go try to calm her down or give her a tissue, something."

Sure, Alex. I'll go console your ex-girlfriend because her ex-boyfriend has a new girlfriend. Totally normal. Happens every day. I groan as I make my way back over to her.

What am I supposed to do, hug her? I place my hand on her shoulder. "It'll be okay, really. This kind of thing happens in all cities. Your insurance will cover it, I'm sure." I'm assuming she's crying over her car and not Alex. Although, I wouldn't put it past her with her futile efforts of snatching him back.

She sniffles through her tears. "It sucks. I never have anyone to depend on. When this stuff happens, it really freaks me out," she says. "Trust me, I enjoy being a single independent woman supporting myself here in Paris, but sometimes, everyone needs help sometimes." Independent woman? An independent woman wouldn't park in a dark alley and then run begging for help when in trouble. An independent woman wouldn't feel the need to call her ex-boyfriend for help.

"I'm sure," I say. Her sobs go in one ear and out the other.

"Wait, let me interrupt your thought before you say anything else." How does she know what I'm thinking? "I *was* looking toward Alex to fill that void in my life, even knowing that he was with you." She pulls out a cigarette from her purse and thrusts it between her lips. "It was wrong and it was a moment of imprudence. I saw the way he looked at you tonight." She reaches in her bag and retrieves a lighter. "He never looked at me that way—oh shit." She clutches the lighter and presses the heel of her palm against her forehead. "He told you we dated for a while, right?"

"I know all about it. Don't you worry," I say with a pit in my stomach.

"Well anyway…" She lights the end of her cigarette and draws in a deep breath. "I knew I was always just a temporary fixture in his life. He had been looking for you for a while, and then when he found you again, he couldn't get rid of me fast enough." She blows a puff of smoke in my face. I turn my head away from the stench and wave it away with my hand. "Oh. Sorry about that," she laughs. "So even though you probably thought you had something to worry about tonight, you really don't. Alex is yours and he's not going anywhere." She places the cigarette back between her lips and wraps her arms around her stomach. "Freaking cold out." She bounces up and down on the balls of her feet.

"Yeah. Kind of," I say. I haven't been standing out here as long as she has.

"Don't get me wrong, I'm jealous as hell. But the jealousy might be more for the fact that he has someone and I don't. It just sucks sometimes." She pulls the cigarette out of her mouth and blows the smoke in the other direction this time.

"Kiera, I can't imagine going through that. That really must have hurt, and I'm sure it doesn't feel any better hearing this from *my* mouth. But I'm being honest. I couldn't imagine hearing that from someone I cared about." Why do I suddenly feel guilty for being the cause of someone else's pain? I didn't do this.

She pulls a tissue out of her purse and blots the dripping mascara from her cheeks. "Really, I'm over it. I'm just grateful that you let him help me tonight. If I were you, I wouldn't have let him come."

"Anytime," I say with a slight smile. "Where do you live, anyway?"

"I live a few miles away in an apartment building." She points down the darker part of the alley.

Alex stands up from behind the car and wipes the dirt from his hands. "Kiera, your spare doesn't have enough air in it to get you to the gas station. You're going to need to have it towed tomorrow. Want me to call you a taxi?"

"Why doesn't she just come stay on our couch for the night? We live just a few blocks away," I holler over to Alex.

"Chloe, can I speak to you for a moment, in private?" he grumbles, waving me over to him.

"What's up?" I ask when we're somewhat concealed behind her car.

"Are you out of your mind? She's psycho," Alex shouts in a soft voice.

"She's not that bad. Just a little lonely," I explain.

"No way, I'm calling her a taxi," he says, speaking loud enough for her to hear.

I won't argue with him. It's his ex-girlfriend. I don't want to make things weird for him. I'm just relieved that she's not as bad as I made her out to be. Well she is, but I think now that she knows I have her pegged, she'll back off.

I walk back over to her, pull out a piece of paper from my bag and write my number on it. "Here's my number." I hand her the torn paper. "If you ever need something, call *me*," I emphasize.

Maybe if she were to prefer me to Alex, everyone might feel a little less awkward.

"Chloe, you're really sweet. I'll call you if I need something, and you can feel free to call me too," she says, scribbling her number down on a piece of paper. "Alex, you were right about her. I can understand what was so important about her now. I'm sorry for trying to interfere."

"Thanks Kiera," he responds, raising his untrusting eyebrow. "You're smoking again?"

"Only when I'm stressed." She rolls her eyes and drops the cigarette to the ground.

"That shit will kill you," he says.

She jams her foot over the cigarette and grinds it into the ground. "Whatever. We're all dying soon anyway," she winks at him.

She's crazy. I need to remember that.

CHAPTER EIGHT

LIVING

IT'S BEEN SIX MONTHS, three days, and fifteen hours since I woke up in this life, a life where Alex and I are allowed to be together with two whole minds. It's like I'm a different person, a new person. It may not be real, but it's real enough for me. I enrolled in classes at the local university, a dream I never thought would come true. I'm accepted here, and the only reason people stare at me now is because I don't speak French, not fluently anyway. Regardless of whether or not I'll be here for four years, I feel like I'm at least moving in the right direction.

The best part about this college thing is that I have a couple of classes with Kiera and Julien. Julien is Kiera's new love interest, and I'm thankful he took her attention off of Alex. They've taken me under their wing and shown me the ropes. Kind of.

When Kiera mentioned enrollment to me, I couldn't have been more eager. I thought Alex might sign up for some classes too, but he decided to take on more shifts at the café instead. It's clear the guy likes to work. I think he likes to be around people all day.

"Hey, Chloe, do you want to grab a coffee with Julien and me after class?" Kiera yells over to me. She's bouncing down the corridor with her fist strangled around the collar of Julien's shirt, dragging him in her shadow.

"Sure, I'd love to," I say, as I reposition my bag over my shoulder. "Alex doesn't get out until four today. So I have some time to kill."

"Can't wait," Kiera squeals. I'm not sure I know anyone with as much energy as Kiera has. She's hard to keep up with sometimes.

Since Kiera and Julien are still somewhat new together, she tries to drag me along on most of her dates for "comfort," she says. For someone who seems as if they have the confidence of a panther, she seems to turn into a pile of mush around him.

It could be the fact that he looks like a French model, with his black spikey hair, glowing emerald green eyes, olive complexion and a toned to perfection body. Definitely her type. Then again, I'm not sure I've met a type that isn't hers, surfer boy included.

I don't mind tagging along with her. She does make my afternoons entertaining when Alex has to work, but he still isn't thrilled about my newfound friendship with her. It sort of just happened. Once I gave her my number the night she had the flat tire, she began texting me and calling me daily, multiple times a day, actually. I think she really was just lonely.

At first, I thought she was up to something—trying to create some weird friendship with me to get closer to Alex, but the more we started talking, the less she even mentioned Alex. It's nice to have a girlfriend, I'll admit. I've never had one before, and I could instantly see what was so great about having one. It would be nice if we didn't have *Alex* in common, but it's becoming less of an issue every day, especially now with Julien in the picture.

She met Julien about three weeks ago during one of her shifts at the café. According to her, it was like a romantic love scene out of a *chick flick*. He was sitting at a table, relaxed in his chair, one leg crossed over the other and a book in hand. When Kiera greeted him from behind to take his order, he placed his book down on his lap and stared up into her eyes for the longest three seconds she's ever experienced. Kiera said she could barely get a word out of her mouth, and before she figured out how to, he asked her out for dinner that night.

An hour later, she was at the apartment digging through my closet, freaking out, and telling me every detail about her encounter.

Over the past three weeks, she's been with Julien pretty much every single night that she hasn't been working. And the nights she is working, Julien sits at a table staring at her like she's the goddess of fine pastries and coffee. It's kind of weird, but who am I to judge weirdness.

The buzzer chimes in the hallway, informing everyone that classes are about to start. I feel like this is my eighth class today. The last two were three-hour classes. I keep reminding myself that this will pay off, but then I realize I'll most likely not make it through a full four-year program. I have hopes though, and that's why I stick with it.

Thankfully, this one is only an hour and it's the last class of the day. I actually love this class. It's Psych 101 and it's taught in English. I think the professor is a retired psychiatrist. Considering how many times I've been diagnosed with different psychological conditions, it's nice to be taught the information, rather than being tested for it.

With my eyes locked on the sluggishly ticking clock, waiting for the minute hand to reach the twelve one more time, I grab my books and wait with my bag in hand ready to jump the second I hear the buzzer. The shrill indication that the day is done sounds and I head toward the door, following the other sixty students exiting the classroom.

As I walk by the whiteboard and the professor while fussing with the twisted strap of my bag, Professor Lane locks his eyes on mine and waves me over to his desk. "Chloe. A moment, please?" Come on. Seriously? I was so close to being free for the day. What could he possibly want from me?

I break out of the slow moving line of students and walk up to the old wooden desk in the corner. Papers are piled neatly in dozens of stacks, and Professor Lane takes a seat on his leather desk chair. The seat makes a deflating noise as he places his weight down on it. He slides on his reading glasses and presses them up his nose with the tip of his pointer finger. His eyes never leave mine. What's with the look? I feel his burning stare creating a hole through the middle of my face.

"Chloe. Have a seat," he says, pointing to the wooden chair in front of his desk.

"Is there a problem, Professor?"

"Have you had any prior experience with psychiatry?" Besides being poked and prodded multiple times a week from age seven and on? "Nope."

He raises his eyebrows at my response and then looks down at the stack of papers. "I was marking up the tests yesterday, and I came across yours." He shuffles through the pile until he settles on one of the papers. He pulls it out from the rest and places it flat on the desk. "You were the only one in the class who got every single answer correct." He removes his glasses and looks me straight in the eyes. "I'm curious, Chloe, how are you so knowledgeable on the subject matter?" He places his glasses back on and glances back down at my paper, looking surprised.

Uh. This is my mind. Of course I'm going to get a perfect score.

Is he accusing me of cheating? My cheeks fill with heat and my hands become clammy. I'm not sure how to explain my extensive knowledge to him. The truth will sound more like an exaggerated lie. But do I really owe him an explanation? I didn't cheat.

"Ah…well…my mother and uncle suffered from severe cases of schizophrenia, and I spent many days in and out of doctors' offices with them. I guess I picked up more information than I thought." I laugh nervously while repositioning my bag over my shoulder.

"I see," he says, eyeballing me above the rim of his glasses. "Well then. Job well done." He hands me my paper with a large red-circled A at the top.

"Thank you, Professor." I stand up from the chair and pivot my direction toward the door, hoping to get there before he has the opportunity to ask me anything else.

"Oh, Chloe?"

I stop short. Shit. Wasn't fast enough. Nerves are gnawing at my skin as I turn around to face him once more. "Yes, Sir?"

He stands up from his chair and takes a couple of steps in my direction. "I've been doing this a *very* long time." He moves in closer, and his voice lowers to a whisper. "You be careful with what you're doing. It doesn't always end well." He rests his forehead into his hand and briefly closes his eyes. When his eyes reopen, he nods his head as though trying to show his disappointment. "Go on now," he shoos me away.

With blood draining from my face, I turn around and dash out into the hallway, slamming my body up against the nearest wall. My scorching cheeks feel as though they've been depleted of all color. How did he know? Does he know? Is there something written on my face that says crazy person? Maybe he meant something else. I hope he meant something else. What am I saying? Of course he knows. He's another figment of my mind. I think. I'm so lost, even here within my own thoughts. I still don't know what's real and what's not. Is anything real at all? Alex has promised me that he's real. But is it my mind that's making him say that?

With unsteady steps, I make my way through the crowded corridors, and I realize everyone is looking at me. Everyone here knows my secret. Everyone knows they are just a figment of my imagination.

I make the last turn toward the main exit and a passing student slaps a piece of paper into my chest. I welcome the unexpected distraction.

I peel the torn pink sheet of paper away from my body. It's some kind of invitation to an off-campus party. I continue walking with it in my hands, inspecting the details and pondering if it would be fun to attend. I wonder if Alex would be interested in going to this kind of thing.

Before I can read the last word on the page, the paper is ripped out of my hand, and Kiera bounces up and down with excitement. She shrieks over to Julien, "We're all going to a campus party Friday night. I'm so excited!" Her voice is piercing, and Julien recoils from her excessive noise, and I cup my hands over my ears, scrunching my eyebrows together. I'm gathering Julien has no clue what she's even yelling about. He understands some English, but for the most part there has been an intense language barrier between us. I'm sure he's just chalking it up to her normal insanity. "It's going to be so much fun," she continues. Her giggles become obtrusive to the surrounding students who are staring at her as if she has some kind of contagious disease. "Chloe, we have to go shopping." Her shrieks have turned into a singsong tune as she grabs my arm, pulling me through the exit.

I rip the paper back from her. "I have to ask Alex first. I don't know if this is really his thing," I say, attempting to slow her down.

"Chloe, we have to go," she pleads. "Alex will be fine, and if he's not…tell him to suck it up and do it for you." She dances around in a circle with her lips pulled into a tight smile.

I'm not sure what's so exciting about this, but it's pretty clear the girl needs to get out more often. Like I should talk. We've kept ourselves cooped up in our apartment since we moved in. Maybe getting out wouldn't be the worst thing in the world.

"I'll talk to him. But, no promises," I say.

"Okay. I need coffee. Come on," she says, her squeals resuming.

Yeah, that's exactly what you need, Kiera, something else to give you energy, I groan to myself. I'm constantly reminded of why Alex didn't see in her as a girlfriend.

We take the only available table left in the café. Alex is running around like a mad man. It looks like he's waiting on all twelve tables today. I doubt he minds. He likes it when it's crazy. More tips.

"Hey, baby," Alex shouts from the back counter. Everyone in the café turns to look at me, and I suddenly want to climb under a table. I hate when he does that. Everyone is whispering about me now. He hustles over and gives me a quick passing kiss. "Class out already?" His voice floats after him as he continues running from table to table.

"Yup. You look busy, huh?" I say.

"It's been pretty wild today, but no complaints." He flashes me his crooked grin and wipes the sweat from his forehead with the back of his sleeve.

Kiera pushes me out of the way to get in front of Alex and in his way. "Hey Alex." Her voice is stern, but endearing. "Yeah...we're going to a party on Friday night. Okay? It's going to be you, Chloe, Julien, and me. It'll be fun. Say okay, okay?" Kiera rambles.

I doubt Alex comprehended a word of what she just said. As he's side-stepping from the right to the left, trying to get past her, he grabs her shoulders and moves her to one side. "Eh, I don't know, Kiera. I'm not the party animal type," he says, heading back into the kitchen.

The second Alex pushes back through the kitchen doors Kiera grabs his wrist and whips him to the side. "Suck it up, Alex. You'll be fine, and Chloe wants to go too. So, we're going. Okay? Good."

He rolls his eyes at her. "Okay, okay. Calm down. We'll go. Chloe, just make her stop talking and we'll go," he laughs, pulling his hand out of her grip. "I have to get back to my other tables. Do you guys want the usual?"

"Whenever you have a free second. Don't worry about us." I shoot him my apology eyes and give him pouty lips.

No more than a second after Alex has left, I turn around to find myself in the middle of a Cabaret. Kiera is straddling Julien at our table. She's doing some weird dance and her tongue is so far down his throat that I think he might have actually swallowed it. I feel my lunch from three hours ago reemerging. Why do I keep agreeing to be the third wheel on their dates? I should have learned by now.

I move back over to the table and drag the chair out as loudly as possible. They don't even flinch. How is this restaurant behavior? *City of Romance* or not, it's gross to watch.

Alex looks back at me, witnessing the awkward display of affection between the two lovebirds. He sticks his tongue out to the side, crinkling his face into a gagging motion. His goofy expression makes me laugh through my nose, startling the hot couple out of their moment of affection. Kiera whips her head around to look at what's causing my obnoxious laughter and gives Alex the evil eye, causing us to laugh even harder. Kiera looks back over at me, rolls her eyes, turns back to Julien, fists the collar of his shirt and pulls him back in for more tongue action.

I turn my chair to stare out the window, hoping my periphery will lose sight of them. Alex returns to the table and places the tray down sternly, causing a slight crashing noise. "Time for Coffee?" Alex asks, shoving a mug in between their faces.

Kiera pushes his hand away, preventing an interruption.

"I have a feeling you're anxious to get away from them today. Why don't you take the bike?" Alex whispers into my ear.

"Eh, no. I'll be okay and safer taking the metro," I laugh, kissing him on the cheek.

I still don't know why he bought that thing. He knows how much I hate it. Yet, he's still convinced I'll have a change of heart someday soon. I ride on the back of it with him sometimes, when I have to, but I refuse to drive that thing myself. There's no doubt that I'll end up face first on the side of the road.

"Guys," I clear my throat. "I'm gonna get going. But don't let me interrupt your *coffee date*." I make sure to add in my air quotes.

"Chloe, don't leave," Kiera shouts while wiping the smeared lipstick off the skin above her top lip. "I'm sorry." She giggles like an idiot, looking back over at Julien. "Were we making you uncomfortable?" She grabs my hand, not allowing me to run away like I want.

"Uh, not so much uncomfortable as grossed out. You two should be careful not to swallow each other's faces," I snort.

With no laughing response in return, Kiera translates to Julien what I said. "I am so sorry Chloe, do not leave," Julien begs in his thick French accent.

I laugh. "Thanks guys, but I have some things I have to do anyway. I'll see you at class tomorrow."

They both wave goodbye, unfazed by my exit. They're probably thrilled I'm leaving. Whatever. I need to get to the grocery store. I really want to make Alex something special tonight. Maybe something to set the mood…

* * *

I walk through the aisles in the grocery store, debating on what I might be able to figure out how to cook. The only things I ever watched my mother cook were eggs, bacon, and spaghetti. Considering her cooking was far from edible, I might want to shy away from what I watched her attempt. I'm pretty much on my own. I think lasagna might be easy to whip up. I'm sure all I need are those ribbon noodles, tomato sauce, mozzarella cheese, and cottage cheese. I'll grab a baguette, a bottle of wine, and some tiramisu to complete my chef-d'oeuvre.

I need a pot, pan, spatula, and…oh yeah a strainer. I can do this. Easy as pie.

* * *

Cooking wasn't as hard as I thought it might be, and I can't see how I can go wrong with lasagna. I'm sure he'll like it. I light the second and last candle on our small table, and run to the bedroom to put on my tight fitting jeans and my blue and white-striped low-cut shirt that Alex always compliments with a wandering eye. Tonight's the night. After months of trying to find the *right time*, it feels like it's become a running joke. Life has done a great job of getting in the way of *right times* and I finally agreed with his theory of waiting it out. When I agreed to his waiting game, he quickly lost interest in waiting.

"Chlo?" he calls, breathless from jogging up the stairs.

"Be right out," I yell, spritzing one last touch of perfume.

"What's…all this for?" he asks, his eyebrow arched as he watches me walk down the hall.

"I just wanted to do something special for you tonight. You've been working so hard and so many hours. Here's me thanking you for doing that." A proud grin spreads across my cheeks.

He hands me a rose, like he does many nights. The rose pokers, as I call them, line the streets, eyeballing every man who walks by. If you make eye contact, a rose is poked against you. Most people wave them away, but Alex usually bites the bait. He arcs his head around me, peering over to the display on the table. "You cooked, huh?" he laughs. Is my cooking a joke?

I thought maybe he would forget about the last couple of breakfasts I've attempted to make. They didn't turn out so well. "Don't worry," I say. "I bet tonight's dinner came out pretty good," I reassure him.

"What did you make?" he asks, walking closer to the table.

"Lasagna." I straighten his plate so it lines up between his place setting. "It was pretty simple, so I'm sure I didn't mess it up." I pull his chair out.

"You got wine, too?" He wraps his hand around the bottle, twists it to look at the label, and responds with a satisfied and agreeable look. Truth be told, I grabbed the first bottle I saw. I know nothing about wine. "This looks like a wonderful dinner. This was wonderful of you, and…" He looks me up and down with eagerness, letting his eyes linger on certain areas. "You look amazing too." His fingers wrap around my wrist, pulling me to him until his lips meet my cheek. "And you smell…" He inhales through his nose. "Mmm." A mischievous grin pulls at the corner of his lips. I raise an eyebrow and smirk, responding to his gesture.

"This was a set up, wasn't it?" He wraps his arm around my waist. "Are you trying to seduce me, Chloe Valcourt?"

"Nah. I'm just a tease," I wink.

"I think I've had enough of the teasing," he says, letting his hand slide down and cup my butt. I playfully slap his hand off and point to his plate.

I wag my finger in front of his face. "You have to eat first."

I watch as he stabs the fork and knife into the lasagna. The knife must be dull, considering his struggle to cut through the noodles. I guess I had a bit of a rough time cutting the slice too. When he finally separates a bite size from the rest of the portion, he places the piece in his mouth with a struggling look on his face.

"So? How is it?" I ask, my eyes pleading for a good response.

His eyes clench shut and his lips pucker.

"Is something wrong?" Crap. Strike three, for me.

He pulls up his napkin and spits the mouthful into it. He clasps his hand around the stem of the wine glass and brings the rim to his mouth. I see the liquid cut in half, and it's clear that I did something very wrong with the ingredients. When he places his glass back down, he stabs his fork back into the lasagna and flips over the piece on his plate.

Shit.

He throws his head back and releases a rumbling laugh. But I'm not joining in with his hysteria. Not only is the lasagna scorched and black on the bottom, but the tinfoil from the pan apparently baked onto the piece I served him. I must not have noticed. I drop my head into my hand with humiliation.

When his laughing fit ends, he must notice the distraught look on my face. He straightens his shoulders and clears his throat. "You know what? It's fine. It's a common mistake. Besides, we have bread and wine, and I'm sure they're both great." He grabs the bottle and reaches across the table for my glass.

"I had nothing to do with cooking either of those," I say, smirking. "We have pre-made dessert too." I give him a cunning grin.

Two hours and a bottle of wine later, we're both laughing. At nothing. Wine makes everything funny. Really funny.

I push my chair out from the table and place my weight on my legs to stand up. But my body feels like it's being anchored to the seat. I try again and use the table as leverage this time. I lock my knees together and hold myself upright as my head swirls in beautiful circles. Oops. I might have had a little too much to drink. The thought of why I'm feeling the way I am causes an unstoppable roll of giggles. I don't even care that Alex is looking at me cock-eyed. His eyes are so striking that he can look at me however he wants.

"Are you okay?" he asks, questioning my behavior.

"Yup," I chirp, giggle, and hiccup. I try to focus my attention on placing one foot in front of the other. But it just doesn't seem to be working, and that's funny too.

I plop myself down onto the ground and shove my head into my knees, laughing even harder. Why can't I stop laughing? I like laughing. It's fun. And this floor. Who would have thought wood could be so comfortable. It's like a pillow for my butt. It's nice.

"Oh boy. We better get you to bed," Alex says, wrapping his arm under my arms.

After a few more stumbling steps, he scoops me up and carries me down to our bed.

Once I'm lying in our amazingly comfortable bed, I don't plan on moving. And just as I think I'll wake up in this outfit tomorrow morning, Alex pulls my shirt over my head and then slides my pants down to my ankles and throws them both across the room. All right! It's time, finally.

I reach up to cup my hands around his cheeks, hoping to pull him down with me. Instead, he moves out of my sight and returns with one of his large t-shirts and slides it over my head.

"Good night, Chloe," he grins, sweeping my hair off my forehead.

My eyes close without effort, and I feel a darkness that I haven't felt in a long time. It's pulling me in with force and it's definitely not as inviting as I'd like to remember. The walls are spinning around my head like a tornado and I feel nausea creeping in.

Here or there, darkness spinning into barreling waves of wooziness.

I squeeze my eyes even tighter, hoping for the spinning sensation to stop, but it doesn't. It speeds up. Is this from the alcohol, or something else? I force my eyes open and see that the walls of our bedroom are liquefying into hardwood floors, one by one until they all become replaced by hundreds of padded tiles.

CHAPTER NINE

THE DARK PARTY

SEEING THROUGH THIS HAZE is nearly impossible. I feel as though I'm walking through the woods on a dark, rainy night with fog so thick I can hardly see my foot move in front of me. It's unsettling. I reach my hands out, seeking the padded wall that I know stands within the short distance. In just two steps, my hand brushes up against the smooth, plushy, plastic surface.

I don't want to be here.

I push my fists into my eyes to rub away the blurriness. It only works a little. Darkness seems to be battling the light in my life and I'm not sure if I'm here, there, or in between. I allow the darkness to remain. It feels safe here. For now.

As my eyes come into full focus, I feel warm linen sheets draped over my body. Thank God. I'm back in my bed. The thought of fighting the darkness by giving into it causes my brain to feel as if it's twisting into a tight knot.

The sun slinking in over my windowpane burns and causes a hammering pain against my temples.

Surveying my surroundings, I see that Alex is still asleep. I want to wake him and tell him about my nightmare, but I feel his body breathing heavily against mine. Sweat is dripping from his forehead and his fists are clenched together. I smooth my hand over his arm to wake him, but as usual, he startles with the slightest touch. He jumps up, panting and gasping for air. "Is she okay? Is she okay?" he shouts.

"Is who okay, Alex?" I ask, maintaining calmness in my voice, as I do most times when this happens.

When I interrupt the thoughts in his head, he stares through the wall in front of us until he realizes that he was having another flashback.

"Car accident again?" I ask.

"Yeah," he responds, his eyes are desolate and glossed over.

He's been having reoccurring nightmares at least once a week. They usually wake him from a sound sleep, but sometimes I have to pull him out of his own mind. I feel bad that he's revisiting this painful incident in his life, and I wish I could help him. But I don't think I can. At least he brushes it off and moves on with his day as if the memories don't bother him. I just can't understand how they don't.

"You had a fun night, huh?" he asks, winking at me. "You're a lush, Chlo," he laughs, amusing himself more than me.

"Very funny." I rake my fingers through the dozens of snarls in my hair. "I've never had alcohol before." And my voice sounds like I swallowed a sour lemon.

"Wait. You've never had a drink before last night?" His face contorts with disbelief.

"It's not as if my mother was going to serve alcohol to a minor whom she had locked in her bedroom." I give him a *duh* look.

"Good point. Well, now you know when to cut yourself off I guess," he says, flicking my ponytail out of my hand. "Do you have a headache or anything? You had quite a bit for someone your size. I just didn't question you because I didn't think it was your first drink."

"I feel fine." Except my pounding headache, and the fact that I ended up in a padded cell after blacking out.

*   *   *

It's four o'clock and I have one hour before Alex will be home. I stare at myself in the mirror, questioning how I can make myself look party ready. Being my first party and all, I have no idea what to expect.

I go a little heavy with the darker eye makeup and smudge on some vivacious red lipstick. I curl my hair and pull it up into a high ponytail. I think I look the part for a college party now. As I apply the last spritz of perfume, I hear the front door open. I hope I didn't overdo it with the makeup and dress.

"I just need a few minutes to get ready, and then we can go," Alex shouts from the living room.

"No problem. I'm just about ready too," I say, glancing in the mirror once more.

I slip the skintight dress over my head and stretch it down over my hips, wiggling around until the hem sits evenly over my thighs. Now, for the tricky part, heels—something I've never really gotten along with. I step into the blue, four-inch, peep-toe pumps, and steady myself against the sink. I laugh at my imbalance. I'll probably look like I'm walking on stilts all night. But they sort of complete my outfit, and I'm sure Kiera, a.k.a. miss fashion queen, will approve.

"Okay, ready?" I ask, smoothing out a wrinkle on the hem of my dress.

The second he turns around, his mouth gapes open, and I can see his eyes tracing a line from my heels up to my face. Mission accomplished. I wink.

He walks over to me, places his hand on the small of my back, and pulls me in against him, allowing me to feel every part of him. "I won't be able to keep my hands off of you tonight," he utters, purposely inhaling my perfume from the crook of my neck.

"Good. It's about time," I whisper.

"You look amazing and ridiculously hot," he says, kissing the sensitive spot right below my ear.

"You're not so bad yourself." I reach up, resting my lips on his chin and leaving a red lipstick stain behind.

"If we don't go now…I don't think we'll ever leave here tonight…or ever for that matter," he says, gripping his fingertips around my hips. "Maybe you should put your running pants on so I'm not fantasizing about you all night," he laughs and pulls me to the front door.

"How are we getting there?" I'm hoping he doesn't suggest the scooter. This dress won't work on that thing.

"I called a taxi to come get us."

* * *

The place where the party is supposed to be is dark and looks like an abandoned warehouse. Now that we're here, I think it's safe to assume that this isn't a university-sponsored party. There's no food, the windows are boarded up, the floors are sticky, and there's spray-paint covering every inch of the exposed brick walls. It's kind of creepy in here. The nicest things in here are the makeshift bars in each corner.

The loud music, lack of oxygen, and the multi-colored flashing lights that are moving to the rhythm of the music is making me dizzy, and I haven't had a drink.

"Chloe," Kiera shrieks. She sprints toward us, pulling Julien behind her, as usual. She's wearing a tight red mini dress with a slit way too high up her thigh, complimented by patent leather black heels that have to be higher than mine. They make her look as if she's almost six feet tall, and she's probably only 5'6. And I thought *I* had gone a little overboard.

"You look nice, Kiera," I say with as much enthusiasm as I can fake.

"You look hot, Chloe." She curls her fingers outward like a claw and makes some kind of hissing sound. "You trying to make Alex jealous with all of the other men checking you out?" She slides her sinful smile in Alex's direction. "Oh, there's one now." She points to a man passing by, staring at me as if I have a set of blinking lights hanging from my chest.

Alex's smile turns into a straight line across his face and he squeezes my hand, assumedly confirming her analysis.

"Anyone want a drink?" Kiera asks.

We both say yes, although with an understanding that I have to take it easy after the occurrence last night.

*　*　*

So much for that idea, I think to myself. The drinks keep coming, and they are too good to pass up. I probably should have stopped three drinks ago, but I'm okay. Plus, Alex has a ride coming for us in a couple of hours, and this is probably the most fun I've had. Ever.

I laugh as I notice Alex looks like he might have had a couple too many drinks as well. He's suddenly turned into a dancing machine, and he's a good dancer. He notices me watching his moves, his perfect crooked grin spreads across his lips, and he lunges for my arm to pull me onto the dance floor. He intertwines his arms around my body, pulls me up against him, and continues his smooth dance moves against my body. The movements are making me crazy. He lowers his lips to my collarbone and skims his teeth along my skin. This building desire is becoming torturous. Can someone have a heart attack from this much tension? I suppose one of us would have had one by now, because we're killing each other.

He drags his lips up my neck and to my ear before whispering, "Thisss is fun." His words are slurred and breathless. "Good call on the party." He lifts my hand and twirls me around in a circle. But the twirls don't stop, only my body does. "You haven't had too much to drink have you?"

"Have *you*?" I retort, tugging at my riding hem.

"I stopped about an hour ago, but I probably had one too many," he snickers.

"Just one?" I raise an eyebrow, questioning his response.

"Oh please, you look like you've had two too many. I think it's time to call it quits," he says, turning into supervisory mode.

Whoa. Not quite appreciating this whole ordering me around thing he's trying out. After living with overbearing parents, the last thing I want is any sort of parental figure in my life. If I have too much to drink and get drunk, so what? I'll learn my lesson. I am so sick of people telling me what to do, even Alex.

"I'm just going to have one more. Kiera just went to go get the next round. I'll be done after that," I laugh, trying to blow off his condescending tone.

"No Chloe," he says, his words surging with firmness. "I want you to stop. You've had enough." His voice carries over the paused music, and embarrassment washes over me as everyone looks at us.

"One more won't freaking kill me, Alex. Let me live a little," I say, thrusting myself out of his arms.

I try to walk away from him, but he grabs my shoulders and spins me around, forcing me to face him. "Chloe, if you black out, it's not the same as someone else blacking out. You know this," he says, arching his head down so his eyes are inches from mine. "Please, I'm begging you to stop."

"Alex, really. I'm okay." I don't know how else to prove my point. I get that he's angry, but he'll see that I'm just fine. It's just one more drink, and it's not going to change anything. I fidget my way out of his grip again and spin around to face Kiera who's bouncing over with her head bobbing to the music.

"Here, Chloe! It's sangria. It's ama-a-a-zing and it tastes like p-u-u-unchhh!" she sings, proving to be more drunk than I am.

I finish the drink within a couple of minutes, and regret is instantaneous. The lights above turn into strobe lights and the room is spinning out of control. Conversations are garbled and I have a developing pain in my head.

I take a couple of steps backwards and lose my balance off my four-inch heels. I knew that was coming. My back hits the wall, and I slink down to the ground for comfort, forgetting about the sticky coating on the cement floor.

Déjà vu.

Alex is hovering over me, tugging at my arms, trying to pull me back up. I don't want to stand up. The numbness feels too good, and sleep is calling my—no wait…it's singing my name.

"God dammit," Alex shouts. "I knew I shouldn't have let you have another one. Chloe." He continues hollering in my ear, but it becomes muffled and muted as he cups his hands around my face.

My name is the last thing I hear before the obscurity takes over my mind. I think I must have passed out. I definitely had too much alcohol, and now I feel like I'm sitting in a dark room, waiting for my consciousness to kick back in. I don't feel much of anything, which is good I guess. But my eyes are too blurred to see, and my limbs are too numb to move. I feel overcome by a sense of creeping discomfort. I hear noise that sounds like something moving around, and I hear my name, but I can't quite make out who is calling me.

"What are you doing back here?" A jumbled voice growls at me from a distance.

"Chloe?" Alex yells. Where is his voice coming from?

"Chloooe?" Kiera's words slur into a whine. I don't see her either.

I still can't answer or move, but I suddenly feel my body being shaken with violence. I should be more scared than I am, but I don't feel like this is actually happening. I feel like I'm listening to a movie.

"How did you figure out how to come back here?" the voice I don't recognize shouts again. "Answer me, now." His voice becomes threatening.

There's an emerging sense of pressure on my face and a throbbing sensation on my cheek. I'm starting to feel more desperate for an answer as to what's going on or where I am. My eyes never remain blurry for this long, and I'm sure whatever is happening isn't good.

I hear a nearby rustling and a series of loud thuds. "You're here too? Are you looking for trouble?" His laugh is wild and sardonic. "What am I saying? You don't even know your own name, idiot." Just as I question who he's yelling at, the sound of his trailing voice is followed by the sound of flesh being pounded. There's no response from whomever the voice is speaking to, but I hear a continuation of loud thuds.

Thud. Thud. Whimper. Thud. Clarity.

My eyes clear up. I'm sitting in the middle of a white padded room. The thuds are coming from the adjacent cell. I creep over to the barred window and pull myself up to look in. I see Alex's head bobbing around along with a wrestling noise. Without knowing what's going on, I hear his door open and close, followed by my door opening. It's Franco. I should have known the voice was his.

"Well, are you going to talk, or what?" he asks, his voice sounding more meek than usual.

"T-tell m-me why you're holding us hostage and I'll tell you whatever you want to know," I say, jittery and surprised that words actually come out of my mouth this time. I don't feel as scared right now. More like brave.

I wasn't expecting to have this confrontation right now, especially not when I've had way too much to drink. I just wanted to enjoy myself at a party tonight, but of course, this has to happen instead.

He fists his hand around a chunk of my hair and pulls my head back, forcing me to look up at his bloody nose. "I will let you go when you give me what I want, but until then, you are my prisoner and so is your stupid brain-dead boyfriend."

"What the hell do you want, Franco?" I shout, my words forceful and aggressive.

"You know exactly what I want. You know damn well that your mother took it from you and hid it." The surety in his voice tells me he honestly thinks I have something that belongs to him.

"I have no clue what the hell you're talking about. So, unless you want to give me another hint, you might as well knock us both back out, because I won't be of any help to you."

It only takes one swat from the back of his hand to push me back where I want to go. I guess that was all I needed to say.

Light reenters and clears up my unsteady reality. I'm back in the loud, dark basement-like room that I had passed out in. Alex is still hovering over me, trying to pour water down my throat. Kiera is holding a cool compress over my head, and Julien has his hand on my knee for...moral support, I guess.

Alex is breathing heavy and sweat is dripping down his temple. "Chloe, can you hear me now?" he asks, his voice much softer and calmer than it was before the darkness swept over me.

"Yeah," I groan.

He grabs the back of his neck and stands up to release a long sharp exhale through his pursed lips. I guess he isn't planning to conceal his anger for too long. "I told you not to drink anymore," he says, his voice louder. "Why couldn't you just listen to me?"

"Chill out, Alex," Kiera snaps at him as she pulls a cigarette out of her purse.

"I'm sorry," I say. "I should have listened. I was just having fun." I try to explain my lack of reasoning while rubbing the soreness out of my cheek.

"Yeah. Alcohol will do that to you. But I know you know that it can be dangerous if you overdo it, which is what you did." He sounds like he's trying to inform me of the repercussions I've already experienced.

"Did you pass out?" he asks with a weird look on his face.

I roll my eyes at him. "You know what happened, Alex. Don't play dumb."

Immediate regret sets in as the words come out of my mouth since Kiera and Julien are standing less than two feet away from me.

He widens his eyes, glaring at me and trying to tell me to shut my mouth, without saying so much. "H-how would I know what happened? I'm assuming you passed out?" he says, trying to cover my last statement with a lie.

"What is she talking about, Alex?" Kiera asks, lighting the end of her cigarette.

"I don't know," he continues.

"Shit, Chloe. What's going on with your face?" Alex asks, tracing his finger under my nose. He pulls away his blood-covered finger and wipes his hand on his jeans. "He got you, didn't he?"

I guess he can forget about hiding the truth. I can see the concern deepen, and I know full well why I have a bloody nose. I'm sure he does too. I also have an idea what's been causing our random headaches and my bloody noses. It's all kind of clear now.

"Yes, he hit me. He wasn't happy with you, or me. Although, I think you set him straight. Either that, or you pissed him off more."

Kiera pulls the cigarette out from between her lips and stomps one of her heels. "What the hell are you two talking about?"

Alex stands back up, turns toward Kiera, and points in the opposite direction. "Go away," he demands, with no further explanation. Yeah. That might work on her. Or not.

Instead of leaving, Kiera takes two steps closer toward Alex and points her finger in his face. "Nooo way, not til' you tell me what'ssss going onnn? You two are acting psycho," she thunders through an intoxicated slur.

We both can't help but to laugh for a split second. "Leave," we say, echoing each other.

Kiera storms off, dragging a bewildered Julien behind her. The poor guy is ending up to be no more than an accessory in her life.

Alex pulls me off the ground and slides his arm underneath mine and around my back. "Come on," he says. "I called the cab a few minutes ago. They'll be here in a minute."

* * *

I'm a rag doll on the couch, sipping water through a straw, focusing on not getting sick again. Rather than Alex appreciating my desire to sleep with my head in a toilet, he's more worried about what happened with Franco. "Now will you tell me what happened?" he asks, his voice calmer this time.

I have no energy to fight him on this one. It will be much easier to give in. Plus, the sooner I tell him what happened, the sooner I can go make my bed up on the bathroom floor.

"Franco was demanding that I tell him where something is. I don't know what he's referring to, but he said that my mother took it from me and I should know where it is."

Alex is enraged, red, and I can see his veins pulsating against the skin of his forehead. "Shit."

"It's fine," I say. "I told him that unless he wanted to elaborate on what he is looking for, he could just put me back into an unconscious state, because I have no answer for him. That's what he did. Granted, he knocked me back out with his hand, but at least I got out of there. I didn't feel him hit me, if it makes you feel any better." I force an uncomfortable smile.

"Yeah, I feel much better now, Chloe." He's fuming, pacing and cracking his knuckles. He looks lost in thought, and I can't imagine what he could be trying to figure out.

"I won't drink like that again. Okay? If I don't end up in that situation, we won't have to deal with Franco anymore, hopefully," I say, shoving my head into the contours of the plush sofa.

"You kind of acted like an idiot tonight," he says, disappointment clouding his eyes. "I was worried and trying to take care of you and you acted ridiculous. You weren't acting like the Chloe I know. You were acting like...Kiera." He shakes his head with a saddened expression. "I didn't like it."

"Alex, you don't need to always protect me. I was acting like an idiotic college student. Oh well. I learned my lesson. You don't need to harp on it, okay?"

"Okay. I'm going to bed." His voice is absent of any emotion.

"You have nothing to respond with?" I ask, cupping my hand around my ear. He's infuriating me. I feel enraged at the thought of him trying to control me. Haven't I dealt with that enough in my life? I don't need to get it from him too.

"You're drunk and you're in a fighting mood. Just go to bed, and we'll talk about this in the morning." He turns and heads to the bedroom.

I follow him, hoping I don't need to drop myself into the bathroom on the way.

With the walls feeling as though they're closing in on me, I manage to make it down the hall and throw myself backwards onto the bed. The fetal position and putting my pillow in a chokehold sounds like the best bet. Maybe it will even make the room stop spinning. "You can't go to bed mad at me, you know," I mumble into my pillow.

With no response, Alex takes off his shirt and jeans and steps into a pair of shorts. I figure he'll climb into bed and comfort me until I feel better, but instead he rolls over to face the wall. I can't believe he's still angry with me.

I turn over, inch myself closer to him and curl my arm halfway around his body, hoping he'll turn over and talk to me. But he doesn't budge.

"Please talk to me," I whisper.

He rolls over to face me, releasing an annoyed sigh. "Chloe, I'm not angry. I'm upset and I'm wracking my brain, trying to figure out what the hell we are going to tell Julien. That was really dumb of us."

"Why don't we just tell them the truth?" I ask with hesitation, knowing that he'll probably disagree. "Wait, what about Kiera?"

With bitterness in his eyes, and a scowl on his face, he looks at me like what I'm saying is absurd. "Yeah, obviously her too." He closes his eyes and nods his head, looking as if he's trying to think straight. "What good is the truth going to do? It will just be another person who thinks we're crazy."

"Well, we are crazy, and if they don't like it, then they can go away," I say matter-of-factly.

He places his hand on my cheek, and glides it back to my ear, pulling my face to meet his. "Chloe, if you want to tell them, you can. But you need to know that *they* might laugh and make you feel as crappy as you did when you were living with your mother. Our situation is a little hard to believe, especially to any normal person who thinks life is just one straight line."

"Well, if they leave, they were never our friends to begin with. I can't sit here and lie every time I see them though. It will make things complicated. We'll just have to take the chance."

* * *

"What time is it?" I grunt, flipping the alarm clock around.

I rip the pillow out from underneath my head and smother my face with it to block out the noise. Who would be banging on our door this early? Or is it just my head that's creating the noise? Nope.

Never mind, there it is again. It's definitely coming from the front door. "Alex, wake up." I nudge him in the side.

"Chloe, go back to bed," he whines.

I growl with frustration. "No. Someone is knocking on the door. Go get it." I nudge him again.

With a loud sigh, Alex clambers out of bed, pulls on his jeans and walks to the front door.

"What the hell, Kiera? It's seven in the morning. Didn't your parents ever teach you any manners?" I hear the door slam. "Whoa! Wait! Come back here! Hey! Where are you going?" Alex yells after her.

"Chloe? Where are you?" Kiera hollers from down the hall.

I groan in response.

"Sit up right now, and tell me what happened last night. I'm not leaving until you do."

I rub my eyes, pained from the brightness of the sun, and I see Kiera standing over me with her arms crossed and her cheeks red. "Kiera, it's freaking seven in the morning. Give me a break." I let out a forceful but fake cry.

"Nope. Start talking," she demands.

Alex walks back in and I watch as she awkwardly tries not to notice that he's only wearing jeans. But it's obvious her eyes keep getting dragged toward his bare chest.

"Alex, put your shirt on so wandering eyes over here can stop trying to avoid your half-naked body," I fume, slamming my head back into my pillow.

"Hey," she says, putting her hands up in defense. "I wasn't looking. I didn't even notice...ugh, put a shirt on, Alex," she repeats after me.

Alex laughs, throws his shirt on with an egotistical glimmer in his eye and struts out of the room.

Kiera makes her way over to the bed and bounces down next to me. "Well? Are you going to start talking, or what?"

I feel the nausea return with the motion of my shaking bed. "Kiera, look. Alex and I... we're not like you."

CHAPTER TEN

TRUTH BEHOLDS THE BLACKNESS

I START AT THE BEGINNING and tell her everything, wondering when she is going to hightail it out of the apartment. It's evident that my story isn't disturbing enough for her, because she's sitting here staring at me like I'm the coolest person she's ever met. If I were sitting where she is right now, I'd be looking at her with pity, wondering what looney-bin she must have escaped from. I guess she's a better person than I am.

I finally pull myself off the bed, and stumble over to the window, trying to avoid eye contact with her. "So, now you have the truth. Feel like running off yet?"

She jumps up, follows me over to the window, and grabs both of my shoulders, turning me to face her. "No," she says. "I want you to teach me how to do it." Her words are stern, but concise.

I try hard to stifle a laugh, but it seems to burst out of my mouth like a cannonball. "Kiera, I can't teach you. There's something broken in my brain that forces me to live like this. Trust me, you don't want it."

With her hands still on my shoulders, she shakes me back and forth, re-mixing the stale liquid that remains in my stomach. "You get to experience multiple lives. Why *wouldn't* I want to experience that?" she says, sounding bewildered but also oddly thrilled over my incurable psychological condition.

I did decide to leave out the state of my other life. I have a strong suspicion she might have a change of heart once she finds that out.

"You want the reason why I'm not going to condone you trying to acquire this ability?" I ask.

She shrugs. "Sure."

"It's not that I think it's even possible for you to do so, but maybe you should know everything before you make the odd request to learn how to have a twisted condition, like the one we suffer from. Yes, I said suffer."

"Chloe, I don't care about anything else. I want to help you guys," she replies, seeming unaffected by anything I've just said.

I snap my shoulders out of her grip and take a few steps away from her. With a scowl pulling across my face, I curl my lips in disgust at a person who thinks they could just come out of nowhere and help us. We're so beyond help that it's just depressing. "I appreciate that you want to help, but you can't help. You should just live your simple life in one place, here in our illusory world," I say impudently.

I'm jealous of her easy life. I wish my life could just be unassuming as well. Even though I can tell that I've taken my anger and hostility too far with her, I haven't quite gotten to the point of regret yet.

She isn't saying anything. Instead, she's glaring at me in silence. After staring for a brief moment, she turns and walks out of the room as if we politely ended our conversation.

"So, what…you wake us up and then storm out of our apartment?" Alex yells after her.

She doesn't respond with anything other than slamming our door, which causes me to wince from the pounding in my head.

Alex returns to the room, pulls the covers down, and slides back into bed. "Geez, what did you say to her? I've been trying to get her to do that for six months now," he jokes.

I shrug. "I offended her, I guess."

"Oh, is that why she ran out? Did we scare her off?" he asks with a little too much hope in his voice.

"No, not exactly. She wants to become like us." I still can't believe the audacity of that request. "I told her to stick with her simple life."

Alex pulls his eyebrows in with a look of disappointment. "Ouch, Chlo. That's pretty harsh. Why would you say something like that?"

Whatever. I don't care. Anyone who thinks that my life has been all cupcakes and rainbows has another thing coming to them. Her life *is* simple compared to mine, and I would do anything for that.

I keep replaying the look she had on her face when she left. Why would that have hurt her so much? Was it really that mean of me to tell her to enjoy her life? Although, if Alex is shocked at what I said, maybe I was a little out of line, especially considering how much he can't stand her.

"Ugh, fine. I'll go after her...right after I get a few more hours of sleep."

"Whatever you want," Alex moans, turning over and pulling the blankets around his back.

I pull the sheets back over my head and clench my eyes shut to try and block out the sun. I toss and turn for more than a half-hour until I convince myself that I'm never falling back asleep. The second I shut my eyes, my memories of everything that's happened in the past twenty-four hours become more vivid. I'm going to go find her. This is annoying. I rip the covers back off and let my feet drop heavily to the ground.

Alex rolls his head over and peers out of one half-open eye. "Chloe, what are you doing? I thought you were going back to sleep?"

"I have to go find her. I feel bad now," I whine, slipping on the first thing I can find in the closet.

"What?" he groans. "Are you just going to go bust into her apartment at eight in the morning?" A hazy laughter follows his question.

"Well, yeah. That's what she just did to us, isn't it?"

"You two are crazy. I'm going back to sleep. Wake me when you get back from your rampage."

I lean over and kiss him on the cheek. I toss my key and phone into my pocket and leave.

I've tried calling Kiera ten times, and she's not answering. On top of that, I've been walking for over thirty minutes. Her apartment seems much further away than usual, especially feeling as shitty as I do.

I pound my fist on her door a number of times before I hear feet scuffling across the floor. The door flies open and Kiera is standing in the doorway with red puffy eyes.

"Geez, Kiera," I say. "I didn't mean to make you *that* upset. I'm sorry. I didn't mean any of it. You caught me off guard, and I reacted like an idiot." I bow my head, trying to show remorse.

"Kiera, who's at the door?" A familiar voice shouts.

"No one, Dad. I'll be back in a minute," Kiera replies.

"Dad?" I ask.

"Yes, I called him when you upset me and he came over to talk to me. Is it a problem?" she asks, her words snide, and her eyes surly.

I thrust the door open wider and push her arm out of the way so I can walk in to confirm whose voice I'm pretty sure I just heard. With an absurd amount of confusion, my hands tremor with apprehension, causing each step I take to fall short of my racing mind. The corner I need to turn suddenly feels as if it's a mile away, and I can hear her words repeating my name in an echo from behind me. I reach the angled wall, and pivot myself around it to confirm my analysis and disbelief.

"Dad?" I ask again.

Kiera places herself as a blockade between her father and me. Her eyes are blazing with rage, and all I can do is feel sorry for her.

"Yes Chloe, this is my dad. What the hell is the problem now? Is he not good enough to be around you either?" she asks, waving her hand in front of my frozen stare.

I look over her shoulder to see her *dad* lift his finger and place it up against his lips. A pleading look is etched onto his clean-shaven face. I can see he doesn't want me to say anything, but how can I not?

"Um. Hello, sir..." I say, my eyes like daggers.

He places his hands in his pockets and walks toward me. "Hello, darling. Are you a friend of Kiera's?" he asks, sounding fatherly.

I cock my head to the side and look him straight in the eyes. "Yes."

He pulls his hand back out of his pocket and reaches out to shake my hand. I can't give into this, and I refuse to return the gesture. I look at him then back at Kiera before I turn to head for the door.

Kiera grabs my arm from behind and forcefully pulls me backward. "Where are you going, Chloe?" she questions, digging her fingers into me.

I turn back around, directing my attention solely on her. "I can't do this. I was coming to apologize, and I'm sorry if I hurt your feelings this morning, but I have to go."

I whip my arm out of her grip and sprint out of the door before either of them has a chance to interject again.

I wonder if Alex knows who Kiera's dad is? Or is this just one big unusual coincidence? It seems unlikely that it would be a fluke, but I can't be sure of anything anymore.

As I'm rounding the last block before arriving at our apartment, my phone vibrates in my back pocket. I retrieve it from my pants and see "1 new message" flash across the screen. It's Tomas's phone number. It says: *"Can we meet later? We need to talk...meet me at my office at 10:00 a.m."*

I pick up my pace out of anger and march up the stairwell, skipping a stair in-between each step. I jam my key into our door and shove it open. I don't see Alex in the living room, which means he's probably still sleeping off the one too many drinks from last night. Regardless, I stomp into our bedroom and find him snoring away. This can't wait.

I jump on the bed and his eyes snap open. He shoos me off and turns over onto his other side. I shake him again with a little more force and he grabs his pillow and shoves it over his head. "Let me sleep," he whines.

I rip the pillow away and place my ice-cold hands on his cheek. "Do you know who Kiera's father is?" I ask.

He groans and clenches his eyes. "What? I'm sleeping. Can't this wait?"

"Um no, this can't wait," I say. "Do you know who Kiera's father is?" I ask again, but with more vigor.

With one eye still nearly closed, he scrunches his nose upward. "No, I never met her father. It was never that serious. What is this all about?"

"You swear you don't know who her father is?"

He finally sits up and throws his head back against the headboard. "Chloe, why would I lie about that of all things? I told you we dated. I'm pretty sure that's a bigger deal than who her father is."

Well, if he really doesn't know who he is, he's not going to take this well. I give him another minute to clear his mind from his haze. He needs to be completely coherent to digest this.

"Well, who is it?" He throws his hands up in the air, clearly aggravated with all of the drama from this morning.

"Tomas is her father," I say. "How did we not know this? We've never seen Tomas with anyone, especially a daughter."

"That's completely impossible, Chloe," Alex replies, shaking his head at me.

"Fine, then you go over to her apartment and see for yourself. When I was there, he hushed me and gave me a look, warning me not to say anything. I didn't. Instead, I left. Then I got this text message a few minutes ago." I pull out my phone to show him the evidence.

After he reads it, he doesn't say another word. He gets up and grabs his clothes on the way into the bathroom. I hear the water pipes whistle and the shower crank on and then the shower curtain screech over the rod.

Okay, well I think he took that well, I think to myself. The shower doesn't last long, maybe five minutes tops. I hear the shower curtain rip back across the metal rod and the medicine cabinet slam open and shut a couple of times, telling me that Alex's anger has yet to subside. There's no question in my mind that his hatred for Tomas just grew that much more in a quick ten-minute span of time.

The door swings open and Alex is clothed, his wet hair doing nothing to hide the veins popping from his forehead.

"Maybe you should calm down," I say, taking a couple of steps toward him.

He doesn't move. "Absolutely not. That man just crossed the final line with me. What else is being hidden from us? Can you even imagine? Your uncle has been hiding a daughter from us. How does someone do that? Better yet, how has Kiera been hiding the fact that Tomas is her father, or the fact that you two are now related?" His words fly out of his mouth, each one louder than the last.

"You dated my cousin," I say, curling my lip in disgust.

"Chloe, not now," he begs. "We're going to his office. It's nine-thirty, and we need to get going. Let's go." He pulls his coat off the hook.

As we walk down a few blocks, Alex slows down. "I don't know why I care so much, but this is just annoying me. Isn't this pretty aggravating to you?" he asks.

"Well, yes. It's frustrating, but in all honesty, it's not like we've ever asked him if he had any children or a spouse. We both just assumed he didn't, you know…due to the lifestyle he maintains."

"Yeah, I suppose you're right. But why does it have to be Kiera? What are the odds of that happening? It's almost like it was a setup or something," he continues. "This is actually starting to make sense finally."

"What's starting to make sense?" I question.

He nods his head and clenches his fists. "Nothing, I'm just talking to myself."

I grab his hand to calm down, and to try and force some blood back into his whitened knuckles. "I just think we need to give him the benefit of the doubt."

He squeezes my hand with a gentle grip and lets out a frustrated sigh. "Sure."

I walk ahead of him to reach Tomas's door first. I knock three times before I hear footsteps approaching the other side. As the door opens, I'm greeted with an unexpected smile.

We both have a seat around his desk. I cross my legs and cup my hands over my knee. "Well, start talking, Tomas. I think you have a lot to share with us."

"Why, whatever do you mean, dear? I just wanted to see how you were feeling. Alex informed me of your party foul last night," he laughs.

I look over to Alex with a questioning look. "You called Tomas?"

Alex takes his jacket off and folds it neatly across his lap. "Yes, Chloe. I wanted to know if there was something different I had to do when you passed out from drinking too much. As I had warned you, people like us can't afford to just pass out. He's the one who told me where you most likely ended up."

I can't really argue with that, but we're skipping over the reason why we came here today. "Tomas, I'm fine. I've been fine since last night. However, I'm thinking an explanation might be in order. You know, in regards to our little encounter with Kiera?"

Completely uninterested, Tomas continues to fidget with a pile of paperclips on his desk. "Kiera, dear? Is she that girl you've been spending so much time with?"

With anger storming through me, I walk over to his desk and sweep the paperclips onto the floor to get his attention. "Yeah, your daughter? Don't worry though…she's not here. You don't have to play your mind-games anymore."

Tomas pushes the chair out from underneath him and leans forward, hovering over me and erupting into laughter. "You must not be serious, dear. I do not have a daughter. One would remember such an act." His eyes narrow at me.

Alex stands, rolls his sleeves up, and crosses his arms over his chest. I think it's just for effect, but just in case, I tug on his arm and pull him back down to his seat.

I stand on the balls of my feet, inching myself higher until I'm eye to eye with Tomas. "Are you going to sit here, look me in the eyes, and tell me that I didn't just see you two hours ago at Kiera's apartment?"

Tomas nods his head in disagreement. "What a ridiculous accusation," he laughs. "I was asleep for God's sake. I was right there on that couch." He points over to a mess of freshly ruffled blankets and two flattened pillows leaning against the armrest.

My chest tightens as I consider the possibility of imagining everything I just saw. Was I still asleep or passed out from last night? What is going on? I need an explanation, and I need one now. I need to hear it from Alex's mouth.

"Alex, did Kiera come over to our apartment this morning?" I ask, seeking verification.

"Yes. Why are you asking, like you weren't the one dealing with her?" His eyebrows pull together, looking confused.

"Did I or didn't I go chasing after her when she left?"

He nods. "You said you were leaving. I heard the door open and close, and then you woke me up around nine-thirty."

Tomas is looking down, pinching his lip, and appears to be deep in thought.

"Why don't I take you both over to Kiera's apartment and settle this confusion?" I suggest.

Alex stands up and throws his jacket back on. "That's a great idea. Let's go," he says, wrapping his hand around mine.

Tomas doesn't move, instead he stares at me with a blank look. "I will remain here. I'm sure you can get all the proof you need from your dear friend Kiera," he says, scratching at his chin.

I cross my arms and shoot a glaring look at him. "You can't make this easy, can you, Tomas?" I turn toward the door, but turn around with a fleeting question. "When did you shave your beard?"

He runs his fingers over his chin and his eyes circle around. "Hmm." He shrugs. "You don't need me, dear. The answer is right in front of your nose." He throws his head back and laughs wildly.

Neither Alex nor I say a word as we barge out of the office in a rage.

I'm exhausted from the amount of walking I've already done today. It's not even eleven, and I've probably walked six miles.

We stop by our apartment and grab the keys to the scooter. Most of the time I'd rather die walking than get back on that thing, but I'm too tired to walk at this point. I haven't put up much of a fight riding with him, but I feel sick every time I get off it, and after last night, who knows what I'll feel like by the time we get to Kiera's.

"Can you go slow? I still don't feel well," I groan, flipping my leg over the seat.

He hands me my helmet. "Yup. Here." He pulls in a deep breath and holds it, forcing his face to redden. As he blows the air out of his nose, he swings his leg over the scooter and clips his helmet on. "I don't even know what we're doing anymore." He speaks so softly that I question whether he meant for me to hear him.

I don't know what he means by that, and I hope it's not regarding something I've caused. We both thought Paris was going to bring us a simpler life, one that was only surrounded with happy things. It was for the first few months, but now it seems like we're going down another dangerous path.

I sometimes wonder what life would have been like if I were still living at my parents' house. What if I never fell out of that tree or ended up in a coma? Would we be here? I try to believe that everything in life happens for a reason. But when logic fails, it makes you wonder.

My pulse speeds up as we approach Kiera's apartment, and it's not from the toe-curling ride. My stomach is churning at the thought of my misperception deepening even further. We hop off the scooter and walk around to the back of the building and approach her door.

"Let me talk first, okay?" I say.

Alex pulls his helmet off and jostles his fingers through his still perfect waves. "I just want to know what's going on, Chloe," he responds with a clenched jaw.

I knock and place my ear against the door to listen for any signs of her coming. I don't hear anything, and I can see the rage in Alex growing deeper. I lift my hand to knock again, but Alex stops my hand before I can place it on the door. He balls his hand into a fist and pounds brashly.

I tug on the leather sleeve of his jacket and restrain his arm from winding up again. "Alex, if you scare her off she's not going to answer the door," I whisper.

I reach into my bag and pull out my phone. I flip through the few numbers I have until I find hers. "Maybe she went out. I'll send her a text. *Kiera, we really need to talk. I can explain my behavior from earlier. I want to make things right. Come over for dinner tonight?*"

I hope she responds.

Alex slides the phone out of my hand and retrieves his. "What did you say to her?" he asks, reading the text message.

He hands me back my phone and types a message on his phone.

I raise my eyebrows, questioning who he's sending a message to. "Who are you sending that to?" I ask.

"I'm asking Tomas to come over for dinner tonight too. If they both come, we'll resolve this confusion tonight. Then this can be over with," he says.

"Or make things really uncomfortable…"

As I'm picturing the possible scenario of what could happen tonight, my phone vibrates and startles me out of my visionary smog. "It's her. She responded."

Alex's head jerks up with alert. "What'd she say?"

I begin thumping my thumbs against the various keys on my phone to respond. "She said: 'Fine, but you have a lot of explaining to do. I'm bringing Julien.'"

Alex pulls his phone back out of his pocket, checking it for a third time in the last sixty seconds. "Good. Now, let's just hope Tomas writes back." His posture stiffens and his neck cords stand out. I get the sense he's going to explode one of these days if something doesn't give. "Let's just get to the store so we can buy stuff for dinner." He hands me back my helmet and turns back around without another word.

Before I pull my helmet over my head, I skate my hands around his chest. "Hey," I say into his ear. He turns his head and looks at me from the corner of his eye. "Should I make lasagna?" I ask in a sweet voice, trying not to laugh.

With a chuckle, he turns all the way around and pushes my helmet down over my head. "I think it would be safer for our guests if I cook dinner tonight, sweetheart," he says with a cunning grin.

"Oh please, like *you* know how to cook." He hasn't touched a pot or pan since we ended up here. I'm willing to bet my chances that lasagna would be better than whatever he can muster up in the kitchen. We might be better off ordering takeout.

"I'm better than you," he says, clicking his helmet into place. That's the last of the discussion before his phone vibrates. I grip my hand around his arm, trying to see what the phone says. "What does it say? Is he coming or not?" I ask.

CHAPTER ELEVEN

FAMILY DINNER

ALEX IS WHIPPING AROUND THE KITCHEN, tossing pans around, seasoning everything, and taste testing along the way. Where did he learn to cook like this? I'm sort of mesmerized watching him. We usually get take out, or eat something that can be microwaved. This is the first time I've had a chance to see his skills around the kitchen. By the looks of it, I have a feeling whatever he's preparing will taste a lot better than any of my attempts at cooking.

I lean over the kitchen island with my chin resting on my hands. I can't help but to gaze at him, study the way his muscles bulge every time he lifts the pan or stirs the sauce. Can my hormones explode? Is that what's going to happen to me if we don't end this waiting game soon? God I need this man. I need those hands that are around the dishtowel to be around me instead. I watch as he steals a taste from a spoon, and I find myself licking my lips in response. I can't figure out what the hell has gotten into me. I've lost all control. He has stolen my control.

It's six o'clock. They'll be arriving soon, and I'm now realizing I should have told them two different times so they wouldn't arrive at the same time. If they do, they'll know something's up, which it clearly is. Technically, they forced us to this measure.

I hear a weak knock on the door, and I know it must be Tomas. It's not hard to decipher Kiera's personality from anyone else's even by the way she knocks. I open the door to greet Tomas, who has made an effort to comb his hair and shower. He actually smells clean, and that's a first.

"Hi Tomas," I greet him with a smile. He's giving me a strange look, which tells me to lessen my excitement. I can't make him suspicious.

I open the door wider and wave my arm out to welcome him into our apartment.

"Am I late for the tea party?" he asks, his words sound sharp and suspicious. *Tea party?* Oh right. How can I forget that my uncle has convinced himself that he's the Mad Hatter and we're all in some kind of wonderland. With the amount of times I silently call him a freak, I can't help but wonder when that word is going to blare out of my mouth. Although it would just encourage him, I'm sure.

"Can't a niece invite her favorite uncle over for dinner?" Yeah, that was believable, Chloe.

Tomas walks into the living room just as my phone buzzes on the kitchen counter. I find a message from Kiera saying she's running a few minutes late. That worked out well, I guess.

"Tomas, have a seat at the table. Would you like a glass of wine or a water?" I ask.

He sits down at the table and crosses his hands over his lap. "I can trust a water. Water."

I nod. "Water it is." I turn on my heels, eyeballing Alex. Freak, freak, freak. I grab a glass of water from the kitchen and return to Tomas's side. "You okay? You seem more miserable than usual..."

He pulls a handkerchief out of his pocket and wipes the forming beads of sweat off of his forehead. "Yeah, yeah. I'm okay. Round and round. Spinning and twisting, as always."

I place my hand on his shoulder, attempting to show my sympathy. "I'm sorry to hear that. Do you have a cold or something?"

He clasps his hands together and brings his fists up to his forehead, covering his eyes. "No."

"Fair enough," I say, walking back in to the kitchen.

I watch him from the kitchen, paying close attention to his trembling hand as it reaches for the glass of water, and the difficulty he's having to keep the glass steady against his pursed lips. Something's definitely wrong with him. I poke Alex and point out his unusual behavior. Alex scrunches his forehead and looks at me with confusion. I shrug my shoulders to let him know that I'm just as confused. You know it's bad if we're both questioning Tomas's peculiar behavior.

There it is, the knock on the door that will probably push Tomas over the edge. I now regret agreeing to stir up this trouble. We're not the type that should be looking for trouble. Trouble seems to find us just fine.

I wrap my hand around the doorknob and force myself to invite in the expectant wrath. Kiera stands in front of me with a look of anger, hurt, and resentment. I can't really blame her. She's holding Julien's hand for support, and he looks miserable and uncomfortable. He must really care about her if she convinced him to walk into *this* drama.

I do the only thing that comes to mind. I lunge forward and wrap my arms around her neck. I whisper into her ear, "I'm sorry. Please forgive me." I'm hoping that's all it'll take, because in a few minutes I'm going to need to come up with a whole new set of apologies.

"Apology accepted, Chloe. No more weirdness, okay?" she asks with a bitter smile.

I can't respond. There's about to be so much more weirdness, and probably more than what she can handle. I don't even want to think about what's about to go through Julien's mind. He definitely didn't sign up for this.

I gesture for them to come in. "Come on in. Dinner's almost ready. Drinks?" I look back and forth between the two of them.

They remove their coats, and I extend my arms out to take them.

"What do you have to drink?" Kiera asks.

"Would you like wine or water?"

She turns to Julien and covers her mouth trying to stifle a giggle. "We'll stick with water, especially after last night."

I take a couple of steps closer to the dining area where Tomas is sitting. "Sure thing. Why don't you two go have a seat in the other room, and I'll get your drinks." I point to the living room, which is partially out of sight from where Tomas is sitting.

As I step out of Kiera's way to let them go by, it only takes a second. "Dad?" She tucks her hair around the back of her ear. "What are you doing here?"

Tomas doesn't flinch, and he doesn't look at her. He's acting as if he can't even hear her, but this place isn't that large. He heard her.

"Dad?" she calls again, her voice uncertain.

He still doesn't move. "Chloe," Tomas calls over to me while maintaining his focus on the empty wall in front of him.

"Tomas, what are you doing? Say hello to your daughter?" I point over to Kiera.

Tomas's nostrils flare and the corner of his lip curls down into an angry sneer. "I already told you. I don't have a daughter. Why are you doing this?" he snaps at me. "I should have assumed this was a cat and mouse trap. I'm the mouse, aren't I?" His body stiffens and his veins pulsate around his eyes. This isn't going to end well. I know this now.

"Dad, what are you talking about? It's me, Kiera, and why would you say I'm not your daughter?" she chokes out, folding her arms over her stomach. Shit. Dammit. I didn't mean for this to happen like this. I really should be deported back to that padded cell.

Tomas places his face in his hands. "I. Do. Not. Have. A. Daughter," he repeats again, glaring at me out of the corner of his protruding eyes.

Kiera brushes by me and grabs Tomas by the arm. "Look at me," she cries. "What's the matter with you? I just saw you this morning. You take off for eighteen years and then suddenly come back into my life a few months ago, and do this? What the hell is wrong with you? You're a complete asshole, you know that?"

I feel horrible. I shouldn't have interfered. Shit. Shit. Shit.

"Chloe did you know this was going to happen?" she growls at me. The look on her face is one that she would give to her worst enemy. Not her supposed best friend.

I shake my head. "I didn't," I say, narrowing my eyes at Tomas. "Is this not the man I saw in your apartment this morning?" I ask.

"Yes, Chloe. This is who you saw this morning. My father," she says as she slaps Tomas across the face. "If you will excuse us, we'll be leaving now." She snatches her purse from the coffee table and slings it over her shoulder. "I'm sorry Alex, I'm sure you've been cooking for a while. I don't want to be rude to you and Chloe, but I cannot stay in the same room as this neglectful lying piece of shit." She rips their coats back out of my hands and rushes toward the door.

"I'm so sorry Kiera," I say. I don't know what else to say. I'm still not even sure I can make sense of this.

"Wait. Why did you invite him over here? You just met him this morning, didn't you?" She turns around and her face crumples with despair.

Alex walks up behind me and places his hands on my shoulders, for support, I think. "Not exactly. Talk to me for a minute?" I sit down on the couch and pat the cushion next to me. "Please, let me explain, Kiera."

With a reluctant look in her eyes, she follows me to the couch but doesn't sit. She crosses her arms across her chest, and remains standing, hovering over me. After a minute of staring at each other, she sits on the arm of the couch.

"Kiera." I let out a loud sigh. "Tomas is my uncle." I pause, allowing her to take this information in slowly. I wish I was allowed to take in this information slowly. "I just met him about a year ago."

"What?" She cocks her head to the side. "Is this some kind of sick joke?"

"I was starting to think that myself." I let my eyes rest on my knees. I can't look up into her pain stricken eyes. I know how she feels. "I'm sorry he's so confused right now. I'm sure you know that he isn't *right* in the head."

Kiera waves her hands in front of her closed eyes, warning me to stop. "Wait, wait…who is Tomas?"

My heart is throbbing, and the words I need to say feel stuck in my throat as I point over to Tomas. "That's Tomas. Isn't that your dad's name?"

Her eyes widen, redness fills her cheeks, and tears well up in the corner of her eyes. She's trembling and looks at Julien with a frightened look and then looks back at me. "No, Chloe. My dad's name is—wow, okay. I don't feel—" The color on her face drains almost instantly. Her eyes roll back, and her body goes limp. I leap toward her to catch her before she falls, but I get pulled down with her.

"Kiera," I yell, trying to peel her off the ground. She must have passed out.

"Kiera," Julien yells, lifting her up and away from my struggling arms. He places her on the couch just as Alex runs over with a wet rag. Julien takes the cloth and pats her forehead with it. "Tell me wh-what is happening?" Julian spits out his stuttering attempt at English. Alex responds in French. I'm assuming he's explaining what might be happening.

While they're busy trying to wake Kiera, I approach Tomas. I kneel down next to him and yank on his arm, forcing him to turn toward me. "This is out of your control, isn't it?" I ask, keeping my voice quiet.

"I've been sleeping…a lot. I didn't know why, and I don't know why, but there's always a reason," he says, his eyes dead of any emotion.

"Who is he, Tomas?" I tighten my grip around his wrist.

He shrugs. "Did he speak to you when you saw him this morning?" Tomas asks.

"Yes. He said it was nice to meet me. He appeared to know who I was since he shushed me from behind Kiera's back."

"Yes. Yes. We all know you who are, dear. What did his hair look like?" Tomas asks.

"I couldn't see. He was wearing a…"

"Fedora?" Tomas interrupts.

"Yes," I respond, swallowing the uprising bile in my throat.

Tomas squints his eyes shut and pinches the bridge of his nose. "Franco, Simon, James, and Tomas. Tick-tock. Tick-tock."

"What?" I ask, shaking his arm with force.

"I'm tired," he whispers. His face whitens and his eyelids close. What the?

"Alex, can you help me," I yell.

Tomas is slouched over, and he's sliding sideways off the chair. Alex leaves Kiera and Julien to help me, and catches Tomas just as he's about to fall over. His dead weight is too much for Alex, and he gently eases him onto the floor beside the table. He checks his pulse.

"What the hell is going on?" I shout, knowing no one else is going to have an answer.

"Chloe, calm down and go help Julien. Kiera's waking up, but she's obviously confused. She could use some water, why don't you go get her a glass." Alex says, taking control as usual.

I run a glass of water over to her, and she manages to get herself upright and onto the couch.

"You okay, Kiera? What happened?" I ask, trying to hide the panic in my voice. I don't think I'm doing a good job, though.

"I-I don't remember. Who is that over there on the ground? Is he okay?" she asks, concern growing in her voice.

I stand in front of her blocking the view of Tomas. "It's just my uncle." I'm hoping that's enough to get her to calm down for a minute. "Why don't you just take a couple of deep breaths, and drink this water. I'm sure you'll feel better in a moment."

I can hear Tomas waking up, and I'm fearful that everything is going to start all over again.

"Alex, is he okay?"

"I don't know yet," he responds.

I turn back around and Kiera has regained her complete awareness. She stands up to face me and places her hand on my shoulder, pushing me to the side.

"Dad? Are you okay?" she asks, throwing herself onto the ground to help him up.

Here we go again. Worst idea ever.

"Oh, darling, you're here. Yes, I'm okay. Your dad will always be okay, sweet girl." Tomas's uncharacteristic voice comforts Kiera.

Alex and I look over at each other and then back at Tomas. "Tomas?" I question.

He looks at me and gathers his brows in toward his nose. "Tomas?" he repeats, followed by a throaty laugh.

"Dad, why does she keep calling you Tomas?" Kiera asks, with a weary voice.

"I'm not quite sure, buttercup. She's a strange girl, huh?" He's speaking of me as if I'm not standing right here. *I'm strange*?

"Are you out of your mind, Tomas?" I shout.

"Young lady, please. My name is not Tomas, and I'd appreciate it if you would stop calling me that. Your mother would not approve of your behavior, would she?"

"Well, if you aren't Tomas. Who the hell are you?" I shout, pounding my fists against my thighs.

He stands up and brushes the non-existent dust off of his pants. "Why don't you start with Uncle?" He arches his eyebrows.

I pace back and forth, trying to suppress my anger. "Uncle what? There's a whole freaking lot of you, isn't there?"

"Chloe, what are you talking about? Are you okay?" Kiera asks.

I can almost see the steam pouring out of Alex's ear as he cups his hand over his mouth, looking like he's trying to quell a bursting outrage.

My unknown uncle wraps his arm around Kiera's neck and pulls her into his side. "Darling, would you mind if we left? I'll take you home."

"Sure, Dad," she says, as she reaches across the couch for her and Julien's coats. "Hon, why don't you go rest? I'll check in with you tomorrow. Alex and I can try to help you find a doctor if you aren't feeling any better," Kiera says to me in a therapeutic voice, accompanied by a look of pity. She feels sorry for me? She thinks I'm the one who needs help? Holy crap. She's in a world of shit right now and she thinks I'm the one who should go talk to someone. Why do I even give a shit? If she wants to go live happily ever after with her daddy who pretty much escaped from a mental institution, she can.

Alex still hasn't blinked or even shifted his weight. I think he's afraid to open his mouth, and I think I'm afraid to say anything else too. I might actually speak my thoughts out loud.

Julien waves good-bye with a lost look and leans over to give me a weak hug before following Kiera and my uncle out of the apartment. As the door closes, Alex blows the pent up steam out of his tightened lips. "What just happened?" he asks, staring through me. "No. No, you know what? Let's go." He pulls both our coats off the hooks. "We're going after them."

I hold my jacket out in front of me, hesitating to put it on. "Alex, I don't think that's a great idea. We don't know what's going on with Tomas right now. You're the one who keeps saying your're sick of this. Let's just leave it alone right now."

He shoves his second arm through his jacket sleeve, and whips up the zipper, creating a ripping noise between the pieces of metal. "No. We're going to go find out."

I slide my arms through my sleeves and follow Alex out the door, but with reluctance. I don't think this is a good idea, and I'm sure he *knows* it's not a good idea.

We're soaring down the street without knowing whether or not Tomas had his car or if he came by foot. "Where are we going?" I yell over the wind.

"To Kiera's," he shouts. I'm not sure if I heard him correctly. The scooter engine is whining in my ear and I can hardly hear myself speak.

* * *

Alex hammers his fist against the door. I'm not sure I would have announced our arrival like that. Tomas, or whoever is still in there, isn't going to willingly answer the door for us. I think it's clear he's hiding something.

I can hear a body rubbing up against the inside of the door. "It's them," Kiera's muffled voice whispers from the other side.

I hear more shuffling, followed by no noise. After minutes of waiting, the door finally skulks open, revealing an angered Tomas, or whoever he is.

"Tomas?" I ask.

He walks out toward us and pulls the door half closed behind him. "You need to leave and go home. Kiera cannot know anything," he says in a gentle but firm voice.

"What did you say, Dad?" Kiera pulls the door open and looks at everyone with confusion.

"It's nothing, sweet girl. You've had a long day and I don't want Chloe filling your head with any more junk right now. Why don't you go to bed? I'll handle them."

She nods her head wearily and narrows her eyes at us before turning around and storming down the hallway into her bedroom.

After the door slams, Alex takes a step in toward my uncle, cornering him against the door. "How could we tell Kiera anything if we don't know what's going on?"

He places his hand on Alex's shoulder. "It's in your best interest if you don't know who I am. Let's just say I'm making your life a lot less complicated." He moves his head closer to Alex's ear. Alex recoils from the closeness. "Take your girlfriend home, and forget about anything that happened tonight."

Alex looks at the hand that's on his shoulder, and I can see his rage growing. "No." Alex's voice elevates into a higher pitch. "Tell us who you are. Now." Alex shoves the hand off his shoulder.

My uncle reaches behind him, grips the doorknob, and slips back inside, slamming the door in our faces. The sound of multiple locks clicking into place follows.

Alex pulls me away from the apartment. "Do you want to go home or stay here?" he asks.

"What do you mean *stay here*? For how long?" I ask.

He leans up against the brick of the building and slides down onto the ground. "I'm staying until he comes out of there so I can find out what's going on. But if you don't want to stay, I'll take you home."

I remain standing and watch as Alex's head burrows into his knees. "Where are we going to stay? Right here on the ground?" I ask.

"Yes, right here. It might be a long night," he says.

I let out a loud sigh and lean up against the wall, planting myself on the ground next to him. "I'll stay, I guess. I just don't think we're going to gain anything from it." I'm not sure I understand why this is so important to him. It's usually me who's insisting on solving every problem or figuring every loose end out.

* * *

With the onset of a rustling noise, my stomach tenses with apprehension of more confrontation. Alex jumps up to his feet, ready and willing to continue this losing battle. I think I'm the one getting tired of this now. He urges me over to the bush outside of the front door and we both duck down.

Alex brushes the hair away from my ear and places his arm around my neck, pulling me in close. "We're going to follow him to see where he goes, okay?" he whispers.

"I guess," I shrug.

The door opens, and my uncle walks out. His manner is uneasy as he peers over his shoulder, searching his surroundings.

"What am I doing here?" he asks himself. His eyebrows scrunch together and he scratches his cheek, looking from side to side.

I don't think we have to follow him. I don't think we need to question who he is right now. I think the only thing we need to wonder is how long he's going to remain as Tomas.

CHAPTER TWELVE

LOST IN A MIND OF MIRRORS

I PULL DOWN THE EXTRA SHEETS, blanket, and pillow out of our closet and bring it down to the living room.

I fluff the pillow and place it against the armrest for support. "How's your head now?" I ask Tomas. "Would you like some pain relievers or something to drink?"

His hand is wrapped around his head, placing pressure on his temples. "Better, but unsteady. Are you sure you don't mind me staying here for the night?" he asks with audible tension growing within his gravelly voice.

"It's fine, Tomas. Get some rest and we'll catch up in the morning," Alex reassures him. "Yell if you need something."

Alex takes my hand and escorts me down to our bedroom. Once inside, he closes the door and locks it.

"Why are you locking the door," I ask.

He takes a couple of books off the nearby bookshelf and wedges them under the door. "To keep us safe."

"Do you think he's going to *turn* again tonight?"

"Who knows? I just need to keep you safe." He tugs on my arm and pulls me into his chest, wrapping his arms around me. "How does this sort of trouble keep finding us, Chlo? It's exhausting. You know?"

I close my eyes with momentary comfort from the warmth of his chest and the soothing rhythm of his beating heart.

* * *

I'm sure he slept with his eyes open all night, and I feel bad for not keeping him company, but fatigue won that battle. My memories flick on like a light, and the knot in my stomach makes me wonder if Tomas is still in our living room or if he broke out while we were asleep. I wonder if we'll ever get our answers.

When I lift my head from my pillow, my eyes are drawn to the inconsistent pattern of colors left on the sheet below. I look for evidence on my face, and when I pull my hand away, I find it. Blood. I sit up, tilt my head back, and pinch the bridge of my nose.

Alex's eyes grow wide when he notices the bloody mess left behind on my pillowcase. I don't want to know what my face looks like after smothering my face in blood all night.

He wraps his hands around my face and tilts my head back even farther. "Oh my God. You're bleeding. Did you cut yourself?"

"How would I cut myself with a pillow?"

He lowers his head, looking up at my nose for a mark that I'm sure he won't find. "I'll grab you something. Don't move." He runs into the closet and returns with a facecloth. He wads up the cloth and presses it under my nose. "Does it hurt?"

I squint my eyes from the pressure. "No, it doesn't. I just wish I would stop getting so many bloody noses."

"What do you mean so many? The only one I know about was after you passed out at the party. Have there been other times?"

"Just one other time, a few months ago. It's not a big deal, really," I try to convince him, hoping he won't go ballistic over this.

"Okay well, let's just…" He stops midsentence and clutches the top of his head.

I drop the rag from my face and turn my attention toward him. "You okay? What's going on?"

"My head," he grits his teeth together. "It's throbbing." His face drains of color.

Another beating. That's what this is. Franco is beating the shit out of us.

"Do you want ice? Should I rub it?"

"It's going away. It's like this stabbing pain that comes on out of nowhere and then disappears as fast as it came on," he groans, rubbing the sides of his head.

"Do you think Franco has something to do with this?" I ask, dropping the idea in his head.

"If we're both experiencing odd physical abnormalities, then I'd say there's a good chance he has something to do with this. I think we need to get out of those cells."

"You do?" I'm somewhat taken aback by his change of heart. I figured he'd want us to stay in there forever, and after dealing with Franco those last few times, I probably wouldn't argue with him. I have no idea how we're going to find a way out—not with both of us coming out alive.

"I'm going to go check on him. Please stay here."

I hear him walk down to the living room and into the kitchen. I hear his fist slam into the wall, followed by a slew of profanity. He storms back into our bedroom, whips the closet door open, and pulls clothes off the hangers. "He's gone."

More like he's lost track of where his mind is.

"I wonder where he went, or who he is right now," I say.

I drag my tired body out of bed, knowing we aren't going to get comfortable again. Our hunt is about to continue. I'm tired. I'm sick of this. I want to forget about Tomas. I want to forget that Franco owns the decision whether we should live or die. I don't want to be held hostage, physically or mentally anymore. I want to wake up somewhere normal, somewhere without confusion.

Alex pulls a sweatshirt over his head and whips his hat off the bureau. "You know what's weird?" he says. "We both know how sloppy of a person Tomas is, but whenever he left, he folded the blanket and the sheets perfectly and placed them in a neat pile on the coffee table."

"That's because he isn't Tomas," I say.

"Well, who do you think he is then?"

"I don't think anyone knows, including Tomas."

"Great. It's clear this isn't getting settled today, and I have to work tonight. I want you to come with me."

"Is Kiera working tonight, too?" I ask.

"I think I saw her name on the schedule for tonight."

"Good. She won't be able to run from me, and psycho uncle won't be there to drag her away before she answers my questions."

"No brawls, Chlo." Alex laughs and places a kiss on my forehead. "I'm going to go make breakfast and secure the apartment."

"I'll be out in a few."

I step into the shower and twist the faucet all the way right, letting the steaming hot water melt my nerves. I need to understand what's happening. There's a reason for all of this. There has to be. I just wish I knew why my dreams had to be so complicated. There has to be some kind of logical meaning or reasoning for all of this. Yet, even if I spend a lifetime in this alternate state of mind, I'm still not sure I'll have full clarity.

If there are only four personalities, and if in fact he's dealing with uncontrollable personality shifts right now, Kiera's father can only be one of three other options. Two of which I'm sure he's not. The only option would be James, and that doesn't seem like it should be an option. However, according to my mother's secret letters, and the stories my mother and Tomas both shared with me, it's hard to think of any other possibility. James is the only one left. Although, there *could* be more than four personalities, I suppose. Maybe it's just that no one knows of more. Maybe one was just created. Maybe more will be created. I can't help but wonder if someone's brain could explode from such drastic imbalance.

What's worse is that Kiera could be in trouble. Her vision is so clouded right now. I don't know how I'm going to tell her that her long lost dad isn't who she thinks he is. She probably wouldn't even believe me, especially when I break the news to her that he has multiple personalities, half of which she'd be terrified to meet.

I wonder who Kiera's mother is, or where she is for that matter. Maybe I don't want to know. It's amazing how in the dark Kiera is about all of this. Unless she isn't. Maybe she's just a good liar, like her father.

I pick up my phone and start a new text to Tomas saying: *"Who are you right now? I know what's going on."*

Within seconds my phone vibrates with a return message saying: *"It's Tomas. I know you know, but I still don't know who he is. Sorry."* He? I love how he talks about himself in the third-person, as if he were multiple people rather than multiple personalities.

I guess Tomas is officially no longer a resource for me. The only way I'm going to get to the bottom of this is either through Kiera or the source of the problem himself.

*   *   *

"What time is she supposed to be here?" I ask Alex, watching as he runs around prepping his tables.

He places the ketchup bottle down on the last table and straightens both of the placed napkins. "I don't know. I think both of our shifts started at six."

It's six-thirty. With a heavy feeling in my stomach, I make my way to the back corner table and sit down with my eyes fixed on the front door, waiting for it to open.

When the door opens, my heart stops as I wait and hope for Kiera to come bouncing through the entryway. No such luck. My breath hitches when I see who *is* coming through the door. What is *he* doing here?

I slouch down behind my book, hoping he doesn't see me. I don't want any more awkward encounters. The other day was as much as I could handle.

I peek over the top of my book and see him heading straight for me. Crap, crap, crap. Shit.

"Ms. Valcourt," he says. "It's a pleasure to see you here. It's also a little out of the ordinary. I don't typically see many of my students in this café." Couldn't he just pretend he didn't see me? God.

I place my book down and clear my throat from the forming lump. "Hi, Professor Lane. This is one of my favorite places, actually," I say, slinking down farther into my chair.

"I've been coming here for many, many years. You have good taste," he says, his voice monotone. His eyes narrow and then widen. "I just can't help but wonder what would drag you to *this* particular café?" His glare is making me uncomfortable. It's making me feel as though he can read my mind and knows the exact reason why I know of this place.

"Oh," I squeak. "My boyfriend works here." I point over to Alex.

The professor looks over to Alex. I watch as the professor's face contorts with an odd expression. "*He's* your boyfriend?" he asks. "The wanderer." His words are so soft that I'm not sure he intended for me to hear them. Did he just call Alex the wanderer?

"Do you know him?" I interrupt his intense stare in Alex's direction.

"No, I don't believe I do." He shakes his head with a confused look. "Ms. Valcourt, I hope you did not forget about what I said to you last week. Please, make sure you are careful in the decisions you make. They can affect a lot more than you are aware of." His forehead begins to glisten, and his voice sounds shrill. "Have a good night, Ms. Valcourt." He tips his hat and leaves the cafe. He never ordered anything.

Alex approaches me the second my professor exits the door. "Who was that?" he asks, concern coursing through his eyes.

"He's my professor, my psychology professor. My psychology professor who sounds like he knows more about my life than he should. Classes are being put on hold for a bit."

"That might be the best idea right now. I don't like the looks of that guy, and I definitely don't like the way he's making you feel right now. He looks kind of off too. Maybe you could just drop that class?" I know he's trying to be supportive, but there's too much going on right now. The thought of school doesn't have a place in my dreams right now.

I feel I've been barricaded into a corner, unable to do anything I really want. Even within my dream, reality isn't what it should be. Alex kisses my cheek, "Sorry, Chloe." A table shouts for the check and Alex hustles back into the kitchen.

While I fixate my eyes back on the front door, I convince myself that Kiera isn't coming. I pull out my phone and dial her number. I hear two rings followed by a click.

"Kiera?" Please say something. Please.

I hear heavy breathing but no voice.

"Kiera, it's Chloe. Are you okay?" Dread is seeping through my nerves, numbing my body.

"Help me," her voice cries softly.

"Kiera, where are you? Can you tell me?" I'm trying to stay calm, so I can keep her calm, but I'm having a hard time hiding my fear for her.

The phone clicks, and I know she's gone. I redial her number again, and it doesn't even ring one complete time when the phone is clicked on again.

"Chloe, do not call Kiera's number again or I will take her cell phone away from her. Do you understand me, young lady?" he says politely, but the threat is emphasized behind each word.

"If you just tell me who you are, I'll leave you alone," I retort, attempting to sound tougher than I feel.

"Like I've told you before, Chloe, this isn't a concern of yours. Please allow my daughter and me to live in peace," he says evenly, as if this conversation is ineffective.

"Are you hurting her?" my voice croaks.

"Jesus. Who do you think I am? Franco?" he laughs. "No darling, I don't hurt people. I'm the *only* normal one. So, let it go," he pauses, breathing heavily into the phone. "When you can do that, maybe you and I can be friends too." He sighs and ends the call.

I slam my phone down on the table, furious, upset, and baffled. I kick the chair out from below me, and rush over to Alex, pulling him to the side of the café where no one can hear us. "He has her."

"Great," Alex says, ruffling his fingers through his hair. "Do you have Julien's number?"

"Yes, but I can hardly hold a conversation with him." Still. After months of trying to learn French, I still can't hold a functional conversation with anyone in this country.

"I'll call him," he says, handing me his apron. "Go take that table's order." He points to a couple who just sat down.

Seriously? I've never waited tables before. I don't know what I'm supposed to do. Well, I do. Not in French, though.

People are waving their hands in the air, attempting to get the attention of the staff. I look around, reminding myself that I'm now the only person here who can take orders. This should go over well. What about not being able to speak French does Alex not understand?

With hesitation, I walk up to the table and greet the man and by the looks of it, his wife. Let's hope I can survive on the twenty words I actually know. *How do I say what can I get for you, in French?* Think, Chloe. "Que…puis-je faire…pour vous?"

They both look up at me and offer a kind smile. It's clear to them French is not my native or secondary language. I'm not sure if I even said what I intended to. So embarrassing. I can feel my cheeks burning, and I think it's noticeable to them, too.

"Don't worry Miss, we both speak English. We'll have two baguettes, a soup de jour, and two espressos," the man says with an appreciative sigh.

I jot down their order and take the menus from the table. "Merci," I blurt out, without placing an accent over any of the letters. Embarrassment is now an understatement.

I head to the back counter and punch the order in on the computer register. This is easy. If I was a little more fluent, I could actually handle this job. But I'm only given one second to bask in my own feeling of success before Alex comes out of the back room.

"Julien's on his way over to Kiera's apartment right now. He said he would send you a message when he found out what's going on. Whenever he sends it to you, let me know." He takes the notepad and pen back out of my hand and greets the table whose order I just took.

He seems so angry, even angrier than I am. I know his frustration isn't geared toward me, but his moments of happiness have been vague and less frequent this past week. Not that I can blame him, but I miss us. Just us. Without the drama. After we figure out what's going on with Kiera, and we make sure she's safe, I'm letting this all go. Tomas is going to be the demise of my relationship with Alex if I let this continue.

Maybe we should just stay locked in that cell for as long as possible. It creates happiness here, a feeling we need in order to sustain the life we want to live.

I return to my table, plop down on the chair, and twiddle my thumbs for over an hour until my phone buzzes. It's Julien. I feel a boulder drop into my stomach as hundreds of thoughts cross my mind. I open the message, but I can hardly make out one word of the French.

I run over to Alex, waving my phone at him. "It's him. I can't understand what it says though."

I watch as he squints at the phone, translating the message. His eyes widen and his eyebrows pull in toward his nose. With an unsettled gaze, he unties the back of his apron with his free hand and allows it to drop to the ground.

"We need to get over there. Now," he says.

CHAPTER THIRTEEN

SYNDICATED ALLIANCE

"I GUESS MY PLAN WORKED quicker than I expected. Nice to see you both again," the unknown personality says.

"Where is she?" I brush past him, darting my eyes around the room for any indication. I have to find her.

Tomas's alter ego takes a seat on Kiera's living room futon and caresses the pleats of his perfectly pressed pants before resting his hands on his knees. He pulls in a sharp breath and lifts his chin and eyebrows, directing his attention solely on me. "Now, please keep your voice down. She's sleeping, and she's fine," he says with a dubious grin. "I think it's about time we have a little chat." He looks over to Alex, and nods his head toward the door. "Alex, you are free to go, son." His words exude confidence.

Alex throws his head back and releases a bellowing laugh. When he re-collects himself, his lips unfold into a straight line and his eyes narrow on my uncle's. "Absolutely not. Psycho."

"Very well, then. I'll just cut to the chase." My uncle clears his throat as his Adam's apple bobs up and down. "Chloe, I'm not who you think I am." He shifts his weight uncomfortably on the futon and once again smoothes the pleats out of his pants.

Alex and I both remain standing, watching his eyes jitter around and his mouth utter words filled with air. It looks as if he's practicing what he is going to say before he says it.

I sigh heavily, debating whether I should even participate in this conversation. "And who exactly do I think you are?"

"Don't you think I'm Tomas?" he questions, tilting his head to the side.

"I know you aren't Tomas."

He perks ups. "Well then, I guess we got that awkward explanation out of the way," he chuckles. He couldn't be so ignorant to think he's really off the hook that easily. In truth, I don't give a damn who he is. He just needs to get away from Kiera.

"Which one are you?" I play into his riddle.

His eyes glow with excitement. "Why, whatever do you mean?" A devious grin grows wide across his cheeks. Oh, for God's sake.

"Are you going to tell me, or not?" I shift my weight onto my other foot. My patience is running thin, but I can't let him know that I care.

"Not," he replies, waggling his eyebrows with amusement.

"Fine," I say. "Have it your way. Alex, are you ready to go?" I lift Alex's clenched fist and lead him toward the door.

"Guess you don't—you don't want to know, huh?" he stutters. I've got him right where I want him now.

"Nope. I don't care. Tell Kiera we were looking for her." I shrug my shoulders, trying to appear unfazed. As I close in on the front door, I notice a distressed look growing upon his face. Beads of sweat are forming on his head. He's unclasped the top button of his shirt, and his hair is starting to fall out of its perfectly combed back place.

"Don't you want to know if she's okay?" He tries to pull me back into his trap.

I place my hand on the doorknob and twist it open. I shake my head and focus my attention on the path outside of the door. "Oh. By the way…my mother has been looking for you for quite a while. You might want to give her a call…James."

I turn around just in time to see the stupefied look on his face. A look of knowing that I've figured him out, and that he has lost his one and only secret.

Just as I place one foot out of the door, I hear scuffling from down the hall, and I turn to see Kiera wobbling toward us with smudged mascara running down her cheeks, clothes that she had been wearing yesterday, and a look of displacement.

"What's going on in here?" she garbles with a hazy look.

"Kiera, why don't you come with us," Alex offers, reaching his hand out to her.

She walks toward us with an empty look behind her eyes, fear apparently keeping her in a frozen mental capacity. I pull her coat off the coat rack and tuck it under my arm. I press my hand against her back to urge her out of the apartment, leaving James alone, dumbfounded and without control.

* * *

I wrap a blanket around Kiera's shoulders, and Alex squats down beside her with a cup of tea. "You feeling any better now?" He places his hand on her shoulder, giving it a squeeze. "Julien said he'd be here in a few minutes."

"Why did he...?" and a furtive expression sweeps over her face. "Put me in there? I don't—I don't get it?" Her words are hardly audible. I don't understand how she could have ever thought of him as being normal or safe to be around. Parents don't typically take off from their young child, and return, seeking them out as an adult, not without a good reason behind it. I can't say whether or not I would have been any less gullible in her lonely life situation.

"Put you in where?" I question, pushing the hair away from her reddened zombie-like eyes.

"He locked me in a closet all day." She nods at her own disbelief. "He never said why. I should have never let him back into my life." She lets her head fall forward, probably avoiding our sympathetic looks.

"Kiera, what is your mother's name? Where is she? Do you know?" Do I even want this answer?

She sniffles and closes her eyes briefly. When she reopens them, she focuses on the teacup clenched between her fingers. "She died when I was five. Her name was Melanie."

She died. She's dead. "Was James around when she died?"

She crinkles her forehead and pulls her eyebrows together, appearing to try and recall the memory. "No, he had been away for a few days. I think. He traveled a lot." Oh no. It all makes sense to me. It's all fitting together like one sick fucked up puzzle.

I look at Alex, wondering if he's thinking the same thing I am. His mouth is in a straight line, and his focus is on the ceiling. If he hasn't figured it out, I'm certain he will shortly. "What did she die from?" I ask, covering her trembling hand with mine.

"The police said she ended her own life. She jumped off of our balcony," she says. Her chin is trembling, and tears pool up in her eyes. "My dad, James, left after that. No one could find him. It was as if he disappeared off the face of the earth." She seems lost behind her own words. Yeah, I'm thinking running away might be a better term to use. Any murderer knows not to stick around after the job's done.

"Disappeared?" I question. I know I should stop pushing her. She's been through enough today, but James is out there, loose. I'm questioning the similarities between him and Franco, or if Franco just takes over when least expected. "How did you end up here, then?"

James lived in Southborough, Massachusetts with my mother. If he had a daughter there, why would she be here, in Paris? Maybe she isn't actually here in Paris. Maybe she is just part of my mind. Or maybe I'm part of hers. Although, we are related, maybe we're connected too.

Kiera leans over toward the coffee table and places her teacup down. "I was told that I needed to be protected, and that I couldn't live at home. I was sent to live with a foster family for a while. I only stayed with them for a couple of years, though. After that, I stayed with another family for a bit, and then four others until I turned eighteen. The day I was legally allowed to live on my own was the happiest day of my life." She smudges more dripping mascara off with her thumb and sucks in a long breath of air. "So, that's the story."

I wrap my arms around her and squeeze, hoping to take even just an ounce of pain away. Nevertheless, she pulls away. She places her hands on my shoulders with a firm grip and wipes her face clean of all emotion.

"Chloe...was I imagining it, or did you tell me that Tomas/James is your uncle?" she asks, pain and puzzlement still reeling through her bloodshot eyes.

"You aren't imagining it. James *is* my uncle. He's my mother's brother," I say matter-of-factly.

Kiera backs herself up to the edge of the couch, and then stands up to distance herself from me. "What is this? Some kind of sick joke?" she asks, clutching the fabric of her shirt over her chest. How did I just become the monster in all of this? It's not like I've known about this all along. I have to deal with this just like she does.

"No. More like an odd coincidence. I swear I had no idea we were related, who you were, or why we even met. You didn't seem to care when I told you the other night? What changed?"

"I convinced myself that I had imagined you saying that, and that whatever I thought you said, couldn't be real. How would any of that even be explained? It's impossible, even." If only she knew I was questioning whether *she* is even real.

She whips her coat off the back of the couch and makes a quick dash for the door. As if this whole thing was planned, a knock sounds from the other side of the door. Kiera stops and stares at the door, waiting for something to happen. She takes a few steps backward, most likely terrified of what might be standing on the other side. But before I can remind her that Julien was on his way, he shoves the door open and falls to his knees before her.

"Kiera, êtes-vous d'accord?" He wraps his arms around her legs, burying his face into her thigh. The worry and pain on his face lets me know how much he cares for her, which she desperately needs right now.

"He asked her if she was okay," Alex whispers to me, translating the French words.

"I figured," I respond.

Alex grabs me by the arm and pulls me into the kitchen. "Do you think James killed her mother?" Alex asks.

I press my fingers into my forehead, attempting to rub the stress away. "I think *Franco* killed her mother."

Alex opens each cabinet door, appearing to look for something, but it might just be peace of mind. Each door slams one after another before he stops to face me. "Chloe." He stops and turns toward me. "How many are there?" he asks.

"I know of four," I shrug. "There could be more I don't know about though."

"Awesome." He slams another cabinet. "This is just getting better by the second. I've had it, Chloe."

He's had it? With me? With this? This is out of my control. Doesn't he realize this? "We need Tomas back, and we need to tell him what's going on, so he can give us some insight," I say.

Alex grips the back of his neck and clenches his jaw. "How do you suppose we do that?"

"We need to get James here, and keep him here until he turns back into Tomas," I say.

He waves his hands in front of his face. "No, no, no. That's a bad idea. He just had Kiera locked in a closet for an entire day just to get you over there, to do what? Wave his identity in front of your face like a riddle?"

"Okay, I get it. Then, we'll just have to wait for him." I'm totally losing this battle right now. I promised myself when we got Kiera back, I'd let this go. But I can't.

Alex grabs my shoulders, his grim eyes blazing into mine. "Chloe, this is killing me," he says, pulling me into his chest. "I can't keep going like this."

"What are you saying, Alex?" What is he saying? His frustration is killing me. This whole ordeal is pulling us apart, and if I let it, it will get the best of us. I have to make this better, somehow.

He nods his head, appearing not to have an answer or response. "I don't know, Chloe."

We both look over to Kiera and Julien who seem to be in an unbreakable and speechless embrace. I can't imagine what she's going through or what she's been through, but knowing that she's family now makes it harder to walk away from this. I don't even want to think about how she's going to react when I tell her about each of James's personalities. Although, I suppose she must have a clue, especially after what happened with Tomas the other night.

"Kiera, we should probably talk some more," I speak up, interrupting their silence.

"What else is there to know?" she asks, her voice remains timid as she twists her multi-colored bracelets around her wrist.

I walk over and extend my hand to her, hoping she'll find comfort and follow me. "Come back over and sit down. I'd rather get everything out in the open and not have you find out any more secrets."

She takes my hand and follows me to the couch. I position myself to look directly at her while I search through my foggy mind for the right words.

"James was born James." I stop and let her question what that means. With a confused look on her face, I continue. "As he grew older, he became Franco, Tomas…and Simon as well," I trail off again.

Her head recoils and her eyes narrow. "I don't understand."

"James suffers from a type of multiple personality disorder. He also has some of the same abilities that Alex and I have. The problem is James doesn't seem to have any control over which of the other three personalities he has taken on.

"I can only speak from my experience, now having met three out of four of them. Tomas as a person is harmless—he's a professional nut. Franco is a murderer and should be locked up. From what I've heard, Simon is a mute—nothing more. James, though, he isn't supposed to exist anymore, which makes this even more complicated than necessary."

"I—I…don't understand," she says. Her eyes search mine, appearing to try and decipher whether I'm crazy, she's crazy, or everything I'm saying is sadly factual.

"I'm sure this is a lot for you to take in. I just figured you should know what's going on," I say.

Kiera grips her hands around her bouncing knees. "I don't even know what to say or think right now," she says, looking over her shoulder at Julien, who's sitting at the edge of the couch with an even *more* lost look on his face. He probably doesn't understand anything I just said. Lucky him.

"Wait!" Kiera yells at me as if I were on the other side of the room rather than just six inches away.

"What?" I ask.

She's shaking her head as if she doesn't really want to know this answer. "Where did you meet Franco?"

I stand up and pinch my fingers around a sore spot on my neck. How do I explain this? "Uh…well…he's holding Alex and me hostage in some abandoned basement of a mental institution. He wants something from me, and I don't know what it is. And until I come up with it, he's going to keep us there…unless he chooses to kill us."

"Wait. You're there now?" she asks, incomprehension obscuring her hazel eyes.

"Yes. I told you that you wouldn't want to live like we do. It's not as exciting as it appears to be."

Kiera looks up at me with a combination of anger and sadness. "I still want to help."

I stand up and take her teacup from the coffee table and walk over to the kitchen sink. Why would she or anyone want to help us escape from a serial killer? It's just stupid to put yourself in that kind of danger.

"That's a nice gesture, Kiera, but I'm afraid it wouldn't be possible. Besides, he'd kill you." I speak loudly enough for my voice to carry into the living room.

The second she digests my words, a light bulb must flash in her head. I walk back into the living room to see her eyes large and glossed over as she picks at her limp bottom lip. When she notices me round the corner, her eyes flutter to mine. "He killed her, didn't he?"

"Who?" I ask knowingly.

"My mother? He killed her, didn't he?" Her words seethe through her tightened jaw.

"I don't know. But it's the first thought that entered my head too," I say.

Alex walks forward and places a calming hand on my shoulder. "Ladies, we shouldn't jump to conclusions. I'm not defending Franco in any respect, but we should probably not assume anything right now."

Kiera jumps up out of her seat and begins pacing around the living room, gripping hunks of her hair. She's mumbling to herself and her eyes are bugging out of her face. When she stops short and looks over at Alex and me, she drops her hands to her side. "I'm going to Massachusetts and I'll get you guys out of there. That's what I'm going to do," she says, whipping her phone out of Julien's hand and then punching various buttons.

Alex's face reddens as he approaches Kiera and pulls the phone from her hand. "Didn't you just hear what Chloe said? He'll kill you. This isn't a joke," he snaps.

Kiera jerks the phone back. "Yeah, I heard her. I get it," she says, sneering at Alex.

"How do you plan on getting there?" he asks with a hard expression.

She stares at Alex for a moment, giving him a stern look before her face drops in defeat.

I cross my hands over my lap and stare down at the whitened creases within my knuckles. "Kiera, we appreciate your concern, but there's no reason to risk your life for us. Besides, freeing us is a little more complicated than just getting past Franco and unlocking a couple of doors."

I can't be the one to tell her about Alex's condition, or the fact that he needs to be released and then put into a safe place, for the sake of his own well-being. I'm not quite sure what his original plan was when he wanted to run away from the institution, but having the chance to think about it now, he most likely would have gone back to his incoherent state within hours, and I would have needed to figure out how to care for him, and find a place for us to hide out. It's kind of scary that I didn't think of that before.

I stand up, and grip my hand around Alex's arm. "Kiera, can you just sit down and stay here for a few minutes? I need to have a word with Alex."

I drag Alex into our bedroom and close the door softly behind me.

"Chlo, what's the matter?" he asks, sitting down on the edge of our bed.

I walk over, sit down next to him, and twist my body to face him. I lift his hand, embracing it between my hands and bring it to my lap. "If Franco hadn't stopped us in the institution, what was your escape plan?"

He looks down at our intertwined fingers and drops his eyelids. "Would you be mad if I told you I hadn't thought that far ahead? I was so eager to be free and to be with you, that I wasn't even thinking past the block of time that I would have been in a fully coherent state."

I smooth my thumb over his knuckles trying to comfort him. "Baby, do you know how dangerous that could have been for both of us?" I'm just as much to blame for not thinking it through though.

Now we're at a point where we do need to figure out what's going to happen if we *can* manage to get away from Franco. It's not like we're going to just prance back into the institution after being missing for almost a year.

"Now that we have a chance to think about this, I don't know what we're going to do when we do leave those cells," he says, lifting his chin. "It's all I've been thinking about for the past few months." He releases my hand and clenches both of his fists against his legs. "Why do you think I was so against going back there in the first place? We seem to be okay in this alternate state, and I just wanted to stay put for as long as possible."

This can't be the only solution—living in a comatose state forever. "There has to be something else?" I say.

"I guess you'll have to keep me locked in a closet somewhere so I don't hurt you or myself." His eyes drift from mine, focusing only on the wooden floor below our feet. "Being free doesn't sound like the best option anymore."

I never thought I'd want to purposely keep myself locked in an abandoned institution, but if that means I can remain in this alternate state with Alex, than what he's saying actually makes sense. "I get it, Alex. Here, you're fissure free." I offer a smile. I understand that it will be the only way we can both live together. It has to be here in this dream of a reality, without complication. But then again, for me—I don't know if I'll be able to remain unconscious once Franco isn't keeping me that way. I guess there's a possibility that I'll have to live part of my life in that horrible cell, alone. The realization of what I've been hoping and fighting over for the past year just settled into a disturbing understanding.

Alex peers up at me, his blue eyes troubled as he tucks a loose strand of hair behind my ear. "I think you're finally understanding why I want to stay away from Franco for as long as possible."

"So, what do we tell Kiera? The truth?" I ask, looking down toward my lap, allowing the loose strand of hair to fall back over my eye.

He nods. "I'd rather her not know about my situation, and I don't want her opinions and suggestions. I think we just need to be clear that she must let us handle this ourselves," he says.

"Then that's what we'll do," I agree with a tight-lipped smile, a forced one at best. "Wait. How can Kiera even get to Southborough? Isn't she just...part of our minds here?"

"We shouldn't question what she's capable of." As strange as his words are to me, I somewhat understand what he's getting at. Alex stands up and pulls me behind him, leading us back down to the living room. Halfway down the hall I see the front door had been left wide open. Shit.

When we enter back into the living room, Julien's coat is still hung over the side of the couch, and we both sprint back toward the front door. Once we enter into the corridor, we see Julien running toward us mumbling something in French.

"Julien couldn't stop her," Alex groans.

I slap my hand around Alex's arm, pulling him to look at me. "Alex. Can she drift?"

He shakes his head, partially looking like he doesn't want to tell me, partially looking like he's unsure. "I don't know."

CHAPTER FOURTEEN

FACING THE END

I SHOUT AT TOMAS to open his door, praying and hoping that he's there. Alex pounds on another spot of the door above my head, yelling Tomas's name.

It's been a couple of hours since Kiera took off. We've searched everywhere for her, at her apartment, the cafe, and the school. It's clear that she is following through with her plan, but we need to find a way to stop her from the mistake she's about to make — if that is in fact what she's trying to do.

"Tomas," Alex yells through the thick wooden door again. "Let us in. Now."

I have my ear up against the door, listening for noise, but I don't hear much except for a clicking that I can't quite pinpoint. Alex reaches for the doorknob and twists. It's unlocked, and Alex shoves the door. Tomas is hunched over his desk, pounding on the keyboard of his computer. He doesn't flinch at our sudden existence or acknowledge us in any way.

"Tomas?" I call out with angst distorting my voice

He lifts his bloodshot eyes from his screen and looks at us but doesn't say a word. I walk behind him to see what he's typing, and I see that he's entering a bunch of numbers into a spreadsheet.

I place my hand on his shoulder, startling him into gasping for air. "Tomas? Are you okay?" I ask.

He swings his chair around, dodging my gaze. "No, not okay," he growls. "What kind of question is that?" He flips his chair back around to continue his data entry.

I take a couple of steps backward, feeling worn down from his unpredictable reactions. "Tomas, we know what's going on," I say.

He stands up and kicks his rolling chair across the room. He throws his arms up into the air, his reddened eyeballs bulging out as far as they will go. "No you don't," he says, scowling. "I don't even know what's going on."

"James is back," I say, backing further away from him.

Alex comes to stand in front of me, protecting me from his assumable wrath, but Tomas's mouth drops into a wide upsetting frown and his eyes droop halfway down his face. "I've lost all control. I'm done," he says in a whisper, sounding as though he were only speaking to himself. "I'm in trouble, guys. We all might be in trouble."

"Are we in trouble because James is back? I didn't think he was dangerous." I say, hopeful to correct his theory.

"James is only dangerous in the sense that he can eliminate me, and if he replaces me, I can't help you anymore. On top of that, James isn't aware of where or what Franco is up to right now."

Tomas sits back down and buries his face within his hands, lost and without any more thoughts or ideas. We're losing this battle, and I fear we're moving closer to the inevitable permanent darkness that is waiting for us on the other side. Our options are disappearing and so is this false happiness.

If Tomas can't help us, we need to figure this out for ourselves. As much as I want to ask Tomas for help, and explain to him the severity of the situation with Kiera being on her way to confront Franco, it's hard to determine how long Tomas will be in this state of mind. What if while he's helping us, he transitions back into James? God only knows what will happen to us then.

Lost within my thoughts, Alex pulls me to the other side of the office. "Chloe, we should leave. I don't trust Tomas right now," he says, wiping the beads of sweat off his nose.

I shrug. "We can't leave, Alex. I need to make sure we're okay back at home, " I say, searching the room, looking for the tanks Tomas used on us before.

"You don't even know how he set that tank up last time. He did something so we'd only be out for fifteen minutes, remember?" he says. "You don't even know if Kiera will be there."

"Something tells me I need to go back and check on *things*."

"Chloe…" He grabs me by the waist and pulls me toward him. "I don't think it's a good idea. Let's not."

"Alex, give me a chance." I pull myself out of his loose grip and approach Tomas.

"Could you tell us how you gassed us last time? How did you make it so we were only gone for fifteen minutes?" I stare at him, waiting for an answer. But with my fears coming to a reality, I can tell he's fading out again. I think we need to get him out of here before James makes another appearance.

Alex kneels by Tomas's side and taps his face to see if he can get a reaction. Tomas doesn't flinch. Alex slides his shoulder under Tomas's arm and lifts him to his feet. I help on the other side and wrap my arm around Tomas's back while we drag him out of his own office.

As we reach the door, Alex slides it open and shimmies Tomas out. We lower his back against the wall until he's sitting on the pavement. He's completely unconscious. I'm sure not for long, though.

We both settle back into the office, and Alex secures the door. We need to keep ourselves safe while *we're* unconscious, and Alex seems to be taking extra measures of precaution by blockading the door. He moves furniture up against the door and slides bookshelves in front of the windows. He wipes his dust-covered hands off on his pants and rests his head on one of the walls, gasping for air. I can see the frustration on his face, and I know he's getting tired of this. Sometimes I still wish I never ruined his drift the way I have. He had it so good before he met me—living each day at the beach with nothing other than peace and happiness—nothing to worry about. Now, I'm here and I've made his life crazy, creepy, messed up, and chaotic. I'm not sure I can understand how he continues to love me through all of this. It's as if our relationship has caused some kind of havoc on our internal universe. We feel like soul mates, but sometimes it seems as if we're each other's kryptonite.

I walk up behind him, and trace my fingers along the curve of his spine, startling him away from whatever thought was running through his mind. He turns around, wraps his arms around me, and pulls me into him. "I'm getting tired of this," he says.

And there it is. I knew it. He can't deal with this situation, or me anymore. Maybe I should just figure this out myself. It's clear I've pushed him too far. Or this situation caused by me, has pushed him too far. Either way, his life is a mess because of me.

I pull myself from his hold, looking past him. "I know, Alex. I've pushed you too far. I'll handle this myself. I don't want to make you do this anymore. You don't deserve this," I say. My chest tightens, listening to my own words.

He doesn't respond. His expression is cold and dark—it's a look I've never seen. I have no idea what's going through his mind right now, but I do know that we're running out of time. As much as I want to sit here and analyze his words and thoughts, I know I have to do this now or Kiera could potentially get us all killed.

I brush past Alex, grab the tank of gas and the mask connected to it. The dials on the tank don't make any sense, so I turn the only knob I see.

"Chloe, stop," Alex yells, rushing over to me. He pulls the mask from my hand and hovers over me. "It's not that I don't want to go with you. I just don't think there's a reason for us to go."

"I've dragged you into this far enough. Why don't you just go home and get some sleep. I'll deal with this myself." I pull the mask back out of his hand.

He's giving me another empty stare, one I still can't resolve. "Chloe, I don't want *you* to go either though," he says, covering his hand over his squinting eyes.

How could he even suggest that? He knows if Kiera gets to Franco, anything could happen. How can I not go? I'm the only chance we all have.

I place my hand on his chest and push him away. My heart aches, seeing the pained look in his eyes. "Does she drift, or not?" I ask him.

He doesn't respond. He just stares at me, biting the inside of his cheek.

"Alex, I'm going. I have to," I whisper.

"No," he says. "You don't have to, but you're so stubborn that you'll never listen to me anyway." The sadness that was just filling his eyes has turned into anger. He's not thinking rationally. Why is this only clear to me? Franco is going to do something to Kiera, or us. It would be even worse if Kiera managed to overcome Franco and then released Alex and me. Either way, it will end badly.

I narrow my eyes in response to his condescending tone. "Fine, then I guess I'm just stubborn. You'll thank me someday, though. You will."

Alex walks to the door and removes the pieces of furniture to clear an exit. "Chloe, let's just stay here. There's no purpose in going back."

As he's moving the last of the items, I pull the mask over my face. I grab Tomas's desk chair, swing it behind me, and fall to the cushion. Just as I feel the haze begin to set in, Alex turns to see the decision I've made. I don't think he thought I was actually going to go through with this. He must have assumed I'd follow him out of here if he threatened to leave, but it looks like I just proved his theory wrong.

"Chloe, wait." He races over to me. "This isn't supposed to happen like..." are the last words I hear as a thick black sheet covers my world again.

The chair beneath me falls through the floor...

The painted walls soften, the gas mask liquefies into my skin, and the clothing over my body loosens. A faint yellow glow appears from a small box window in front of me and my body conforms to the floor below.

The conversation down the hall is clear and concise, and it's one that I was hoping not to hear. She *is* here. I knew it. How did I know it? I shake off the confusion and refocus on the commotion.

Here against the dry, crackled padding in the dark, I can vividly imagine what the conversation looks like. And it's not pretty.

I slide against the wall, approaching the invisible door that I now know exists. My mind is being torn from the blistering conversation between Kiera and Franco, and then the thought of Alex's angry and hurt eyes makes me double over in pain. He's probably trying to figure out how to drag me back out of here somehow. In the case that he does figure it out, I need to do what I came here to do. Quick.

I stand up against the wall and listen for an opportunity to interrupt their dialog.

"Did you kill my mother, or not?" I hear a hand slap against skin, and I pray that it was Kiera's hand slapping Franco's face. But would he really allow that to happen? "Answer me, you animal," Kiera shrieks.

"Maybe I did, maybe I didn't. It's too late now though, isn't it, love?" Franco says in a slithery voice. "So, should Daddy buy you a puppy now, or what? What is it that you want from me?"

"Let Chloe and Alex go," she growls.

Hearing a hooting laugh from Franco, I feel relieved to know he finds that request to be humorous. I'm hoping that means he does not intend to appease her demand.

"You want me to release your cousin and her pretty little boyfriend?" He rips with laughter again.

"That's exactly what I just said." Her words don't miss a beat. Her mission is clear and her attitude is relentless. Enough so to get her killed.

"I'll make a deal with you, sweet-cheeks," Franco says. "I'll let them go, but I'll lock you up in their place." I can hear him scratching the husks of his five o'clock shadow as he waits for her response.

"Fine," she complies. She agreed. No, Kiera. No. "I'll do that if it means you'll let them go. I'll trade places." Her firm words muster up a sick feeling in my stomach.

I can't believe she just offered to do that for us. Why would anyone offer herself up to this monster? If he did kill her mother, he'll probably get the same thrill out of killing her as well. I doubt she has anything to offer him, not like I apparently do.

"Stop," I yell, instantly filled with regret.

I hear them both scuffling down the hall toward me, one with firm footing, and the other being dragged against her will.

"What are you doing back here? How the hell do you keep getting back here for that matter?" Franco's voice sounds enraged as he smashes his face into the bars of the tiny window opening.

I refuse to give him the satisfaction of an answer. "Do not allow her to trade places with us. Alex and I can deal with this."

Franco nods and backs away from the window as a satirical laugh echoes from the hall. "I don't think I like this love-fest going on here. As a matter of fact, it's making me quite uncomfortable." I hear him fussing with something metallic.

"Kiera, please leave. You don't know what you're getting yourself into here," I plead.

"Chloe, I'm not leaving until he admits to killing my mother," she snaps.

This wasn't about freeing Alex and me. She wants answers. Reasons. The truth. I can't I say I blame her for that. However, the chance of getting Franco to admit to something like that is about as likely as Kiera leaving this place unharmed.

Still unable to see Franco or Kiera, I can tell that silence isn't a sign of good things happening or things to come. I can nearly hear the gears within Franco's mind grinding against each other. He's probably going to lock Kiera up in here now too.

I grab the bars of the window, and try to lift myself up off the ground to see if I can get a look at anything in the hall. For the struggling second in which I'm able to hold my weight up, I see Franco deep in thought standing in front of Kiera whose legs are tied to the chair she's seated on. The metallic noise was caused from the chair scratching along the cement ground. She's a fighter. Great. And She's restrained now too. I lose my grip on the bars and fall back down to the padded floor. I try once more to pull myself back up, expecting to see the same scene. Instead, shock bleeds from my eyes. In a matter of five seconds, everything has changed.

CHAPTER FIFTEEN

WHEN ONE DOOR OPENS...

THE LOCK ON MY DOOR CLINKS before gliding open. I take a few steps backward, trying to gather the words that should be said and the thoughts that should be acted upon. I never expected this chance and now that I have it, I don't know what the right decision is. I find myself pacing in circles, trying to regain my composure. It's hopeless, though.

I move toward the shadow standing within the threshold of my escape. Freedom awaits me, but is it only for me? With only one foot into the hall, I succumb to an ounce of clarity.

"Chloe, let's go." Kiera grabs my arm and pulls me ahead. "Who knows how long we have," she cries out as her shadow turns into a colorful blur.

I pull my arm from her grip and switch directions. "How did you get here?"

"Later. I'll explain everything later."

"No!" I shout. "How are you here?"

"Do you want my help or not?" she says, ignoring my questions. I do need her help. I'll badger her later.

"Come here," I say.

I run through the wet musky hallway that I've only had the pleasure of seeing from afar, which I'm now seeing was a better experience than being up close and personal with the stained blood covered walls and floors. This must be Franco's stomping ground. I wonder if this is where he's conducted all of his crimes. I shudder at the thought.

I can hear the anger coursing through Kiera as she stomps her feet behind me. "What are we doing, Chloe? Let's just go unlock Alex's cell and get the hell out of here. This isn't hard," she says with irritation creeping into her voice.

I greet Franco's unconscious body, which is flattened to the ground. His arms are in different directions and his legs are jumbled in a mess.

"Is he dead?" I ask, backing away from a potential crime scene.

She shakes her head and shoves her hands into her back pockets. "He's just unconscious." She kicks him with her foot. "As he was walking by, I grabbed one of those syringe things from his coat pocket. I don't know how long he'll be out for, though."

She's a genius and a product of Franco. Of course, she outsmarted him at his own game. All kids do that to their parents at some point in their lives. "Help me drag him into the cell I was just in," I say, lifting his limp arms from the ground.

"Shouldn't we just go release Alex first?" Her voice carries down the hall as she continues toward Alex's cell.

"No. He's staying there," I say. I try to pull Franco's weight without Kiera's help. I know she's going to start in on me, and I just need to get him in there. It's my only hope.

"What the hell is wrong with you? I just took care of the problem so I could free you both, and now you're going to leave him locked up?" she yells, throwing the keys over her head and into the wall.

"Just trust me right now. I'll explain everything to you once we get Franco locked up."

She lets out an exaggerated sigh and walks back over to Franco's body. She grabs each of his ankles and helps me drag him, not so smoothly over the cold, wet, uneven floor. Once we reach the open cell I have inhabited for the past year, we drag him into the room and drop him into the far corner. This feels gratifying, no, more than that: euphoric. I reach into his lab-coat pocket and pull out a half-dozen syringes. I know these will be my only ticket back to Alex.

I yank on Kiera's arm. She won't move. She looks like she's trying to hypnotize Franco's unconscious mind with her rage filled eyes. Maybe realization is catching up with her.

Closing this door feels like I'm closing the back cover of a bad book. It's over now. I don't have to read that again.

When the lock clinks, Kiera doesn't let a second pass before she whips me around and shoves me into the bloodstained wall. "What are you doing, Chloe? Go let Alex out now."

I remove her hands from my shoulders and place them down by her side. "Look at me, Kiera," I say, trying to keep my voice even. "Alex isn't the way I am on this side. He's not okay. I don't think he wanted you to see him like this, because he's embarrassed of himself." Her head jerks back slightly and her eyebrows pull in with confusion. "In this part of his life he's incoherent, unable to think, and in the dark. He doesn't know who he is or who anyone is. He doesn't speak and he doesn't interact. He needs to stay here so he can live his other life in a constant state of happiness." I feel nothing but guilt for releasing Alex's secret. I knew if I didn't tell her there wouldn't be much I could do to stop her from releasing him, though. "Does this make sense?" I can see my words have caused a ripple in her understanding. You think you know someone, and then you suddenly find out how wrong you are.

Kiera reaches for my hand and engulfs it between hers. "Yes. I think. I'm so sorry, Chloe. I guess I understand why you wanted to remain locked up the way you were. However, what are *you* going to do? You seem the same in both parts of your life. Why do you want to stay here locked up, for no reason?"

I shrug. The answer is so simple, but it might sound crazy to someone who doesn't feel the way I do. "I love him. That's all this is about. I want to stay with him, any and every way I can."

Kiera's eyes remain focused on mine as if she were trying to figure out a difficult math equation. "That's a pretty crazy kind of love," she snorts. "I hope I never become that deranged." Her smirk lightens the tension between us. "Well, shall I lock you two loons here in your love nest...err...padded cell?" she teases. "Wait, how do you guys eat and drink in here? Obviously you've been kept alive somehow."

"It's a long story, but an old friend is taking care of us—making sure we're fed and hydrated. It's okay, really." I'm not sure I'm doing a good job of convincing her of this. "Please. You're going to go back home now, somehow...right?" I ask, still trying to figure out how she got here.

"Yes, I'll be fine," she chuckles. "Actually." I knew that was too easy. "Chloe?"

"Yeah?"

"You know, since we're related, and I'm James's daughter and all, I might be able to drift like you and Alex."

"Maybe," I say. "But, Julien won't be wherever you go."

"I know. I'm just saying, maybe I could give it a try sometime." She smiles with amusement.

That must be how she got here. Maybe she doesn't even know how she got here. Maybe she was so focused on helping us that she just ended up here.

I walk over to where Kiera threw the keys and pick them up, fumbling through all of them to find one that looks like a match. I unlock Alex's cell and walk into the new home we'll share. I see him hunched over in his usual spot against the far wall, and I slide down next to him, placing my body under his lifeless arm. It's heavy, but this is where I need to be.

"Thanks Kiera. I'll see you at home," I say, smiling with gratitude.

She glides the door shut and I hear the locks click into place. She throws the keys in through the window and they land next to my ankle. "Bye, Chlo. Be safe," her voice trails off as she walks down the hall.

I give Alex a kiss on the cheek and whisper, "I'm sorry" into his ear. I'm sure he's pissed and going crazy right now, but maybe when he finds out how much I helped our situation, he'll feel differently. His hand tightens around my shoulder, and he leans his cheek against the top of my head. "I know you're in there, Alex. I'm sorry if you're angry at me."

I hear a door in the distance open and close twice, followed by footsteps closing in on our cell. Ashley slides my door open and looks at me with bewilderment. She's holding a tray full of food in her hand. She moves in closer to me and points to Franco's cell. "Dying?" She asks.

"No. I am not as bad as he is. Please keep him fed as well." She places the tray of food down in front of us. "Whatever you do, don't let him out." I lower my head and lift my eyes. "Do you understand?"

She nods her head in agreement. "Killer?" She looks over to the conjoining wall between my cell and Franco's.

"Exactly."

She turns around and scurries out of the cell, closing the door behind her. I hear her feet tread quickly down the cement hall, followed by a metal door opening and closing. At least we're being fed. I still know Ashley isn't a permanent solution. I try to put it in the back of my mind, but now that Franco is detained, I should probably come and check on things more often. I have to stay focused on the fact that

Franco still thinks he needs us, and now he's going to need Ashley to stay alive as well.

I remove all of the syringes from my pocket and place them on the ground between us. I take one, and puncture the needle into my arm. I nestle my head into Alex's chest and inhale a deep sigh of relief. With a racing heart, and a feeling of melting through the floor, I'm satisfied to know that everything is perfect right now.

My head sways from side to side, and I feel like a heavy raindrop racing toward the ground...

My body liquefies into a hard chair and the weight over my eyelids release, allowing me to focus on the surroundings of Tomas's office.

Everything seems okay, except—

Alex isn't here.

* * *

I tread at a quick pace down the hall to our apartment. I'm a little uneasy, wondering what Alex's mood might be like after I did what I just did. With a lump in my throat, I open the door and walk into the living room. The door was unlocked. He's here somewhere. Not in the living room, though. I walk down to our bedroom and turn the corner hoping and expecting to see him lying in the bed. But when my eyes settle on reality, I see that he's in fact not here either. At least I hope he's not.

"Well, aren't you just an ignorant little pest?" Franco grumbles, standing up from the edge of my perfectly made bed.

"Wha—what are you doing here? Where is Alex? What did you do with him?" I ask, trying to stop my uncontrollable quivering.

"Oh relax. Your little boyfriend is probably at work. Maybe." He raises an eyebrow and scratches his chin. "I think," he laughs, waggling his eyebrows up and down.

I know he's just trying to get under my skin, but the sound of his words make me feel sick. He takes a couple of steps closer to me, forcing me to take a couple back. He cocks his head to the side and smiles. "You sent me here. Now, you get to deal with it. Good job, love," he smirks.

I can hear my heart beating through every vein in my body. The combination of anger, hate, fear, and anxiety is blending into an impending eruption. "How the hell did you get into my apartment?" I ask.

"Don't worry about it," he responds, surveying every inch of my bedroom.

"Get out now," I demand. I don't know why I'm using anger as a defense. I know where it will get me.

He closes the remaining space between us, forcing my back up against the bathroom door. He looks down at my shoulder and traces his long, perfectly manicured finger along the seam of my shirt. "You really aren't that intelligent, are you? Do you really think it's going to be that easy to get rid of me?" he whispers into my ear.

I clench my eyes and twist my head to move further away from his face. "So what, are you just going to sit here and watch me?" My voice crackles, and with my desperation growing, his back straightens a little more. He knows he's winning.

He wraps his fingers around the middle of my arm and squeezes so hard my circulation cuts off. "No, you're coming with me. And if you don't make it easy, I'm sure you can use your imagination on what I'm capable of." He sighs in a melodic tone. "I'd rather not get into detail about it, so I hope you'll just cooperate." His signature sadistic smirk grows over his pursed lips.

My initial instinct is to fight back, but the thought of what he would do to Alex, myself and, or Kiera, doesn't make the fight worth it.

I snatch my arm out of his grip. "So then, Uncle Franco, where are we going?"

He takes a few steps toward the bedroom door and gestures for me to walk out. "Less questions, more moving. Let's go."

I nudge past him and walk toward my bureau. "Considering we both know I won't be back tonight, I'd like to grab a few things."

He walks out the door and into the hallway, but still blocks any sort of escape. "Make it quick, buttercup," he grunts.

I rip open my top drawer and pull out my cellphone. I keep my hand in the drawer, trying to make it look as if I'm looking for clothes. I turn on my phone and send Alex a text message that says: *"HELP! Franco is in our apartment and is trying to take me."* I pile up an armful of clothes, wrap them around the phone, and shove everything in a bag as I walk into the hall.

Franco is waiting less than two feet away from my bedroom door, leaning against one wall with his foot resting on the opposite wall.

"Please take your foot off of my wall. Do you have any manners?" I ask, curling my lip with disgust.

He scrapes his foot down, leaving black marks behind. "Are you ready to go, princess?"

I cross my arms over my chest, flinging my bag under my arm. "I'm not going with you. I've changed my mind. In fact, if you'd like to kill Alex, Kiera, and my, you can go right ahead. Because we both know that by doing that, you won't get that little bit of information from me that you've been looking for. If you want to know what I know, I suggest you change your plan of action."

It takes everything I have to portray a false sense of arrogance in this moment. I know I'm playing mind games with a murderer.

"I see," he says, rolling his eyes into the back of his head. Well then, if you aren't going to come with me, what am I supposed to do?" he asks himself, sounding quizzical. He taps his finger under his chin, appearing to be deep in thought. But with how shallow his mind is, I'm sure his thoughts have already hit a brick wall.

"Leave?" I say, pointing to the front door.

He reaches over and with a delicate grip takes my arm into his hands, sliding his grip down to my wrist before pulling me in against him. Fresh cologne and the scent of cigars fill my nose. "Now, Chloe, we both know that is not an option." He pinches my chin between his thumb and forefinger and tilts my face toward his. "The only option we have here is for you to tell me what your little secret is. Once I know, I'll be happy to leave you alone, and even let you live your little fairytale life here in this illusory world you think you've created."

I actually do wish I knew what this supposed secret is. I rip my hand out of his grip again and re-tuck the bag of clothes under my arm. "What exactly are you looking for from me?"

"But I thought you knew?" he says in an unsettling, singsong voice.

"If I knew, I likely would have told you by now just to get you the hell away from me," I say.

He narrows his eyes and runs his fingers through his perfectly slicked back hair. "Chloe, quit playing your games with me. You know I'm looking for that damn locket. Now tell me where it is." His voice lowers a number of octaves, and I can sense aggression reemerging in his voice.

"I don't know anything about any locket," besides the fact that we returned it to the bottomless ground within the Catacombs. I still can't help to wonder what the meaning behind this locket is. I find this beat up thing lying on the rock in the middle of an underground cemetery, thinking it must be nothing more than someone's lost item. Yet, it resulted in a citywide disturbance, causing us to look death in the face while being forced to return the locket to the precise location where I had originally found it. Maybe I shouldn't have returned it. Maybe things would have turned out better than this. Maybe it holds some kind of answer to life. The thought makes me roll my eyes, knowing that I'm being held hostage for an item I can hide in my pocket.

"Well Chloe, I must admit, you have been on the receiving end of some good genetics. You have been granted the gift to lie. It's impressive. But coming from the better liar, you aren't getting past me. I know you know where that locket is, and you are going to tell me how to find it." He slams his fist into the wall, leaving a gaping hole.

I place my trembling hands behind my back, trying to hide my fear. "Or what?"

He closes his eyes and nods, stifling a silent laugh. "There is no, 'or what?' I've already taken care of that part. I'm a professional, Chloe." His face lifts with a derisive grin. "Let me clear up a few of *my* lies for you." He clears his throat. "Lie number one: Alex isn't at work. I also have his phone, and I apologize for not responding to the cute little S.O.S text message you sent him a few minutes ago." He stops and looks up to the ceiling, as if he's trying to recall his next thought. "Lie number two: Kiera didn't outsmart me. Well, actually, I guess that was kind of a good act. Let's just say she'll be safe soon, too. I'd like to get to know my daughter a little more before killing her," he chokes with laughter. "And lie number three: you are not a good liar," he whispers. He wags his finger in my face, clicking his tongue between his teeth.

With fury building through my body, I throw my fists into his chest, pushing against him with every ounce of adrenaline gushing through my body. "Where is Alex? Tell me," I cry, giving him exactly what he wants.

He grabs my wrists and shoves me backwards. My head crashes into the wall, and it swells with pain. "I wouldn't worry about Alex. I know where he is," he says.

That's the problem. The crazed look is growing on his face, and his eyes are beginning to twitch. "Here's the deal, love. For every day that passes and you haven't told me where I can find this locket of yours, I'm going to make sure Alex is even more uncomfortable than he currently is. How does that sound?"

I have no clue what he means, no idea where Alex is, and no thoughts on how I'm going to get away from him. Franco's mind games are beyond my realm of understanding.

"So what's it going to be, love? Shall we get this over with today, or should we beat a dead Alex to the—oh I do apologize, I meant to say...horse. Horse. Shall, we beat a dead horse into the ground?" he snickers.

His wordplay makes me sick, and I'm ready to give in to him. He won't move his eyes from my face, and I feel myself becoming weaker with his motives of interrogation.

"Fine. I'll tell you. But you need to show me that Alex is okay first, and you need to tell me what's so important about that stupid locket." Did I just agree to show him where that locket is? I have no idea how to find that thing again.

"Very well. That sounds like a fair deal to me," he humbly agrees, as he makes his way toward the door.

CHAPTER SIXTEEN

LOST. FOUND. GONE.

I SLIDE INTO THE FRONT SEAT of the black sedan that Franco has claimed to be his own. The car smells like rubber and stale cigar smoke. But I find the stench to be a distraction from the speed in which we're driving. We fly around sharp corners, down steep hills, and around unfamiliar back alleys until we pull over onto a low curb. There are no doors and no windows on any of the surrounding walls. The alley looks to be barren and lifeless, making it hard to imagine where we could be going. All I know is, Alex better be there.

I push the heavy door open and slide out, peering around the outside of the car with hopes of recognizing where we might be. But before my entire body is out of the car, Franco grabs my wrist and pulls me in the opposite direction. The seemingly endless cobblestones that we've been walking over flatten into a smooth surface, and the path we've taken appears to be curving into the poorly lit opening of a brick wall.

The entryway is small and tight, and leads directly to a single stair that looks to disappear beneath the slight opening. As we approach the step that descends into a black hole, Franco leads the way, disappearing into the ground below. I follow closely behind him, but even with his hand wrapped around my wrist, I can't make out a hint of anything past his elbow. The stairwell has unraveled into a tight spiraling decline leading into a cool, sweet smelling confined space that doesn't appear to be opening into anything other than more steps.

My chest tightens, and my breathing becomes shallow. I can't tell if it's attributed to my nerves or the lack of available oxygen in this confined space.

After minutes of endless stairs, I see the coiled stairwell open into a barely lit corridor, which is lined with jail cell looking doors. I already know where we are, and I had hoped that I would never end up back here in the Catacombs again. I follow the mere shadow of Franco who's leading me down the hallway. He's giving me enough space so that I could run if I chose to, but I'm worried that Alex is in fact down here, so I won't run. And he knows it.

The black cell doors conceal a darkness that I can't see beyond, and I'm not sure I'd want to see in if I could. As we approach the end of the walkway, I see a pair of dirt-covered hands curled around two bars. I run past Franco and up to the hands I love.

Alex's grime covered face is pressed up against the inside of the grated door. He looks weak and his pale complexion is glowing through the smeared filth.

I squeeze my hands around his, pushing my head up against the bars to get as close to his head as possible. "Are you okay?" I whisper. My heart is pulsating in my ears and pounding against the metal that separates us.

I feel his hands grip the bars tighter. His head hardly nods, but it's enough for me to notice. "Do not tell him where it is, Chloe. Do you hear me?" he says, merely whispering the words through his clenched jaw.

I flinch my head back, surprised by his words. "Are you out of your mind? You'll die in here," I say, trying hard to hold back the tears that are about to pour from my eyes.

"I don't care. You don't understand what will happen if you…"

We're both interrupted when we hear a large thud hit the dirt ground. I turn and force my eyes to focus through the darkness. I can't see anything, and I'm fearful this will become another one of Franco's ploys. I take a couple of small steps toward the unrevealing darkness until I come to the beginning of a shadow. The shadow doesn't resemble a tall object, but rather one that is flat on the ground. I take another hesitant step forward, and my eyes focus on Franco's shoes. He's lying there, apparently unconscious. I kick his foot with the toe of my shoe, wondering if it will cause any movement. But he doesn't flinch.

With no movement, I walk closer to his head and after a minute of my eyes adjusting to a darker surrounding, I see that he's still breathing. I nudge him again to be sure he's unconscious, but he still doesn't twitch.

I return to Alex's cell and clench my hands over his. I stare at him for a moment, hoping to clarify my own confusion. But my blank stare alerts Alex and he shakes the bars below his hands. My eyes refocus on his, and I nod. "He's passed out."

Alex's eyes widen with hope. "Go grab the key that's in his right front pocket. If you feel any movement within his body, run back here," he says. He releases his grip from around the bars and waves me off.

I'll never understand how he thinks so quickly. It always feels as though I freeze whenever I'm in a moment that requires immediate attention. It's like my brain doesn't work that fast. With cautiousness, I make my way back over to Franco and pull his pant leg away from his body, fearful of making any physical contact with him. I slip my hand into his pocket, and pinch a key between my thumb and forefinger.

I unfold my hand, revealing an ancient looking copper skeleton key. Where could this key have even come from? It has to be over a hundred years old. Whatever the case may be, I shove it into the keyhole and twist it to the right. Alex uses what must be left of his energy and pushes the door open.

He falls into me and wraps his trembling arms around my body, shoving his face into my shoulder. He kisses my neck, then my cheek, and then the top of my head. He's close to squeezing the air out of my body he's holding me so tight. "Let's get this over with," he whispers.

With the dim light glowing over his body, I can see he's been beaten badly. He has contusions on his head, and his eyes are both swollen and red. "What did he do to you?" I try to sound strong for him, but I sound as frail as he looks.

"It's not important right now," he says faintly.

With his arm around my shoulder and the little amount of support I can actually offer, we make our way into the darkness where Franco's body lies unconscious. We only move three feet into the unlit walkway before we're overcome with bewilderment. "He's gone?" I mumble under my breath.

With no more confirmation needed, I pull Alex in the opposite direction, dragging both of us back to the winding stairwell. I have no clue how I'm going to get him up these stairs as weak as he is, but we have to get out of here. I push Alex ahead of me and keep my hands on his back for support. He does what he can to pull himself up by the railing, but the hundred or so steps accompanied by a lack of oxygen are going to wipe him out. I squeeze around him, and grab his arm, pulling him up each step, one at a time. By the time we reach the top, I fall backwards. He holds himself up, hunched over, with no color in his face. His eyes are half shut and his mouth is trying to wrap itself around as much air as possible.

I pull myself back up and place his arm around my shoulder. "Come on. We're almost there," I say.

As I pull us both out of the entrance to the underground cemetery, I see Franco's likely stolen car is still parked on the curb just a few feet away. I'll go ahead and assume he didn't find another exit. I don't get it. I don't want to get it. I'm thankful to have us both free for the moment, but Franco is like a horror movie. He's always lurking around a corner, waiting for his moment to jump out and scare the hell out of me. I need to be one step ahead of him.

I know I don't want to go near his car, as tempting as it is. I see cars passing by at the next block, and I'm thinking it might be a main street where we can find a cab. I drag Alex down the street, while compulsively checking over my shoulder in fear of being followed.

I feel relieved once we arrive at the street, knowing that we most likely won't be attacked in plain view of the hundreds of passerbys. I see a cab in the distance, and I shoot my hand into the air, flagging it down. The cab pulls off onto the side of the road and I help Alex into the car. The driver looks back at us and takes a double look at Alex, who looks like he just crawled out of a hole, which he did. The cab driver shrugs and floors it.

I direct the driver to take us to the café since I'm worried about going home, knowing that Franco now knows where we live. As we approach the café, I see the lights are off, and there's no sign of anyone in there. Then I realize it's Sunday, and it's closed.

I help Alex out of the cab and fling his arm around my shoulder.

"Around back," Alex mutters, pulling a key out of his pocket.

I drag him around the back of the café, and he fumbles around trying to get the key into the lock. I take the key from his unsteady hand and slide it in. As soon as the door gives way, I pull Alex inside and set him down on the floor against the wall. "I'll be right back. Just stay here," I say, rubbing my thumb up and down his dirt-covered cheek.

I run to the front of the café, looking for something to feed him. I don't know if food or water will help him, but it's all I can do. I grab a few stale pastries from behind the glass display and a couple bottles of water from the fridge.

As I approach Alex, I see that his head is cocked over, and his body looks even more limp. I break apart the food into little pieces and hand feed him. I tilt his head back and pour the water into his mouth. He chokes a bit, but manages to get the rest of it down. After minutes of helping him, I see some color fill his cheeks. His half lidded eyes perk open and he lifts his hand to reach for mine.

"I think you have a concussion," I say.

He tries to laugh. "Thank you, Dr. Chloe."

"This is all my fault, and I'm so sorry," I cry.

He places his hand on my face and brushes the loose strands of hair off my forehead. I smile to let him, hoping to ease some of his discomfort, and I lean over to wrap my arms around his neck. But before my arms make it completely around him, he pulls back.

He places his hands on my shoulders, keeping me at a distance. His focus becomes determined and he pulls his eyebrows into a crease. "Chloe."

"What's the matter, Alex?" The way he says my name is making me uneasy. Something else is coming. Something bad. My heart is pounding so hard against my chest I think I can hear it.

With a dark look in his eyes, he glances past me toward the wall, unable to look at me. "You need to go home," he whispers.

I clutch my hands over my chest, confused and scared. "I am home, silly." My voice sputters as I try to sound upbeat.

A grave expression appears on his face as he looks down to the ground. "No," he says. "You need to go home to your mother and father. We can't..."

I cup my hand over my mouth, shaking my head, knowing what's about to come out of his mouth. "Don't even finish your sentence, Alex." My breath shudders.

He throws his head back against the wall and squeezes his eyes shut. "We can't be together, Chloe. We're a poison to each other. We're so far from being what each other needs. I'm so sorry," he groans. "Saying this is killing me right now, but I need you to be safe, and that isn't here with me. This place is no good for us. I need to go back to my home too, to Celia."

I can't breathe, and I think my throat is closing in. My heart feels as if it might have stopped beating. I don't know what to say or what to think. I've been afraid of him leaving me, but I never actually thought he would. Do I beg him not to do this? Do I cry so he knows I'm hurt? Or do I pretend like I'm okay? I feel weak, sick, and as if my brain suddenly isn't collaborating with my heart. I don't understand. How can he do this to me? With every leap and bound we've overcome just to be together—why would he just throw it away?

My burning eyes stare into his, and I can see the pain overwhelming him as well. But if he's in as much pain as he appears, why is he doing this?

"So that's it? You're just leaving me?" I whimper in a croaky voice.

He doesn't answer me. Instead, he places his hand on my face and tries to pull me in.

"I can't." I pull my head back, feeling his fingers slip off my face.

Why wouldn't he want me to go back to San Diego with him? I can't go home. Doesn't he understand that? I'd rather be locked in a cell down in the Catacombs.

With tears running down my cheeks, I narrow my eyes at him. "You know I can't go home, Alex. I'll find somewhere to go. You don't have to worry about me," I say with tears continuing to sizzle over my fiery cheeks.

As I back away, Alex grabs my arm. "It's not like that," he utters through his nearly closed mouth. His tight grip around my arm slides down to my hand, and I feel something slip inside of my palm. I squeeze it, wondering what it could be. But not quite caring what it is, either. He releases my hand. "Go, now." He swallows hard as a tear pools in the corner of his eye.

I try to take him in for one last second, a second I'm sure will be the last time I see him. The man I thought I was going to spend the rest of my life with. I don't think my heart could ever take another one of these moments. Maybe this *is* for the best. Maybe we've caused each other too much trouble. As my eyes trail from his eyes down to his lips, I see him mouth the words, "I love you."

How could this be love? This is unreal. That's just it. He isn't real. That must be it.

I flee out the back door and around the corner to a main street. I look back once more, just to see the dream I've been living fade into a non-existent blur.

I don't even remember who I was before I met him. I don't know how to get back to that now. So much life has happened in the past year and a half, and now it's like it never happened. I feel empty and lost, left without any direction. No one will ever love me like he did. I'm crazy, and not even living a real life right now.

* * *

I try to convince myself this is it—the last time I'll see Tomas's office. I pull the gas tank over to the chair and sit down with the mask in my hand. When I can convince my mind that this world here doesn't exist, it will be like I was never here. There will be no trace of me in this drift. I have to force my mind to believe that. I have to forget about this place. It's *not* real and neither my mind nor my body can live here anymore. I look at my clenched fists and uncurl my fingers to reveal a tiny folded piece of paper that Alex placed into my hand. I can't imagine this says anything more than what he already said, and I'm not sure I can emotionally digest any other explanation from him right now. I place the note in my pocket and try to push it out of my mind.

I turn the dial on the tank and place the mask around my face, close my eyes, and pull in a long breath. This stupid fake life has turned all of my dreams into nightmares once again.

As I fall through the black tunnel that's ironically foreshadowing my future, I try to erase my memories, my pain, love, hate, sadness, and happiness.

For the first time in my life, I like the darkness. I actually wish it were darker, and I wish I could just stay here in this in-between place.

When my eyes open to the padded cell that I've feared for so long, I feel Alex's unconscious body leaning on me, and it's just another reminder of what will no longer be. I wonder if this part of Alex would have done this to me? I lift his arm off my shoulder and place it back down by his side. I take one look at him as I walk toward the padded door, and I see a tear trickling out from beneath his closed lid. Unable to look at him any longer, I unlock the cell with the key that was still clenched within my fist and I walk out, closing the door behind me.

When I walk down the hall, I find Ashley in the hall, leaning against a wall next to a rolling cart with hospital food. I approach her and place my hands over her cold bony shoulders. "Please promise me you will continue to keep Alex fed?" The words get caught in my throat and a sob follows. I cover my mouth to hold back my visible pain.

Ashley wraps her arms around my neck and whispers into my ear, "Feed." She releases her arms from around me and looks me in the eyes. "Always."

I nod my head to say thank you without speaking. I walk past her and out toward the metal door that exits back into the cold world. From behind, Ashley yells after me, "Lost."

CHAPTER SEVENTEEN

A NEW ENDING

THIS BEACH ISN'T THE SAME, which I suppose is the point. I've heard before that pain can never remain the same day after day, and I find that to be true. Instead of my pain getting less, it has increasingly gotten worse. I took love for granted. I took our relationship for granted. Moreover, I took Alex for granted. I did too much damage to his life and I can understand why he wouldn't want to be with me anymore. I wish my tears would run dry and I wish my heart would stop pounding every time I see a mirage of his reflection in the water. I wish I could do it all over and try harder.

I've been here in Charleston, South Carolina for almost two months. A one-way train ticket was supposed to be the key to my freedom. However, it was only a doorway to more misery. I figured living in a warmer climate and being near the ocean would ease my pain, but it hasn't. I got a waitressing job to make the days go by faster and it does help sometimes, but when I think about making the days go by quicker, what am I really crossing the days off for? How many days left until I'm ninety, alone, and miserable? Alex is never coming back. He doesn't even know where I am. I wish I could check on him, just to see how he's doing. I wonder where he is, if he's happy, and if he's moved on.

I went to look for the note he placed in my hand while we were saying goodbye. I searched every pocket of those pants a thousand times, but I couldn't find it. I would do anything to know what it said now, but I'm sure I can assume it was some sort of apology for breaking my heart. I still don't understand how you can love someone but not act on it? It makes no sense. I know he loved me, and I know love doesn't just disappear. But that doesn't explain our ending.

I'm renting a small studio apartment a mile away from the beach and a half mile away from the coffee shop I'm working at. It's real life. I thought it would be better than it is. But how could real feel right after I've experienced living in a dream?

I left all of the walls white and all of my furniture is a solid wooden finish. Everything is simple, like a padded room, where I belong.

The knock on the door interrupts my staring contest with the empty wall in my living room. I open the door with the same forced smile I wear every night at seven o'clock. "Hi Maryanne. How are you tonight?" I speak loudly enough for her old ears to hear.

"Your coffee, dear." She hands me a Styrofoam cup filled with black coffee. My nightcap, my check-in. "Just checking in on you," she smiles. "Oh, Chloe, you remind me so much of my daughter." Her hand trembles as she touches her fingertips to my cheek.

"I'm sure she's watching over you, Maryanne." I force another smile. Poor thing. Her daughter died ten years ago, but she remembers her as a teenager, rather than the fifty-year-old who left her.

A good mother who outlived her daughter meets a daughter whose mother wished she wasn't a mother. Life isn't fair like that.

I think she's lonely, but I also think she's waiting for me to make myself disappear some day. It may be the stark white walls, or the black circles under my sleepless eyes that make her think that. But whatever the case, she's a nice lady, and she makes me feel a little less alone here.

Once she leaves, I return to staring at my ceiling, finally realizing how white, white really is. It doesn't turn into anything now like it used to, and white has become just white. Boring because I don't drift anymore.

I'm still debating whether it was a good idea to start taking a stabilizing medication. The doctor was understanding and seemed as though he'd seen thousands of people with my exact case. He wrote me a prescription as if it were an antibiotic for some kind of infection. I'm not complaining, but now I'm wondering if it wasn't the best thing for me. I liked it for a little while, but now I miss having the ability to *go places*. I'm too normal, and I wasn't born to be normal. It's uncomfortable.

I've decided to skip a few nights of my medication, curious where my mind might take me.

I lean back on my bed and focus on the whiteness of my ceiling. I close my eyes and attempt my breathing exercises. But just like the last two nights nothing happens. Nothing.

I dream, but they're stagnant. I can't communicate, I can't feel, and I can't smell. It's a simple nighttime dream. Nothing more.

My dreams sway from the first time Alex brushed the wet hair out of my face as I was drowning, to the first time I tasted cotton candy and thought he was going to kiss me. Then of course, there was our first kiss, which always seems to replay in my head like a broken record. Even in my dream, I still get butterflies and a knot in my stomach. That warmth, the feeling of my heart intensifying, the comfort, it's nothing that I could ever imagine feeling with anyone else.

Tonight my dreams are leading me to Paris and to the cafe. It's the one spot I never wanted to see without Alex. It's our spot. But we don't have a spot anymore. There is no *we* anymore. I suppose it's nice to see that the cafe is busy and full of people. Even the café moved on. It's the way it should be.

I sit down at an empty chair in the corner, happy to know that no one will interact with me in a regular dream. I see a new, unfamiliar waiter delivering the food and drinks to people. I wonder who he is. I see the kitchen doors swing open and another waiter bustle through. He's walking backwards, careful to make sure the door doesn't hit the tray he's carrying. As he turns around, I see that my dream has created another version of Alex. A bleak smile grows over my lips. It's nice that I can revisit him—even if only in my mind. It makes my pain disappear, momentarily. It's almost like giving into an addiction or a craving. I watch him carefully as he delivers the food to the table he's waiting on. But as he turns around to head back into the kitchen, something catches his eye. Me. He stops dead in his tracks and walks toward me. His eyes never blink or move from my face. When he approaches me, he lifts my hand off the table and kisses it softly. But I can't feel it, and I can't feel him. These damn dreams aren't so real anymore. God, I miss him. It hurts so much. I need him.

"You have to leave. Okay? It's not safe for you here. I'm so sorry, baby. I love you," he whispers into my ear. He drops my hand from his, and I know the dream is over. This *is* just a dream. Why does he get to live in my dreams and I don't?

With pain returning to my chest and my brain reminding me of why I need to stop dreaming, I stand up and take one last look around. Just as I consider closing my eyes to end the dream, something else catches my attention. Franco. He's sitting at one of the tables. He's sitting with...Professor Lane. They're both watching every one of Alex's moves—studying him like a lab rat. I try to call out to him, but my words just float above his head.

"Professor, have you found that map that will lead us to The Black Gate?" Franco asks.

"I'm getting closer," the professor says with a wry smile.

The Black Gate? The Professor and Franco know each other? No, no. What am I saying? This is just a dream—images that my mind is creating. *This isn't real...right?* I question myself.

I feel sweat dripping down my neck, and my heart wrenching in pain. My eyes open and all I see are white sheets, white walls, and a white ceiling. *Just a dream,* I remind myself. Then again, aren't my drifts just dreams too?

*   *   *

It's been two weeks, and I still haven't officially drifted off anywhere. My stale dreams don't allow me to interact. I can only watch scenes like a movie. I'm still trying to decide if I'm cured from the ability to drift, or if it just takes a while for that medication to move out of my system. My dreams *have* become more intense, which may or may not be a good sign. Most of them include Alex, and a lot of them include Franco following Alex around. It doesn't make any sense.

I've tried to talk to Alex in my dreams and I've told him what I've been up to, where I've been and what I've been doing. He only smiles at me though. I don't think he can hear me.

I wish I could get closure. I need closure. My dreams have created a permanent opening, and it's like a waterspout of salt that bleeds into my open wounds.

Day fifteen of trying to drift, I actually felt the darkness floating toward me. But my mind snaps out of the haze quicker than I am able to find myself in any other reality.

Last night was different, though. It wasn't a dream. I know that. I felt the darkness. The dizziness. Life sucking me up into a vortex. My dreams don't do that. I found myself at the cafe for a split second — it was only a second, but it gives me hope that I'm getting closer.

*　　*　　*

The world whizzes by as I stare out of the train window, wondering if what I'm doing will help, or if it will cause more pain. I have to follow my heart though, and that's back to Southborough, Massachusetts.

CHAPTER EIGHTEEN

JUST A VISIT

I RELOCK THE CELL DOOR, lean up against the padded wall, kiss his cheek, and beg him to help me. I know he doesn't hear me, but something about his arm being around me feels right. I'm not sure where my drift will take me. I don't visualize a place. I visualize Alex.

White padding, a heavy arm, darkness blending with a Parisian glow...

It works. Alex is the key to drifting. I should have known. It's always been about him.

The drift takes me to Paris. This confuses me. Alex isn't in Paris, I don't think. He said he was going back to San Diego. Yet I end up here at our old apartment. There has to be a reason. Or at least I have to think there's a reason.

I wonder if he rented the apartment out to someone else or just abandoned it. I'm here, so now I have to know.

I slide my key into the lock and find that it turns with ease. I walk in nervously and take one step inside before I fall to my knees. His scent is all it takes to knock me down. My dreams never include smells, making this the first time I've inhaled his scent in the past three months. He's still here. He lied.

I walk into what used to be our bedroom, and when I look around I become puzzled by the sight of Alex's clothes piled up on the bed, his shoes scattered around the room, and a small lump of *my* clothes sprawled across his pillow. He definitely still lives here, and I'm questioning why he was lying about us *both* going home. Maybe he *was* just trying to get rid of me.

I open the top drawer of the dresser that I used to occupy, wondering what I'll find. All of my clothes are still folded perfectly how I left them. On top of my clothes is a folded up note. And it looks similar to the one I lost. My hands tremble as I pick the letter up. I unfold it and find Alex's handwriting. It reads:

> *Chloe,*
>
> *This is the hardest thing I've ever had to do. But I'm doing this to keep you safe. I love you more than anything, but Franco would have killed you if I didn't do this. I made a deal with him, so he'll never bother you again.*
>
> *I know you probably hate me for what I had to do, but Franco is watching us, and I had to make it look real.*
>
> *The whole thing, everything was a setup. I finally told him to bring you to me so I could say good-bye, and I would then do as he wished.*
>
> *Please don't do anything to try and fight this battle. He's stronger than you even know, and this is the only way to keep you safe.*
>
> *Don't ever think I have stopped loving you. Every second I have to be away from you will be the most painful second of my entire life.*
>
> *This is not your fault and never has been. I don't want you to think that. This is how it was meant to be. Things will be okay, and things will end up the way they should be. But right now, I need you to be away from me.*
>
> *I love you, Chloe.*
> *Always yours,*
> *Alex*

What? Tears spill from eyes. My mind is spinning, my heart is pounding, adrenaline is spiraling though my body, but all I can do is cry. I'm crying for all of the nights I cried for him, for all the seconds that he's been in pain for losing me, for all of the dreams that were just dreams, and for all of our lost days apart.

I want to fix this, but he's made it sound like there was no chance of doing so. I have to be able to outsmart Franco, somehow. I can only assume Tomas and James must be long gone by now, and they won't be of any help. And if everything was a setup, so was me drugging Franco. Was Kiera part of this set-up too? I wonder if Alex knows that I drugged Franco in the abandoned institution—if he knows that's *how* he got here. This is my fault. His plan may have been inevitable, but I helped him along.

That's the answer though. I have to make him conscious there in the institution again.

In the midst of figuring out how to accomplish the impossible, I hear the doorknob of the front door turn. Blood drains from my face and my heart pounds in my ears. I slip underneath the bed and wait to hear who it is.

Only able to see a few inches off the ground, I see Alex's feet enter the room and slightly hop forward as if he were being pushed. Just after he passes by the bed, I see Franco's shiny polished shoes inches behind him.

"Night night, lover boy," Franco sings to Alex.

I hear a clink of metal, followed by a locking sound. Franco leaves the room and I hear the springs creak within the couch in the living room. What the hell? Is he living here with Alex?

All I want to do is climb out from under the bed and lie down next to him. He'll be so mad that I came back, but I know he'd be happy to see me, even if only until realization kicks in. I rest my chin on my arms trying not to make any sounds.

It's only been seconds, and I hear snoring coming from the living room. The wait is killing me. He's so close.

"Alex?" I whisper softly, trying not to startle him.

I feel the bed bounce, followed by a soft smothered grunt. I climb out from under the bed and I pull myself up to my feet. A gag covers his mouth and his frightened eyes are blaring out of his face. I place my finger against my lips to show him I know to be quiet.

I pull the gag down below his mouth and he continues looking at me with a darkness glossing over his swollen eyes. He's looking at me as if I am already marked for dead.

"It's okay, Alex. I'm going to get you out of here," I say.

"I'm so sorry. I'm so sorry, baby," he cries.

I hush him and replace the gag back around his mouth in case Franco comes back. The anger emanating through my body has encouraged an idea that I have to try, now, while Franco's asleep.

I tiptoe over to the French windows, snatching Alex's keys from the bureau on the way. I glide the window open just wide enough to where I can squeeze through it. I lean out and reach for the escape ladder that I never understood the use for—until now.

I reach the ground and run over to Alex's scooter. I stare at it, angry for a moment, knowing I have to face this demon of a vehicle again. But it's for Alex, who has given up his living rights to a psychotic man just to keep me safe. I can do this…for him. I force a slow exhale out of my pursed lips, calming myself as I swing my leg over the seat. If I think about this for another second, I'll chicken out. It's now or never. I twist the key in the ignition and gun it.

Over the course of the ten-minute ride, I think I may take five breaths total. I feel as if I am going to crash each time I take a turn. Somehow, I make it in one piece. I walk into Tomas's unlocked office and head straight for the glass cabinet above his desk. I've seen him take bottles from it each time he was concocting some kind of drug. Something helpful must be in here.

None of the liquid filled bottles are labeled, except for one that says ketamine. He put a small description underneath that says, "Caution: For long term catalepsy." I think I've heard of this before. I'm sure this is the stuff that knocks you out, but I have no idea for how long.

With a little more confidence, I straddle my leg back over the scooter and make it back to the apartment in half the amount of time. I won't be able to make it up to the window since the ladder is too high off the ground. I didn't even think of that when I left or jumped down from it. I guess I'll have to take my chances with the stairs.

Before I approach the front door, I fill a syringe with the liquid and clasp my fingers around it, holding it behind my back. I grip my free hand around the doorknob and twist with a slow movement, careful not to make any sound. I push the door open enough to hear Franco still snoring on the couch. He's in a black t-shirt and jeans, attire I've never seen Franco sporting. He must be comfortable with this living situation. Asshole. I remove my shoes to avoid footsteps and cautiously approach him from behind. Without a moment's hesitation, I jab the needle into his upper arm, plunging the liquid in with force. His eyes flash open with fury and his hand shoots up to grab my arm. But he swings his arm right past me, almost as if his brain is disconnected from his body.

The drug seems to be working quicker than I expected. His teeth grind together as his eyeballs roll into the back of his head. I remain hovering over him until his breathing elongates.

I pull the set of keys out of his pocket and sprint back into the bedroom.

Alex's eyes are filled with terror and question. I remove the gag from his mouth and begin trying different keys on the handcuffs. "We're going to need to get Franco contained somewhere, but once we do, he'll be restrained. *Everywhere.*"

I slide the last key in and the handcuffs unlatch, releasing Alex's hands. The red welts covering his wrists are a clear indicator that this has been going on night after night—and it's all because of me. I lift up his hand and examine the multiple scabs and scars, but his injuries are clearly the least of his worries.

He pulls me onto his lap and wraps his hands around my face. "Chlo…look at me. How did you—what did you do?" he asks, his chest heaving in and out.

"I went to Tomas's office and found a drug to make him unconscious. That's why we have to get him somewhere quick. I don't know how long it will last," I say, losing myself within the depths of his eyes.

He studies me, looking as if he's trying to piece together the chaotic mess our lives have become. "I'm so sorry for hurting you," he moans.

"We'll have time for explanations later. Right now, we have to get him somewhere. Are you able to help? I'm afraid I can't do this alone."

He perks up. "Yeah, I know exactly where he's going. His car is downstairs. Let's get him down there," Alex says, pulling himself up to his feet.

He lifts Franco and throws him over his shoulder, and I hold open each door of the back stairwell as we barrel toward the first floor.

Alex shoves him into the backseat of the car face down. We race down familiar side streets until we get to the same dark unlit side street that I wasn't fond of the last time I was here.

I wasn't sure how Alex was going to manage to lug Franco all the way down the hundred spiraling steps, but we're almost to the bottom, I think.

Within a few steps from the stairs, I see Alex pulling one of the cell doors shut. The locking sound follows, and with the final clink, an immediate sense of relief overcomes me. I can't even wrap my head around what we've been through because of this monster. Is this really the end of him? Can we now put this problem to rest? I can only ask questions that I know will never be answered, but I guess having Franco locked up in both realities will be as comforting as it gets. "He's still being fed at home. I asked Ashley to continue feeding him."

"Who is Ashley?" I realize now that Alex wouldn't remember her. She's not part of our drift. She's real. And he isn't familiar with real.

"A friend from the institution. Franco had convinced her to bring us food when he was holding us captive. Once I traded places with him, I asked her to continue keeping him fed. She's scared of him, so she agreed."

"Why not just let him die?" He seems to disagree with my humanity.

"I am not him."

"Do you trust her?" he asks.

"As much as I trust anyone else," I shrug, avoiding his questioning gaze.

"You don't trust anyone," he reminds me.

"I know."

He tugs on my hand to stop me from avoiding the look on his face. But I keep my focus planted on the ground below our feet, knowing the next question he's going to ask. "So, someone you don't trust is responsible for keeping us alive right now?" His words come out quickly and with a subtle harshness.

"What other options do I have, Alex?" I have sole responsibility now of making sure that we are being taken care of in a world neither of us want to be a part of. That's not exactly fair to question the decisions I've been forced to make alone.

"You're right. I'm sorry. I suppose we're safer now than we have been all year being watched over by Franco."

"It's just temporary until I figure out a better solution."

The ride back to our apartment seems slow and full of apprehension. We have so much to catch up on and I don't even know where to start. The pain I've felt and lived through for the past few months was unbearable, but I suppose it could have been prevented if I had read Alex's note. Who knows what has been going through *his* head for the past three months, knowing that I didn't have his note.

I climb into the comforts of the bed that I had shared with Alex for so long before my heart fell to pieces. It still has the same scent and warmth, but it almost feels like we're starting on page one again.

"I'll start," I say, clearing my throat.

I can see the relief on his face, but also the fear of what I might say.

"That day in the cafe when you broke up with me, I thought my life was ending. My heart ached in ways that I had hoped to never feel again after we lost each other last year. I was hurt, confused, and angry. But the worst part was that I chose not to read the note you gave me."

The corners of his lips droop and the color on his face drains, probably from knowing I had been carrying around the agony for so long, and yet in the end I still came back here.

He places his hand on my chin and lifts it up, forcing our eyes to reconnect. "I found the note in Tomas's office. I knew right then that you hadn't read it and that my chances of seeing you anytime in the near future were probably non-existent," he says, looking back and forth between both of my eyes.

"I didn't even notice it was gone. I didn't want to read it. I didn't want a lame excuse for an apology, or another reason why we couldn't be together. You were pretty convincing that day. However, when I finally decided that I *wanted* to read what you had to say, I obviously couldn't find the note."

He runs his thumb across my cheek and presses his lips over the tip of my nose.

"I had to keep you safe," he says.

I close my eyes and nod. "I moved down to South Carolina and tried to start over there. Every day I tried to figure out how to get over you, but I couldn't. Everything reminded me of you: the ocean, the sky, even the white walls in my tiny apartment."

He pulls my head to his lips and wraps his arms tightly around me. "I am so sorry you had to go through that. I'm so sorry that I couldn't come after you, especially after I knew you had lost the note. I was so worried about you. I figured you would move on and try to forget about me. And I wouldn't blame you. I don't know what made you come back, but I can't even begin to tell you how thankful I am that you did."

The emotional tidal wave slamming over me forces a steady stream of tears to rush down my cheeks. "I missed you so badly. I need you, always. I can't live without you. It's not possible."

He reaches around my head, tangling his fingers in my hair and pulls my face to his, forcing his lips against mine. The images of what I went through over the past three months fade away with each second that our lips remain entwined together.

He pulls away, but still holds my face in a firm grip, looking deep into my eyes. "I spent every night lying here dreaming about you, questioning everything I thought was supposed to happen, thinking about what I would do when I had the chance to see you again. Chloe, I need you." His words trail off as he parts my lips with his again.

There's no time to analyze what he means by, what *was supposed to happen*. I don't care right now. With adrenaline turning into an aggressive need, Alex falls backward onto the bed and pulls me down with him. Breathing seems unnecessary with our faces as close as they are. It's as if the oxygen between us is being shared, causing my lips to tingle from the force of our insistent thirst. With Alex's uncontrolled hands clutching each article of my clothing, and his, I feel every inch of my skin melt into him.

His hands press firmly into the small of my back, holding me tightly as he traces light kisses from my lips down to my collarbone. "I want you, Chloe. Now," he says, his voice is gruff and deliberate. His desires are more than clear. "Today is our someday. Today is the day that I can't get past without feeling every part of you, inside and out." His words make me melt into the mattress, and I surrender myself to him.

The warmth from his body flows through me, giving me a new reason to love him. This feeling of belonging, completion, need, and desire, all jumbled together in a fragile mess within the depths of my heart tells me that whatever we have, is with us forever.

With each movement of our bodies working against each other, my heart pounds harder, my breaths become weaker, but my body aches for more. The soft murmurs escaping his throat and the look of hunger in his eyes become replaced with bliss from a desired connection that we've both longed for. Oh wow. This is—. There aren't words. "Alex," I breathe. His eyes hover over mine, looking at me as if he can see into my soul. If he can see it, he'll know that it lives for him, it exists because of him, and it will survive with him. The intensity of this moment is causing my emotions to mesh within my physical senses, confusing the need to laugh and cry. I can't decipher which I need to do more. But as the minutes pass, the solid element we've both become blends together in a rhythm of bliss, and I now understand the reason for waiting—to feel him become a part of me in every way. We're now one. Even if it wasn't his reason, he was worth every long second.

Cradled in the nook of his shoulder and chest, I lie still trying to even out each breath I take. He squeezes his arm around me and kisses my cheek. "I love you," he whispers with a shuddering breath.

"I love you more," I say, pulling away slightly, seeing a new look in Alex's eyes—one I can't quite figure out. But it's a good look, and that's all I care about.

After lying in each other's arms for hours, I sit up against the headboard, contemplating what's next for us. I have to know, "What was Franco keeping you for? What was he making you do?"

Alex props himself up on his elbows and focuses on the wall in front of us. "I had to give him injections—keep him focused. He was trying to eliminate Tomas and James. He was also worried about losing consciousness in *this* reality. I made a deal with him that if he let you go and forgot about the locket, I would help him sustain his life here. I guess the idea of being free and only one person made him happy, and for that he kept me around. But he chose to hold me as a prisoner any moment I wasn't being of any use to him, as you saw."

"Tomas and James are gone?" I question.

"For now," he answers. "The important thing is that Franco can't hurt us again. But I'm afraid to ask what's going on in those cells at home?"

I never had the opportunity to tell him how *well* I fixed things. "Actually, things couldn't be better. We're both locked in a cell together there, and Franco is locked in a separate one. No one can hurt either of us," I explain with a haughty grin, knowing that was the only thing I did right.

"How are we both locked in one cell?" he asks. A grim look shadows his face. I know what he's worried about. "Aren't you nervous I'll hurt you?"

I nod. "You won't." I wrap my hands around his. "All that matters is we're together and Franco is locked up, in both places."

"That's good," he says. But I can tell he still sounds somewhat unsure about this. "You know, we haven't had a smooth road. It's actually been pretty rough terrain." He laughs a little and traces his finger in swirls over my knee. "We deserve more than this. We should be able to have a normal life together. And after having months to think about what I would do if I got to talk to you again, I kept wondering what you would think about moving home to San Diego, or even to your new home in South Carolina?"

"Together you mean, right?" I pull in a quick breath and hold it, waiting for his answer.

He wraps his arms around me, squeezing gently, comforting me, soothing my pain, and consoling my fears. "Always and forever."

"No more Paris?" I love this place, but I do question if it's the right place to live.

"This isn't where we belong. Vous ne parlez pas français."

"What does that mean?" I laugh.

"Exactly." He nudges his shoulder into mine.

"Okay, fine. One point for you." I walk my fingers up his chest, marveling at the softness of his skin. "So, Alex Levette. Tell me, how were you so confident that you would talk to me again?" I wish I was blessed with that confidence.

I can see the wheels turning in his head, trying to figure out a response. Why does he have to think of a response? "Well...I knew Franco wouldn't live forever. I knew I had already managed to wait twelve years to talk to you once, so I figured at worst, what would be another twenty?" He pinches my chin and pulls my face to his. "You will always be worth the wait."

I cover my lips over his, tasting him. Memorizing him. "You're amazing. You know that?"

"What city or town did you rent an apartment in?" A flicker of excitement lightens his eyes. I guess he really does want to get out of here.

"Charleston. It's a nice area and the people are all very friendly. I think you'd like it," I say. "Wait. What about Kiera? And when do you want to leave?" I look past him and out at the perfect view I'll have to say good-bye to again.

"She's fine. Just don't worry about her right now. I want to leave at the end of the week. It will give us enough time to pack and wrap things up." He skates his fingertips down the length of my arm, reigniting my nerves.

"Oh." I flip over onto my side, craving more of his touch. I'm not sure I'll ever have enough now. He wraps his arms around me and pulls me in. "I could live here...forever," I say, nuzzling into his chest. "I don't care where we are as long as your arms are always around me."

"Fine with me," his husky voice whispers in my ear. "I do need to run a couple of errands tomorrow morning though. But tomorrow night I'm taking you on one last Parisian night out on the town."

I can't stop staring at him, trying to take in every inch of the face I've missed. My emotions feel like they've been wound into a tight knot, and I can't wrap my head around everything that happened tonight. I think part of me is petrified of waking up from a dream and finding out none of this is real.

"This is all real, right?" I ask, sweeping my hands across the curves of his torso. A grin tugs on his lips, making me want to touch him more.

He looks down at my hands and intertwines his fingers with mine. "Everything in *Paris* is always real."

"I dreamt of you every night for three months," I say. "My dreams felt so real and I sometimes wondered if they were. But when I woke up every morning, I felt like there was a knife lodged into my chest as I realized you and I were just a memory." Even while I'm telling him what I went through, I feel the sting of pain run through me as a reminder of what I felt every morning we *weren't* together. He looks at me, pained, and his hand slides up and down my cheek, comforting the ache that's oozing through my words.

"You don't need to dream about me anymore, Chlo. We're together, and we are real, so damn real. We are not a dream, but this feels so good, it's hard not to confuse us with one," he says, pulling the sheets back over us. "This is real too. And I will never get enough of this."

I feel whole again, and as if the gaps in my heart are closing back up. I might need to lie here for the next three months, just to make up for lost time.

* * *

I didn't dream last night, and it was a pleasant change. I never thought of it before, but a dreamless night leaves you wondering if everything in your world is finally right and there's nothing left to dream about.

CHAPTER NINETEEN

THE START OF THE BEGINNING

ALEX HAS BEEN GONE FOR A WHILE today, and I can't imagine what he's doing. He promised he'd be home by five, though. This sucks. I am going to miss this place. I'm sure we'll come back to visit, but it was our first home together, and it will always hold a special place in my heart. It will always be *our* place—our dream within a dream.

I've been leisurely folding all of my clothes and placing them into the boxes Alex brought home this morning. Although I'm not sure where all of our stuff is going to go when we get down to Charleston. "I wonder if the apartment I was renting in our real life will be there in our drift?

"The apartment will be there, but the people you may have met won't be." He gives me an off look. "Did you meet anyone?" I know what he means by that.

"Just a sweet old lady who was my neighbor. She watched over me."

I can see the relief wash over his face. "I'm glad you had someone."

* * *

With the Eiffel tower in plain view, I'm starting to question where we could be going. We don't usually go this far. We take a sharp turn and head toward an elevator at the base of the tower. I squeeze my hands around his. "Where are we going?" I ask, but I already know. I've waited for this since the first time I saw the Eiffel Tower.

He looks down at me from the corner of his eyes and gives me a wry look but doesn't say a word. He approaches a man near the elevator and engages in a conversation that I can't translate. I try to pick apart each word, searching my brain for the meaning, but nothing's coming to me. His hand tugs on mine as we're escorted past an incredibly long line of people who are also waiting to go up the tower. We follow a man into the elevator and within seconds, we ascend upward into the sky.

Halfway up, the elevator stops and I'm a little confused as to why we're stopping here. But as the door opens, the escort steps outside of the elevator and gestures for us to follow.

"Monsieur and Mademoiselle, this way." Another host escorts us to a table overlooking the city skyline. My heart flutters at the first sight of the view. It's breathtaking.

"Wait until you see the view from the top," Alex says, pulling my chair out from the table.

"We get to go all the way up too?" I squeal, like a child.

He places his finger in front of his smile, urging me to lower my voice. I look around, noticing the quiet romantic diners who surround us. "Of course," he says. "We just need to enjoy our dinner first, if that's okay?"

"I think it'll be just fine," I snicker.

We relax into our seats as our napkins are draped over our laps. This type of dining is something that I've only seen in movies. Being treated like royalty is something I could never get used to, but for tonight, I'll indulge.

"Our meals have been pre-ordered, but I'm sure you'll like what's coming," Alex says.

He seems so quiet tonight. I'm sure he's going to miss this place. He's been connected to this city for far longer than I've even been around. Maybe we shouldn't leave. He's sacrificed so much for me already, and he kind of made it sound like we were leaving because I wasn't adapting well enough here. I could try harder to learn the language and get a job. Maybe we could belong here.

He pulls my hand over to his and massages the top of my knuckles with his thumb. "I promised you I'd take you up here some day," he says, leaning in toward me.

"You did. I remember that day very clearly. Thank you for keeping that promise," I smile coyly. "Are you sure you want to leave here? We could make it work, you know."

"We need to move on," he says. The sureness of his voice makes it clear that he's thought this through.

* * *

I drum my fingers on the table while watching Alex take care of the bill. "Ready?" I'm struggling to conceal my eagerness, but I've waited so long to see the top.

Alex dabs his mouth with his napkin, almost as if he's getting joy from dragging this out. With a sly smirk, he stands up and offers me his hand. "Yes," he winks. "I think we're ready now."

* * *

The elevator doors glide open, revealing the most incredible view I never could have imagined. I grip Alex's hand and pull him out onto the viewing deck. My eyes are drawn to the river, my favorite place in the city. It looks even more beautiful from up here. I wrap my fingers around the railing and lean over, taking everything in and inhaling the intoxicating scent from the clouds.

Alex pulls his phone out from his pocket and snaps a few pictures of the skyline. "Chloe, smile," he says, sliding in next to me. He holds the phone up in front of our faces and a broad smile stretches across his cheeks. "I want to remember this moment forever."

After he slides his phone back into his pocket, I turn back around to lean against the metal barrier. I want to take in this sight for as long as I can. "This is astonishing, Alex." My words jitter from me, shivering against the cool breeze of a low bearing cloud. "I'll never forget this, ever."

He removes his jacket and places it around my shoulders. He briskly runs his hands up and down my arms, forcing warmth back into my skin. As the tremors in my upper body subside, he leans in closer against my back, wrapping his arms around the front of my chest. "I love you, Chloe." His words are whispered softly into my ear.

As his words drift off with the breeze, he releases his arms from around me. I turn to see why he let go. And for a second, I glance from side to side trying to find where he could have gone. But when my eyes drift down, I'm quick to notice where he went. My eyes flash between his, focusing on the flushed look on his face, the straight line across his mouth, the knee he's kneeling on, and the black suede box he's clutching in his trembling hand.

I feel my knees nearly give out as my breath becomes so shallow that I'm not sure if I can actually take in any more oxygen. I clasp my hands together, throwing them against my pounding heart. My mouth falls open from shock and tears pool over my lashes.

He pulls in a shuddering breath and forces an anxious smile as he reaches into his pocket and pulls out a tissue for me. "Chloe Valcourt," he begins. Oh my God. "We're young, we have our whole lives ahead of us, and if we were normal, I'd say this is ridiculous and way too soon. But, you and I, we're one of a kind. We have something that can never be ripped apart. Our lives need to grow together, and I need to be with you forever. If I ever have to go one more day without seeing your smile, or hearing your voice, I might not make it through that day. You *are* my life, you *are* my love, you *are* my reason for being, and I promise to spend every day of my life loving you, caring for you and being your best friend, the one I've always promised to be. Chloe." He pulls in a deep breath. "Will you do me the honor of becoming my wife?"

His hands are unsteady and his lips are quivering with anticipation while I try to take in everything he just said. I need a minute, but only because I want to remember every single word for the rest of my life.

"Yes, I will," I cry with delight, whipping my arms around his neck.

My knees give out and I fall into him, stopping myself inches from his face. Our eyes lock as his hand reaches up to cradle my cheek. I move in, crashing my lips into his with more passion, more love, more emotion than we've ever shown each other. Words can't describe how I feel at this moment, and this is the only way I know how to show him. With our lips dancing in a slow progression, I can feel his feelings and sense his thoughts.

After minutes of being lost in this frozen moment of time, his lips begin to slow and become firmer against mine. He pulls away, smiling sweetly with a slight quiver in his bottom lip. "Ca—can I give you the ring?" he asks, breathless.

I slap my hands over my mouth. "Yes," I chirp.

He stands up on both feet, and pulls me up with him, never moving his hand from my back. His other hand is now shaking so hard he's having a hard time opening the box. When he manages to separate the opening, I'm blinded by the unexpected sparkle. It's more beautiful than I ever could have imagined. The band is white gold and the diamond has a bluish hue. It's large and surrounded by dozens of tiny little diamonds that look like sparkling dust. I'm amazed at his taste. I'm amazed by him.

His unsteady fingers remove the ring from the cushioned slit, and he effortlessly glides it onto my finger.

"It fits perfectly," I croon, admiring the striking beauty. "I guess you really do know everything about me," I giggle.

I hold my hand out in front of me, taking in the new symbol of our past, present, and future, knowing that this moment in time is the start of everything we've worked for. Everything is right, and everything is the way it was meant to be. Dream or no dream. This is real to me.

A little elderly lady approaches us from behind. She's wiping her tears away. "So, when's the wedding?" her voice shivers as she places her hand under mine, lifting my palm so she can see the ring.

I look over at Alex to see if he has a response since I haven't had a minute to consider the thought of a wedding.

"Friday, ma'am. This Friday." His voice is serious and his words are firm and thought out.

"Friday?" I shout, shocked and wondering how we could pull something off so fast.

"Don't worry. I have it all planned out," he says with his beautiful crooked smile.

"God bless you both." The old lady smiles and leans in to kiss me on each cheek, and then Alex as well.

She makes me wish I had any family member worthy of calling with this type of excitement. Although, I'm sure Celia will be over the moon when she finds out, and that will be enough satisfaction for me.

Now that both of our emotions have settled down a bit, I see Alex fall against a nearby post. He pulls his collar away from his neck and stretches his head from side to side. "Hey, are you okay?" I ask.

He lifts his head up and smiles with a somewhat embarrassed look on his face. "Be thankful you never have to propose to anyone," he laughs. "It takes everything out of you, trying to keep your excitement in check while also praying that the answer is *yes*."

"Did you really think that I would say no?" I ask, smoothing my hand over the slight stubble on his cheek.

"It's just that, we're young, really young," he explains.

"Yet, we've experienced more than most people our age," I say, agreeing to his reason. I wouldn't care if we didn't have a reason. I love him. He loves me. It's simple. "Age is just a number. We both know that this is right and that we're meant to be together. I didn't question it for a second." I stand up on my toes and pull his face down to mine. I press my lips into his and then pull back slightly. "I love you more than anything in both of our worlds. You and I...we're an endless dream."

He pulls me in tightly against him and kisses the top of my ear. "We're more than a dream, Chlo. Real is only what you make of it. If you want us to be real, then we're as real as it gets."

When he pulls away, he leads us over to a bench on the inner part of the viewing deck. "Is Friday good for you?" he asks, lifting my hand to admire the ring on my finger.

I wrap my arms around his arm and rest my head on his shoulder. "Now would be good for me," I say. "Mrs. Chloe Levette," I let out an exaggerated sigh. "It has a nice ring to it, don't you think?"

"It's beautiful." He rests his chin over my head. "I am the luckiest man in the world."

CHAPTER TWENTY

UNTIL LIFE BECOMES SIMPLE

IT'S BEAUTIFUL, PERFECT, ELEGANT, and really hard to button up the back, I laugh to myself. I'm exhausted from trying to put this thing on. With much discomfort, I sit down on the edge of the chair in front of our floor length mirror, staring at my reflection, gazing through my own eyes, wrongfully feeling sad on what's supposed to be the best day of my life.

I wish my mother didn't despise me. I wish I had a sister or a friend. I wish someone would be standing here with me right now, helping me with my dress, make-up and hair, or telling me silly stories about my past. Isn't that the way it should be? I have no idea how I'm going to finish getting this dress on. I can't even ask Alex. The last thing I need is bad luck right now.

I pull myself back up, twisting and turning until I somewhat have the back of the dress twisted around to the front, but I still can't reach. I let out a loud groan of frustration and Alex knocks on the door in response.

"Are you okay in there, Chlo?"

"Yes," I say. "I just can't...get this dress buttoned myself." I blow my bangs back out of my face for the hundredth time.

"Okay, hang on," he replies.

"No!" I shout. "You can't come in. It's bad luck." I pull the curtain out from the wall to cover my body in case he comes in anyway. I hear him laughing outside the door, and for a second I get angry that he's poking fun at my frustration. But as the door opens, shock replaces my anger when I see Celia walk through. It is a good thing I haven't put any make-up on yet, because I have a waterfall of tears cascading down my cheeks.

"Hi sweetie," she says, choking back her own tears. "I'm sorry I'm late. Alex didn't give me much warning," she giggles. "Honey, you look beautiful. Would you mind if I helped you finish getting ready?" She wraps her arms loosely around me, careful not to lean against my dress.

I can't respond with anything other than more tears.

"Shh, it's okay," she hushes, wiping the tears away with her thumb. "Chloe, I'm so happy that you and Alex have found each other. I know I've said this a million times, but you two were meant to be together ever since you were seven years old. I knew in my heart even then that you two would find a way to be together someday. Seeing you in this dress right now reminds me that everything in life really does happen for a reason. I know your conditions have seemed like a curse throughout your life, but you two wouldn't be who you are, or together, if it wasn't for it." She wraps her arms around my neck and sniffles the rest of her tears away. "Okay, enough with the mush, let's get this bride ready."

She pulls me back over to the mirror and twists the dress back to where it should be. Her fingers are nimble and quick as she fastens each clasp, and then smoothes the back of the dress, allowing the train to lie flat across the floor. She holds her finger up to me and smiles before running out into the hall.

She returns with a large bag that she whips open with one swing of her hand. A curling iron, hairspray, and hairpins are just the beginning of what flies out.

After a half hour of inhaling burning hairspray, my eyebrows being plucked, and having my skin pulled way too tightly around my hairline, I feel the last pin jab into the center of my hair, followed by Celia's fingers raking out the last strands on the top.

"Time for make-up," she chirps, turning me around to face the mirror.

It only takes her a few minutes to put the finishing touches on my face. I feel ready. I try to stand up and get a closer look in the mirror, but she waves at me to stay seated.

"Chloe," she says, her voice suddenly quite serious. "I have a couple of things for you." A smile trembles across her lips.

She pulls out a garter from her bag. It's blue, lacey, and forces warmth in my cheeks. "Here, put this on. It's your something blue," she winks.

She shoves her hands back into her bag and pulls out a pearl bracelet. She lifts my hand and clasps it around my wrist. "This bracelet is an exact replica of a bracelet Alex's mom used to wear." She laughs quietly to herself. "She always said it brought her luck. But she only started saying it after she met Alex's dad. She had it on the night she met him, and she never took it off after that. Well, not until the night of the accident, strangely." Her eyes glaze over for a moment. I can sense the superstitious thoughts running through her mind. "Anyway, at home, in our real world, the bracelet was left to me. But because I'm still in the institution, I don't have it. Now, since you two have chosen to live your life here in this beautiful world your minds have created, I wouldn't be able to get my hands on it. However, I found this one that looks exactly the same." She places the string of pearls around my wrist. "I realize it isn't old, but the meaning behind it is from a long time ago." She shrugs and offers me a cheeky smile. "When you two finally reconnected, I knew Alex's mom would have wanted you to have it had she been alive on your wedding day." She chokes, tears welling up in her eyes again and in mine as well. "No, no." She yanks a handful of tissues from the box behind her. "You can't cry." She blots the tissue under each of my eyes. "Make-up! We can't ruin the make-up."

I pull in a deep breath and roll my eyes up toward the ceiling, attempting to stop any incoming tears. Celia taught me that trick the last time she gave me a makeover.

"Okay, here's the last thing." There's more? Geez, Celia. "It's your something new." She hands me a little blue, suede jewelry box bordered by gold lining. I open it, finding a pair of pearl earrings that match the bracelet. There's also a note in the box. I pull it out and place the box down on the chair next to me. I unfold the note and read:

> My Dearest Chloe,
> This is your something new. One of these you can touch, and the other you can feel in your heart. Alex lost his mom, and in a sense, you lost yours too. I took Alex into my life and cared for him, as his mother would have done. You will now be my daughter-in-law, and I want you to know that you can always look at me as a mom in your life. I will always be here for you, and give you advice. I will get mad at you when you

screw up, and I'll be proud of you when you do something
wonderful. Therefore, from today on, you never have to feel
like you don't have a family, because today, we become a family.
        I love you, and always will.
        Celia

Before I even have a second to digest the sweet words written on
the note, Celia pinches my chin and tilts it up toward the ceiling.
"Do not cry," she laughs.

"Are you two done in there?" Alex yells.

"Just one minute," Celia shouts back to him. "Why don't you go
ahead and take your car down there. We'll be leaving in just a second."

"Thank you, Celia," I say. "This means more than I could ever
explain to you. That day when you did my hair for the first time, and
looked at me like I was…pretty, I wished that you were my mom. So,
this note is answering my wish in a way." I wrap my arms around her
until she peels me off.

"Stop," she cries. "No touching. You'll smudge." She waves her
arms around, panicking that her masterpiece will be ruined. "Okay,
it's time." She takes my hand and squeezes her fingers around mine.
When she releases my hand, she moves behind me and lifts the back of
my train to help me out of the apartment and down the flights of stairs.

I wish I knew where we were going. Alex begged me to let him keep
it a secret, and because I have an idea as to where we might be going,
I let him have that surprise.

The car ride seems to take forever, and my heart is racing with
anticipation. I can't believe I'm going to be a married woman by the end of
this hour. It still feels strange, but right—incredibly right at the same time.

The car pulls up to the exact spot I had hoped it would. The river,
our river, it's the best place I could imagine having our wedding at, and
I'm glad that Alex thought the same. I take a look around before I step
out of the car, and I see Alex standing by a bench. He's clutching a
small bouquet of red roses, and he looks amazing in his tuxedo. My
heart flutters, and my head trembles inside.

"It's time, Chloe," Celia says in a soft voice as she steps out of the car.

She meets me at my door to help me out and I slide out with
caution, being careful not to catch my dress on anything. I'm greeted

by a light spring breeze caressing my face. The sun warms my skin, and my eyes focus on Alex, who's gleaming, watching my every move as I make my way down to him.

Time seems to be crawling with each step closer. My heart has been skipping beats since I left the car, and I wish I could fast-forward myself into his arms. The river is sparkling behind him, and the sun is creating a glow within his translucent blue eyes. Everything at this moment feels like perfection.

Three steps to go until I never have to let go of him again.

"Hi," I say, my words come out in a soft whisper.

"You…you are the most beautiful thing I've ever seen," he says, nodding with a blissful smile as he hands me the bouquet of roses.

"You look amazing in that tux," I say, wrapping my fingers around the stems.

He encases my free hand within his and brings it to his warm chest. It steadies my unsteady nerves and allows me to concentrate on just being here with him.

The man standing before us clears his throat, and his words float through the air. "Do you, Alexander take Chloe to be your wedded wife and to live together in marriage?" he begins. "Do you promise to love her, be faithful to her, care for her and never leave her for as long as you both shall live?"

"I do," Alex says, without an ounce of hesitation.

"Chloe, do you take Alex to be your wedded husband and to live together in marriage? Do you promise to love him, be faithful to him, care for him and never leave him for as long as you both shall live?" the justice of the peace asks me.

"I do," I say, looking up through my eyelashes to see Alex's eyes filling with tears.

"I love you," his lips mouth the words.

"I love you," I mouth back.

"Please accept this ring as a symbol of my love and our unbreakable bond," Alex repeats after the justice of the peace.

With the ring on my finger, and the one I'm sliding onto his, I feel complete.

"I now pronounce you man and wife." The man smiles at us both. "You may kiss your bride." He nods at Alex with a wink.

I can hear Celia's ferocious claps as she jumps up and down, squealing with delight. Alex places his hands around my face and gingerly pulls my lips to his. The cage of butterflies that used to be cooped up within the confines of my body has opened and released the thousands of flutters that once warned me we weren't forever— that the moment wouldn't last. Now I know, this moment is ours forever. I'm free from loneliness, and I'm freed from darkness. When our lips part, we will be known as one, our lives will forever be connected. I will be his, and he will be mine.

He pulls away slightly, searching both of my eyes. "Thank you for freeing me," he says, smiling with his eyes. "With you, I will always be fissure free. You saved me."

Celia lunges at us and wraps her small arms around us, as far as they'll go. "Welcome to the family, Chloe," she squeaks, trying to hide the crackling sobs behind her smile.

"My mom would have been so happy today. She would have loved you, Chloe," Alex smiles, squeezing his arm tighter around my waist.

As his words end, another cool breeze comforts us and I can't help but to think that the two breezes we've had in the past thirty minutes have been Alex's mom. I hope she's with us, and she's watching with pride. As the breeze ends, Alex glances up to the sky with a glowing grin. I guess he's thinking the same.

"Ready for our reception?" Alex looks over toward one of the riverboats.

"Reception?" I question, looking back and forth between Alex and Celia.

"What kind of wedding did you think this was going to be?" he laughs.

He takes my hand and leads us onto a boat that looks similar to the one we had been on before.

As we walk through the boat to the back, we're greeted with thirty or so strangers who are all clapping for us, and we're escorted to a small table in the back of the boat where we only sit long enough to enjoy a bite of food. The rest of the night we spend dancing and laughing under the sparkling glow of the Eiffel Tower.

"Quite the last night to spend here in Paris," I say, wrapping my arms around Alex's neck.

He places his head on my shoulder and brushes his lips against my neck. "I try," he whispers as I feel a smile grow against my skin.

"One more song, Mrs. Levette. This is for you." His words hum. Beethoven's *Moonlight Sonata* chimes in our ears, and the song reminds me of all the great moments that have led us up to this point. We seal the last dance with a kiss that outlasts the length of the song, and when I open my eyes, the crowd on the boat is standing around us in a circle, all holding tiny votive candles in their hands, all smiling at us. Alex grabs my hand and shoots it up to the sky, announcing his *win*, and the crowd cheers with excitement.

Alex, Celia, and I gather our things and boisterously depart from the boat. While trying to manage my shoes in one hand, and the train of my dress in the other, I fall a few steps behind Alex and Celia. When I stop halfway down the dock to get a better grip on my dress, I feel a small hand wrap around my wrist. I look down toward the sensation on my arm, and my heart races with confusion. I look around to see if I can find where he could have come from, but no one is left on the boat. I look back down toward the little boy who can't be more than three years old. "Hi there, sweetie," I say. "Where are your mommy and daddy?"

He doesn't answer, but instead wraps his little hands around my leg, pressing his cheek up against my thigh.

CHAPTER TWENTY-ONE

CROSSING THRESHOLDS

"FLIGHT ATTENDANTS, PLEASE PREPARE for takeoff," the announcer recites on the loudspeaker.

My hands grip the armrests, and I clench my eyes shut as tightly as possible. My legs continue to bounce up and down with jitters running through every one of my nerves, and I have to keep reminding myself to breathe.

Alex's hand pulls on my hand, forcing my grip to release from the chair. He places my hand in between his and moves in a little closer. "It's okay. This is all normal."

"Why do we have to fly, again? Couldn't we just drift there?" I laugh. The plane is bumping along the runway, and we're picking up speed. "Besides, how many times have you been on a plane?" I ask pointedly.

"More times than you. And I think you should experience flying. So, we're flying," he chuckles.

"It's not funny," I scold him. "I'm scared we're going to crash." My words come out a little louder than I anticipate.

Alex cups his hand over my mouth, his eyes large and worried. "That's not something you yell out on a plane," he says, attempting to shush me. "Besides...this is a dream. Not a nightmare. We're not going to crash."

The plane speeds up even faster until the pressure pins me back to the seat. I can feel the plane lift off the ground, and I clench my eyes shut again. I try holding my breath, hoping it will help with this pit in my stomach, but nothing seems to help. "If this is a dream, why do I feel like I'm going to throw up?" I grumble.

"Just look out the window," Alex says.

I shake my head, keeping my eyes closed. "No way. I'm fine just like this."

He cups his hand around my chin and turns my head to face the window. "Just look. It looks just like the view from the top of the Eiffel Tower."

I peek through my squinted eyes to see millions of beautiful lights below, and I understand why this is part of my dream. "It's beautiful," I say quietly.

"Do you feel a little better now?"

"Yes," I say. "As long as we don't drop from the sky or anything."

"Chloe," he yells through a whisper. "Quit saying that stuff, you're freaking everyone out around you."

"Sorry."

"Why don't you just close your eyes for a little while," he says.

He takes the complimentary blanket out of the bag, wraps it around me, and pulls my head down onto his shoulder.

Being so late at night, I don't have to struggle too hard to fall asleep. My mind is enjoying the replay of our perfect wedding, the vows, the kiss, and the dances. I wish I could relive that every night.

Once my mind gets tired of recalling every little detail, I feel myself doze off into a deeper and darker sleep, inviting in the sounds of a soft giggle coming from what must be a child.

Where is that sound coming from? It's dark and I can't see anything, and I'm asleep. Why am I hearing this?

I force my eyes open and startle Alex who, by the looks of it, was on the verge of falling asleep.

"Are you okay?" he asks, concern darkening his eyes.

I shake my head. "I'm not." I bury my head in my hand. "Something strange happened when we left the boat and I didn't tell you about it."

"What do you mean?" He pulls my hand away from my face. "What could have happened?"

"Uh," I sigh. "It wasn't really a big deal, but a little boy came up behind me and took my hand. I asked him where his parents were. He didn't answer me, but instead wrapped his arms around my leg." My eyes drift down to my lap. I'm questioning why it's bothering me, but he gave me this weird feeling. "It really freaked me out."

Alex rubs his eyes to pull himself out of his half sleep haze. "Chloe." He laughs a little, but it sounds somewhat forced. "I'm sure he was just confused and thought you looked like his mom."

I shrug. "Maybe."

Alex's eyes start closing again. "I'm sure it was nothing. I wouldn't worry about it." He sounds bored with my train of thought. Maybe I'm overacting. He was just a lost random little boy.

Alex's eyes shut and his head drops to my shoulder. "He looked like you," I whisper in his ear.

*   *   *

Landing sucked. I almost had a panic attack. Who would have thought a plane could stop that suddenly. I thought for sure we were going to drive right off the runway. I'm not so sure I'll be in much of a rush to fly again after this trip.

Alex didn't seem too surprised when he walked in to see my empty little apartment. He said it kind of looked like my room at the institution. I didn't really know how to respond to that, but I guess the last time I felt the way I felt here was when I was in the institution.

"Let's go check out the beach," Alex says. "How far away is it?"

"You do know it's only five in the morning, right?" I mutter through a yawn.

"We slept on the plane, we're good." The eagerness in his eyes tells me he's not giving up until I show him to the beach.

I groan, accepting that we aren't getting any more sleep. "It's not too far, just a couple of blocks away."

Walking hand in hand down the streets of Charleston, I can tell he already likes it here. "It looks like a town from another era down here, huh?" he says.

I smile. "That was part of the reason I chose this place. It has history and beauty. I never really explored too much, but I'm sure we have plenty of time for that."

We plant ourselves in the sand, and sit in silence, taking in the fresh ocean air.

"Did you say that little boy looked like me?" he asks as if he just remembered what I had whispered into his ear last night. I thought he was asleep. Whoops.

"I didn't think you heard me."

"I was half asleep, and I guess it just popped back into my head." He looks over to me, his eyebrows raised with curiosity. "What were you suggesting by saying that?" I'm not sure I'm getting out of this one.

"I wasn't really suggesting anything. I just found it kind of strange."

"Hmm," he sighs. "I'm sure it was just a freak coincidence."

Alex stands up and brushes the sand off his pants. How would you feel about maybe finding a new place to rent, one that might fit a larger bed? Maybe even one I'd fit in?" he grins.

"I was going to suggest that, don't worry," I laugh.

Alex closes his eyes and takes in a deep breath of the ocean air. "I think I'm going to like this place, here with my wife."

* * *

"Wait, don't go in yet," Alex scolds with laughter.

He lifts me up and shoves the door open with his foot. "We need to do this right, Mrs. Levette."

I squeal as he rushes the door and throws me down on the couch.

We had rented the apartment a week ago and ordered furniture to be delivered before we moved in. Now that it's here, today has become our official move in date.

"I want to go see the furniture in our bedroom," I say with a flirtatious grin.

"Whatever you want, Mrs. Levette." He grunts while pulling his shirt up and over his head. He tosses his shirt across the living room, scoops me up, and carries me down to our new bedroom.

Our night blended into morning, a Monday morning. "Our honeymoon's over I guess," I say, skating my fingers along the ridges of his back.

He rolls over and sweeps the hair off my forehead. "It's not over. I just have an eight hour shift in the middle of it." He runs his fingertips down my shoulder, making me wish neither of us had to earn a living. "It's not fair that I have to work today and you don't," he groans.

"Shouldn't money just appear in our dreams?" I laugh.

"I think we've made this dream a little too real to expect money to rain from the sky."

I shrug and sigh. "Oh well, I guess." I fling the sheets off of us. "You'll know where to find me when you get done with your shift." I unzip my backpack and pull out my bikini while shooting him an evil smirk.

"You're a brat." He throws his pillow in my face.

"And you're going to be late for work." I whip it back at him.

* * *

Our new favorite dock has become our meeting place for when one of us gets off a shift. The beach is empty and quiet and it's the perfect spot to relax. With my eyes closed and my face soaking up the sun, I feel something soft bounce off my ankle, startling me out of my cloud. I glance down and see a small beach ball rolling around a couple of inches from my feet. I lean forward, pick it up, and look around to see who might have lost it. But there really isn't anyone close enough that might have thrown it. I look up at the dock above my head, and my mouth gapes open with disbelief. It's him again. The little boy with blond curls has his head hanging over the edge. I place my hand above my eyes as a visor from the sun, looking straight up at him. When he notices my focus, a large smile grows across his face and he waves at me with eagerness.

I stand up and look for the end of the dock. When I fix my eyes on the end where the wood meets the sand, I sprint over to it. But when I look down to the end of the dock, I see nothing but water at the end. My gaze scans the beach, looking for any other hint that this little boy actually exists, but there's no one in sight.

When an unexpected hand lands on my shoulder, I jerk around to see who it is. When I gasp with shock, Alex places both of his warm hands on my shoulders and looks at me with concern. "What's going on? Are you okay?"

"I just saw him again, that little boy from the wedding. He was there." I point toward the end of the dock. "And he dropped his ball on me from up there."

"What ball?" He searches behind me, looking for a hint of what I might be talking about.

When I turn around to show him, I see that it's gone.

"Chloe, I think you're still suffering from jetlag. Why don't we get home and take a nap." He takes my hand and pulls me in the direction of our apartment. Reluctantly, I follow him. I know what I saw, and it wasn't a result of exhaustion.

"Alex, I'm not suffering from jetlag. Why don't you believe me?" He thinks I'm making up stories, or seeing things. Maybe both. I know I'm not imagining this little boy.

He doesn't respond, but instead continues dragging me along. I pull my hand out of his and stop so he'll stop too.

"Why won't you answer me?" The irritation in my voice is obvious.

Alex looks up to the sky and pulls in a sharp breath. "Because." He throws his arms up. "I don't know what to say to you." He's getting angry, and I'm not sure why. He must really think I'm making up stories. Why won't he even consider that something unusual might be going on?

"Let's go sit down for a few minutes," he says in a soft voice, sounding apologetic for the way he just snapped at me.

We walk over to the next dock and sit down on one of the benches overlooking the water. He grips his hands together and rests them over his lap. After a couple minutes of silence, he says, "I saw him too, and I've been trying to figure out who he is. I haven't said anything to you, because I haven't quite figured it out for myself yet." He doesn't look up at my widened eyes, at my gaping mouth, the redness on my face from the anger within me. He just continues staring down at his fidgeting hands, pretending that I'm not going to blow up at any second.

With my mind racing and searching for an answer, I twist my body to face him, staring at his bowed head. "Why have you been making it out like I'm crazy then?" I ask, grinding the sand beneath my feet. "Who do you think he is?"

He keeps his eyes set on the wooden planks below us. "I really don't know, Chloe." He wraps his hand around his neck and sighs.

I try to calm myself down. I try to remember that we're in this together. I try to remind myself that things aren't always what they seem, even in my dreams.

I place my hand down over his unsteady fingers. "This might be out in left field, but have you ever considered the thought of having a child?" I ask.

He pulls his hands out from under mine and snaps his head up to look at me. "Why are you asking me this while we're in the middle of trying to figure out who this little boy is?"

I drop my head into the palms of my hands, resting my elbows on my knees. "I don't know. Don't you think it's weird that he looks like you?"

Alex directs his gaze back toward the ground. "That's ridiculous, Chloe. Besides, I am worried about having kids. What if he ends up like us, or worse?"

"You think our child would be a he?" I ask.

"He or she, whatever the case would be, I'd be worried for them," he says.

I sit up straight, turning to face him again. Hurt seems to be playing its part in my heart as I realize now that maybe we should have spoken about this before getting married. "I always thought I would have a baby or two. I never really thought to ask you how you felt on the subject. I shouldn't have assumed I guess…"

A pained expression grows on his face as he places his hand on my lap. "Chloe, I didn't say I didn't want kids. I just haven't really thought about it. Besides, wouldn't you be worried about what they might be like?"

I take a minute to ponder whether I'd be worried for our future child ending up like us. To me, the answer is simple. I would love him or her no matter what they were like. "Yes, and no. I mean you have to realize that my outcome would have been a lot better if my mother didn't treat me and raise me the way she did, and as for you, you may have been completely unaffected by your condition if you hadn't gotten into that car accident," I shrug. "My condition has prohibited me from doing most things in my life, but I never thought of it as stopping me from having a family, I guess."

Alex slides his finger under my chin and lifts my face so my gaze meets his. "Chloe, if you want to have children, I would never argue with that, but it doesn't mean I won't worry about them."

"I love that about you," I grin. "That means a lot."

"I'm not sure either of us is ready right now, though."

"I'm not ready right now either, but do you think that little boy is connected to us in some…way? If you know what I mean?"

"No, I don't know what you mean?" His words come tumbling out of his mouth. Why is he making me spell this out? I know he knows what I'm thinking.

Fine, if he wants me to make myself clearer, then I will. "What if that little boy belongs to us?"

He clears his throat and stands up from the bench. With a fake throaty laugh, he says, "That's impossible. I think you would have known if you had a baby." Making me feel foolish for asking such a question isn't going to sway me from my thoughts.

I tug on his hand and pull myself up from the bench. "Alex." I raise an eyebrow. "He looks just like you. There's no denying that."

He closes his eyes and takes in a long deep breath. "I know he does. I'm not denying it."

CHAPTER TWENTY-TWO

BEING OUT OF THE KNOW

ANY TIME WE'VE BEEN TO THE BEACH over the past few weeks, Sammy, our cute little blonde-haired mystery boy has shown up. He doesn't ever appear to be with anyone, which I can't help but find odd. He's a little young to be wandering around by himself. Yet, by the way he speaks, he sounds wise beyond his age.

When he sees us he usually approaches Alex with a ball and begs him to play. Although the situation is beyond strange, I think it's adorable the way Alex has become so engrossed with him. I just wish I could get more information out of him.

We both find ourselves worrying a lot about where he is when he isn't with us. I've tried asking him where he goes when he doesn't see us, but anytime I ask, he gets upset and runs off. Alex doesn't say much about it, and it makes me wonder what he's thinking. I try to consider that when I find myself nagging him with questions.

Other than entertaining our little buddy when we're on the beach, we've both been working a lot. The nights when neither of us is working turn into date night, making married life exactly how I imagined it would be. I love every second of it. It's hard to believe it's been exactly one year since Alex and I attempted to run away together. I never expected that day to turn out like this.

I gently nudge Alex out of his deep sleep and kiss him on the cheek, pulling the sheets over his shoulders. "Happy one year of escaping our imprisoned life," I whisper in his ear.

He turns over, props himself up on his elbow and looks at me carefully. "Has it really been a year?" he asks, with a raspy and tired voice.

"Crazy, huh? I was thinking we should celebrate tonight," I say, pushing a blond spiral away from his forehead.

"You got it." He smiles, but it's quick to fade as his eyes close again.

I playfully push him back over and he flops backward on the bed, "You're so lazy," I giggle.

He pulls the pillow over his face, muffling his words. "Love you, have fun at work."

The second I step outside, I regret not looking out the window before I left the apartment. It's raining, and not the drizzly annoying rain, but the large thud, get you soaked in thirty-seconds type of rain. It's just another reason why we need a car. We've been in a debate about the need for a car for the past couple of months. I want one, and he's made it abundantly clear that he doesn't. I'm just not sure why. Although, I can guess the car accident might have something to do with this. And I suppose I can understand that.

I throw the hood of my zip-up sweatshirt over my head, and walk at a fast pace, being careful to avoid the three-inch deep puddles—not that it'll matter by the time I get to work since I'll be completely drenched anyway. The rainstorms here are nothing to joke about.

I keep my head down, attempting to keep the rain out of my face, but I'm alarmed when I hear a small shriek coming from ahead. When I lift my head up, I see a woman and a small boy walking ahead of me at a quick pace, carefully avoiding each puddle. The mother is holding an umbrella, and she's tugging on her child's arm, dragging him through the streets. The little boy is pulling back on his mother's arm, trying to pull his hand out of hers. He's almost to the point of throwing himself onto the ground to get away from her.

Just as they're about to turn a corner, the little boy gets his way and slips out of his mother's grip. He twists around and runs in my direction.

"Hey," I shout to him.

I run in his direction, first to help him, and second to see the woman pulling him down the street. But before I can get close enough, the woman turns around and grabs him by the arm and he goes flying back in the opposite direction screaming, "Mama."

The mother looks up at me with a look of fear that's draining her complexion of color. I become so startled with awareness that I stop and grab a hold of the nearest wall to keep me from falling.

"Kiera?" I cry out.

I try pulling myself along the wall for support, but she takes off fast, pulling the little boy behind her. What the fuck is going on?

The wall lets me down, and my legs give out below me. The first thought that enters my mind is an unfortunate one. I consider the possibility that Alex and Kiera's past has resulted in this little boy being their child. It would explain why the little boy looks like Alex and why she looked so afraid to see me? It's obvious that she knows something, something I'm not supposed to know. How could he not tell me? How could I have not known? Why would I just be finding this out now? Where has this little boy been all along?

I don't even know what to think right now. I can't imagine that Alex would have kept this a secret. We took vows to always be truthful with each other, and now I find this out? But this makes no sense. If that little boy is around three, or so he looks, that means that Alex was with Kiera a year before we met. He said he hadn't been with her the three years prior to when we met. This isn't adding up.

So now what? Do I ask Alex? I have to. I should have known this was all too good to be true, just like everything else in my stupid discombobulated life. I can't go to work right now. I feel sick to my stomach. I'm going to be sick. I run back to our apartment and shove the door open, startling Alex who sits straight up.

"Are you okay, Chloe? What happened?" He jumps out of bed and starts toward me. "Sweetie, you're soaked." He sprints into the bathroom and grabs a towel for me.

I place my hands on my hips and step forward with my teeth clenched together. "When were you going to tell me? Huh?" I walk a little closer. "How long were you going to let me think he was just some random little boy?"

The color drains from *his* face, giving me confirmation that he knows something.

He walks closer to me. "What are you talking about?" he asks, placing the towel around my shoulders.

"That little boy is your son, isn't he?" I shove my finger into his chest.

He takes my hand and moves it away. "How many times do I have to tell you how ridiculous that thought is?"

"I just saw him with Kiera. *Now* what do you have to say?" I ask, narrowing my eyes at him.

"You found Kiera? She's here, in Charleston?" he asks. He truthfully appears perplexed. But I'm not buying it.

"Oh please, like you didn't know," I snap back.

"Will you stop it?" He slaps his hands down by his side. "I did not know Kiera was here. She shouldn't be here, okay?"

"Why *shouldn't* she be here?" Anger is searing through my body, and I feel like I'm seconds from my skin ripping open and exposing the Hulk within me.

"Because, she was gone?" he says simply, as if the answer should have been obvious.

What kind of answer is that? My stomach is churning with pain. "Have you been cheating on me?" I ask, trying my hardest to conceal the hot tears that are burning the back of my eyes.

"What?" His voice plunges with sadness. "You think I'd...cheat on you?" He says the word *cheat* as if it's a cuss word, and he buries his eyebrows below his lashes, looking disgusted that I could suggest such a thing.

"Well, why is she here then? Why is she with that little boy? Why does that little boy look like you?" I can't stop the interrogation. I want answers, and I want them now. He knows why she's here and he knows who that little boy is. And I know I'm not giving up until he tells me what the hell is going on.

"I suppose you won't accept me saying, I really don't know, as an answer?" Is he seriously offering me a cheesy smile right now? I'm about to slap him, and he's trying to make a joke.

"No!" I shout. I release an exaggerated groan and the incessant nerves creeping up my body cause me to start pacing the room in circles.

"First off, I did not cheat on you." Hearing those words calm my nerves only a little. But it's obvious by his introduction that there's more to this. Stuff he's been hiding. "But?" I say, widening my eyes with a clearly ticked off scowl.

I watch as his Adam's apple bobs up and down along the center of his throat. "Second, I never even slept with Kiera. So, you can get that thought right out of your head. I truly don't know why she's here."

"What?" Hearing this actually surprises me. I sort of just assumed that they had *been* together in every way. "Wait. Was I your first?" The question causes my face to burn from a fiery blush. The topic still embarrasses me I guess.

"Yes? Why is that so shocking?" He's clearly insulted by my question.

I place my hand on his arm. I think it's my turn for a peace offering. "I'm sorry for accusing you."

"You have to stop assuming I'm trying to hurt you. No matter what happens in our life, I'm never doing anything other than trying to protect you. Haven't I made that clear?" He pulls his arm out from under my hand, and my stomach immediately twinges with pain. "How can I prove it to you? Defying myself to be a slave for Franco in order to keep you safe wasn't enough of a reason for you?"

My eyes fall toward the ground. Suddenly, I'm the asshole. "You have, and I'm sorry." I turn back for the front door. "I'm late for work."

Alex's fingers wrap around my wrist and he pulls me around to face him. "I will never do anything to hurt you, Chloe. Stop thinking it." He pulls me in against him and places a kiss on the top of my sopping wet hair. "Whatever surprises life throws at us are meant to be surprises." Yeah. And I hate surprises. If my life were mapped out with detailed instructions on what road to take, I would take the road most traveled. I yearn to be normal, and I know I'll never have that.

My walk back has turned into a run. At least the rain has stopped, but my mind is still cloudy, trying to figure out the meaning of Kiera reappearing, and why that little boy looks like Alex. My head could probably come up with four hundred different reasons for it, but for whatever reason, I'm not supposed to know this answer. I don't know if I have the ability to let this go, but for the sake of my marriage, it might be in my best interest to pretend. Somehow, I need to promise myself that I will attempt to live a normal life and stop probing at each crazy event that happens to me.

I try to clear my mind throughout my shift, but I start to feel guilty for attacking Alex the way I did. He didn't deserve that. The little boy has blond hair and blue eyes—so do millions of other little boys. Kiera being here is still irking me, but I believe that he doesn't know why she's here.

I watch as the hour hand ticks on to the four, and I lace my fingers through the tie on the back of my apron. With the bell chiming on the door, I turn to greet one last customer before the end of my shift, but I see it's Alex who's standing in the doorway with a bouquet of flowers.

I walk over to him with a sheepish grin. "I should probably be the one giving you flowers," I say with a pout.

"Forget about it. It's been a year since we somewhat ran away together. Even if it's only in our minds," he laughs and hands me the flowers. "We're celebrating tonight, whether you're crazy or not," he grins.

"Where are we going to celebrate?" I raise an eyebrow. "My cell or yours?"

He laughs softly and places his hands around my shoulders, looking me expressively in my eyes. "Baby, we're locked in one love cell, together. Remember?" He blushes, and I know he's trying to hold a serious expression.

I slap my palm against my forehead. "Oh, right. I forgot."

"We're just going to the beach. I packed us a picnic."

"I guess that'll do too."

We sit on the empty beach, covered with a blanket to hide from a cool breeze. We both sit quietly watching the sun dip down into the ocean. "You've been kind of quiet," I mumble, shoving the last of my sandwich in my mouth. "Everything okay?"

"I'm just thinking, that's all," he says.

"I was wondering what that pained expression was?" I laugh, but he doesn't laugh with me.

"I was just contemplating our life," he sighs and stares down at his knotted bracelet. He clears his throat, and I immediately know he's going to drop a bomb on me when he does that. "You want me to be honest with you, right?" Color is disappearing from his cheeks, and I think mine as well.

With the sudden sensation of a boulder bouncing into the pit of my stomach, I say, "Yes, I do."

"I need you to understand something, and I need you to respect something for your own good," he says, staring at me straight in the eyes.

"Oh…okay," I choke out. I feel my eyes becoming larger, and I'm losing my thoughts while looking at his colorless complexion.

He grabs my hands and I can't help but recall other times he's started a conversation like this. "You know how I was able to live in another time, right?"

"Yes." I already think I know where this is going, but I'll hear him out.

"Maybe we should just pretend like I'm psychic and I know what the future holds. Would that be easier for you to deal with?" he asks, squinting one eye shut, anticipating whatever reaction is brewing in my mind.

His question hits me hard. I've always wondered if that may be the case, but hearing the truth makes me wonder what else I should be questioning.

He knows what our future holds.

He has always known.

And that is why he's usually so calm about everything.

"Oh. So you know what lies ahead of us, and I don't?" I funnel the sand through my hands, trying to push my focus onto something else besides the rupturing jealousy coercing through my body. "Let me guess. You're not going to tell me what you know." I can't help but unleash the hostility in my voice. I already know his response. If he wanted me to know I would have already been aware of this little hidden secret.

"Chloe, I hate that I know what our future holds. I want to experience life just like you get to. Knowing what's going to happen takes the excitement out of life, and it's almost like a punishment. I don't want to hide things from you, but I do, to protect you from losing the good things in life." He places his two hands around my fist that's releasing the mist of sand, keeping the grains bottled up inside of my hand. "Could I ask you for the biggest favor I'll ever ask you?"

"Can I say no?" I tighten my eyes and look out into the darkening ocean, feeling trapped like the sand that's being smothered within my clenched fist

"Yes, but I would beg you to change your mind. Do you trust me?" he asks.

I sigh with annoyance. "Yes, unfortunately."

"So that I don't have to feel like I'm hiding things from you, could you manage to go through life knowing that I might know *some* of what's in store for us?"

"Why can't you just tell me what's going to happen? Or what if there's a specific occurrence that I want to know about? Would you tell me then?" I can't control my voice from escalating with an uneasy excitement.

"I don't want to. That's not the way life should be lived," he says. "Besides, I don't know what's going to happen every moment, but I have drifted to other times and I've seen certain changes occur in our lives. I don't usually know when they happened or how they happened, but it's almost like I get to read the last page of every chapter of our life. I feel like I'm cheating life, and it's a horrible way to live. I want you to enjoy life the way it's meant to be lived. Would you do that for both of us?"

"Can I just ask you one question?"

"No, because I know what it is."

"It's not the question you think I'm going to ask, but okay." I know I probably sound more irritated than I should.

"I was nervous, Chloe. That's why it took so long for me to come talk to you. Just because I took the fun out of life's surprises doesn't mean you didn't make me nervous. I didn't know when we were supposed to meet, or how. You could have told me to go away two hundred times before you would actually agree to get to know me." His eyes lose focus and he snickers, relishing in his own memories.

"How did you know that was my question?" I ask, now wondering if he can read my mind too.

"Because I know you would have asked one of two questions if I agreed to answer them. And I'm sure that would have been one of them. Am I wrong?"

I laugh and nod. "That was precisely what I was wondering. Well, one of the things."

He releases my hands, allowing the sand to escape. "Do you hate me?" he asks, nudging me back and forth.

"Hate you for feeling cursed?" I press my cheek into his shoulder. "I feel bad that you can't enjoy life like you want me to. It's sad." I've never wanted anything other than a normal life, and at least Alex is giving me that option.

With the winds picking up, we wrap up our picnic and head back to our apartment. Our walk is quiet and full of my own murky thoughts. I have so much I want to ask and know, but I can't. I don't know if I'd be strong enough to keep these types of secrets from him.

"Hey so, what's the weather going to be like in sixty-one days from today?" I ask, shoving my shoulder into his.

"Funny, Chloe," he chuckles, attempting to conceal a smile.

"Who wins the world series in 2015?" I ask, looping my arm around his elbow.

Alex wraps his arm around my neck and pulls me into his body. "Shush. That's enough," he roars with laughter.

"Would you rather me ask you these questions, or more serious ones?" I test with a more grave tone.

"I'd rather you pretend like I didn't know the truth." He squeezes me a little tighter.

*   *   *

My eyes are heavy and my mind is pulling my consciousness to a sedated location. We seem to have our nights and mornings a little mixed up, and exhaustion seems to be getting the best of me in the comforts of Alex's arms, within the contours of our bed. Just as my mind is on the brink of barrenness, Alex whispers unexpected words into my ear. "You're going to be an amazing mom some day." He seals the words with a soft kiss on my forehead, and I increase the depth of my breathing to assure him that I'm asleep and didn't really hear what he intended only my unconscious mind to comprehend.

CHAPTER TWENTY-THREE

BETTER LEFT IN THE DARK

IT'S TAKEN ME A LITTLE TIME to accept that Alex has already lived through parts of our future, and I'm still not sure if I can wrap my head around it. I thought it was weird when we were able to visit an earlier era, but I never considered the fact that Alex could have known what *our* future holds. Now that I know we're capable of doing it, I often feel tempted to look for myself. But whenever I bring up the thought, he begs me not to. He wishes he didn't know anything of what is to come. He said he hasn't drifted to any future times since we met, but the few times he did it was enough to show him too much of what he shouldn't have known.

I've been trying to put it out of my head since he told me last week, but questions keep popping up in my mind and I'm struggling to mask the urge to ask him a million questions. On top of that, the thought of Kiera wandering around the area with that little boy is still puzzling me.

The worst part is, I actually miss Kiera, and I wish I could have her back as a friend. I wish I didn't have to think that she had some deep dark secret that I was never even tipped off about. It worries me to think that I knew her so little, that she could potentially be in cahoots with Franco. I guess I can only hope that she disappeared from my life for a different reason.

All I know is, the amount of unanswered questions piling up in my life is becoming more of a burden than anything else, and chasing the definition of normal is becoming tedious. It seems that the harder I try to accomplish normalcy, the farther away the goal becomes.

Not only have I not seen Kiera since that weird rainy day, but also, sadly, I haven't seen the little boy since then either. I hope he's okay.

When I express my concerns to Alex, he appeases me by telling me not to worry and says everything is fine with the little boy. But of course that just brings up more questions on how Alex knows about him. I have my speculations, but no proof and no answers. I feel like I'm living my life on edge, waiting for each new page to turn and reveal another surprise, but the surprises are only in my life and for my benefit. Because this is only happening within my mind.

I'm not sure how much more I can take. There's only one way to release the intense suspense I've been feeling when I think about what might be coming. I have to give into the urge. I have to try and drift to a future time. It's the only way to fix myself.

I don't know how to do it and I don't know if it will work since I'm already in a drift right now, but I feel like I should just try. I won't tell Alex. I would already know what he knows, so I don't think it would be an issue. And plus, it's not like I'd have to keep any secrets from him—we'd just be on the same page. I know I'm trying to convince myself this is the right thing to do. But I know it's not. I also know my mind is going to win this round.

I have a half hour before Alex meets me here on the beach, and there's no one around. The clouds are a perfect focal point to help me briefly lose myself, and the darkness is calling my name. I lie back and stare through the sky, picturing myself older and with Alex. I can see our hair starting to gray, our skin not as tight, and our hands still interlocked walking down the shores of a beach. With a deep breath, I focus even harder on what I want to see.

The sand below me turns into a solid formation of plastic, the sky glows with a white light, the water vaporizes beneath me, and one by one, each cloud turns into a solid panel on the wall.

I swallow hard, pushing away my fears, but the temperature drops, and a shadow of darkness covers me with fog. I shift my weight to regain my bearings, but pain shoots through my stomach. The alarming sensation snaps me out of my drift faster than I had planned. The sight I'm faced with startles me into a panic. My hands grip the padding of the floor, and I grit my teeth together as each of my nerves wake up with an unexpected all over discomfort.

My abdomen is swollen. Very swollen. My ankles are swollen, and my back is aching from the position I've been sitting in for months.

I can't comprehend the outcome to this, or how this will work. I never thought this far ahead or considered this possibility. What if this happens here, in this padded room? I need to know how much longer I have. I don't even know if this is current or in the future.

I have to assume this is in the future. I've always had a connection with my physical feelings in both my mind and body, and I haven't felt any kind of *this* type of discomfort, until now.

From the looks of it, it's been eight or nine months since the discomfort began. How will I know when I have to come back here to make sure we are safe?

I can't have a baby in this room.

It has to be on the other side, where Alex is conscious and we're not confined without any medical assistance.

I never should have come here.

Through each moment of pain, I close my eyes and visualize my life back in Charleston, sitting on the beach and staring at the clouds. With each second of the pain subsiding, I feel a sensation of relief. I feel the sun warming my body, the breeze cooling my face and I open my eyes, left with a desire to kiss the sand below me.

I'm breathless and a wreck. Kids are not a good idea for us. It's just something I'm going to have to get past.

I hear the sand crunching behind me, and I try to take a few quick breaths so Alex won't see the likely flushed look coating my face.

He sits down next to me and puts his arm around me. "How was your day?" he asks, kicking off his shoes and twisting his baseball cap around so he can see me.

"Fine," I respond. I know my voice sounds dejected and flat. And I know he's going to ask me what's wrong, so I keep my eyes drawn to the sand to prolong the inevitable.

He leans his head around to try and get my attention. "Hey? What's wrong?" Well that took three seconds.

"Nothing," I laugh, trying to hide the remorse that's driving through me at ninety-miles an hour after seeing the slippery when wet sign.

He leans back and lays his head over his crossed arms. "Hmm. Okay, I don't believe you, but if you don't want to talk about it, that's fine too."

I pull myself together, lean back to be with him and look at his nose, since I can't look in his eyes. "I'm really okay. I'm just tired I think. Don't worry." I force an unquestionably fake smile.

He sits back up and slides his shoes back on. "Let's get home then. Maybe you just need..." He coughs through the word "me." Then he clears his throat. "I mean a good night's sleep," he grins impishly. I'm going to try and ignore his insinuation, because the thought of what could result from that now, takes most of... No. All of the fun away.

We walk home along the shore, cutting through some back roads, making small talk about work and the weather. I can't think of anything else to say, and my mind can't seem to get rid of the image of myself sitting in a padded cell, very pregnant and very miserable.

As we climb into bed much earlier than usual, Alex pulls me in, turns on the charm, and lets his lips trail across my neck. His hand slides under the back of my shirt and smoothly begins pulling it up. I'm currently having an internal battle. My body is so weak in his hands.

Pain. Fear. A baby in a fucking padded cell.

"Stop."

He laughs and skates his hand around my back and over to my stomach.

"Alex. Stop." I pull away, creating a few feet of space in between us. "Not tonight. I'm sorry."

I've never said no. I've never wanted to. I don't like the way this feels. Any of it.

"Oh, sure. I'm sorry...I didn't mean to..." Embarrassment flashes across his flushed skin.

"It's fine." I sound like a bitch. But it's not like an explanation would exactly fix that right now.

I fluff my pillow and turn over to face the opposite direction. "It's not you Alex, don't worry." I shouldn't have just said that. I sense the thoughts stirring in his head.

I feel him sit up in bed and flick the lamp back on. "I wasn't worried it was me, Chloe. I'm worried about why you've been so quiet and what's going through your mind. I didn't just meet you yesterday, you know?"

I sit up and bring my knees to my chest with a discomforting twinge caused from my heart and stomach wrestling with each other. "We should probably start being more careful again. Maybe you should get birth control or something?" I plant my face in my knees.

He leans over and kisses the top of my head. "I agree with that. I know we stopped worrying so much lately, but I don't think either of us is ready for what could happen." I don't think he has any idea of what that really means. Clearly, what I saw, wasn't part of one of his future visits.

He lies back down and turns the lamp off. We both lie there silently in the dark, both staring up to the ceiling. I'm counting down the seconds until this conversation continues.

"Chloe, what made you all the sudden become concerned about that? Don't get me wrong, I'm not arguing with you, but it just seems a little out of the blue."

And there it is. I can't lie, but I don't want to tell him what I did either. My silence will probably answer the question for itself.

"Chloe?" His voice breaks through the unbearable silence.

I sit up and bow my head down. "I'm sorry."

"You didn't," he whispers. I can hear grief filling his voice.

I lift my head and look at him, hoping if he looks me in the eyes he won't get as upset with me.

"Why would you do that? I nearly begged you not to, and not for my sake, for yours."

I cover my hands over my face, and suck the smothered air up through my nose. "Okay, well it's too late."

He places his hand on my back. "What happened when you were wherever you were?"

"Me, pregnant..." I trail off, not sure how to continue.

"Well, that's okay, isn't it? We decided we wanted to have kids." He settles back down into his pillow, thinking that's the worst of it. "Just please, Chloe, don't be tempted to keep doing what you did. It's so bad for your life. Trust me," he says, letting me off the hook way too easily.

"Alex, I was very pregnant in the padded cell, alone and next to your unconscious body."

His hand twists into the back of my shirt. "Are you sure?"

"I know what I saw and felt. So, that's why I want to be careful."

"Chloe, you know it doesn't matter if we're careful or not. If you experienced it, it's inevitable. You've technically already lived through it," he explains. His voice and thoughts are abrupt and bursting through his mouth.

"I don't understand that?" Yes I do. I don't want to understand that.

"You're not supposed to…" he snaps back. "Everything will be the way it's supposed to. Just please, don't… just don't do that again. It's going to ruin everything."

"Alex, trust me. I don't want to see anything else. Can we just go to sleep? I can't think about this anymore."

He leans over and kisses the side of my head and rests his head back down. I hear him breathing heavily after only a few minutes. Even though I was the one who was exhausted, I have a feeling I won't be able to sleep tonight. I'm afraid to go to sleep.

After hours of stirring, my eyes find their way closed, and I fall heavily into a deep sleep, pulling my nightmares back into revisit my fragile mind. I keep seeing the same scene I lived through this afternoon. Except the movie in my head stops before I see the outcome or any acknowledgement that everything turns out okay like Alex is promising.

I don't believe that this can happen if we do everything possible to prevent it. It's what I'm going to do. We have to. He can't be aware of what I'm going to live through, or he would have been more careful in the first place.

Reluctant as I've always been to go visit any type of doctor, I'm going tomorrow. I want to take as many precautions as necessary. I don't know if sex with Alex here in our drift can make me pregnant there, but I want to take as many precautions as necessary. Therefore, whatever pill they can give me to prevent what I saw today is what I need. Maybe I should see if Ashley can smuggle birth control to me in the institution. Who knows what's going on in that cell?

* * *

The waiting room is filled with pregnant women, reminding me of what my stomach looked like yesterday. It's an honest reminder of how not ready I am for any of this. I pull a magazine from the table beside me and go through the motions, trying to focus on what I'm reading. But with my leg twitching, and the lady beside me rubbing her belly, I can't concentrate on anything else. I can only hope they call me in soon.

After an hour of bouncing my knee up and down and coming close to the verge of multiple panic attacks, I see a clipboard appear from the door, followed by hearing my name.

I lower my head with embarrassment for a reason I'm unsure of and hurry through the door. I'm escorted to a nearby room and handed a hospital gown and a cup. At this moment, I consider my options of escape. I don't want to do this anymore, and I'd rather just give up that part of married life, which I'm sure Alex might have a thing or two to say about. But it is what it is.

While I hesitate to reach for the gown and the cup, the nurse closes the door behind her. I'm locked in. The walls are moving in closer, and the ceiling and floor are crowding my five-foot-tall frame. I need air. I clutch the collar of my shirt and pull it out as far as it will go. But it isn't helping. My head feels like it's filled with water, and a buzzing noise circulates around me. I hear muffled words in what sounds like the far distance, but the room is like a box. Just as I feel like I might fall backwards, a cold hand is placed down over my knuckles. "Dear? Are you okay?" She taps her fingers on my hand again. "Is this your first time here, hon?"

My eyes dart to the hanging pictures of smiling babies and then to the dozens of pamphlets on *how to prevent pregnancy*. When the queasiness in my head tempers, I try to reconnect my senses and focus my attention back on the nurse, who's now observing me as if I was a two-headed monster. "Yes, it is," I say quietly.

"This is just a normal procedure. It's nothing to worry about." She smiles kindly, and I can see by her expression that I'm probably not the first newbie to freak out in this room.

I laugh nervously and move toward the door that we just entered through. "You know, I just saw the time, and I actually have to be at work in twenty minutes." I force out another sheepish laugh. "I'll reschedule on my way out. I apologize for wasting your time."

The nurse places her hand on my shoulder. "Ms. Levette, if you've never done this before, it would be a wise decision to stay. I'd be remiss to let you run out these doors without seeking protection for yourself if that's what you originally came here for."

I know she's right, and I know I'm just uncomfortable, but I suppose this *is* necessary, or I wouldn't have come. A flash of the bloody padded cell whizzes through my mind, and the image is enough to persuade my mind back to the exam table.

She lifts her other hand with the gown and the cup and holds it back up to me. "Please, do yourself a favor," she says in a kind voice.

I take the items from her hand and watch as she walks out of the door, leaving me here alone with these damn four walls that will probably close in on me again once the doctor arrives. I attempt to work through the cold sweat that seems to be interfering with my ability to think straight, but I do as she asked and return the cup back on the counter.

I hop up on the paper-covered table and pinch the back of the gown shut. I settle on the edge, impatient and uncomfortable as I wait.

Three light taps on the door sound before it opens. The nurse pokes her head back in, looks at me, smiles, picks up the cup, and turns to walk back out. "The doctor will be in shortly. Everything will be over before you know it," she says as she closes the door again.

Cold and awkward, I remain seated on the table for what must have been a half an hour. Three knocks on the door sound again and the doorknob twists, as does my stomach. A female doctor with short blond hair, large unblinking eyes, and a straight line for a smile, enters the room.

She reaches her hand out to me without looking up from her clipboard. "Hi Chloe, I'm Dr. Faith."

I shake her hand, and feel a little more at ease, but I'm not sure why.

"So, I hear that you are here to acquire birth control?" she asks, jotting notes down on my chart.

Flushed, I nod my head in agreement. It would be wonderful if she could lower her voice. I can't imagine how many people in the hall just heard that. And I don't want to think about the amount of people who will be eyeballing me when I do the walk of shame out of this room.

"Hmm," she says with her eyebrows pulling. "Chloe, I want you to do me a favor and lay back for me." She pulls the paper liner on the table backward and taps the headrest. I lie back. Sweat beads on every inch of my skin and I clench my eyes shut. I'm not sure what I'm hiding from right this second, but the darkness makes me feel better. I hear her press a button under the table, which causes me to recline backwards until I'm lying flat. I feel so vulnerable and uncomfortable.

I continue waiting with my eyes closed, trying to imagine I'm somewhere else. Now would be a great time to drift. My nerves are building up with an awful anticipation until I feel my gown shift to the side and a cold object placed on my stomach.

"I need you to hold still for just a moment," the doctor instructs.

I open my eyes to see a little black monitor next to the table.

"What is that?" I ask, my breath suddenly sharp and not flowing out of my lungs, as it should.

"It's an ultrasound machine," she says matter-of-factly. "I'd like to confirm the positive pregnancy test you just took."

I don't need to hear anymore. That's all it takes. My mind shuts off and I'm lost within the confines of my brain. I'm drifting, I'm not conscious, and I'm not unconscious. I'm just in oblivion, trying to avoid the ultimate outcome of my unlikely future.

Something cold and wet is covering my head, and I try to peel my eyes open. "Chloe? Can you hear me?"

My eyes open to see the black screen has been turned off and pushed back into the corner of the room. Please tell me she didn't just say what I think she did. My life is as good as over. I'll probably die there in that padded cell.

"Did you confirm it?" I ask, my voice trembling with fear.

She sits down on her stool and rolls herself over to the side of the table where I'm sitting. "I'm sorry, Chloe. Your ultrasound was inconclusive. It showed that there was in fact no fetus in there. You likely suffered from a chemical pregnancy." Her words come out as if she says them hundreds of times a day. Is losing a baby this common? Must be, since she's handing me a pamphlet labeled "How To Cope With A Loss."

I feel relieved, but worried by what the definition of a chemical pregnancy is. I find my hand smothering my chest, feeling for my heart, and waiting for it to steady. "What does that mean?"

"It means that you *were* pregnant, but unfortunately, the fetus didn't make it. There isn't a definitive explanation, but the fact is, there is not a baby at this time. However, I would like to have you back to check on you once more next week," she says, pushing the button under the table, elevating me to a sitting position.

"Do you mind if I ask why?" I should try to remember how to blink my eyes. I think I'm in shock. I think I'm confused. I think I'm not happy about this.

She scribbles something within the notes of my file and clips the pen into the clipboard as she looks up at me with the same straight face she first came in with. "Standard procedure for these occurrences."

With no questions left, the doctor looks back at the charts, hangs it back up on the wall, and reaches for the door. "I'll see you next week, Chloe." The door closes, and I hear the doctor knocking on the next patient's room.

I feel startled with information, left here alone to digest the fact that I actually had a baby growing inside of me, and now it's gone. It was a baby made from Alex and me, and now it's gone. I suddenly feel guilty for feeling the amount of relief I felt for that split second. I shouldn't feel that way about a baby that never got a chance at life — my baby that didn't make it.

Unexpected tears trickle down my cheeks, and I wish that Alex were here with me.

CHAPTER TWENTY-FOUR

WHAT WILL NOT BE—WILL BE

WHEN I TOLD ALEX WHAT CONSPIRED at the doctor's office, I fell to pieces, and he fell with me. Watching as his mouth dropped open, his eyes saddened and the color on his face washed away, my heart broke even more. Neither of us are ready for the responsibility that we almost had, but knowing that we lost it, makes it more wanted.

My timing isn't good since he has to leave for work only minutes after we finish discussing our unknown loss. I can only imagine how long his shift must seem to him. Because for me, I know I only want to be in his arms right now. It's the comfort I know I need. Instead, I'm sitting here feeling sick to my stomach from dwelling on what could have been.

I curl up on the couch, wrap my arms around a pillow, and cry myself to sleep. My heart feels heavy and I just want to go back to the way I felt ten hours ago. Visions of a tiny baby being happy in our arms are stolen by a dark shadow. Birthing a baby on the white padded floor, leaving behind only streaks of blood, and my body flattened to the ground burns my mind. The vision of Alex and I lying on the floor together next to our toddler who's about to take his first step appears and disappears just as fast when I hear the front door open. My body startles out of my unwanted dream, and I feel Alex's cold body climb on top of me and cradle me tightly within his arms.

We lie on the couch, half asleep and half awake, focused on how cruel life can be. "We can still have a baby, Chloe. This doesn't have to be the end," he says, his voice strained.

"I don't know. Having a baby in a padded cell doesn't sound too wonderful," I remind him.

He pulls in a long sharp breath near my ear and rests his head back down on my back. "That is not your end. Trust me." After being entangled on the couch for hours, my tears have worn me out and forced me to fall into a shallow sleep. Alex lifts me up and brings me down to our room. But when my body rests comfortably on the bed, I am awoken by a wave of nausea. These feelings of sickness have come and gone since I left the doctor's office, but right now, the feeling doesn't seem to be subsiding. I think I'm way too emotionally wound up.

I clench my eyes shut and pull in a few deep breaths through my nose, trying to force the queasiness away. And by the fourth breath, I feel fine again. I hope a good night of sleep will reset my body and mind to feeling less like I've been run over by a truck.

When morning arrives, my eyes open to the sunlight peeking in underneath the curtains. For a split second, I forget about yesterday. I forget about the padded cell. I forget that I'm only living in a dream.

I try to continue feeling calm and forgetful while I pull myself out of bed. But I'm instantly reminded of pain when a throbbing headache smothers the top of my head.

I throw some bread in the toaster and pour a tall glass of orange juice. Once my stomach begins to digest the food and juice, my headache subsides and again, I try to put yesterday behind me and move on. I have to.

I clamber into the shower, trying to paint the image of a happy life with just Alex and me. The thought of that future doesn't excite me as much as seeing a child, but I'm sure it will become our normal, just like everything else has.

I step out of the shower and dry myself off while looking in the mirror. I try to avoid eye contact with my red, puffy eyes. I don't want to see how sad I look.

*   *   *

I smooth my hand over Alex's shoulder with a subtle attempt at waking him from his deep sleep. We have a shift together this morning, and it's a relief to know we'll be together at least.

His eyes peel open, red and puffy as well. "I know. I'm coming," he groans.

I rub his shoulders, remembering that he's feeling the same pain I am. He groans again, but with comfort. "Let's just try and focus on today and today only," I say, placing my chin on his shoulder.

He turns over and pulls my face into his. With a serious and thoughtful expression, his eyebrows crunch together. "We'll always have each other," he says, placing a kiss on the tip of my nose.

*　*　*

We each go our own way once we enter the coffee shop. I'm running the counter and Alex is waiting tables. We exchange lots of smiles and goofy faces throughout the morning, and it makes me feel a little better, like everything is normal again.

But normal only lasts for so long until another wave of nausea overcomes me. It strikes me as odd this time. I haven't been crying today, I haven't been upset, and I haven't felt worked up. Could it be a stomach bug? Maybe it's still from the leftover hormones.

I attempt to breathe through the sick feeling, but this time none of my tricks are working. I can feel it working its way up my stomach, and my brain tells me to run to the bathroom as quick as my feet can carry me. I barely make it into a stall when my toast and juice reemerge from four hours earlier.

As I wash my hands and rinse out my mouth, I look into the mirror, seeing my current reflection exhibit a green hue, one that might scare the customers off. I splash cold water on my face and cup some more water into my mouth. When I lift my face again, the green has turned into a subtle pale pink. It'll have to do.

When I emerge from the restroom, Alex makes immediate eye contact with me, giving me a questioning look. I wave him off to try and assure him that I'm okay, but I can see he isn't buying it. He continues bussing his few tables, while convulsively looking over his shoulder to glance in my direction.

Getting sick has caused me to feel unsteady and dizzy. It has to be a bug. I just need to sit down for a few minutes. With my head in my hands and my elbows resting on my knees, my head starts to spin with wonder. Maybe the ultrasound was wrong and maybe the test was correct. Could ultrasounds be wrong? I mean, it's kind of clear whether something is in there.

* * *

It's been a week since my dreadful doctor's appointment, and I have to go back today for a follow up. I tell Alex he doesn't have to come, and that I'll be okay, but he isn't taking no for an answer.

His hand is wrapped tightly around mine, and I can tell he's eager for some real answers too. I've been losing my breakfast every morning for the past week, feeling tired all-day, emotional, and hungry as well. They're clear symptoms of pregnancy, and none of this is making any sense.

A nurse, different from last week calls me into the office. Alex stands up first, pulling me behind him. I don't feel nervous or apprehensive like I did last time. I just want an explanation.

The nurse places a cup and a gown on the counter. "Go ahead sweetie, I'll be back for the cup in a couple of minutes."

I do as she asks and place the cup back on the counter. The second I sit down on the table, all of the horrifying memories from last week come flashing back. I clasp my hands together and smooth out the fine lines on each finger until my hands turn white with loss of circulation.

Alex comes to my side and soothingly rubs my back. "It's okay, Chloe. We're going to get some answers today. Maybe she can give you something to make you feel better, you know?" I know he's trying to make me feel better, but in truth, I don't think much is going to help me.

I can't look anywhere but down at my hands right now. Again, I don't want to be here or ever come back here again. The knot in my stomach is making me nauseous, and I hope it subsides so I don't have to run to the bathroom in this stupid gown.

The nurse reappears to collect the sample and dips her head down to look at my face. "Would you like some juice? You aren't looking so well, dear."

"Yes, please if you don't mind," Alex responds, answering for me.

She returns with a small cup of apple juice, and I sip on it warily, hoping it works. The nurse leaves with the sample, and my tensions increase. What if the doctor comes back and tells me something different from what she thought last week? Is it even possible? Minutes pass, as does my nausea, thankfully.

The doctor knocks before entering the room and sits down on the stool next to the table.

"Dr. Faith, I'm Alex, Chloe's husband. Could I ask what the status is?" Alex asks eagerly, bouncing his knees up and down.

"Alex, it's a pleasure to meet you. As you already know, I'm Dr. Faith." She clears her through before continuing on with the results. "Chloe, Alex, as strange as it is, the test results still came back positive, just as they did last week. I'm going to have to do a more thorough exam to rule out the possibility of an ectopic pregnancy."

"What is that?" I blurt out.

The doctor stands up and pulls the ultrasound machine over to the table. "It's when the embryo implants itself outside of the uterus. We would have to terminate it if that were case. But before we start worrying, let's take a look with a more in-depth ultrasound scan.

She presses the button under the table, and once again I'm lying flat and helpless. I hold my breath for whatever is about to happen, and she pushes the gown to the side and presses the ultrasound wand around my stomach.

Her right hand is searching, while her left hand clicks keys on the ultrasound machine. After what seems like forever, she shuts the screen off and removes her gloves.

"There is no baby anywhere in there. This is a very abnormal occurrence, and I'm afraid I don't have a better answer for you. My suggestion would be to wait a month and check back here to see if the hormones dissipate from your system. In some rare cases, the hormones linger for a while after a chemical pregnancy or a miscarriage. Those hormones could cause you to feel like you have pregnancy symptoms. My best advice to you is to hang in there." She offers a half smile. "I know that's not what you wanted to hear, but it's all I can say."

Relief doesn't exactly describe my feelings. I'm still not satisfied with her answer, but what other choice do I have other than to accept what she has said?

"Thank you for your time, Doctor," Alex says, shaking her hand.

He lifts my clothes off of the chair and places them on my lap. "Are you okay?" he asks.

I shake my head dismissively. "This doesn't make any sense."

Alex places his hand on my head, combing his fingers through my hair. He whispers, "I know," under his breath and kisses my forehead.

I step down from the table to get dressed, but another wave of nausea hits me. It's not going anywhere but up this time. I run to the bathroom, feeling my stomach inch up through my throat. As soon as my body is completely empty of every liquid and food that I've ingested today, I fall back against the wall and the tears begin. I feel so sorry for myself. Everything is always an uphill battle for me and us.

Alex hands me a cup of water and helps me up off the ground. "Are you going to make it home? I'll call a cab. We need to get a car. I'm sorry I've made us wait so long on getting one. I'll take care of it this week."

"Alex, it's okay. I can walk. Don't worry," I reassure him.

"Don't worry?" he repeats. "How could I not? You're sick. I have to take care of you, Chloe."

"Really, I'll be okay." I try to convince both of us.

*   *   *

Over the next couple of weeks, I religiously check my stomach in the mirror for any indication that it has grown or changed in any way. I know what the ultrasound showed, but I don't believe it when I've been as sick as I have been, starving, tired and emotional all of the time.

CHAPTER TWENTY-FIVE

WHEN TWO SIDES DON'T MATCH UP

HOW MUCH LONGER CAN THIS GO ON? It's been a month since my fourth visit to the doctor, getting the same results each time. Inconclusive. I'm inconclusive. So is my damn brain.

I'm still left with no answers, and I'm still sick, hungry, and tired. On top of that, I swear I've felt movement in my stomach, but there's nothing in there.

Alex is starting to think everything is in my head and that my mind is making me believe things that aren't true. "The mind can do crazy things if you allow it," is what he keeps saying. I want to say, yeah...no shit. Hence the reason I'm living permanently in a dream.

It's aggravating me that he thinks I'm causing myself this much discomfort. But I guess if I were on the other side, watching him react this way to apparently nothing, I'd be wondering about the cause as well.

My mind has been busy speculating possibilities, and I think I know what I have to do. It's going to be the only way to rule out the other possibility.

I lie down in my bed, close my eyes, and visualize my haunting nightmares.

Ten, nine, eight, seven... please let me get an answer...

I peel my eyes open and lift Alex's heavy arm up from around my neck and then lift his other hand off of my stomach, a stomach that isn't flat anymore. My current reality is beginning to set in. So is a nagging pain in my stomach. It causes me to flinch and gasp. It's how I remember it in my drift. This was the reality I saw, and this is why the tests keep coming up positive.

I am pregnant in my real life. I look over at Alex, knowing that at some point, we conjugated our marriage in this not-so-blissful padded cell. The thought of how that occurred, or who initiated it, bewilders me. Nevertheless, it happened. All I know now is, I need to get myself the hell out of this place before I give birth down here.

I pull myself off the ground with accompanying aches and pains and suddenly feel the burden of having extra weight on the front of my body. I place my hands on my stomach, feeling around my now foreign curves. A smile overwhelms my face when I realize that I didn't lose something I didn't know I needed. I wonder how this will all work. I wonder if Alex will be able to be a part of this baby's life.

* * *

Once Franco hears me moving around in the padded cell, he begins banging on the wall and yelling obscenities at me. He shoves his face into the barred window on the conjoining wall and threatens my life, Alex's, and the baby's. "I've been keeping you alive," he shouts. "You owe me now."

Keeping me alive? I laugh, knowing there's nothing he can do from the constraints of his padded room.

"Why don't you go ahead and rot," I reply, trotting out of my unlocked door.

His sardonic laugh echoes down the hall as I near the exit. "This isn't over, Chloe. The second you think you're safe..." I let the door slam between his final threats.

After sneaking out of the abandoned basement, I'm blasted with New England's cold air. I wrap my arms around myself as I scamper over to the nearby hospital. I'm thankful it's only a few blocks away.

I wait to be seen, keeping my fingers crossed that no one recognizes me. I've been a missing person for over a year, and I have no idea how public that information is.

A nurse appears out of a door and calls my name, but the closer I get to her, the alarm sounding in my head screams at me to run.

"Chloe?" she shouts as I turn in the opposite direction.

I turn around in what seems like slow motion, hoping not to cause a panic. "Hi, Nurse Charlie," I mutter, keeping my focus on the ground below her feet.

"Hey there. Why don't you come on back with me," she says. Her voice still has sweetness to it. I hope that's not a switch she's going to flip when we get behind closed doors.

I'm so stupid, I shouldn't have shown my face anywhere in this area. What was I thinking? We enter into a room, and she gestures for me to have a seat.

She closes the door and crosses her arms over her chest. With her head cocked slightly to the side, she gives me a puzzled look. "Chloe, you have been missing for over a year. You have a different last name, and you're—you're pregnant?"

I shift my weight, trying to find a comfortable position as Charlie studies every inch of me, trying to figure out an explanation. "Look. If you're going to turn me in, just get it over with. I was desperate and I needed to see a doctor. I had hoped against all odds that I wouldn't run into someone that would either recognize me or know me. But of course, I have to run into you."

She holds her hands up, seeming insulted by my words. "Chloe, slow down. Tell me what's going on. I'm not some evil witch who wants to ruin your life. But I am concerned about you. You look like you're about thirty-two or thirty-four weeks pregnant. Am I correct?" she asks.

"I—I don't really know," I say.

I tell Charlie everything, assuming she'll only believe about a quarter of it. When I work up the courage to glance up at her face, I kind of get the idea that she actually cares.

She has a tear running down her cheek, and it takes me by surprise. "I believe you, Chloe. I do. Dr. Greene had gone over your case with me many times before he was let go, and I found you fascinating, and I was even a little jealous of the way you could escape from a crappy life. I was never allowed to encourage your abilities due to the state in which you were admitted to the hospital, but I silently supported your desires." Her eyes are sincere, and her angelic face comforts me. "Your little baby there needs to be with both of his or her parents, and that can't happen if you're locked up again."

"That's why I'm here." I look down at my stomach and caress my hands over my bump.

"I don't have access to your records at the institution, and I'd be willing to consider you as any other patient here if you promise me something," she says, placing her hand over my shoulder.

"What is it that I need to promise?" I lean my body away from hers, craving the space she's taking up.

"If you get into any trouble, ever, I want you to call me—whether it's regarding your pregnancy, or either of your lives, I want to help you. Okay?" She doesn't wait for me to say okay. I'm assuming the desperation on my face answers her question since she pulls me in for a hug.

I can't control my emotions as I wrap my arms around her, falling into her, into someone in this life that seems to care. "Thank you, Charlie. Thank you." I pull away. "You aren't going to call my mother, are you? Because I'd rather be locked up than see her."

"No, I will not call her." She taps her delicate fingers over my shoulder. "Let's take your vitals and find out how you're doing." She switches her demeanor from a friend back to a medical professional and urges me over to the scale. She jots down a number and proceeds to take my blood pressure. "Do you want to find out if it's a boy or a girl today?" she asks, smiling like a friend.

The words make my heart slam against my chest. I hadn't even considered the thought of finding out.

"Yes, I would love to know." I'm trying to control the excited cheering going on inside of my head right now.

As she begins preparing my arm for blood work, she looks up with a little concern. "What are all of these marks from?" She skates her finger along multiple lines running down my arm. "You aren't doing…" her voice lowers into a whisper, "drugs, are you?"

I shake my head fervently. I know what the marks are from. It's from Franco keeping me unconscious with whatever shit he was pumping into me. Bastard. "God no. They're from injections to keep me unconscious." Her face twists with a look of disgust. "Who would have…?"

I shake my head. "Please, don't ask." She holds her hands up again, agreeing to my requests. "Okay, fine. Will you tell me where you are living right now?" She pulls my arm from my lap.

This isn't going to go over well. I sigh, prolonging my answer. "Below the institution, in a cell. It's the only place I'm safe, and the only place that will allow me to live my other life in Charleston. The problem is, my pregnancy is only occurring in this part of my life," I explain, leaving out the part about Franco residing in the cell next to me and Alex being my cellmate and the reason for my pregnancy.

"I see," she says, carefully pricking my skin with the needle. "Well, it's unsafe and unhealthy for you to be leaving your body in that cell." She fills two vials of blood and places a bandage over my arm. "Well." She peeks her head out of the door, looking down each direction before pulling her head back in. "This is completely unprofessional and I'd lose my job if anyone found out, but will you come stay with me until the baby is born? I'll care for you and help you. You need someone, and I know you don't have anyone else…here."

Move in with her? What would I do with Alex? I don't know about this. "I couldn't impose on you like that, and I can't leave Alex." I pull my sleeve back down to my wrist. "Thank you, though."

It's my only option right now, but I don't want her to risk her job over the decisions I've made.

She kneels down in front of me, looking up at me with her large jade eyes. "Chloe, I insist. You are both welcome. You both need care."

I peer down to my hands and nod. "If you're sure, I would greatly appreciate it."

She stands back up and moves about the room, cleaning up from the blood work. "After your appointment, I'll take a lunch break and I'll bring you to my house. We'll stop and get Alex on the way. Does that sound okay?"

"Yes, thank you," I mumble through more tears. Damn hormones.

"You got it." She smiles and hands me a box of tissues.

"The doctor will be in, in a minute. I'll meet you back here when you're through. I can't wait to hear what you're having," she says with a large friend-like smile.

I climb up on the table and fidget with the paper beneath me. By the time the doctor peeks her head into the door, I see that I've shredded the paper into hundreds of pieces.

She looks down at the table and then back at me while reaching her hand out to shake mine. "Hi Chloe, I'm Dr. Row. How are you feeling?"

"I've been pretty sick for a while now. I'm hoping that it will subside soon," I say, keeping the amount of information I give her to a minimum.

"Usually morning sickness begins to lessen around twenty weeks, but sometimes it can last throughout the entire length of a pregnancy.

But I'm hopeful you'll start to feel more normal soon. I hear you'd like to find out if you're having a little girl or boy today?" she asks.

"Yes, I would love to," I say, trying to control the outflow of tears again.

"All right, I'll do the ultrasound first and then a normal exam to make sure everything is the way it should be."

I lie back on the table as she turns on the ultrasound machine. She brings the wand over to my stomach, and there it is. Here in my real life. My precious little baby appears front and center.

My heart feels swollen with happiness and joy, and I only wish that Alex could be here to experience this moment with me.

"Can you see what the gender is?" I lift my head, looking over at the monitor with anticipation.

"Yes, just one second. I need the baby to flip around a little…more." She pushes on areas of my stomach and I watch as the baby's feet hit the area where the ultrasound wand is.

"I see five little toes right there. Do you see that?" she asks, pointing to the screen.

"Yes," I say, falling in love with a foot, reaching out to the screen as if I could touch him or her.

"Here we go. I can see what the gender is. Clear as day with this one. Would you like to know here, or would you like me to write it down so you can open it with your partner?"

"I'd love it if you could write it down." I didn't even think of that. Now I can share the moment with Alex.

She scribbles a word down on a piece of paper, folds it up and places it in an envelope. "Of course. Congratulations, Mommy." She types a few things into the computer and minimizes the screen. "It looks like you're about thirty-three weeks along. I'll want to see you again in three weeks."

"Thank you, Dr. Row."

I pull myself together, trying to compose my excitement as I rush out the door. Charlie's waiting for me around the first corner and grabs me by the arm. "Well, is it a boy or a girl?" she asks, bouncing up and down on her toes.

I show her the sealed envelope. "I'm waiting to find out. I want to open this with Alex," I reply with a silly grin.

"You'll have to tell me as soon as you can," she says under her breath since we're now in view of other patients. "Ready to go?"

"I am."

Sitting in the front seat of Charlie's car, my eyes are burning a hole through the envelope clamped between both of my hands.

"I don't know how you haven't ripped that thing open yet," she says, looking at it too.

"It's hard, but I need to experience this with Alex."

*   *   *

I run into the basement of the institution, and pull Alex up to his feet. His body responds, but his eyes stare through me with his normal blank stare. He follows me like a zombie, and I'm thankful he didn't put up a fight. Maybe somewhere in his head, he knows this is what's best for all of us.

*   *   *

Her house is very nice. It's settled deep within a newly developed neighborhood and has a perfect white picket fence. As we walk through the doors, I see that everything is very neat and tidy, clean and well kept. She brings us down the hall to an empty bedroom and walks inside. "Thank you again for letting me bring Alex. I'm glad I got him out of there. You don't even want to know what that abandoned basement looks like. It would give you nightmares." I couldn't stand the thought of leaving him there without me.

"Will this room be okay for you too?" she asks, sweeping a spec of dust off the bureau.

"Honestly, we were okay in the basement of the hospital," I laugh. "So, I'm sure this will do."

"Well then, hopefully this will be a little more comfortable for your growing body," she says.

"Thank you, Charlie, really."

"Well, I have to get back to work. I assume you'll be asleep when I get home." She winks, insinuating that she already knows I'll be back in Charleston. She gives me a tight hug and shrieks, "Good luck," into my ear.

It's almost like having a friend again. I lead Alex over to one of the twin size beds and urge him to lie down. He doesn't put up a fight. I'm sure his body is aware of the difference in comfort. I lie down in the other twin size bed on the opposite side of the room, holding the envelope in my hand. I should have thought of this sooner—I won't have this envelope when I wake up. I get back off the bed and walk over to where Alex is lying. "I know you're in there, Alex." I curl my hand around his and pull the piece of paper out of the envelope. I smile at the word and lean my lips down to Alex's ear. "It's a boy." I kiss him gently, and I feel his fingers tighten around mine. I wonder if he did hear me and understands.

The comfort of the mattress soothes my aching muscles and contorts the swollen areas of my back. It won't be hard to push myself back into a drift, my *happy* place: Charleston.

When my eyes open, I'm lying comfortably in my own bed with a large smile stretched across my face. I glance over to the clock and see that I have to be at work shortly. Today is one of those days where Alex's shift ends and mine begins. I won't be able to share this news with him until tonight. The wait is going to kill me.

CHAPTER TWENTY-SIX

THE NEWS

I WALK IN TO THE COFFEE SHOP just as Alex is taking off his apron. Once he spots me, he runs over and pecks my cheek. "How are you feeling? You hanging in there today?"

"I'm great, actually. As a matter of fact, I want to do something fun tonight." I take his apron from his hand and tie it around my neck. "I'll meet you at the beach after work?"

"You got it, baby," he says, kissing me again.

* * *

Work dragged on forever, but because the restaurant traffic died down early, my manager let me leave an hour early.

I'm racing down to the beach, excited to surprise Alex early and with a surprise I know he'll love. But when I approach the area where we normally meet, I see him kneeling down talking to the little blond boy. We haven't seen him or Kiera in months, but here they both are.

The poor little guy is covering his face crying, and shockingly, Kiera's standing behind him with her arms crossed, her eyes rolled up to the sky, an annoyed look on her face.

Alex appears to be comforting him and pulls him in for a hug. As he's doing that, I run around to the other side of the dock to get close enough so I can hear what's going on. When I enter into hearing range, I overhear the conversation between the two of them.

"I need mommy, she'll make me feel better, like always," the little boy cries into Alex's shoulder.

Mommy? I wonder who…

"Sammy, it's not time yet. We've talked about this, little man. Mommy can't know about you yet. We have to keep you a secret, remember? Daddy loves you, but you need to go back and stay with Cousin Kiera for just a little longer. But you know what? I don't want you to worry, because I have a feeling mommy's finally going to find out about you real soon," Alex smiles and shuffles his hands through Sammy's blond curls.

I place my hands over my heart, and my breath hitches a bit. I knew it.

"Alex?" I call out to him.

His head shoots up with a look of concern. It's a look as in he's been caught hiding a secret. But as it turns out, I don't really need an explanation because I already know the outcome.

"Chloe, it's not what you think," he says, nervously jumping up and brushing the sand off his knees.

"Yes it is," Kiera says, checking her watch. "Guys, I gotta run. I have a date in Rome...in two years, and I have to be there in five minutes."

"Kiera!" Alex gives her a scolding look.

"Kiera?" I say.

She nods and rolls her eyes. "We're related. I can drift. I'm not from this world you think *you* created. I'm from the real world too. I just like it better here." She gives me a cunning grin. "End of story. We'll catch up soon, but right now, my Italian stallion is waiting." She flutters her eyelashes, whips around and struts off into the blinding sun.

I shake my head at the Kiera I've known and still love. Having answers now and knowing that she isn't working for Franco is as much confirmation as I need.

"I know everything," I say to Alex, clasping my hands around my stomach. I take his hand, place it on my stomach, and whisper, "It's a boy, and I think we should name him...Sammy."

A broad smile sweeps across Alex's face and he wraps his hands around my back, pulling me in. "He's amazing, Chloe. He might look like me, but he's just like you—talks like you, acts like you and he drifts like us. But it's okay." He looks down at Sammy and pulls him into his leg. "He's in control and really likes to visit from the future," he laughs. "He is one smart little guy, Chloe. He's so lucky."

With his words stirring different thoughts and emotions within my head and heart, I feel two small hands wrap around my leg. I look down to the dazzling big blue eyes looking up at me.

"Mommy?" he smiles at me. "Is it time yet?"

For a preview of Book 3, turn the page.

WHEN FULLY FUSED
BOOK 3: SCHASM SERIES

Content subject to change in editing

PREFACE

I HOPE THIS WORKS. I mean, it has to work.

"Sammy, can you get mommy a glass of water?" I ask, watching him put the final touches on his stick-figure drawing.

I wonder if I'll forget about him. I wonder what will happen to all my memories. I watch the little head of blond curls bounce over to me, happy, and carefree.

"Here, Mommy. Here's your water," he says with a gratifying look.

"Thank you, Sammy," I respond with a lump forming in my throat.

I carefully place the glass of water down on the counter and kneel down to Sammy's level. "Come here, sweetie," I say, wrapping my fingers gently around his little arm. I pull him in close to me.

"What's the matter, Mommy?"

CHAPTER ONE

SOUGHT AFTER GOLD

I'M NOT SURE WHY PEOPLE TELL YOU not to cry over spilled milk. Are they talking to the parents, or to the children who are spilling the milk? This is the third spill I've cleaned up today. Messes suck, even in a drift. I wish my mind could figure out how to clean it up without me having to get down on my hands and knees.

Just as I'm peeling up the last piece of macaroni from the tiled floor, a brash knock on the front door startles me into thumping my head under the table. It's only eight in the morning. People seriously have no common courtesy these days.

Rubbing my sore head, I push the loose strands of hair off of my face and try to look presentable for whoever is ignorant enough to be knocking at this time of day.

I separate two of the blinds and peek out before opening the door. Great. Another *salesman*. I wish these people would just give up. I unlatch the chain, twist the deadbolt, and open the front door only a crack. "Can I help you?" I ask in a snide voice.

"Hello, ma'am. I don't mean to bother you so early in the morning, but could you spare a moment of your time?" the opulently well-dressed man asks. Looking at him a little closer, he doesn't look like a typical door-to-door salesman. I'm no expert in the fine clothing department, but I'm sure his shimmering grey suit and snakeskin leather shoes are probably worth more than a car payment for my new little Prius out there.

"Now really isn't a good time, sir. If you'd like to come back later, my husband will be home around five tonight." I attempt to close the door, but his fingers wrap around the edge, holding it firmly in place and making it so I can't close it.

"Alex is not the one I need to speak with. It's you. And I'm nicely asking you for a moment of your time, Chloe." His voice has lowered a bit and sounds more like a growl.

I press both of my hands against the door and push it harder without concern for the man's fingers that are wedged between the threshold and the door. It closes enough so I can attach the chain at the top to constrict the door from opening any further. "What do you want?" I ask, hiding my face. I can't believe they're here now. I look over my shoulder to make sure Sammy isn't witnessing another one of these incidences.

He's not, thankfully.

"Go away. Leave me the hell alone."

"Where is it?" The man shouts with aggression growing in his voice.

"Where is what?" I play dumb.

"Where is the damn locket?" I swallow hard. This locket has become a dark shadow that follows me around. No matter how fast I run or how hard I try to hide from it, it's always lurking around the corner.

"What is it with you people and this stupid locket? I don't know anything about any locket, or its whereabouts." I twirl my finger in the air, gesturing for him to turn around and leave. I know he can see my hand through the opening where his fingers still have a grip on the door. "Bye-Bye now." I press my entire body up against the door, pushing as hard as I can. I hear the man groan from the pain of his likely broken fingers. He tries to pull his hand out and makes it as far as his knuckles. Only for the fact that I want him to leave, I loosen my weight against the door. He slides his hand out and I slam the door shut, locking each of the three deadbolts.

I fall against the door and crash the back of my head into it. I can't deal with this anymore. There is no break from this. I hate that I'm subjecting Sammy to a life I promised I would never give him. I want him to be able to go outside and play and live like a normal four-year-old. But how can I when we're being constantly watched with a pair of binoculars? We have no clue how many people are after the locket. And if it were up to me, I'd go find that damn thing again and gladly hand it to the first person that asks for it. It's of no use to me lying on some rock in the Catacombs. Nevertheless, whenever I say the word locket around Alex, it's as if I unleashed some demon that should only be known about, and never spoken of. It's been an uncomfortably touchy subject over the past four years. As it should be, considering how many people are after the damn thing, and me for that matter. I know there is a deeper explanation for it—after all this is something concocted within the confines of my broken mind. I'm just not sure I understand the reasoning behind a secret that my mind must be keeping from my unconscious.

*   *   *

The sun is beginning to dull and dip down below the horizon. I've been standing here, staring blankly out of the kitchen window, waiting for Alex and not another psychopath to pull into the driveway.

"Mommy, I'm hungry." Sammy's voice pulls me out of my trance. He tugs on the back of my shirt and looks up at me with his beautiful Alex-like eyes. "Can I have a snack?"

I kneel down in front of him and pull him into my chest. "We're having dinner in a half hour. We're just waiting for Daddy to come home." We have the same conversation every day at five o'clock. Now he's going to give me his best puppy dog pout and scuff his feet against the linoleum tiles.

"Fineeee," he whines and meanders out into the living room. He's such a good kid. We're so lucky with how understanding he is and always has been with our constant moving around, and running away from any means of a solid foundation. If things stay like this, I don't know how we'll be able to handle him attending school. We can't just rip him out anytime someone comes knocking on our door. I feel disappointed in myself. I need to protect him from this life he's falling into. And protection doesn't always mean running. It means fighting off whatever is pushing us away.

Alex pulls into the driveway. I watch him remove his aviator sunglasses and hook them up on his window visor. He catches me looking at him from the window, and it's easy to tell he can read the words written into my expression. His lips sag downwards and his shoulders slump as I see the shoulder belt fling behind him. It takes him less than fifteen seconds to make it from his car to where I'm standing in the kitchen.

We don't exchange words at first. He wraps his arms around me and nuzzles his head into my shoulder. He smells like fresh soap, as if he just showered. He pulls away and places his hands around the sides of my neck. He leans his head down to meet my eyes and looks at me intently. "What happened?"

What is he waiting for me to tell him? I'm sure he can guess what happened. We get a good solid month before we're found again. And we've been living in this house for exactly thirty days today. It's almost as good as clockwork.

"Another one came by today," I tell him the obvious facts.

He pulls me back into his chest and runs his fingers through the loose messy knot of hair piled on my head. "Sorry, Chlo." He whispers his apology as if it were his fault. He can't protect me every second of the day, but sometimes he acts as if he was placed in my world only to protect me.

I kiss his nose and pull out of his tight grip. "It's dinner time," I say with a forced smile. He doesn't move. He just stands there, watching me bounce off of each corner in the kitchen, preparing to remove the casserole from the oven.

"Chlo, stop." I don't want to stop. Because when I do, he's going to want my attention. He's going to want to tell me we're leaving again. He's going to tell me we have to keep running. And I am so sick of running.

"Just let them catch us, Alex." I wrench open the oven and whip an oven-mitt from the hook above my head. "Just give them the damn thing. I don't want it, and I don't need it."

Alex drops the handful of forks onto the counter and fists his hands through his hair. "You don't know what you're talking about." Anger fires through his eyes. He's been trying so hard to protect us, but we're being stalked. Every time Alex thinks he's outsmarted them, he quickly finds that not to be the case.

"Yes," I respond softly while picking up the dropped silverware. "I do." My reassuring words don't have any effect over him.

He gently retrieves the forks from my hand and places them down on the three napkin settings on the table. "I'm sorry. I just thought we would lose them for a little while if we moved back here."

"Thirty days is all we ever get from them, Alex."

He drops down into his seat and lets his head fall into his hands. "Shit. I should call Celia and make sure they didn't get to her too," he says, standing up and sliding his phone out of his pocket.

"I already called and warned her. She said a man stopped in front of her house, but never approached the front door. She's fine, don't worry."

He inhales sharply and closes his eyes. "I am so sick of this. We are never going to be able to live a normal life here."

"Here? There's evidently nowhere."

"I know." He pulls the chair out from the table and sits down. "I was obviously wrong again."

"So, now what? Should we leave this world behind, go back to a place where your mind doesn't work and my mind can't stay planted in one place? Because, to be honest...that doesn't really sound like a better option to me." I pull Sammy's chair out for him to sit down. "This is the only way Sammy can have two parents. Do I have to remind you of this?" I comb my fingers through Sammy's hair, now regretting what I just said in front of him.

"We're in trouble, Chloe. I don't know what else to do," he says.

"We're always in trouble," I groan. I place Alex and Sammy's plates down in front of them. "At least we can have a little normal here." I nudge my head toward Sammy.

"So we should just keep running?"

"It's better than the alternative—a world where we can't be together." I sit down at the opposite end of the table.

He stabs his fork into the pot roast and looks up at me with a crumpled face. "Why didn't you call me today when it happened? I told you I would always take your call at work, Chloe."

He just started there a few weeks ago, I didn't want to get him in trouble. I know how important this job is to him and our family. "It was nothing that couldn't wait until you got home."

"I just wish you would have called, okay? When this happens again, I want you to call me."

Okay, so I'll be calling him tomorrow, I'm sure. When we were in Charleston, I had a different man at my door every day. It was as if they thought their lame salesman acts weren't new to me—as if I didn't know why they were really there. I won't let them in. They know that and I know that. What I don't know is why we're running from something that won't go away no matter where we are. I'm sure Alex knows. I'm sure he has more insight. And I'm sure he just doesn't want to tell me, as always.

I place my fork and knife back down on the table and I set my eyes on his. He looks over at me and nods his head, silently begging me not to ask what I'm about to ask. He knows because I ask every day. I'm hoping he'll give up and tell me one of these days, but it won't happen without me wearing him down first. It's been four years of me begging to know what he knows. He claims to not know much more than I do, but sometimes he says it's best if I don't know. So I have to assume there's something important he's hiding.

I suck in a deep breath, trying to swallow my once again growing anger. I look over at Sammy, hoping to shift my mind onto something else. Asking this always causes arguments and I'm tired of fighting.

Of course, Sammy is staring at me, nodding his head just like Alex. While I know he's just copying what he sees, I can't help but to wonder what that little mind knows, and if he knows too much, as well. Now having nowhere else to look, my anger resurfaces. "Just tell me," I say, softly.

"No, Chloe. Drop it." He clears his throat and looks over at Sammy. "Hey buddy, what did you do today?"

I take a deep breath and attempt to blow out my uprising rage. We've been over this a thousand times, but it still eats away at me. I never should've put that locket back. If I didn't, maybe I would have gotten some answers on the importance of the stupid thing. I'm being followed by strange men, here in what is supposed to be our dream of a life. Alex won't tell me anything. He wants to keep me in the dark, to protect me, against what, I still don't know. It drives me nuts. I'm the one being followed. It's a necklace with a picture of an old couple in front of a freaking rock. I can't really understand what could be so damn important about it. And if it is so important, and it supposedly belongs to me, I should know why.

"All right, buddy. Go watch TV for a little bit, and I'll come join you in a few," Alex says, standing up with his plate.

Sammy bounces off into the next room, and I stand up with my plate as well. "What's your problem, Alex?" I say, speaking to him like this hurts me. I hate when we argue. And we only argue about this. The topic gets brought up far more often now than it has in the past, but only because these salesmen are showing up too often for my comfort. Here I thought I was wearing them down, and as soon as I feel like I've gained some leverage, they increase their attempts to retrieve the information. Maybe Alex doesn't want to tell me because he thinks I'm weak and I'll give them the answers they're looking for. And honestly, I'm not sure I wouldn't. If it meant we could live in peace here, then I would do whatever it takes to have that.

"Chlo, I'm really tired of having the same argument over this matter. You've promised me time after time that you would drop it, for me. So, why can't you?" He huffs as he drops his plate into the sink.

"Because, the situation is getting worse. I feel like I'm constantly being watched and monitored. I have no idea why. Yet, I have a strange feeling you do." I can't control the anger seeping through the cracks in my voice. I keep thinking I'll break him down. But he's as strong and persistent as I am. We're both fighting a brick wall. "Put yourself in my shoes for a minute. How would you feel?"

He places his glass gently down into the sink, and turns around to face me. He opens his arms and purses his lips into a pout. "Come here, baby."

Those blue eyes and perfect lips get me every time. Whenever I focus on them, my anger always diminishes, which is why I try to avoid looking at him when I'm trying to convince him to give me answers. But now it's too late. I've fallen into his trap. His eyes have dragged me in like a magnet, and my body is now pressed up against his. The warmth of his embrace makes me forget why I'm angry. It's almost like he knows he holds that power over me, and he uses it to his advantage. He rests his cheek on my head and whispers, "Sorry, Chlo. Hang in there. You'll have some answers soon."

I jerk away. The anger is back. It's spiraling around my stomach and electrifying all of my emotional wiring. "What do you mean, soon?" He's never hinted at me actually finding out this deep dark secret. Why now?

He pulls me back in and hushes me. Seriously? He's actually hushing me? His arms are wrapped so tightly around me that I'm getting the sense something isn't right—more than a secret he won't share. "Love you, Chlo," he says with a deep inhale. "Let's go see what Sammy's up to." He's great at changing the subject. And now I'm faced with two options, ruining the night with an argument that I won't win, or giving up as always and spending a nice quiet night with my husband and son.

"Okay." I comply, even though my head screams to keep battling.

I release a heavy sigh, making it known I'm not letting this go, but merely dropping it for now. He sits down next to Sammy on the living room couch, wraps his arm around his little body, and kisses the top of his messy blond curls. "Ready for bed, bud?"

"No, Daddy! I have to watch this first." Sammy smiles and turns his attention back to the TV.

"Okay, I guess I have no choice," Alex says, his voice rising into a playful octave.

"No!" Sammy shrieks with laughter.

Alex lifts Sammy up over his head and flies him down the hall like an airplane, wind noises and all. Alex likes to put Sammy to bed every night. It's his special bonding time with him. He's been working so much lately that he feels like he's missing out on Sammy's life. This new job at the accounting firm has him on a tight leash, but he enjoys the paycheck, and I appreciate him taking care of us.

He's worked so hard to get to where he is. Over the past four years, he's been taking night classes, interning, and being a gopher for various executives. Finally, a few months ago after we decided to move here to try and escape the freaks following us around, and to be closer to Celia, he applied at a local firm. To our surprise, they offered him a job. We quickly uprooted from Charleston and moved here to San Diego. Since we moved here, we've lived in three different locations in hopes to escapes our followers. They're winning.

"How was work today?" I ask him as he's walking back down the hall from Sammy's bedroom.

"It was good. Same old stuff. Let's not talk about work, or strange men coming to the door. Let's just sit down, relax, and watch a movie. Can we do that?" He lifts my hand and pulls me toward the couch. "How's my favorite girl?"

"Good, now that you're home." I smile and fall into his arms. I flick the TV on and choose the first movie I see on Demand. Alex places his arm around my shoulders and sinks into the couch. "My mom called today, again," I say.

His lips press firmly into a straight line as he lifts the remote and clicks the TV off. "Chlo, you're going to have to answer it eventually. She can't do anything to you. You're a married woman with a child. Maybe she just wants to make things right." I wish she would just leave me alone here. She shouldn't be part of this world we've worked hard to create. She isn't welcome, and I definitely don't want her to see Sammy.

"I don't want to talk to her." I'm surprised she hasn't just shown up here. She's always managed to find a way in before. Maybe she is trying to do things right, but she has done things so wrong for so long, that there is no possible way to make things right.

Not now. Not ever.

Alex doesn't seem to understand this, though. Maybe I've never been clear enough on how horrible she really was to me. He seems to think I owe her another chance. I think that would change if he ever had a glimpse at the childhood he was kept away from.

"You're telling me, if Sammy ever went missing, you wouldn't go to the ends of the earth to track him down?" he asks.

"Of course I would. My mother, though, she can't stand me. It's different with her. I guarantee you there's an ulterior motive to her search. For all I know, she's probably after that stupid locket, too." The second the words leave my mouth Alex's eyes widen, and he presses his fingers into the stress lines on his forehead.

"I didn't even think of that," he says, vaguely.

"Seriously? I was half joking. There's a chance my mother knows about this thing, and I don't?"

Alex responds with a loud groan. I should have figured. Maybe that's why she's hated me so much. That would actually make sense.

"That's it," I shout. "I've had it. I want you to tell me right now what is so important about that old necklace." I throw my weight on top of Alex and pin him down to the couch. I straddle my legs over his waist and place my hands firmly over his shoulders. "Tell me."

"Or what?" he says with a snide grin.

"You don't want to know, what," I say, raising an eyebrow.

He fists his hands around the collar of my shirt and pulls me down, flat on top of him. He crashes his lips into mine and moves his hands slowly up the sides of my shirt. "Or what, Chlo?" he mutters against my lips. I slide my hand between us and unhook his belt, letting my hand wander down under his zipper. My lips slide across his jawline and down his neck, and as he replies with a soft groan, I know it's my chance. I'm playing dirty now. Maybe it will work. I pull my hand out and sit up with a smile. "That's what. You're on probation...from me until you tell me all of your secrets, Mr. Levette."

"Hey now," he whines. "No fair, you tease."

"Alex, I want an explanation." I punch his chest playfully. "You give me what I want, and I'll...give you what you want." I press my lips back up against his.

He whines and flips me over onto my side. "Chlo, it's one of those things you'll know about when the time is right." He sweeps his thumb down my cheek. "You promised you'd stop the future-knowing questions. Remember?" His voice is low and pleading. "Just think of the locket as a piece of gold that everyone's after. Except, it belongs to you. Someday you'll thank me for protecting your secret."

"My secret?" I reply.

"I wouldn't protect anything else this much if it weren't for you and Sammy." He pulls my head down onto his shoulder and places a kiss on my nose. "Please?" He presses his lips against my collarbone. I don't know if he's pleading for me, or for my questions to stop.

As I try to release the consuming pressure building within the walls of my chest, I focus on his moving lips, the crave in my belly, the crickets chirping outside of the window, and...gravel being scuffed against the ground. "Hey, do you hear that?" I ask, propping myself back up.

"Hear what?" he asks, jumping up like he's ready to pounce.

I glance in every direction, feeling claustrophobic in my own house, now wishing we had shut the blinds before sunset. I'm nervous to look toward the front window near the door, but my head naturally turns in that direction when I hear the scuffling noise again.

The darkness outside of the window accents the two tiny white lights shining into the house. I grip my fingers into Alex's tensed arm, and he pulls me off of the couch and lowers me to the ground.

"Stay here," he whispers. He makes his way toward the two lights. As he approaches the window, he slams his fist against the glass and the lights disappear almost instantly. He unbolts the door and unlinks the chain in one swift motion, flinging the door open.

With no further action from Alex, I watch as he hesitantly bends over to retrieve something from the ground. "What the hell?" he asks, scratching his head.

"What? What is it?" I ask, panic still saturating my voice.

"There's no one out here, but there are two tiny flashlights sitting here beneath the window. Someone obviously had to be holding them. But, you'd think I would have at least seen them running off?"

I peel myself up from the floor and pull one of the flashlights from his hand, inspecting it for any hint of who it might have belonged to. "Hmm," I sigh.

"What? Did you find something?" Alex asks.

"Yeah, it says Ocnarf and Co." I flip it over to see if there is anything else. Nothing. "Google it—" Before I even finish my sentence, he's sitting at the computer desk, pounding his fingers into the keys on his laptop.

Unknown. Of course," he says, slamming his hands onto the desk. "I need to call Celia."

Alex pulls his phone from his pocket and presses two buttons before flattening the device up to his ear. "Are your blinds closed?" he asks calmly, probably trying not to freak her out. "Okay. Are your doors all locked?" he continues. "It's okay, don't worry. I just wanted to make sure everything is secure there. Sorry for waking—"

His words cut off. "Mom, really, everything is fine. Go back to bed, and I'll talk to you in the morning." He clicks a button on his phone and drops it onto the desk.

"Everything okay?" I ask.

"I think I freaked her out pretty good," he says, rubbing the tension out of his neck.

"Alex. Clearly, this is getting worse. We need to figure something out. Witness protection or something. I don't know." I shake my head with frustration.

Alex lets his head fall back, and he releases a loud throaty laugh. "Did you just say, 'Witness protection'?" He laughs again. "You do know that's for someone who watched the action of a crime and may be in danger for being a witness, right? I'm not quite sure our situation falls under that category." He walks away, snorting and whispering the words, *witness protection* under his breath.

As I'm peeling the throw blanket from the ground and folding it under my arm, Alex shouts from the kitchen, "I'm having an alarm system installed tomorrow. That will help us out a bit."

Just as I smooth the throw over the top of the couch, I see another light shining in through the window. "Alex, there's another light," I say, keeping my voice soft.

He runs to the door again, but by the time he's close enough, the light disappears.

WHEN FULLY FUSED, COMING FROM BOOKTROPE EDITIONS SUMMER 2014

ACKNOWLEDGMENTS

I don't know where I would be without the love and support of my family, friends, bloggers and readers. You all have played such an important role in this journey I decided to embark on, and I could never thank you enough. But I'll try...

Jennifer Gilbert, my book manager and friend, you have been the most incredible sidekick during this amazing experience. I love brainstorming, planning, and creating with you. You have become a true asset to building my dream. Thank you for being at the end of every nervous email and phone call, as well as talking me off of many ledges. Most importantly, thank you for being as excited for every milestone as I have been. You are truly the best at what you do. Katrina Mendolera, I absolutely love working with you. I feel like you were in my brain and filled the gaps my mind left open. You are an amazingly talented editor and I am so lucky to have you by my side. I look forward to working with you lots more in the future. Marni Mann, thank you for always being there to listen to me for being such an amazing friend. Allie Burke, I love you for stepping in and offering to help me format my moody manuscript. You are an awesome person and a wonderful friend. Jesse James Freeman, an asset to Booktrope and an asset to each of us authors. You are the top go-to guy and I love that I can call you my friend too. I will never be able to thank you enough for bringing me into this amazing team of people. Katherine Sears and Ken Shear, from the bottom of my heart, thank you for giving me the foundation to live out my dream of writing books.

To my two little men, Bryce and Brayden, I know you don't understand why mommy's head seems to be in the clouds all of the time, but when you're both older, you'll understand I was busy making my dreams come true. I hope you both get to endure the same feeling when you accomplish your life-long goals. I love you both more than anything.

Josh, my husband and best friend, you have been the most supportive person in my life. You have encouraged me and pushed me to never give up. You have sat by my side while I drift off into another reality every night, and I thank you for showing interest and excitement in every single sentence I forced you to listen to about the fictional worlds I swear are real. I love you more than words—and I know a lot of words now.

To my parents (Cindy and John) and step-parents (Mark and Evilee) who have always been by my side, supporting my goals with a proud smile. I love you all.

Along with having amazing parents, I have lucked out with an awesome set of in-laws as well. Sue, Rich, and Bob, you never fail to show me your love and support when it comes to this crazy journey of mine, and I thank you for that.

My grandparents, the solid rocks in my life who never change and who never stop believing in me—your stories about how you tell every person you cross that your granddaughter is an author never gets old. Love you both.

Lori, the best sister a girl could ask for. You've been my biggest fan, and you've given me a confidence boost whenever I questioned what I've gotten myself into. You make me feel as though I've done something amazing, and I love you for that.

I could never thank my friends enough for the constant encouragement. Each and every one of you has showed your interest in my obsession, and you have never failed to show me how much you care. I feel the same about all of you.

A special thanks to the bloggers who have been supporting me from day one—you make us authors stand out in the spotlight, and for that I will be forever grateful. Stephanie Higgins (Romance Addict Book Blog), thank you for everything you have done to help promote the Schasm Series. You are truly an amazing person and friend, and I love working with you.

Thank you, Hazel Godwin (Craves the Angst) and Courtney Whisenant (Author Alliance) for being kind enough to endorse this book. Your words mean the world to me.

ALSO BY SHARI RYAN

Schasm (Young Adult Romance) A young woman finds herself lost between what is real and what is imagined, but a chance encounter with a man brings new hope for the future.

MORE GREAT READS FROM BOOKTROPE

The Dead Boy's Legacy by **Cassius Shuman** (Fiction) 9-year-old Tommy McCarthy is abducted while riding his bike home from a little league game. This psychological family drama explores his family's grief while also looking at the background and motivations of his abductor.

Work in Progress by **Christina Esdon** (Romance) Psychologist Reese Morgan refuses to let go of a childhood trauma. When she meets a handsome contractor, Josh Montgomery, she wonders if the walls around her heart can be knocked down to let love in.

The Collection by **T.K. Lasser** (Paranormal Romance) A human lie detector and an immortal art thief are thrust together in a ruthless plot of high stakes acquisition and murder by a black market art buyer.

Dancing on the Edge by **Kit Bakke** (Young Adult) A teenager's touching and fantastical journey through grief. An inspiring story of adventure and travel.

Memoirs Aren't Fairytales by **Marni Mann** (Contemporary Fiction) Leaving her old life behind, Nicole finds herself falling deeper and deeper into heroin addiction. Can she ever find her way back to a life free of track marks? Does she even want to?

Discover more books and learn about our
new approach to publishing at **booktrope.com**.

CPSIA information can be obtained
at www.ICGtesting.com
Printed in the USA
FFOW03n1905050614
5756FF